The Chicago Healer

the chicago HEALER

PAUL H. BOGE

The Chicago Healer

First printing April 2004
Second printing June 2004

Printed in Canada
International Standard Book Number: 1-894860-27-6

Published by:
Castle Quay Books
500 Trillium Drive, Kitchener, Ontario, N2G 4Y4
Tel: (800) 265-6397 Fax (519) 748-9835
E-mail: info@castlequaybooks.com
www.castlequaybooks.com

Copy editing by Larry N. Willard
Cover Design by Essence Publishing and William Ho
Photo of Paul Boge by karin falk photography
Printed at Essence Publishing, Belleville, Ontario

National Library of Canada Cataloguing in Publication

Boge, Paul H., 1973-
The Chicago healer / Paul H. Boge. -- 1st ed.

ISBN 1-894860-27-6

I. Title.

PS8603.O34C47 2004 C813'.6 C2004-901421-8

1

The private jet landed in the pouring rain at O'Hare Airport. The only passenger on board was Lucas Stephens who was typing the final conditions of a seven million-dollar sales agreement on his laptop. Lucas had only been with Empirico for two years but already he was their most productive representative. He owned two houses—a mansion in Chicago and another residence in Florida, which he rarely used. He drove three cars: a Mercedes for work, a Porsche for the evenings and a BMW strictly for weekends. He had memberships at two country clubs and a yacht in Belmont Harbor. Ten people worked directly for him and he earned the equivalent of fifteen lawyers.

Lucas was twenty-five years old.

He got off the plane and was immediately greeted by a limousine driver in his late sixties and three other Empirico employees. The employees were dressed in dark trench coats and had come, as usual, to take instructions from Lucas. He gave them each a quick handshake, then relayed follow-up procedures on fulfilling the company's commitments to their new-found clients. They nodded, got into a nearby Lexus and hurried off to carry out their orders. Lucas got into his limousine and turned on the basketball game while the driver put his bags into the trunk. He flipped open his cell phone, checked his stocks and tried to relax. His trip had only been a week long but he felt like he'd been gone a month. As the limousine drove off Lucas glanced at his watch and took in a deep breath. A jolt of fear ran through his spine. They would be meeting soon. All of them. They would discuss who was making money for Empirico and who was losing it. Fortunately, Lucas' trip had gone well. He'd be okay for this meeting, he hoped. But success was short-lived at Empirico. This trip was already old news. He would soon have to prove himself again.

And again.

The limousine stopped outside of the massive Empirico facility. The baby blue reflective windows surrounding the forty-storey office building allowed Empirico to see out but prevented outsiders from seeing in. An external elevator shaft ran the entire height of the building with spiraling, multi-colored tubes around it to give it the feel of a massive DNA strand. Nothing was too good for Chicago architecture.

The driver held the door open for Lucas who waited a few moments until the game had ended. Basketball always seemed to come down to the last minute—sometimes to the final shot. Lucas got out, shook the limousine driver's hand and thanked him by name.

"Are the games really that important, Mr. Stephens?" the driver asked.

Lucas grinned. "Especially when I have money riding on them."

Two sets of armed security guards greeted Lucas at checkpoints inside the main entrance. His assistant, Anne, came out to greet him. She had short blond hair, an infectious smile and spoke with a Danish accent. Her irresistible and taller than average frame made her look like she had just walked off the cover of a fashion magazine.

"Welcome back, Lucas."

"Thank you. Nothing like coming home."

She gave him the briefing notes for the meeting and managed to touch his hand in the process. "They're just about to get started."

Lucas glanced at the notes and walked past her to a security door. He felt his pulse pounding in his neck. *There's nothing to worry about. I did fine.* But still, his throat got drier. He fumbled through his wallet and found his security card. He slipped it through the lock and entered a long hallway to the rear of the facility. Cameras watched him the entire way.

Two tall men stood at the end of the hallway beside a metal detector. Thatcher and Ridley had both served in Vietnam. Their suit jackets showed a bulge in the side where they kept their handguns. Lucas nodded slightly but they made no response. Although he had successfully passed through the detector and their body searches many times before, Lucas still hated the process. He hated being around them. Sure, they were the boss' bodyguards, but they always gave Lucas a creepy feeling. They could kill him in a heartbeat if they wanted to. And what worried him the most was that, if ordered to do so, they would have no hesitation in performing that task. There was something eerie about being in the presence of those kinds of people.

The guards finished their search and Thatcher opened the door. Lucas walked into the top security boardroom and joined the rest of Empirico's executives known collectively as the Council.

The room stretched out long enough for someone to throw a good football pass. At the center, fifty leather chairs were arranged in four rows in a semi-circle facing a platform. On the platform stood a glass lectern in front of a mahogany desk. A buffet table with crackers, caviar, pizza, sandwiches and every fruit imaginable filled the back of the room. Two pool tables, fifteen leather couches and a full service bar gave the Council members an opportunity to clear their heads during meeting breaks.

Lucas swallowed as he looked around at forty of the world's most powerful executives. They were the brass of Empirico. The air suddenly felt thinner, as though it took twice the effort to breathe. Sweat formed on his forehead. No one had noticed him yet and it occurred to him that he could still run out. Working for Empirico was all that Lucas had hoped it would be, but the meetings—they were different. Sinister, almost. The Council members were tough, like ravenous wolves waiting to destroy anything standing in their way.

Mike Hirdina—early thirties, black hair, strong build—spotted Lucas standing at the door. Mike was the next youngest member of the Council and the closest companion to Lucas. Their eyes met and Lucas let out a sigh of relief. Mike smiled and came towards him. The air felt cleaner. He could breathe easier.

Mike shook Lucas' hand with such enthusiasm that it throbbed after he let go. He shouted out Lucas' name loud enough for the whole room to hear, then said, "Look who decided to finally show up!"

Off to the side, some of the other Council members laughed over a joke one of them had told. When they heard Mike's announcement they looked over their shoulders. When they saw Lucas the smile on their faces vanished, as when someone picks up the phone at a party only to receive bad news. "Wonderful," one of them said. A couple of them raised their glasses pretending to appreciate Lucas' presence. But Lucas knew better. The others returned to their conversations and hoped Lucas would not talk to them.

"You know how it is, Mike. Some of us have to work." Lucas stretched his fingers out of Mike's view. The blood began to flow again.

Mike spoke in a quieter voice. He leaned closer to Lucas. "I hear you signed a deal for seven million." Lucas nodded. "Watch your back."

"Meaning?"

Mike glanced behind him to see if anyone was listening. "Meaning the big boss likes the sales, but the rest of the Council are getting nervous."

"I'm just trying to survive."

"Well, you're surviving a little too well. What do you think happens when you double the output of some of these people?"

Lucas swallowed. The air got thinner again. He reached to a drink tray, grabbed a glass of purified water and finished it in one shot. Lucas spoke in a normal voice, then stopped himself and whispered, "Then what am I supposed to do? Decline sales so some of these guys can breathe easier? Forget it! If they can't handle it they can walk."

"Just remember," Mike said. "There's more of them than there are of you."

"Of me or of us?"

Mike put on a smile. "Lucas. Relax. Why do you think I came to talk with you?"

Lucas reached for another glass.

Claire Chartier made her way across the room to greet him. She spoke with a beautiful French accent that was only partially affected by her American surroundings. She wore a dark business suit with a short skirt, which made her look intelligent and intimidating.

"Welcome back, Lucas. I understand your trip was successful."

He reached out and shook Claire's hand. She grasped it warmly and smiled. She was in her early thirties and Lucas felt she, like Mike, was on his side. He looked into her blue eyes. "How were things in France?" he asked.

"They went well."

"Congratulations."

"I can't take all the credit. Empirico guaranteed the support of a political campaign in return."

"But you closed the deal."

Claire wanted to respond but a sudden shyness came over her. He wasn't flattering her, he didn't think he was anyway, but still her cheeks blushed and she excused herself pretending to need a drink.

Lucas forced his way around the room and greeted the rest of the Council. Every word felt fake. Every smile lacked genuine caring. They didn't see a young kid starting out in the corporate world. Instead, they saw a threat. Brilliance, age, success. He had no place to go but up. He called them each by name but none of them mentioned his. He felt like a foreigner talking to people who either couldn't, or didn't want to, understand him.

He looked around for Mike and Claire and saw them talking with senior Council members. He decided not to join them. Instead, he stood by himself, alone, in the middle of the room. He glanced at the platform, then at his watch. *He should be here by now.*

In an adjoining private room Empirico CEO and founder Caesar Alexander reviewed the latest financial figures. A Cuban cigar burned in an ashtray made of solid gold. He was seventy-two and still possessed the sharpest mind in his company. His puffy eyes had enough pink around them to attract attention. His thinning, gray hair was all that was left between him and baldness. Caesar was shorter than average and carried too much weight for a man his age. But he didn't care about weight. Caesar cared about numbers.

And thanks to the Council, especially Lucas, the numbers looked good.

He stood up from his desk and walked to the window. The thoughts of his recent phone conversation still echoed in his mind. He had turned down a strategic alliance with another drug company. The Council thought it was a good idea, but Caesar wanted no part of it. His offer to buy out the competing company was subsequently turned down. There would be no alliances. Not with Caesar. Not ever.

Claire came to the door. "We're ready for you, Mr. Alexander."

Caesar heard her but did not bother to make any reply. And why should he? He paid her $400,000 a year. He didn't owe her a response. If she didn't like it there were plenty of others to take her place. He looked out the window. His thoughts revolved around finding new markets for his drugs. A slight smile came to his face as he relished being in complete control of charting the course of his company, his empire, his life.

Caesar walked into the Council chambers and immediately the forty members took their places. The talking stopped. It suddenly got very quiet. Caesar looked out over them and felt like a commander in chief standing in front of his soldiers. "Welcome back, one and all."

Caesar spoke in a deep, raspy voice with a thick Italian accent. All the time he had spent in Chicago never had an effect on his speech. He saw Lucas in the last row and gave him a slight smile of approval. Normally, anyone else who had seen the smile wouldn't have thought anything of it. But the rest of the Council knew differently. They understood what the smile meant.

"We've increased our activity in Europe, parts of South America and of course here at home," Caesar said as he moved out from behind the lectern. "But when you concentrate on selling to your current clients and take your eye off of new territory, complacency sets in and it's not long before some other multi-national comes in and screws you over."

Lucas searched his mind for a market, a new product, to tackle. *Where are the sick who are in need of Empirico? Better yet, where are the sick who also have money?*

"We need ideas about where to focus our marketing efforts." Caesar looked out at the Council for suggestions. There was a pause, the kind you get when you're in a classroom and everyone is wondering who'll be brave enough to start the discussion. Lucas felt pressured to stand up and say something but nothing came to mind. Not yet.

Mike was first to break the ice. He stood up, adjusted his suit and cleared his throat. "In Japan and most of Europe the government still buys the lion's share of the drugs. We could concentrate more of our efforts on Europe. I know Claire did well in France." She looked at him and hoped he wasn't assuming she should get up and continue where he was leaving off. He nodded his head at her, then turned back to Caesar and explained why Empirico could beat out other research-based pharmaceuticals in Europe.

Mike sat down and the room went as quiet as it had been before he spoke. Caesar didn't even appear to be thinking it over. He looked around at his band of mercenaries and said, as though he was bored with what Mike had offered, "Any other suggestions?"

Various members of the Council offered their opinion as to where they should invest their energy, one of which was to pursue markets in Africa. Caesar listened patiently and after they were finished he jotted a few things down on a notepad. He took a sip of coffee and focused his eyes on Lucas. "Lucas? What are your thoughts? What do you think about Africa?"

Lucas swallowed. His hands felt sweaty. He took in a deep breath as quietly as he could. As he got to his feet his hand brushed against his glass of water and it spilled to the floor. It drew a few laughs from the Council. Not the funny, supportive laughs a person gets when they are with a group of friends; these were mean laughs, the kind that make an awkward situation even worse. It embarrassed him. *You want something that's really funny? How about your pathetic sales results from last month? I closed millions in my last trip alone. You won't be laughing when your insignificant accomplishments get you fired from this company.*

"I think Africa is a bad idea," he said. It was as though a moat was suddenly dug around Lucas so that he was on an island by himself, separated from the Council. "When it comes to pharmaceuticals, Africa is synonymous with philanthropy, not profit."

"You wouldn't go to Africa?" Caesar asked.

"Not if I had the choice. The only way I'd go to Africa is if the World Cup was being played there." It was supposed to be funny but nobody laughed.

Lucas continued. "Over the last three years the pharmaceutical industry has given more than two billion in financial assistance and medical products to developing countries—most notably to sub-Saharan Africa. It's used to fight diseases like malaria, tuberculosis and also AIDS which, if I remember correctly, has infected twenty percent of the adult population in some African countries, including Zambia."

"What do you suggest?"

Lucas felt the thoughts of the Council. *Now we've got you. You think you're so smart? All right, let's see what you're going to come up with. You're gonna fall right down on your face in front of all of us.*

Lucas' heartbeat went up. He felt the veins in his neck pound. The room froze. Panic knocked at his mind's door but he refused to let it in. "China," he said.

Caesar took in a deep breath and leaned his arms on the lectern. He shrugged his shoulders and looked at Lucas as if to ask for an explanation. "We're already in China."

"I know. But there's even more we could be doing there. Here's how. China is growing tremendously in the production and sale of bulk pharmaceutical active ingredients. Over the last fifteen or so years their pharmaceutical output has experienced an average annual growth rate of twenty percent or so."

"And?" Caesar asked.

"China's companies supply sixty percent of their market. The remaining forty comes from Japan, Europe and the US. That includes us. What we should do now is target the new, up-and-coming players in China. We can provide them with finished products."

Even though Lucas was finished with what he wanted to say he remained standing. He waited until Caesar nodded and then sat down. He glanced at Claire beside him. She smiled, proud of the way he handled himself. But behind her beautiful eyes was a hint of uncertainty.

"Responses?" Caesar asked.

Claire whispered into Lucas' ear. "Something doesn't seem right to me about China."

At first Lucas thought she was offering her opinion of whether China was viable from a business point of view. But when he turned and looked at her he saw there was something more behind what she was saying. The dark blue of her eyes conveyed an uncertainty, a fear almost, about what he had suggested. "What do you mean?" he whispered. Their connection was broken when Mike stood up.

"I think we should go for it," Mike said. "We have to make deeper roads into China sooner or later. We're fooling ourselves if we think we can grow and not increase our presence there."

Caesar contemplated the decision. He liked Lucas' idea about China, but he was surprised at Mike's emphatic support. "Lucas, you're going to China."

A chill went down Lucas' back. He didn't expect to be sent. He just wanted to give out the idea. Besides, there were more experienced members of the Council who had been to China; they should be the ones to go. Lucas fidgeted in his chair, trying to muster up the courage to disagree with Caesar in front of everyone. But before he could, Caesar continued. "China's upstarts are our next target. Mike, you go with him."

Mike nodded and immediately went to a phone that connected directly with Anne, the Danish bombshell at the front. Within three minutes she had Lucas and Mike booked first class with accommodations at the Grand Hotel Beijing. She e-mailed their clothing dimensions to the hotel so new Chinese suits, shirts and shoes would be waiting for them when they arrived. It made traveling so much easier.

Caesar dismissed the Council after giving a final speech that was supposed to give them encouragement. It didn't come out that way. It never did. It sounded more like a warning. A threat. Produce or you're out. Results. Success. No room for failure.

The members left the room but Lucas felt no relief. He closed his eyes and wondered why he had suggested China. *What difference does it make? The Chinese are people like everyone else. It's just another country.* And yet, he couldn't shake the feeling that he had made a mistake.

Lucas was about to leave when Caesar called out to him to join him in his study.

"You don't want to go to China?" Caesar asked as Lucas closed the door behind him.

"I want to go. I just wasn't expecting to take the lead on this. It'll be a challenge to convince the Chinese."

Caesar sat down in his chair and studied Lucas. He felt as though he was staring at a younger version of himself. Raw talent. Brains. Most of all, Lucas had guts.

"Power, Lucas. That's what convinces people. That's all it takes. And we've got plenty of it. We have the ability to make sick people well. We have what they want—we have healing drugs. That gives us power. And as long as we have it we can take this company places we can't even dream of."

"It's just that it's China. It's different out there. The people are different."

"People? People, Lucas, are all the same. They want a good life. And drugs make them think a good life is possible."

"Possible?"

"It doesn't matter if the drugs work. It only matters if people think they will work. We have good stuff here at Empirico, don't misunderstand me. I'm proud of what we've made. But you need to focus on convincing them that Empirico can meet their needs."

"But we can. We do have good medicine."

"I know. But that's not the point. The point is that people want to believe in something. They want to believe there is hope. And that, more than the drugs, is your job. To keep that hope alive in people. That's what makes sales."

Lucas nodded.

"Good luck in China, Lucas."

"Thank you," he said and walked to the door.

"And Lucas?" Lucas turned around. Caesar leaned forward and put his arms on his desk. "I believe in you."

Although Caesar was a tough boss and a hard man to work for, Lucas admired him. He was more than just an employer. He was a mentor, like a manager who roots for his boxer in the ring.

"I know you do."

Lucas walked through the security doors and down a hallway to the parking garage. China was next on the hit list and the formula for success would apply there as it had everywhere else. Concentrate on the sick people who had money and win at all costs. It was Empirico's unspoken motto. It had made Lucas into a successful young multi-millionaire.

But as he left the building he couldn't shake a feeling of uneasiness in his chest. It's the kind of feeling people get when they're waiting to be called into the doctor's office to discuss test results. There was something disturbing about China. Maybe it was the different culture. Maybe it was the different people. But the feeling was more than just nerves.

It was a warning.

2

Lucas got into his metallic blue, two door Mercedes. It retailed for $72,400, not that Lucas would know because Empirico leased it for him. And they would easily have given him another car if he'd asked for one. He sat down and felt the comfort of leather seats against his back. He wasn't sitting in some executive chair anymore. The meeting was over and for that he was thankful.

The underground parking garage attendant waved him through and Lucas cruised into traffic. It had stopped raining so he hit the recline button for the sunroof. He selected a jazz CD, Harry Connick Jr., and sang along with "On The Street Where You Live." He grew up listening to jazz and it used to serve as a separation tool between work and the rest of life. But that boundary was weak now, disappearing more and more each day as he made the continual transformation into a high-powered salesman. What was once just an occupation was now consuming him twenty-four hours of every day.

He stopped off at a roadside hot dog vendor and got himself a double-dog loaded with onions, mayonnaise and relish. He bit his teeth into it and savored the feeling meat lovers have when they're eating their favorite food. He finished the first one in less than a minute and bought a second one and a bottled water for the road. Chicago just had a knack for making great hot dogs.

He took Lake Shore and then Sheridan Road into Evanston just north of Chicago and arrived at the white steel gates in front of his home. He clicked a button and they opened inward. He felt proud of himself. That morning was one of the few times he remembered to close them. His grass was a perfect green. He once paid $1400 per month to have a professional lawn service take care of it for him but he had since given the contract to two engineering students who did a better job and charged half the price.

The driveway wound up a long incline and was decorated with white lights spaced perfectly between poplar trees all the way up to the large, red-brick house. It was 4,500 square feet with seven bedrooms, only one of which he ever used. He had a large pool and a hot tub in the backyard for entertaining large parties. He let the neighborhood children play on the tennis court whenever they felt like it. During the winter Lucas converted it to an ice rink and joined the aspiring players in the area for late night hockey tournaments.

He parked his car in the garage and walked out to the yard. He turned on the outdoor hot tub and pulled back the cover. He felt himself relaxing, as though the water was already rushing around him to calm his muscles.

Out of the corner of his eye he saw a shadow move inside his house. His heart skipped a beat and a moment later he felt a painful rush of adrenaline pound through his body. He walked to the back door, hoping what he saw was just a projection of his exhausted mind. He looked through the window beside the oak door and saw the alarm system was not armed. A surprise party, perhaps. But there were no cars on the street. Burglars? He tried to remember if he had armed the system before he left on his trip. But like so many things that are done regularly and out of habit, he could not recall if he had punched the code before leaving.

He unlocked the door. A few steps inside on the floor lay two tennis racquets. If he hurried in he could quickly grab one. He crouched through the door and touched his hand to the wall and moved it up and down trying to find the lights. He breathed in slow, short breaths and listened for even the slightest sound that could tip him off as to what was going on in his house. He rubbed his hand faster along the wall in search of the lights. Where was the panel? Frustrated, he turned his eyes to the wall. He found the panel and quickly looked back to the interior of the house. He was just about to turn the lights on when he saw them. Behind the couch. Two, maybe three. Colombians angry about the deal in South America. A competing American company bitter about the ground they lost to Empirico. They could be anybody. Whatever would happen here tonight, Lucas promised himself he would buy a gun. Maybe a few.

His heart rate sped up and he hit the lights. Fifty people jumped up and screamed at the top of their lungs. "Surprise!"

Thank goodness. They're not here to kill me.

Business contacts, a few people from the Council, acquaintances from the country club and beautiful women hoping they would catch his eye clapped for him. He looked so stupid, standing there holding a tennis racquet. A smile came to his face. He took in a breath and laughed. He was more relieved than happy.

Anna pushed through the crowd and kissed him on the cheek. Of course. His birthday. He had celebrated it in Toronto five days ago with unlikely business prospects he would probably never see again.

"Happy birthday, Lucas. We're glad you're still alive."

"You're responsible for this mess, of course."

"Welcome home."

At the other end of the kitchen Mike, Claire and a few others waved and came over to greet him. Lucas glanced around the room. His heart began to settle down.

"Thank you for nearly killing me." The group laughed. "And thanks for not being hired hit men." More laughter. "Thanks to all of you for coming." They applauded him. Anna turned on some dance music. He was glad they all took an interest in his life, especially the women—they looked so good. Dressed so sharp. But it was the end of a long business trip. And the end of a long meeting. He was tired and wanted to sit in the hot tub. Watch a game. Unwind.

He wished they weren't there.

The remaining lights came on. More people shook his hand. Some of the women kissed him on the cheek and tried to make small talk. They were recent law graduates, financial planners, marketing consultants. But Lucas was not interested in them. At least not tonight.

He grabbed a beer off the counter and joined some of the boys in the den. Ten guys watched the basketball game on a flat screen TV the size of a large window. The room was a great hang-out with four leather couches, a pool table, foozball, shuffle board and a stand-up video game for decoration. Male bonding at its best. Sports and no conversation. He had only watched a few minutes of the game when Mike tapped him on the shoulder. He spoke quietly so no one around them could hear.

"Some of the other guys want to have a talk."

"Which guys?"

"Just some guys. Not from the Council."

"What about?"

"Business."

No kidding. It was always about business. What else was there in life?

"What kind of business?"

"They just said they hoped you would keep an open mind."

Drugs probably. Or some kind of underhanded stock tip. Keeping an open mind was usually synonymous with keeping one eye closed.

"Tonight?"

"They want to meet right now."

There was only one person who could tell Lucas to do something immediately and that was Caesar Alexander. And Lucas was sure he didn't see Caesar here tonight.

"Tell them I'll meet them after the game."

The game ended at 1:00 a.m. Time zones really got in the way of those west coast games. But the Lakers had prevailed and put on a good show. Some of the girls who came with high expectations and low cut shirts had already left. Mike looked over at Lucas who nodded to him. The fun was over. Duty called.

The glass-sheltered verandah offered a beautiful view of the sky and the backyard. Lucas glanced outside to the pool and saw two women taking free throws at the basketball net.

At the table in the middle sat three men in their late twenties. Richard was an up-and-coming powerhouse in financing. He rode on his father's success and was ready to take their company to new heights. Raymond was a medical genius who studied at Harvard, which is where he and Lucas first met. Danny had recently graduated from Yale.

Lucas and Mike sat down and exchanged obligatory introductions with the three men.

"How was your trip, Lucas?" Richard was the one who had called the meeting. His tone indicated he felt small talk was necessary to butter Lucas up for something he would otherwise not be interested in.

"Successful."

"I knew you'd say that."

"Then why did you ask?"

Richard was off guard. He couldn't read Lucas' attitude. He decided to play him as though he were joking. Dry humor. He cracked a fake smile. "You know the rules. Ask three non-business related questions at the start of every meeting."

Richard chuckled. The other two did as well. He was dying for a response from Lucas. A little laugh. Even a smirk. This was inside the first five minutes of contact. The first five and the last five. That's all that really count in a deal. Lucas looked at Richard and smiled.

"Who said anything about rules?"

All five had a short laugh. Lucas watched Richard reach inside his pocket. He pulled out his cigarette package and put it on the table. Richard's eyes were shifty. His palms seemed a little wet. And he was smiling too much for a man who was otherwise confident. Richard was probably going to start lying.

"I have a huge idea. And this idea is backed by confident analysis," Richard began.

"What kind of idea?"

"We're looking to start up a company. Something big. Something powerful. A confidential business plan has already confirmed that $350 million in financing will be in place, provided certain conditions are met."

Richard handed him a business plan but Lucas decided not to look at it. He had people who looked after the analysis for him.

"Just tell me your idea."

Richard looked to Raymond for support. Raymond adjusted his glasses and cleared his throat. "It's all about pursuing a financially viable company that will put big-time dollars into our pockets."

Big-time dollars? Lucas was ready to leave. He hated those words. Not that he hated money; it was just that big-time dollars usually meant a pathetic product with a great marketing campaign. Besides, he worked for Empirico. Money was going to be a tough sell.

"We know you've got money," Richard said. "But with the incredible potential of this project we're convinced you'll come on board."

"What kind of business?"

Richard lit a cigarette and took in a long drag. "Pharmaceuticals." Richard looked directly into Lucas' eyes and watched for any hint of non-verbal communication.

"I'm already in the pharmaceutical business," Lucas replied.

Richard had thought through the possible ways in which Lucas could have answered. He delivered his counter-response as if on cue. "You are *working* for someone who is in the pharmaceutical business. We're offering you the chance to be a player. We have a start-up. IPO in three months. A new pharmaceutical company complete with a new lab and a talented workforce. And we want you to run it."

"You want me to sell out on Empirico?"

Raymond came to the rescue. "It wouldn't be direct competition. We would be pursuing different markets."

"How could you possibly? Do you know Empirico better than I do?"

Danny jumped in to continue construction on the now collapsing bridge. "I think what we're trying to say is we can become the next Empirico. You at the helm. No one here can do what you do. It's our shot, all five of us, to make it in the big leagues."

Lucas looked each one of them in the eyes. The smoke from Richard's cigarette rose between him and Lucas and seemed to form a barrier between them. The three tried to look relaxed and calm, but their beady eyes gave them away. "You're forgetting one thing," Lucas said.

Richard looked up in hope. "What's that?"

"I'm already in the big leagues."

Lucas stood up and the trio knew they were done for. They had gambled on their fragile relationship with Lucas and lost.

"Feel free to stay as long as you want," Lucas said as he walked to the door.

Richard tried to salvage whatever he could. Maybe there would be a next time. "This wasn't meant to upset you, Lucas."

"Who's upset? You're asking me to shaft Empirico. Have a nice night." Lucas walked out and didn't give them a second thought. He would never run into them again.

The trio left through the glass door and passed by the girls in the pool who had decided to give up on basketball for the evening.

Mike was the last person to leave the party. He and Lucas walked out the front door to the driveway.

"It really is good to have you back," Mike said.

"I guess I won't be back for long."

"Ready for the trip?"

"How do you get ready for China?" Lucas asked.

"Learn Chinese?"They both laughed.

"Any ideas on how to pitch them?" Mike asked.

"I'm working on something. I think we'll do fine. I know we will."

"Right. We'll tell them our drugs will make money, help their people and they'll go for it."

Lucas looked up at the stars. "You think we help people?" he asked.

"Of course. You don't?"

"Sometimes I wonder if we just prolong them."

Mike made no motion for a moment. It was as if the truth of his career was being revealed to him. "I guess that's one way of looking at it, isn't it?"

They exchanged goodbyes. Mike was about to leave when Lucas spoke up. "Mike?" Mike turned around. "You ever feel…" Lucas struggled for the right words before he continued. "You ever feel weird in those Council meetings?"

"What do you mean, weird?"

"I mean strange. Like something's wrong."

Mike's eyes grew wide. He put on a comical grin and lifted his hands like he was going to grab Lucas. "You mean like being in a haunted house?" Lucas laughed at first, but his smile faded when he realized that was exactly the kind of feeling he had at Council meetings.

"That's what it feels like, Mike." The night became still. Almost too still.

"I don't get what you're saying, Lucas."

"I'm telling you, it seems like the Council boardroom is spooked. Especially today. More and more all the time. It's creepy."

"You've had a long day. There's nothing creepy going on."

"There is. You don't feel it?"

"Have a good night, Lucas."

"You don't?"

Mike realized this wasn't a joke. "No. I don't. Now get some rest."

Mike walked through the property to his car which was parked on the neighbor's driveway to prevent Lucas from suspecting the surprise party. He started his Porsche 911 and drilled the accelerator. As Lucas heard the car take off down the street he felt a hollow void in his stomach. Having all those people in his house had masked the sense of uncertainty.

Now that he was alone the uneasiness returned.

3

Lucas changed into his silk pajamas. He sat down at the edge of his bed and wished he wasn't alone. He thought about the seven rooms in his house and wanted them to be filled. The moon lit up his dresser. On top of it stood a series of folded pieces of paper with photos. He looked at each one. There were thirty in all, pictures of his sponsor children from all around the world. His sponsorship provided them with food, clothing, shelter and education. They cost him $900 a month which got paid out from a low-risk financial plan he had set up for them. Having them up on the dresser made him feel better, as though he wasn't really alone. They probably thought about him once in a while, maybe more often. He certainly thought of them. He studied their faces. Some of them smiled, but not with the kind of smile people give when they're really happy. They smiled because they hoped there was a way out of their situation. Some of the pictures showed them standing in front of their shabby homes. Lucas shook his head. *Seven rooms.*

He tried to correspond with them at first but then gave up. Now he signed only the obligatory Easter, Christmas and birthday cards from the agency. What on earth was there to say? Hi, how's your life? Their lives were deplorable. And his was not. It was just that simple. He looked at one final picture of a boy in an African country and felt it hard to believe this child was on the same planet as he was. The boy had no socks or shoes. He wore a pair of shorts and a black suit jacket that was far too big for him—probably something his mother gave him on picture day to try and make him look nice for his friend on the other side of the world.

Lucas looked at the clock. 2:00. He had a sales meeting with a hospital executive in six hours, just before he was to leave for China and he'd be lucky not to fall over dead from exhaustion. Tonight would probably be a good night's rest. Four hours if he was fortunate, maybe uninterrupted. Sleep was never something Lucas got much of. Although he had seen doctors on various occasions he could not understand his sleeplessness. He exercised, ate well and had a positive outlook on life, but still found it took forever to fall asleep. He would have to try harder to convince Empirico to invent something for him.

On top of his dresser were two bottles. Whiskey and brandy. He wanted to go to sleep without touching them, but there was this gnawing, a persistent calling inside him to get up, guzzle both bottles down and hit the hay. No, he told himself and closed his eyes. But the thought of alcohol didn't leave him. At first, it was just there to help him sleep. Now it was part of him. A friend. An enemy.

As if being pulled by a rope, Lucas got out of bed and grabbed the whiskey bottle. He opened it and smelled a waft of alcohol. He poured himself a glassful, maybe two shots worth and gulped it down. It burned momentarily as he closed his eyes. He put the bottle down and wanted desperately to resist picking up the brandy.

Lucas opened it and poured another glass. Two shots worth. He didn't want to drink it but maybe if he did the voices inside would finally shut up, at least for the evening. He drank it down and hated himself for not having the courage to resist. He got back into bed. His head hurt from the rush of booze and he promised himself he would throw the bottles away first thing when he woke up.

He'd made himself that promise before.

The drinks helped him fall asleep. About three hours later he had a dream. Some dreams are strange, which is what makes them interesting, but this one was different. It just seemed so pointless. Lucas found himself standing in the middle of a desert. Lots of sand. Blistering heat. No water. Dry tongue.

And that was it. No other people, nothing to do, no danger. Just dry, hot desert. He didn't walk anywhere and didn't see anything except for sand and a merciless sun above, pounding down on him.

At 6:00 Lucas went for a jog outside. He ate a bran cereal breakfast along with a vitamin. He reviewed his stocks. Then his e-mail. Most of it was junk. Those Internet bulk mail people seemed to find a way to annoy everyone. He got into his Mercedes and decided to listen to the report on business. Anything was better than the incessant dribble of disc jockeys.

As he drove off to his hospital meeting the feeling of uneasiness showed up again. It wasn't jet lag or the alcohol from last night. This was something different.

Something unwelcome.

Lucas waited at the receptionist's desk at the hospital. A friendly Japanese girl came to see him. "Mr. Stephens?"

Lucas smiled and leaned against the desk. "Call me Lucas."

"Dr. Graves will meet with you on the leukemia ward in a few minutes. Would you like me to take you there?"

"I know the way."

Lucas walked down the hallway as fast as was acceptable for a hospital. He subconsciously took short breaths as if to avoid catching whatever was killing the patients. It was as though some green monster was going to jump out from one of the rooms, grab him around the neck and make him prisoner like all the others. He got to the cancer ward and felt a tightness in his chest. *Why do we have to meet on a cancer ward?* He sat down near a nurse's station and tried not to look at any of the patients walking by. They were so helpless. Lost causes, some of them. Maybe most of them. He didn't know. He just wanted for his meeting to be over and to get out. Hospital wards weren't an easy place for Lucas. Especially not after he was expelled from medical school.

"Lucas, sorry about the wait," Dr. Graves said as he emerged from a hallway.

"I can come back later if you want. It's no problem." It *was* a problem because Lucas was going to be on his way to China. But he knew Dr. Graves well enough to know he never canceled any appointments.

"Just give me five minutes?"

Lucas nodded and as Dr. Graves disappeared down a hallway he wished he wouldn't have to wait any longer. The seconds felt like hours until Lucas heard a quiet voice coming from inside a nearby room.

"Are you a doctor?" the voice said. Lucas paid no attention. He assumed it was directed at someone else.

"Are you a doctor?" The voice was louder this time and it *was* directed at him. It was a young girl's voice. Maybe five years old. Lucas stood up and poked his head through the door. He hoped she was not referring to him.

"Hello?" Lucas said, not sure who he was talking to.

"You're not wearing your coat."

Lucas stepped inside the room and saw a young girl sitting on her bed. She had big blue eyes and a precious, inquisitive look on her face. Above her bed hung a colorful painted sign. It read: ANGELINA. She had an assortment of stuffed animals and get-well-soon cards around her.

Angelina had no hair.

"I'm not a doctor."

"Are you a dad from one of the kids here?"

She spoke with a lisp. Lucas looked behind him. *What is taking Dr. Graves so long?*

"No. I… I sell pharmaceuticals." He was about to leave and close the door but Angelina got off her next question before he could do so.

"What?"

"I give doctors the medicine they need to make people better."

"Do you have one for me?"

"What do you have?" Lucas said this knowing full well how she would respond.

"I have 'kemia."

"Which stage?"

"I don't know."

Lucas' tongue froze in five hundred knots. He had counter arguments memorized for various responses to his sales presentations but somehow he felt helpless, almost afraid, in the presence of this sick child.

"We have various treatments for leukemia."

"You can come and stand here by my bed. You don't have to be afraid just because I don't have hair. It doesn't spread."

She was right, of course. But it didn't change Lucas' fear that the green monster was waiting to jump out and tackle him to the ground. He walked to her bed, nervous, as though he was walking through a minefield, and stood beside her. He swallowed, waiting for the monster to appear.

"So what's your favorite ice cream?" she said, tilting her head to the side.

"Ice cream?"

"Yeah. We get it once a week. What's your favorite?"

Lucas shrugged his shoulders. He felt sick looking at her. It was as though the illness was being transported telepathically into his body. "I don't know. Anything, I guess."

"Mine's strawberry."

"Strawberry. That's a good choice."

"Do you think your medicines can help me?"

Lucas wanted to get down on his knees to be at her level but his body wouldn't respond. He fought to maintain eye contact with her. Normally, talking about medicine came naturally for him. Yet somehow his vast pharmaceutical knowledge seemed inadequate now. "Not yet."

"When will you get them?"

"I hope very soon."

"They've told me that before. They've told all of us that."

"All of you?"

"There are thirteen of us here." Angelina pointed down to the other beds sectioned off by the curtains. "We're not going to get better are we?"

"Don't say that."

"The only way kids leave here is if they die."

"People recover from leukemia."

"Not the ones who come here."

Get her mind off dying. Get her onto a different subject. "What's your name?" Of course. An elementary marketing tool. Ask someone their name and use it often to reinforce your interest in them.

"Angelina."

"Angelina, we have the most powerful research facility on earth. We have the best doctors, the best technicians, the best of everything. We can do whatever needs to get done. We have the brainpower and we can solve every problem. There's nothing we can't do when we put our minds to it."

"So where's my medicine?"

Lucas looked deep into her trusting, inquisitive eyes. Angelina had an innocence about her that made it difficult for Lucas to slip into his salesperson propaganda. "It's coming." He knew he was stretching it. The best he could hope for was that it *might* be coming. He looked at his watch and decided to make a break for it. "I have to get going."

"Will you come back to see me?"

"Yes."

"Promise?"

Dr. Graves came to the door. "All set, Lucas?"

Thank goodness. Rescued at last.

"Goodbye, Angelina."

Angelina watched Lucas walk out of sight around the corner. She liked him. She liked all her visitors. But she hated the hospital. She hated being so tired. She hated the pain.

She was about to lie back down when she remembered she hadn't asked Lucas her favorite question. Angelina called out as loud as her soft voice would allow. "Wait! You didn't tell me your name."

Lucas did not hear her.

4

Lucas and Mike stepped out of the limousine at O'Hare and were met by an incredible gust of wind. It would be raining soon. Maybe pouring. Lucas thanked the driver and they headed into the airport.

They passed their bags along a security scanner and went through the detectors. At the security officer's request they opened their laptops and turned them on. A security guard wearing latex gloves rubbed a plastic instrument over their computers. Lucas and Mike took their laptops and walked to their gate. Lucas glanced behind him and saw the security personnel fading away in the distance. He still had the strangest feeling that he should not have accepted this mission. *It's just nerves*, he tried to convince himself.

They sat down in the crowded waiting area. Lucas checked his inside pocket to make sure his wallet and passport were secure. Outside, the wind picked up.

"China. Of all the places in the world, you pick China," Mike said.

"Think of it as space. A final frontier for Empirico."

"There will be plenty of other frontiers for Empirico. Besides, I think it's a long shot."

"That's where we play the best."

Lucas checked his watch, then glanced at a nearby paper. He saw the Cubs had won and he regretted missing the game. He loved being at Wrigley Field. He loved the excitement of being in the stands with a hot dog and hearing the fans shouting around him. He promised himself that when he returned from China he'd catch a game. He looked at another story on the front page; this one was about a phony children's charity scam. He started reading the article and then noticed the name of the reporter. It was Tabitha Samos. Loosing interest in the article he put down the paper.

The attendant called the first-class passengers to board the aircraft.

They stepped onto the airplane and a bubbly brunette showed them to their seats. She tried to make polite conversation but it only annoyed Lucas. He smiled and nodded his head but he wasn't listening.

He sat next to the window. The rain drizzled onto it making the world outside less visible. He relaxed in his large, comfortable chair and closed his eyes a moment, already looking forward to the return flight home. The brunette came by with drinks and took orders for their meals.

The plane backed away from the gate and taxied to the runway. A few minutes later the engines powered up. The plane jerked forward, pushing Lucas against his seat. It raced down the runway and the roar of the engines grew louder. He looked at the runway as the plane lifted off. It quickly moved away, then disappeared behind him, as did the rest of Chicago.

No phone calls, no distractions. He opened his laptop and pulled out the informational package Empirico had prepared on China. He caught the brunette as she passed by. "Excuse me. How much time before lunch?"

"Thirty minutes, sir."

Perfect. Just enough time to review the material.

They landed at LAX at 11:00 and hurried to their connecting flight. They boarded Air China flight 430 to Beijing and after a half hour wait they got their turn to take off.

As Lucas watched the City of Angels fade away beneath him, he recalled the last time he'd been there, especially the day he spent on Hollywood Boulevard. He loved the Walk of Fame—all the tourist shops, the crowds, the names of famous entertainers carved in stone on the sidewalk. He wondered what it might be like to be so popular—to be a movie star with thousands screaming at the premier showing—or to be a rock star in front of a sellout audience. He had caught a movie at the Mann's Chinese Theater. He thought it was *Spy Game* but he wasn't sure anymore. The interior design of the theater with its red carpet and gold-colored statues gave it the feel of an elaborate Chinese temple. He had been in awe. Sometimes architecture can make a person feel helpless. That's how Lucas felt at the theater. Now, on the plane, it made him wonder what his trip to China would be like.

Mike sank back in his chair hoping to get some sleep. Lucas reached into his laptop bag and found out he had forgotten to pack his sleeping pills. He closed his eyes in frustration. He thought about downing a few shots of vodka to help him sleep, but there would be no point in fighting the insomnia until later. He had work to do.

He prepared, then reviewed, a sales presentation. In the US there were about 250 pharmaceutical lobbyists per senator fighting for the pharmaceutical industry. But this was China.

This would be different.

"Wake up, Mike."

Mike opened his eyes from his deep sleep. "Here already?" He looked up and straightened out his glasses. Even in stressful circumstances, Mike managed to find a way to relax.

The customs line ups were still jammed from previous flights. There were a few American businessmen close to Lucas and a Spanish couple in front of him. He was sure he could overhear German spoken somewhere in the crowd. But mostly he heard a steady hum of Chinese. It was like an engine idling that felt louder the longer he listened to it. The signs around him had some English, but most contained symbols that meant nothing to Lucas. The people were shorter, too. They spoke so quickly. Lucas felt as though he was invisible—as though he had stepped into another world.

And all the pushing and shoving. People elbowing and bumping into each other. Lucas got a second jab in the back. He turned around and barked at the Chinese people behind him. He blinked his eyes to wake himself up. Every person seemed to take forever to pass through customs. He wanted to collapse in his hotel room bed and get some rest.

Lucas shook his head in frustration over how slowly the line moved. It was as though someone had tied his legs together and forced him to shuffle along. Mike waited beside him. Lucas noticed his reddening face. "You okay?"

"I feel like someone poured hot sauce down my throat," Mike said without breaking eye contact with the customs officers ahead.

"Just hang on. We're almost there. We'll find our guy with the sign and head off to the hotel. Ten bucks says we can get the Lakers game out here."

They finally got their turn. The customs officer was a thin man, so thin that he looked like he had been extremely ill. He motioned for them to give them their passports and called for another officer to come to his aid. A fat man appeared with a square, expressionless face. If he was thinking something suspicious he gave no indication of it. He clenched his jaw together and looked at Lucas and Mike as if studying their faces could reveal their intentions.

"What is your business in China?" the fat guard said in a heavy accent. He was addressing Mike but Lucas responded.

"Pharmaceutical sales."

"How long?" He motioned with his hand for Lucas and Mike to give him their laptop bags.

"Five days," Lucas said.

"And then?"

"Then it's back to the U. S. of A."

The thin officer took their bags and began to walk off with them.

"You're not taking those bags anywhere," Lucas said in a convincing tone.

The thin officer stopped and put them on the nearby counter where he had originally wanted to place them. The fat officer examined the passports, even the empty pages, to check for irregularities. Lucas rolled his eyes back. He covered his mouth with his hand to hide his yawn. The fat officer was about to ask Mike a question when the thin officer screamed. It startled Lucas.

The fat officer immediately turned around. Other officers seemed to materialize from thin air and crowded around the laptop bags. The crowd became quiet. The chatter stopped. All eyes focused on Lucas.

"What's going on?"

Mike couldn't tell. He perched up on his feet to see if he could get a better vantage point. "I don't know."

The fat officer shouted and two security officers immediately broke through the crowd and headed straight for the two Americans.

"This doesn't look good, Lucas."

"Just stay calm. We don't know what the problem is."

The fat officer turned to Lucas who caught a glimpse of his bag. Instead of a laptop there were packages of cocaine.

"Good God," Lucas said as his heart stopped. His throat swelled up. Sweat formed on his face. The room suddenly felt like a sauna. It was as though he had just witnessed an accident, or received news that a loved one had died.

"You are smuggling cocaine into China!" the fat officer said.

Lucas shook his head. "That's not mine." The hum of Chinese started up again. Lucas became angry with himself. How could he let this happen? He was always so careful. His laptop was with him the whole time. Was it the Spanish couple? The Germans? Someone working for the competition? Whoever they were, they got them. And good.

The officers grabbed Lucas and Mike and pushed them through a set of security doors. The doors closed behind them and the buzz of the crowd was gone. Suddenly, everything turned quiet. All Lucas could hear was his own breathing. All he could see was a myriad of expressionless Chinese faces staring at him. Within an instant he had become an enemy of the people.

The fat officer put Lucas in one room and Mike in another. He locked the door and left Lucas with a guard. Lucas expected the fat officer to return any moment. He was wrong.

"This is a mistake."

"Quiet!" The guard shouted in a heavy accent and stared ahead without looking at Lucas. He was a young guard and he acted overly aggressive to compensate for his fear of sharing a room with a man being held for interrogation.

"I don't have time for this," Lucas muttered to himself. He stood up and banged on the door. "I don't have time for this!"

The guard stood up with fire in his eyes. "Quiet and sit down!"

Lucas took in a breath and exhaled, trying to get himself under control. He approached the guard and looked deep into his dark eyes. Lucas lifted a finger and pointed it at the guard's face. "You are not going to yell at me one more time. You will sit down and you will shut up. Don't say another word. Do you understand me?"

The guard swallowed and debated punching Lucas in the face but chose to sit down instead. Lucas paced around the small room, wondering how long this would take.

He did so for three hours.

Lucas sat in his chair with his suit jacket off. His sleeves were rolled up, his eyes exhausted. The guard sat perfectly straight. Didn't move. Competition for Buckingham Palace. The fat officer entered.

"You are being charged with bringing an illegal substance in to China."

"I want to speak with a member of the American embassy."

"You will have opportunity for this later."

"What's your name?"

"I am not here to discuss the matter."

Lucas reached across the table to the fat officer to offer a handshake. "My name is Lucas Stephens."

The fat officer stood at attention and gave short bow. "Chang Chou."

"Chang. Pleasure to meet you. Have a seat."

Chang thought a moment, looked at the guard and took a seat.

"Chang. This has been a mistake. I can provide you with information on my personal income. It will show that I earn way more than what I could make from whatever was placed in my bag."

"The rules are the rules."

"And I agree. We couldn't have a world if we didn't have rules. But rules are meant for people who break the law. What do you think, Chang? Do you think I would bring drugs into your country?"

"I don't know you."

"That's right. You don't know me. Under other circumstances we'd probably see things eye to eye. But the good news is you don't have to know me. You just have to know my record. Clean as a sheet."

Should I offer him a bribe? Lucas decided against it. The negotiations had just begun. Lucas was on the lower end of the teeter-totter and he could feel he was about to get lifted up. *Don't jeopardize anything now. Just stay cool.*

Lucas looked directly into Chang's eyes. It was good business practice. He could see Chang beginning to see things his way. A misunderstanding. That's all this was. Chang got up. Lucas got up as well. Always a good sign. Chang looked at Lucas. "You are being detained indefinitely in a maximum security prison." Chang shouted something at the guard who got up and grabbed onto Lucas with his huge, powerful hands.

"What are you doing? You have no right to do this!"

Chang opened the door and led the way out. Lucas screamed into Chang's ears to let him go. The walls echoed with Lucas' shouts. At the end of a hallway stood three more guards. These ones wore helmets. They had bands around their arms. And rifles in their hands. They stood at attention and saluted Chang without making eye contact with the criminal. Lucas turned to the other room where Mike was emerging.

"Mike!"

Mike turned to see his friend being taken away. "Lucas!"

Chang shouted. "The prisoner will be silent!"

The guards fastened handcuffs on Lucas and grabbed tight into his upper arms, cutting off his circulation. He screamed at them to let go but they paid no attention. He pulled his arms away as best he could but the guards only held on tighter. They forced him down a set of stairs and through a door to the outside. The bright sunlight blinded him a moment, as if someone was shining a flashlight directly at him. When his eyes readjusted he saw an armored vehicle with the rear door open. The guards pushed him inside and got in with him. They tied a chain through his handcuffs down to the floor. The door closed. The engine started. The vehicle moved on.

It happened so fast. One moment he was on a plane and now he was in the hands of Chinese law enforcers. The jet lag almost made him think it was a dream. But the cold, hard bench assured him he was under arrest in China. All Lucas could see was the expressionless Chinese guards who could not have cared less who he was.

The vehicle came to a stop and a fist from outside banged against the door. One of the guards lifted the lock and opened it. The setting sun came at just the right angle to catch Lucas in the eyes, blinding him a moment. A guard unfastened the chain that connected Lucas to the floor. He grabbed Lucas' arm and forced him through the door. His feet hit the ground and his legs hurt from sitting so long. He closed his eyes to adjust them to the light. But what he saw when he opened them made him wish he had kept them shut. He blinked in horror. What he saw made him feel sick to his stomach. His chest became tight, as though someone had filled his lungs with fluid. He would have lost his balance and collapsed if it weren't for the guards holding him up.

A twelve-foot-high brick wall with five rows of barbed wire angled towards the inside surrounded the perimeter. Guards stood in watchtowers at regular intervals. In the distance, outside the gates, small, frail bodies worked in a field being watched by men in uniform carrying guns.

The guards took Lucas to the intimidating two-story facility. A guard who could not have been more than twenty opened the gate. They passed through and Lucas entered the compound.

They walked along a crushed rock path to an entrance on the side. Two guards with rifles stood at the door as the other guards pushed him through. The moment Lucas entered, he felt a horrible pain come all over him. It got dark. It got cold. But mostly, it got scary.

The guards waited with Lucas in a hallway until another guard appeared. This one was tall. Very tall. He came through a doorway and lowered his head to make it through. He was lean, but fit. The tall guard spoke to the other guards. They discussed their orders and why Lucas was there. A dangerous offender. Dangerous to the people of China. The stench of stale urine and humidity filled Lucas' nostrils. He felt nauseated and tried to breathe through his mouth to avoid vomiting.

The tall guard looked at Lucas with his sunken hollow eyes. They were set back so far into his face it made Lucas wonder if they were there at all. He said nothing. He just turned around and starting walking. The other guards grabbed Lucas and pushed him down the hallway.

The tall guard stopped outside another door and produced a blue uniform. The number 430 was stenciled in Chinese on the shoulders and the back. He pointed at Lucas to enter the room. Lucas got in and the guards followed. The tall guard shouted at Lucas, gave him the uniform, then nodded to one of the other guards who came and unfastened the handcuffs.

Lucas waited for them to walk out of the room so he could change but they showed no signs of leaving. The tall guard shouted again. Lucas hesitated. The tall guard stepped closer to Lucas who only came up to his chest. The tall guard shouted so loud it made Lucas jolt. Lucas turned around and took off his shirt. One of the guards said something and the others laughed. Lucas took off the rest of his clothes and felt as if he was in one of those dreams where a person is naked and everyone around them is staring at them.

The tall guard shouted and two guards grabbed Lucas by the neck and forced him to bend at the waist. Lucas struggled but could not get free. The tall guard made a coughing motion and Lucas coughed. The tall guard inspected Lucas and let go of him. Lucas straightened up, unable to look any of them in the eye. He put on his uniform, the buttons barely fitting around his chest. They grabbed him and led out of the room.

They passed a number of cells on their way down the narrow cobblestone hallway. Lucas caught a glimpse of the decrepit looking people inside. Their bodies were so thin, their hair knotted and greasy. At the end of the hall another prisoner talked out loud to an imaginary friend beside him. He banged his head against the bars as saliva dripped from his mouth.

They stopped outside the last cell. The door was open. There was a bench to the side. The cold, stone floor had water, or some other kind of liquid, on it. A tiny window let in a crack of light. There was barely enough room to stand. A guard took Lucas' cuffs off.

"There's no way."

The two guards behind him cocked their rifles and held them ready.

"I don't care what is going on in your sick minds but I am not going in there!"

The tall guard punched Lucas in the chest, knocking the wind out of him and sending him backwards. He immediately locked the door. Lucas lunged forward but was stopped by the bars. He screamed at them with such force that the echo was heard throughout the block. He continued shouting at the guards as they walked down the hallway, up the stairs and out of sight. His demands for justice went completely ignored.

Lucas had arrived at Xaing Xaing Penitentiary.

5

Fifteen thousand feet above the ground at a dropzone near Chicago, a group of skydivers cued up and got ready to jump. Last in line was Tabitha Samos, a twenty-six-year-old daredevil in search of another thrill. She'd gone hang gliding in the Alps, bungee jumping in Vancouver, canoeing on the Amazon, rock-climbing in Arizona, scuba diving in Cozumel and she had even tried downhill mountain bike racing near the Grand Canyon.

Tabitha had broken a total of twenty-eight bones in her body.

The flight instructor shouted her name. She stepped out onto the wing and looked down. Somewhere beneath her was land, she hoped. The wind rippled through her jump suit and for a split second it went through her mind that there was a chance, however small, of both her primary and secondary chutes not opening. For most people this is enough to keep them on the ground. But for Tabitha, this was what had got her up there in the first place. She took in a breath and flung herself away from the airplane. She turned over on her back and stretched out her arms like a giant star. The plane quickly turned into a small dot. She stared up at the sun and relaxed in the experience of free fall. She raced through the air at 120 mph and wished the next sixty seconds could last forever.

She reached 3,500 feet and recalled the promise she made to her instructor that she would pull her ripcord at this elevation. Now that she was here, it suddenly felt like she could fall another thousand feet without any trouble. Who needed to play it so safe? The closer she got to the ground the faster her heart pounded. This was life. 3,000 feet. The ground was getting still closer, like a fast approaching car in an accident. 2,500. Down at terra firma, the instructor watched her and knew she was in trouble. 2,000 feet. She pulled her rip cord and thought about how living or dying can come down to whether someone was paying attention when they prepared your pack.

The chute raced out and caught the draft. Immediately, her harness ripped into the back of her legs. At ten feet she pulled on the toggles and slowed herself down to a perfect landing. Not a foot to spare.

Some of the other jumpers cheered. Some shook their heads. The instructor approached her with a look capable of melting steel. "We agreed at 3,500!" He had never lost a jumper, but as long as Tabitha was around he was leery of losing his record.

"I changed my mind," Tabitha said with a confident grin.

"Next time it's 3,500. Or you're grounded."

"I've done 3,500. That's for amateurs."

"Which is what you are."

Tabitha smiled and gave him a playful shot in the shoulder. "See you next time."

She walked past him to the clubhouse where she changed into her blue jeans, T-shirt and black leather jacket. She hung out with some of the other jumpers for a few minutes to get caught up on how they were doing. There was talk about a night jump and a trip to South America.

Tabitha threw her gear in the back seat of her mint yellow '67 Mustang convertible and pulled back the top. Her medium, attractive build fit perfectly behind the wheel. She sped off down the highway; her shoulder-length black hair blew in the wind as she put on her sunglasses and popped in a dance CD.

Tabitha hurried up the stairs at the *Chicago Observer* to her cubicle. Some of the articles she had written were pinned on the walls. Her claim to fame was exposing a senior city official who was involved in a mortgage fraud scam. She had recently blown the whistle on a bogus children's charity as well as a group of parishioners who were subsequently convicted of siphoning large amounts of money from their church's offerings. The joy of uncovering the truth. Her desk was clean. Photos of some of her friends were stuck on the side of her computer.

She glanced at her watch and hurried to the boardroom where she and the other reporters gathered to discuss the rapes, the murders, the accidents, the sports teams and any other newsworthy items. Her boss, Charlie Chester, the *Observer*'s resident workaholic editor, stood at the front and finished his cigar. The building was smoke-free but he didn't seem to care. He was a short man, overweight, balding and always wore old dress shirts that were practically see-through. Fat Chester (that was his name when he wasn't within ear shot) listened to some of their ideas for stories and gave his almighty approval or disapproval. Tabitha opened her notebook to some of the leads she had on over-billings, fraud and false business practices.

"Sports?" Chester asked.

"Bulls lost on a last shot by Miami," Forester said.

"Hard to believe they got so close," Chester grumbled. He sucked back on his coffee, which he never got from the coffee maker. He always had a special pot brewing privately in his office. No one was ever allowed to test his private mix and rumor had it there was more than coffee in his cup. "We've also got a lead on a new theater being constructed at Navy Pier."

There was nothing new with this story and Tabitha looked away from Chester hoping to avoid the assignment. Chester glanced over his bifocals around the room. He caught Alex trying to avoid him.

"You're the man, Alex. New theater goes to you."

"You're sure about this, Chester?"

"Of course I'm sure. Everybody loves Navy Pier. Beautiful boats. Homemade lemonade with enough sugar to get you high. The theater is news."

Chester turned around and Alex rolled his eyes. Tabitha sat at the back facing Chester with her chair turned around. She didn't need this meeting. She knew the stories she wanted to cover. Forester had been looking at her off and on, examining her. On one occasion she caught him, forcing him to pretend he was just scanning the room. Chester caught her eye.

"Tabitha?"

"I'm working on a story involving an engine manufacturer. An insider says the company knew the lawn mower engines were faulty but an internal audit revealed it would be cheaper to deal with the law suits than to recall them."

"That'll sell. What else?"

Tabitha grinned. "Sheridan Corvey's coming to town."

The group leaned back on their chairs chuckling and shaking their heads.

"What's your angle?"

"Global faith healer. There are bound to be false claims of recovery. All kinds of people go to his services thinking they get healed. Huge offerings. Maybe he's got a political agenda."

Chester laughed and nodded his head. The rest of them discussed other stories, but Tabitha had already mentally left the meeting. She began working on her leads and thought about the unique angle she could give each story.

"Then I think we're set for today," Chester said as he reviewed his sheet. The group was about to disperse when he suddenly remembered the scrap of paper he was handed before the meeting started. His eyes grew bigger as he clutched the paper in his hand. He stopped them with a shout. "Wait!" Everyone turned to face him. "We have something here. An American caught for drug smuggling in China."

The group sat down. Tabitha let out a sigh. *Who cares? The more drug smugglers in jail the better.*

"Tabitha, I want you to investigate this."

It was an insult. He may as well have asked her to cover the repainting upgrades of the city's light standards.

"You're sure there's something there?" Tabitha asked with enough conviction to question the relevance of a dope smuggler in China.

"This is a senior executive."

"Sounds promising," said Wanda, the gossip columnist.

"He's a big gun for a..." Chester reviewed his notes. The kick in the coffee was slowing him down. "A pharmaceutical company. He of course claims he is innocent. His company wants him back. I think there's a hook in there somewhere."

Tabitha thought the idea was stupid. "You got it."

The group left to pursue their assignments. Tabitha reluctantly walked up to Chester to get the contact information from his sheet. A boring story was one thing. Being assigned a boring story was even worse.

"What's his name?" she asked.

Chester looked over the scrap of paper. Nothing on the first side. He turned it over to make sense out of the scratchings on the other side. Something inside Tabitha suddenly made her feel uneasy. It was as though she was about to hear a jury give an unwelcome verdict.

"His name is Lucas Stephens."

Tabitha stopped breathing. Her legs felt like Jell-O. A knot formed in her throat. Her stomach began to ache. *Impossible. Not Lucas. Not Lucas Stephens.* The room cleared out leaving Tabitha by herself.

She had hoped she would never have had to hear his name again.

Lucas didn't sleep his first night at Xaing Xaing. The smell was impossible to get used to, so was being in a room with no privacy. The bars allowed any of the guards passing by, or the insane person in the cell across from him, to look at him. He spent the evening blaming himself for not being more careful. Why didn't he keep a more watchful eye on his bag? And how did the drugs get put there in the first place? But all that didn't matter. And it wouldn't matter, either. He'd spend the day in prison, the issue would get cleared up and he'd be released. In the meanwhile he was losing time. His first meeting was scheduled for the end of the day and he was a wreck. He hadn't slept in thirty-six hours. A warm bed was already a distant memory.

At daybreak, three guards pulled him from his cell and took him to a room on the main level. It had a window with bars on it and a table with two old wooden chairs, one on either side. The guards sat him down. The team of lawyers would be showing up momentarily to get him out of this hole. Certainly an embassy representative would come as well. He waited for ten minutes and then the door opened.

A guard showed Mike into the room and directed him to a seat opposite Lucas. The guard said something to the other guards and then stood behind Mike. At first the guards had looked upon Lucas as a criminal. Now they looked at him with more anger. More distrust. More revenge.

It brought Lucas relief to see his friend again. A familiar face. It was a welcome change from the other prisoners and guards. Mike wore a pair of dress pants and a shirt, not a prison uniform.

Mike had trouble looking Lucas in the eye. Lucas' black hair was disheveled. He had bags under his eyes. He stank like sweat and urine. His face was unshaven and he looked stressed and enraged.

"How are you, Lucas?"

Lucas didn't answer. He looked behind Mike as though he was expecting to see something that was not there. "Where's the embassy representative? The lawyers? Mike. Where are they?"

Mike swallowed and looked at the guards as if hoping they would help him deliver the news. "They're not here, Lucas."

"When are they coming?"

Mike pressed his lips together. He felt like a doctor giving an unwanted result to a patient. "They're not coming, Lucas."

"What do you mean they're not coming?"

"We're working on it. But the Chinese government is not interested in discussing your release."

Lucas swore. "I don't care what they're interested in." He leaned forward. "I'm not staying here one more minute. You understand me?"

"I understand."

"What about Caesar?"

"He's trying. He's been on the phone with Senator Turtle. They're trying to work something out."

"Then tell them to try harder!"

"Lucas, we're in contact with every government agency. We're doing all we can."

"It doesn't seem like it, Mike."

"The last thing on the Chinese government's mind is an American executive who's been caught—"

"Allegedly caught."

"Allegedly caught for smuggling."

Lucas leaned his head back as though he was in a shower hoping to get some water on his face. He took in a few regulated breaths. "This is going to blow over. I'm going to be fine. This will all work out."

"The Chinese government has told us they will review your case at the hearing."

"Good."

"Not really," Mike said. "I'm told hearings can be scheduled three months to two years from the time of arrest."

The air went out of Lucas. He didn't notice but his mouth was now wide open. "I don't care about the Chinese government, Mike. I don't care what they think and I don't care about their policies. You get me out and I don't care what you have to do."

"Empirico lawyers are discussing your situation with Chinese authorities. They don't think it looks good right now, Lucas."

"Write them a check for five million. Threaten to poison their water supply! What's the matter with you? Be resourceful!"

"You're not hearing me, Lucas."

Lucas began to panic. On the one hand he wanted to avoid believing the situation was real in order to keep his sanity; on the other hand he knew he couldn't lie to himself. The thick walls of reality started to close in on him.

"You're not getting out, Lucas. Maybe not ever."

It was as though he was in a sinking ship with the lifeboat getting farther and farther away. *Stay in control. You have gotten yourself out of bad things before and you can do it again. Just relax and think. Nothing is impossible, Lucas. You can do it. Just stay calm. You'll get yourself out.*

He hoped.

"I've been advised by our government to leave immediately." The guard behind Mike shouted. Mike stood up. "Lucas, we'll get out. I promise."

Mike left his friend in the stinking, hot meeting room at the mercy of two guards and a system they both knew nothing about.

The guards grabbed Lucas. Fear gripped his heart. Reality crashed into hope when he discovered they were going to take him back to his cell. Lucas had served time in prison before and it was not worth repeating. Least of all, not at Xaing Xaing.

The guards lifted him firmly by the shoulders and Lucas struggled to free himself. One of them shouted and immediately the tall guard and another guard came into the room. They all grabbed an arm or a leg and yanked his twitching body from the room. Lucas cursed as loud as he could and yelled at them to let him go. He was dragged down the hallway, further and further away from any chance of release.

His mind kicked into gear. How would he get out? He turned his head to look at one of the guards. He would grab one of their guns. He'd shoot the first two and hold the others hostage. Or he could shoot them all dead and make a break for it. But they were holding on with incredible strength as they carried him to his putrid cell. Escape was going to be difficult.

Four strong, armed men would be impossible for anyone, and it should have convinced him not to try anything. But for Lucas, rational thinking was quickly being replaced with an uncontrollable panic to get out at all cost. It was crazy for him to consider any kind of insurrection. He was about to find out why.

A guard opened the door and Lucas pretended to go limp from exhaustion. He faked an act of crying, anything to get the guards to release their hold. He would get them. And he would get out of this septic tank. They let down his feet but Lucas pretended not to be able to stand. Another guard let go, leaving the last guard to push him into his cell.

With a burst of energy Lucas smashed through the partially closed door. He lunged for the guard's rifle. The group was caught completely by surprise. He managed to get hold of the rifle, but the guard grabbed onto the barrel to keep it from pointing into his face. Another guard grabbed Lucas and prevented him from pulling the trigger.

Lucas clenched his fist and drove it into the guard's throat. The guard was stunned and began to wheeze. Lucas clenched his fist and tried to drive another blow into his throat to crush his breathing passage. Just as he was about to strike again he was grabbed from behind by the tall guard who threw him onto the cobblestone floor. Lucas got up and charged after them.

This time the guards were ready.

The tall guard smashed the butt of his rifle directly onto Lucas' shoulder, separating it on contact. Another guard grabbed Lucas by the hair and punched him in the face. The tall guard kicked him repeatedly in the stomach and groin.

Lucas dropped to his knees and flailed with his arms but could not connect with any of them. A guard rammed the butt of his rifle into Lucas' side, which resulted in a tremendous cracking sound. He fell to the floor but refused to give up. He swung at the tall guard but missed completely. The other three punched him and stomped on him with their boots. A fist hit him between the eyes and Lucas knew his attempt at escape had failed.

But the guards did not stop.

They kicked his body with their heavy boots, driving their heels into his side. One kick landed on his face with such force that his nose broke and began bleeding.

Lucas turned over on his chest to protect what he could. *Enough. Enough. Please. Enough.*

The tall guard got down on his knees. He yanked Lucas' head back, spat in his face and drove his fist in Lucas' eyes. Lucas felt himself drifting off into unconsciousness. His entire body was paralyzed with pain. Blood poured out of his nose and out of his mouth. He couldn't move his feet or his hands. His last thought before leaving his senses was of his young life being taken by four guards who didn't know his name, in a penitentiary few in America had ever even heard of.

My God, Lucas thought. *I'm dying.*

The guards didn't stop beating him until they were tired. They dragged his motionless body into his cell leaving a trail of blood along the way. They locked the door and left him lying there on the way to death.

Lucas was completely alone.

6

Tabitha hung up the phone. It brought her relief to know Empirico had no comment about the Lucas Stephens situation. All Anne, the Danish receptionist, said was that they were doing everything they could to get him out and when they had further information they would issue a press release. Until then, Tabitha could put the story and Lucas, out of her mind.

She pulled out a red folder and wrote SHERIDAN CORVEY across the top. She shook her head. No doubt hundreds of people would be lining up at the wishing well for their chance at healing. No doubt they would be tithing their hard-earned money into the coffers of a multi-millionaire to appease the gods and get their deliverance.

Her acquaintance in the administration department at Mount Carmel University returned her phone call and told her they had a theologian named Edgar Sardisan who might be willing to discuss his thoughts on the upcoming Corvey Crusade. She wanted to know what a religious man thought about supernatural healing and whether a good, respected university like Mount Carmel had been suckered into Corveymania. Tabitha debated about driving the two hours from Chicago to Mount Carmel in South Bend, Indiana to meet with Edgar. Live interviews were always better and Mount Carmel was near Notre Dame University. She loved the Fighting Irish campus and figured she could make a day out of it. Maybe she could meet with Edgar at Mount Carmel in the morning, then drive to Notre Dame and hook up with some friends who were studying there. Maybe they could introduce her to some of their friends. Maybe they could introduce her to someone new.

She left a message on Edgar's voice-mail and wondered what kind of man he was.

Edgar Sardisan hurried down the crushed rock pathway to his class at Mount Carmel. He held a stack of books in his hands as he passed by students, nodding and saying hello as fast as he could. He entered his full classroom and plopped the books down on the desk as proof of how well read he was.

Edgar was a theologian because his father was one, as was his father before him. He lived in a house near campus and drove an import because that's what most of the professors at Mount Carmel did. He wore dress pants, a dress shirt and a dress sweater even when the weather was too hot. He never smoked. He drank on occasion and jogged two miles each day. He bordered the fine line between teacher and friend and often wondered if there should be such a line. He was known to have midnight poetry reading sessions with his students outside on campus grounds under the moonlight. He attended every Fighting Irish football game. Edgar had never married.

He looked out at his students and saw one of them wearing a Fighting Irish shirt. He tried not to notice it. He shifted his eyes and did what he could to shake the feeling that he was only teaching at Mount Carmel.

Real professors taught at Notre Dame.

He avoided looking at the far right side of the room where two captivating girls sat. He had been trying to train himself not to look in their direction. Their tight shirts and jeans were a distraction for Edgar. Why on earth couldn't they just wear some conservative clothing?

Edgar cleared his throat and opened his binder to find his lecture pages. He flipped back and forth looking for the day's topic. But what he saw surprised him. A shock raced through his body. Today's lecture notes were missing. *Where are the notes?* He had reviewed them the night before to prepare yet again for today's lecture, but now they were missing. His face turned red of embarrassment. A lecture without notes was impossible.

"In our ongoing discussions of the relevance of theology we will today be discussing some of the works of C. S. Lewis..." he said as he looked through his briefcase. He had no idea how he would continue. *Where are those notes? Where are they?* The two models over to his right stared at him. He felt their presence and his heart-beat went up. Sixty minutes of off-the-cuff lecturing. Death was a welcomed alternative.

A drop of sweat dripped down his side. He moved his books around pretending to layout the materials he would need. *How could I have been so stupid?* A life preserver appeared in the form of a raised hand from a student at the back.

"Dr. Sardisan?"

Edgar looked up, adjusted his glasses and hoped it would be a long question. "Yes?"

"Why don't we as a class go to the Sheridan Corvey crusade next Tuesday?"

It let the wind out of Edgar's teaching sail. Corvey. He was dearly loved by all the theologians at Mount Carmel. "Corvey?" Edgar nodded wishing it could have been any other topic. "What can you tell me about Sheridan Corvey?" Edgar said still looking into other binders for his lecture notes.

"He doesn't have any educational background and yet he has a growing global following. He earns a boat load of money, puts on an incredible show and lots of people get healed."

Edgar nodded again. He'd read a few articles on Corvey and his student was at least partially right. Corvey performed with a sound and light show that would make a rock band jealous. His salary was rumored to be in the high hundred thousands. And the claims of people being healed? No. No, they weren't healed. Sure, those with sore backs and bad knees got 'miraculously healed' but mostly it was showmanship. Mostly it was a crock.

One of the professors had Corvey's picture on his dartboard. Another two had articles published proving how Corvey was a char-latan trying to destroy sound reason. One professor had even prayed for Corvey to be removed from the world stage. Corvey was a four-letter word among Mount Carmel theologians.

"I'm not sure Mr. Corvey would provide any insight into our

course," Edgar replied with as much tact as possible. Anything to avoid a conflict. Now where were those notes?

"I've never been to a Corvey Crusade," said a man in his early twenties.

Time to extinguish the fire. "People. This is theology. Corvey is pop culture." His comment drew a few laughs.

One of the beauty queens raised her slender arm to ask a question. He could feel her eyes on him and it made him nervous. He made brief eye contact with her and nodded his head to acknowledge her question. "He has more than a million people subscribing to his newsletter. I'd like to see what all the fuss is about."

Deception, thought Edgar. *Corvey is a deceiver.* "I don't think it would be wise." Then Edgar stopped himself. Exactly what did he have to be afraid of anyway? His theology was sound. Why not put it to use? *After all*, thought Edgar, *you build a house knowing it will withstand the rain.* "Tell me why you think we should go," he added, with enough conviction to insinuate that if they could provide a suitable answer then he would schedule their next class at a Sheridan Corvey Crusade. Heaven forbid.

"His viewpoint is different from anything at this institution," said a lawyer who had decided to pursue further studies.

"And he has actual documented healing results," said an engineering graduate.

Alleged results! Edgar wanted to scream it out but contained himself and simply nodded his head. He raised his eyes, looking for more evidence.

A farm boy who had barely made it into the program raised his hand and spoke at the same time. "His core belief system is the same as ours. Why, then, is his ministry so much different?"

His argument convinced Edgar. "You're absolutely right. How can someone with a similar starting point as us get so far off track?"

Allegedly off track, thought the farm boy as he bit his lip.

Edgar looked over the class, avoiding the beauty queens, and saw the excitement in their eyes. How could he deny them the opportunity to explore something they were so interested in? "We'll investigate Mr. Sheridan Corvey at his crusade in Chicago this coming Tuesday."

The room erupted with applause and cheers.

"We'd better travel together and get there three hours early," began the lawyer. "He packs every place out two hours in advance."

The last comment struck Edgar. The church where he preached was never more than half full.

Edgar got through his lecture by discussing what the students hoped to learn from Corvey's crusade. When class ended he gathered his things together and left the room knowing his carelessness in forgetting the notes cost his students a useful lecture. He stopped and talked with some of the students and then walked into the office area and greeted his secretary. She reminded him of his doctor's appointment at the end of the week and mentioned that a reporter from the *Chicago Observer* named Tabitha had called for him. He nodded his head but he wasn't paying much attention. He was more interested in who the Fighting Irish were going to start as quarterback. Their home opener was against the Spartans and Edgar had a bet going with a professor from Michigan State. The loser had to memorize a chapter from Leviticus.

He entered his office and saw two men sitting at his desk. They were Reverend Glenn Handle, the executive vice-president of Mount Carmel, and Don Sheath, chair and associate professor of theology. A scheduled meeting with these two at the university club room was a good thing. A visit in the office, especially unannounced, was always a bad thing.

"How are you, Edgar?" Reverend Handle said.

Edgar's mind began to race. What had he done? His papers were graded on time. He was doing more than his fair share of extracurricular work. He even remembered to buy the reverend a present for his birthday.

"I'm fine," Edgar said as he quickly remembered his manners. "And how are the two of you doing?"

"We're good. Have a seat, Edgar."

Edgar resented them being there. It was their faculty, their school, but it was his office.

"Edgar, we wanted to have a little talk," began Reverend Handle.

Little was the operative word. They had never been in his office before and their uncommon coldness toward him did not put him at any ease.

"What about?"

"We've heard you're planning on taking your students to the Sheridan Corvey Crusade."

The news couldn't have gotten to them faster if it had been about a bomb threat.

"That's the plan. In fact, I was just on my way over."

"To discuss the matter with us first?" Reverend Handle asked.

Edgar had to be careful. They were good men. They meant well. But they were authoritarian. They had worked hard and they had their patch of grass. And they were militant about keeping any weeds from sprouting up.

"To inquire whether you would like to have Corvey speak here next week." The joke worked and the three men had a short laugh. But the two could not be diverted that easily. Edgar tried to steer the conversation as best he knew how. "You are raising a valid point, gentlemen, and your visit here proves, as usual, how much you care about the quality of education here… as I do."

"This is a bad thing. You know that," Sheath said.

"Well, it's not that—"

"It's a bad thing," confirmed Reverend Handle. "Corvey openly criticizes theologians. He calls seminaries cemeteries, his thought process is embarrassing and he masquerades around as a modern-day miracle worker. We have lots of proof about the botched healing attempts."

"I know," Edgar said.

Sheath leaned forward in his chair and focused on Edgar's eyes. Edgar swallowed. Maybe he could bolt for the door. But Sheath's stare kept him seated. It was almost as though he was paralyzed. "So then why are you planning on going?"

"It's like this. We know what we believe. That's why we can engage our ideas in dialogue with Corvey. We're not agreeing with him. It's just that there's a chance for our students to bring their knowledge into combat—that's the wrong word but you know what I mean—with a very different approach to theology. I think the necessity to have our students review Corvey's teachings outweighs the apparent freedom they enjoy in a protected environment."

Sheath and Handle didn't know if this was the start of Edgar's downfall or if he was legitimately exploring a current theological issue. They waited for Edgar to continue.

"A race car is safer in the garage but that's not what it was designed for."

"But it's not designed to be driven off a cliff, either," Reverend Handle said.

"It was a bad analogy, anyway," Edgar said.

"This surprises me, Edgar," Sheath said. "And not in a good way. I would have expected you to set an example."

"Would you rather I avoid confrontational issues, pretend they are irrelevant and don't exist?"

"I would rather you speak with us first."

"I'm speaking with you now."

Reverend Handle put on a smile to assure Edgar this was just a friendly visit and not an inquisition. At least not yet.

"I'd like to see the students write a review of the crusade," Reverend Handle said.

"Absolutely."

"And you prepare one as well."

The two men got up. Edgar said goodbye to them wondering if this had jeopardized his chance for promotion.

After they left Edgar sat down behind his desk. Three hours before he would never have dreamed of taking his class to see Corvey. He wondered in disbelief over his decision to go to the crusade. He tried to discern why he had the urge to attend and finally realized he had absolutely no idea.

It seemed to him that something was drawing him there.

7

Lucas woke up ten hours after his beating. He lay curled up on his side with his fingers and toes still numb. He took in a short breath through his clenched teeth and felt the aching of his broken ribs. He tried to breathe through his nose, but the dried blood plugged up his air passageways. His head felt as though a blaring alarm clock was going off with no one to hit the snooze button. The ringing in his ears was so loud he could hear nothing of the world around him. It might have been day, he didn't know. His eyes were so badly bruised it made it impossible to open them enough to tell.

Everything hurt. More dried blood stuck between the cobblestone and his hair, making it too difficult to lift his head. He lay on the cold ground unable to move, unable to think beyond the pain.

Lucas remained that way for two days.

On the third day, two guards came to bring a slop of something resembling food. They prodded him with a stick and his grunt assured them they would not need to dig a grave for him just yet. They set the bowl on the ground and said nothing to him. As they left Lucas wondered if they would have treated a dog with more kindness.

He forced his eyes open and looked at the bowl. He felt no hunger, which was just as well. His jaw was swollen shut and eating was not going to be an easy task.

He stretched out his fingers as best he could and moved them slightly. The two outside fingers on his left hand were broken. He looked down at his body, bloodied and bruised as it was, and felt sorry for himself.

He pulled his hair free of the dried blood and turned himself over on his back. He thought about letting out a scream to ease the pain, but it would do more harm than good. His dried urine stank up the cell. He smelled as bad as the rest of the Xaing Xaing prisoners.

He turned his head and looked at the bowl of soup (that's what he assumed it was) and decided to try a taste. He raised his head slightly but his abdomen muscles could not lift him. It was as though someone was standing on his stomach. He slid on his back and got close enough to look inside. The bowl had a greenish-black liquid inside with small solid pieces floating at the top. Lucas reached his bloodied fingers towards the bowl. His body shivered from the cold as he pulled the bowl nearer to himself. It looked like water from a backed-up toilet.

There was rice inside; at least he hoped it was rice. He grasped the bowl with two fingers, tilted it and allowed a little into his mouth. His throat began to close up and his eyes watered. He felt his stomach turn over and he thought he was going to vomit. With a concentrated effort he closed his mouth and swallowed. It went down like gasoline. Lucas put the bowl down beside him and exhaled to get the taste out of his mouth.

He had just experienced his first main course meal at Xaing Xaing.

On the fourth day, Lucas managed to sit up for a short period. He breathed with some regularity and his eyes were having an easier time focusing on the dark, dingy, cold world around him. The prison was quiet, or that's how it seemed to him. It may have been loud, he didn't know. All his mental and emotional energy was spent on staying alive, keeping him from noticing the world around him. The headache behind his eyes became so intense it made him wonder if his eyeballs would burst out of his skull.

The stained blood turned parts of the blue uniform into a shade of deep purple. He was barefoot but couldn't remember when he had taken his prison-issued shoes off.

In his mind Lucas imagined a group of Marines storming the compound, blasting the Chinese guards into the next world and freeing him. Choppers by the dozens would be landing any minute. The President himself was probably ordering China to return their illegal prisoner or face drastic trade sanctions. Caesar had surely hired a group of mercenaries, armed with the latest automatic weapons, to invade the prison and butcher every guard responsible for this mistake.

So what was taking them so long to get here?

He struggled to look through his small, barred window at the compound. Prisoners, all wearing the same blue uniforms, worked in a field. Some were digging in the dirt, or cleaning laundry; others worked with hammers and nails trying to build something. Off in the distance, a prisoner, somewhere in his eighties, carried water to a trough for the cows in a neighboring field. Guards with rifles watched them. Everything moved in slow motion.

He heard the hum of Chinese. It sounded like a steady tone of irrelevant chatter. Each word reminded Lucas of how far he was from home. No English—no books, no TV, no phone calls. Nothing. What he wouldn't give just to hear someone talk to him in English again.

He sat down on the ground, exhausted from standing for only those few minutes. In the cell across from him, Lucas saw the prisoner talking to his imaginary friend. A guard walked to their cells, looked inside and went back. It was as though the other prisoner didn't even know the guard had been there. He just kept talking to nobody, or at least no one who could be seen by anyone else. He laughed occasionally, as though his imaginary friend had told a joke. It was an eerie laugh. The man was sick. Skin, bones and living on a different planet.

Seeing a man so crazy made Lucas wonder if that would be his fate as well. Now, more than ever, he wanted a way of escaping Xiang Xiang physically, if not mentally as well. When the guard came by again, the prisoner spit on the bars and laughed and pointed at something that wasn't there.

Lucas' room with a view didn't have such a great view.

The Council had an emergency meeting at 6:00 a.m. Caesar paced back and forth on the podium with his hands behind his back.

This made the Council nervous. Normally, Caesar was composed. Usually cool under fire. But one of his sheep had gone missing and he was going to get him back. The atmosphere grew tense as option after option on how to get Lucas out of China failed.

Mike, still exhausted from his travels, thought about his friend in prison. The sound of Lucas screaming as the guards took him away played over in his mind. Next to Mike was an empty chair.

"What about a free medical shipment to China in exchange for his release?" Claire asked.

"I've already offered it," Caesar said. "There's no word back." He'd go into Xaing Xaing himself if he thought it would do any good. He imagined Lucas sitting in his cell alone and wondered if he'd been beaten. He had to get his boy back. Somehow he would get it done.

But other members of the Council did not share Caesar's point of view. With Lucas out of the way there was a position open. Better yet, their positions were not in danger of being terminated because of some hotshot exec in his twenties. If any of them were in Lucas' position they would be begging Caesar and the Council to get them out. But with Lucas in China and his position potentially needing to be filled they were not as anxious to get him back.

"Can you talk to your friends?" Claire asked.

"The President won't get involved. He said he can't risk it."

"Can we put public pressure on the Chinese to let him go?"

"If the public hears more about one of our executives spending time in prison for allegedly smuggling drugs it will damage our reputation," Caesar said.

"But if they know he's being held in a Chinese prison without a hearing it may generate support."

Caesar nodded his head. "You may be right. Let's organize a press conference. It might get the Chinese to move."

"What about Senator Turtle?" Claire asked.

"He's doing everything he can."

Lucas reached for his fresh bowl of slop. His eyes felt better. He could blink without pain. It didn't hurt as much to move his facial muscles. He picked up the bowl and took a sip. The trouble with his nose clearing up was that it brought back his sense of smell.

When he finished his meal, two guards, one of them being the tall one, walked to the cell and opened the door. They reached in and grabbed Lucas. Immediately, he felt the sting in his separated shoulder and his bruised arms. He clenched his jaw together, trying to absorb the pain. Lucas half walked and was half dragged down the hallway. They pulled him with such force that Lucas finally let go and screamed. But the guards paid no attention.

Screams didn't mean much at Xaing Xaing.

At the end of the corridor was a small room with a wooden chair in the middle. They brought Lucas in and closed the door behind them. No windows, no other furnishings. A guard stood behind the chair with something in his hand. The tall guard pushed Lucas so that he sat down hard. The other two guards held his shoulders down. Lucas' heart began to pound. His stomach hurt—it felt as if an awful case of diarrhea was about to explode. A buzzing sound filled the room. He felt something touch the back of his neck. He pulled his head away but the guards grabbed on tighter. The buzzing sound came closer to the side of his head and he felt a brush pass over his ear. He glanced to his shoulder and saw a clump of his black hair.

Within seconds his entire head was shaved. His hair lay scattered on the ground, dried blood still holding parts of it together. The guard who cut his hair left the room.

The tall guard grabbed Lucas by the arm. His separated shoulder felt as though someone was stabbing a hot knife between his arm and his chest. Lucas winced in pain. The tall guard pulled harder. Lucas fell to the ground. He began to cry.

The tall guard kicked Lucas in the back and yelled at him to stand up. He noticed the dried blood on Lucas' uniform and spoke to one of the other guards who quickly left. Lucas sobbed in uncontrollable bursts. He tried to stop but the tears kept coming. *It's just nerves. I'm going to be okay. I'm going....*

But the sobs only grew louder. The other guard returned. He held out a different uniform with the number 430 crudely written on the sides and the back. The tall guard took it and threw it at Lucas. He shouted at him to put it on.

Lucas unbuttoned his uniform as best he could. The pain made it take longer than it normally would. His bruised muscles and broken fingers made it difficult to complete the simple task. When Lucas finally got his uniform off he was shocked by the amount of blood on it. *Is that mine?*

The tall guard ordered one of the other guards to pick up the old uniform. The guard did and went away to burn it.

Lucas sat naked on the floor in the presence of the other guards. He looked over his body. He saw the massive bruising and closed his eyes. He turned his back to the guards to prevent them from looking at him. As he struggled to put on the new uniform he wondered how long it would take for his blood to ruin this one as well.

The tall guard said something and the others laughed. The tall guard, however, didn't even smile at the joke he made. He just looked at Lucas with those creepy, hollow eyes and watched as he got dressed.

It was there on the ground that Lucas resolved himself to kill the tall guard. Maybe all the guards. He'd find a way to steal one of the rifles and shoot them, the tall guard first. He'd get into one of the watchtowers, he and some of the prisoners, and open fire on their captors. The guards would die. Every single one of them. He'd get the tall guard back for what he was doing. Lucas would put a gun right to his forehead, smile at him, cap off some clichéd John Wayne or Clint Eastwood line, pull the trigger and watch the tall guard's brains splatter out of the back of his head. No matter how or when Lucas got out, he'd end the tall guard's life.

Lucas kept his head down as he finished dressing. He couldn't find the courage to look any of them in the eye.

The next day the guards brought Lucas outside to the work area. His eyes hurt when the bright sunshine shone down on him. As he walked along the crushed rock path he noticed he was being taken away from where all the other prisoners were. The prisoners looked briefly at him, made no hint of a greeting and carried on about their work. It was a cool day. He was underdressed but would find out this was the norm at Xaing Xaing.

The tall guard took him to one of the bathroom facilities. He opened the door and Lucas nearly choked from the stench. He couldn't see inside but it smelled as though a thousand filled-up baby diapers were pressed against his nose. The guards gave Lucas a bucket of water and a wooden handle with bristles. They shouted at him and pointed inside. Lucas wanted to disagree but he had learned better than to disobey them. He stood there. Depressed. Three stinking toilets without running water. The basins beneath caught the excrement. Lucas was to clean the latrines and dump the basins out at the back of the compound. He froze. Not even a pig would be allowed in a place like this.

The tall guard grew impatient. He shouted at Lucas and lifted up his rifle in a threatening manner. Lucas cursed quietly at them and told them he would rather stuff their mouths with the contents of the toilet than clean the stinking latrine. The tall guard yelled again and hit Lucas in his sore shoulder. Lucas dropped to his knees. He picked up the bucket and the brush and struggled to get into the latrine. The guard kicked a rock under the door to keep it open. It wasn't meant to let the draft clean out some of the stench, it was meant for the other guard to keep an eye on him.

Lucas put the wooden brush in the water and wondered if there was more nutrition in the cleaning pail than in his slop. He put the bristles to the ground and scrubbed, back and forth. Back and forth. Back and forth. Over and over again. The smell got so bad that his eyes burned. He switched hands occasionally to relieve the burning in his separated shoulder.

He sat down for a moment. Sweat covered his body. He continued again. When he got close to the refuse container he saw a piece of paper with writing on it. He looked over his shoulder at the guard who was staring at the sky. The tall guard was gone. Lucas looked back at the box, then back at the guard. He reached for the piece of paper.

He went through the toilet paper until he touched it. His eyes darted to the guard who wasn't paying attention, then back to the refuse container. The paper was printed material, but the excrement made it difficult to read.

Lucas heard the guard coming to check on him. He hid the piece of paper in his uniform and continued working. Somehow, the curiosity of what was on that paper made the rest of the task easier to complete. He finished the entire latrine and notified the guard.

The guard brought him back to his cell. Lucas hid in the corner to shield himself from the view of the other prisoners. He pulled out his scrap of paper and held it up to the light of the setting sun. He struggled to see the words. It looked like English.

He spit on his fingers and rubbed the excrement off the paper as best he could. It was the first chapter of a book. For the first time at Xaing Xaing he felt anticipation. It was English. Definitely English. Finally, some freedom from the Chinese language. Finally, something familiar—something he could relate to other than his own thoughts.

He read the first few words and his heart suddenly melted. He shook his head and then rubbed the paper to get a better look as if doing so would bring a different result. He reread the words and closed his eyes in frustration. He felt it was a cosmic practical joke.

He had been wrongfully accused, imprisoned, beaten, forced into cleaning latrines and his only hope of some decent English material was dashed before his eyes. He was miles from home and deserved some kind of break. Anything but this. Of all the millions of books in the world he was stuck with a page from the Bible.

Fate was cruel.

8

Edgar and his students lined up outside the United Center three hours before the start of the Corvey Crusade. When they arrived there were already seven thousand anxious, determined people waiting for the action to begin. Some had been there since morning. Some had waited through the night. The line-ups reminded Edgar of the days, days he didn't like to remember, when he waited against his parents' permission for a rock concert. Now he was lining up for a healing crusade. It felt just as wrong.

Police cordoned off traffic for a block in all directions. The nearby streets became sidewalks. Not only would Corvey pack out the arena, but he'd have at least as many stranded outside.

Bus loads of people poured in, bringing the curious, the skeptical and the desperate who were seeking a miracle. They came from everywhere: Chicago, Milwaukee, Toronto, even as far as Los Angeles and Vancouver. One bus made it from Mexico City. People had flown in from Frankfurt and London. A father had come from the Philippines with his AIDS-stricken child. He had done so five times before.

It looked like a wheelchair convention to Edgar. He studied the faces of those who were visibly sick and wondered how many other people had life-threatening illnesses growing in their bodies without them knowing it. It bothered him to see the sick here. He felt they should be at hospitals where they could receive proper medical attention instead of wasting their hopes on a highly paid, over-advertised master of emotional blackmail.

The doors opened and people hurried into the arena like peasants cramming into a bakery during a food shortage. They wouldn't all get in. Not by a long shot. Many would have to wait outside and be forced to listen via speakers or possibly a big screen TV. Corvey had planned only one crusade in Chicago, but he could easily have booked ten straight days.

Although it was a cool evening, Edgar felt something out of the ordinary. There was electricity in the atmosphere, as though a crowd of football fans were about to cheer for a touchdown. There was an excitement, an anticipation of sorts among the people—or maybe not with the people, maybe it was just there, in the air or something. He couldn't touch it, but it was more real than if he could grab it with both hands. It was something he had never felt before.

Edgar and his class found seats on the floor level. Various groups of people here and there were praying. Some were laying hands on the sick and shouting things. *Poor people*, Edgar thought, *this ministry has really screwed them up.*

Edgar pulled out his pen and paper. No doubt he would be filling up page after page on the theological blunders Corvey would be making. Corvey was known for them.

Edgar read a biography of Sheridan Corvey on the back of a bulletin. It mentioned he had no formal training in any post secondary institution. He had finished grade twelve by correspondence, then worked as a bartender in a night club. He had married a parking-lot attendant at nineteen and by twenty-two they were $40,000 in debt. His wife was diagnosed with heart disease, he was fired from his job and they were forced to live in a run-down trailer. Corvey had hit rock bottom.

He had tried every medical treatment they could afford and found nothing that could help his wife. Completely stressed, Corvey decided to "get religion" and headed into a local church. He got a Bible from the pastor and for three months did nothing but read and pray inside his rat hole trailer. At the end of it, his wife was healed and they soon got out of debt. From then on, Corvey turned pro and never looked back. Edgar put the bulletin on the seat beside him. It was a story he found difficult to believe.

The class discussed what they might see. A real live miracle? Something truly beyond science? A blind man seeing? A deaf woman hearing? A paralytic walking? They hoped they would not be disappointed.

Edgar sat at the far right of the row, next to the aisle, just in case he needed to leave. The lights were being tested. Final sound checks were made. Beside him, a woman was wheeled in by an usher. She stopped next to Edgar.

"Is this taken?" she said with a fragile smile and a slight laugh.

"No, please sit down. I... I mean it's yours."

Her legs were thinner than normal and from the way they were positioned it was obvious she hadn't used them in quite some time. Her head twitched sporadically to the left as if someone was flicking a switch to make her do that. Her hands were bent inward at an awkward angle and her cheeks were sunken. Maybe she was forty years old. She wasn't more than ninety pounds. Most of her blond hair was gone, too. Edgar considered himself a good conversationalist but somehow he felt unsure of himself around her, even scared. He had nothing of encouragement to offer her. Least of all at a healing crusade. Exactly what do you say to someone who is dying?

The seat immediately to Edgar's left was open. He planned it this way so he would have a place to put his Bible and his notes about the mistakes Corvey would be making. He wanted to keep an open mind but with Corvey this was going to be impossible. Plus, he knew what Sheath and Handle were after—a slamfest. Crucify Corvey; then the brass at Mount Carmel would be as happy as a graduate landing his first job.

Edgar's attention was drawn again to the aisle to his right where he saw a man looking for a seat. He had straggly blond hair, a dirty T-shirt, a marked-up face and a large build. He wasn't tall, maybe 5' 8', but the size of him made him look bigger. *Oh please, not here!* Edgar thought. He watched him out of the corner of his eye go past him down the aisle. He relaxed when he saw the biker walk down another row to an available seat.

Then, Edgar caught the biker again. He left the row and came back down the aisle. It was as if someone had said to the biker, *I'm sorry, this seat is saved for my dying friend who's gone to the bathroom.*

The biker walked back in the direction of where Edgar was seated, looking around the area for an empty seat. Edgar turned away and hoped the biker wouldn't spot the seat next to him. It wasn't so much that Edgar didn't like him—he hadn't even met him yet—it was that he wanted his space. But the biker was coming for that seat. He looked at Edgar and squinted his eyes as though he had lost his glasses. He looked in his late fifties—the effects of drugs and hard living had definitely left their mark. "Is that seat free?"

No, No it isn't. It's being saved for my dying friend who's gone to the bathroom. "Sure, help yourself," Edgar said moving his items to the ground. The biker smiled politely to the woman in the wheelchair, revealing his dentures and pushed past Edgar into the seat. What bothered Edgar the most was the biker's smell. A combination of body odor, cigarettes and booze filled Edgar's nostrils, forcing him to breathe through his mouth.

"Thanks." The biker with his big, fat gut barely fit into his blue jeans, or at least they were blue originally. They seemed like the kind of pants someone wore to every occasion if they couldn't afford anything else.

He had a friendliness about him. It reminded Edgar of some of his students. He was happy, ready for a good time. Then again, maybe he was at a healing crusade for the same reason the woman in the wheelchair was.

"You're welcome," Edgar replied, hoping he wouldn't be drawn into a conversation. But fortune was not smiling on Edgar. The biker, however, was. He grinned at Edgar and stared at him until Edgar returned eye contact.

"You been here before?" the biker asked. It was an insult to Edgar. Who on earth would admit they frequented healing crusades—especially Corvey's? It was like asking him, *Hey, do you ever sleep on the streets or wait in line at the soup kitchens?*

"Never been to one," Edgar said with a touch of pride in his voice.

"Me neither. But I hear lots of good things about them."

"I guess. But not everything you hear is true," Edgar said.

The biker let out a short laugh as if someone had reminded him of a joke he'd heard. "You're right about that. I suppose some miracles'll happen tonight."

Edgar nodded politely. "We'll see. Do you believe in miracles?"

The biker looked out ahead and thought for a moment, then turned his head back to Edgar. His happy disposition penetrated Edgar the way light penetrates a room when a cloth has cleaned a dirty window. "I'm not sure," he said.

The conversation had a natural ending there but the biker would not be put off. He smiled again, elbowed Edgar in the arm in a way that bothered him and asked, "What about you? You believe in all this healing stuff?"

Edgar's brain stalled. He searched his mind, trying to think through his position on supernatural healing. "I'm not sure," was all he could manage. And it was the truth.

"Well, I guess we're about to find out!" Without any hesitation the biker pushed out his hand to Edgar. "I'm Jake. Jake Rubenstein."

Edgar shook the rough, broken skin of Jake's hand. He did so out of obligation and was afraid of what he would catch. "Edgar Sardisan."

Jake coughed into his hands the way smokers do when their lungs have been charred with tar and other harmful cigarette components. It sounded awful. Edgar remembered that someone once called cigarettes *Satan sticks* and after hearing Jake's cough he figured they may not have been far wrong. Jake's eyes got watery. He managed to get himself under control but then he coughed again, really coughed. It was loud enough to make even healthy people glad they were at a healing crusade.

The arena filled up to capacity. The doors closed. Outside, the crusade team hooked up speakers and monitors. More than fifty police officers directed traffic. Many people held out their Bibles or touched the arena as though a healing vibe would be sent to free them from their ailments. Others became angry for coming late. Some started crying.

Tabitha ran down the sidewalk and was amazed at the number of people. It reminded her of the days when the Blackhawks made the playoffs. She came up to one of the entrances and searched through her purse.

"I'm sorry, ma'am. We're filled to capacity." Tabitha showed the usher her media badge. He opened the door for her. "Just remember. No photography."

A sure sign that they had something to hide.

Tabitha wanted to be close to the people so instead of sitting in the press box she decided to stand near an aisle. Edgar had returned her phone call and left a message on her voice-mail but she had not yet called him back. She wondered what a professor of theology might think of this event and if he would be interested in coming to one.

Edgar looked at his students. He debated whether he was helping or harming them by bringing them here. Ushers scanned the aisles to ensure there were no empty spaces. The massive choir gathered on the stage. The conductor led them in singing drills. All the while the excitement continued to grow.

Corvey remained in a private room by himself. Four security guards stood outside to make sure that no one, not even his wife, would disturb him. He did what he did before every meeting. He prayed. Usually seven hours' worth. It came with the job. He thought about the sick people waiting in the arena. He thought about the thousands who had been healed in previous crusades.

And the thousands who went away sick.

But he prayed nonetheless.

The band started up and a young man in his thirties came on stage. He greeted the crowd with a lot of religious jargon that Edgar could not tolerate. The crowd stood up, those who could, and the entire arena began singing. Edgar forced himself to hum along. He wasn't looking forward to the half-hour or so of emotional, touchy-feely songs or the sermon (of sorts) that would follow. It made him think coming here wasn't such a good idea.

The songs were sung with such force it felt like a rock concert. The entire arena clapped and shouted as loud as they could. The students thoroughly enjoyed themselves and Edgar was already beginning to work through his explanation to Sheath and Handle about how to rid his students from Corvey's influence. When the singing stopped the lights grew dim. The choir sat down. A single spotlight appeared. Sheridan Corvey stepped onto the stage.

He wore a $2,800 blue suit with new black leather shoes that would never be worn again, at least not by him. His silk tie matched perfectly. His hair was caked down with so much gel that a hurricane would not move it. He was good looking. A little shorter than average. He had a quiet, compassionate way about him as he walked to the glass lectern at the center. Everyone clapped, including Jake who managed to send out more of his stink to Edgar. The clapping turned into cheering. Soon, people stood to their feet, cheering, waiting in anticipation for what would happen.

Edgar was amazed. Corvey got a standing ovation and hadn't even done anything yet.

Corvey greeted the crowd and they quickly settled down. "God loves to hear his creation clapping for Him." He began discussing how much he enjoyed these evenings and how special things were going to happen.

He went into his spiel about the incredible cost associated with the crusade as well as the expense of their ministry to starving children in Africa. He said a voluntary offering would be taken to cover expenses. Edgar loved the timing. The singing left the crowd on an emotional high, and taking the offering before the prayers for healing would certainly translate into the maximum amount of giving. He wondered if the Corvey Crusade team had performed studies as to when the collection should take place so as to maximize the receivables.

Tabitha took notes. She surveyed the audience and saw a mix of blacks, whites, Hispanics and Asians. She saw new leather jackets and beat-up jean jackets. Expensive suits and grubby sweaters. Fancy jewelry and plain watches. Whatever Corvey was pitching it was being bought (or at least it was being shown interest) by various people groups. She checked her watch and hoped she would get enough material soon. If she left in the next half-hour she might make it to the dropzone in time.

When the offering bucket came to Edgar he wondered why Corvey didn't just take a $400,000 cut in pay to help cover the costs himself. He felt more uneasy about the offering money than he did about the healing. It was rumored that Corvey earned $500,000 per year. Other reports had him pegged at closer to a million. Whatever the case, Corvey's salary didn't sit right with Edgar. He passed the bucket on. He would have no part in paying for Corvey's next tailored suit. He looked at the woman in the wheelchair beside him who dropped five wrinkled, dirty dollar bills into the container.

Corvey spoke to the audience about how suffering was bad and how healing was within everyone's grasp. "Sickness has never been God's design for mankind," he said. "God will heal anyone with the faith to believe in a miracle."

Edgar got out his pen and paper and began examining what Corvey said. Within five minutes Edgar had filled up his first page on Corvey's theological mistakes. He shook his head with enough enthusiasm for people around him to notice and hoped his students would be discerning as well.

And then it started. The prayers for healing. Healing was guaranteed as far as Corvey was concerned. He asked anyone in need of a miracle to stand up and reach up to God and those who couldn't stand were encouraged to lift their hands. Everyone else was asked to pray for the healing of those standing (which was more than half the crowd). The choir sang a soft song about healing. Corvey prayed.

Tabitha watched with great interest. She got out of her seat, grabbed her black leather jacket and walked closer to the floor area. A woman in the crowd stood up with a puzzled look on her face. She put her hand on her back and called out to one of the ushers. "My back! My back is healed."

Tabitha jotted it down in her notepad. There was no previous proof of the woman's back pains and no doctor present to confirm the healing. But the woman seemed convinced. Tabitha walked down to her to get an interview but the ushers took her to the front before she had a chance.

Other people all over the arena began experiencing similar phenomena. Corvey encouraged those who believed they had received a miracle to come to the front and give a testimony.

After people gave their testimonies Tabitha managed to interview some of them to get a better understanding of what happened.

"Your back? It's better?" Tabitha asked.

The lady bent down and touched her toes. "Doesn't hurt anymore!" Tabitha asked a few more questions and got the lady's phone number. No doubt some medical investigation would need to be done before a healing could be substantiated.

The students were caught up in the excitement and moved to the front to get a closer look. Jake joined them.

"Want to come, Edgar?" asked one of the students.

"No, thanks." Edgar wasn't sure what to make of it. He didn't want to fall into the sensationalism but he didn't want to remain unnecessarily closed to what might be going on. He continued with his notes listing no fewer than twenty-eight mistakes by the grand showman himself. Edgar had enough incriminating evidence and placed the stack of papers beside him on the left. He looked to his right and saw the woman in the wheelchair. Still crippled, still believing. Edgar crossed his arms and decided he could stand it for another five minutes before having to bolt out of this charade.

Tabitha listened to the testimonies and wasn't sure what to make of them, either. The "miracles" that were testified to by those supposedly healed were nothing of the extraordinary. There were claims of back pains disappearing and sore wrists or bum knees that felt better, but nothing to do with cancer, diabetes, blindness, or paralysis. Nothing really tangible. In her heart Tabitha disliked the Corvey Crusades because they seemed to prey upon innocent people who, in healthier circumstances, would never surrender their emotions, or their wallets, to this man. But she did want to see a miracle—even a whole slew of them. Not only would it make for a good story, but there was something about seeing a sick person not get well that bothered Tabitha.

She witnessed enough testimonies to write a summary of her less than eventful experience at the Corvey Crusade. She got more phone numbers of some of those who had been healed (or who claimed to have been healed) and would follow up with them to see if, or when, the same problems reappeared.

Tabitha left early. The thrill of a night sky dive pulled her out of the arena and into her yellow Mustang. With any luck, she might even get in two jumps.

Corvey had the choir sing another song. He lifted his hands and looked at the ceiling. Tears flowed from his eyes. "There are others here tonight who are still sick."

Edgar looked at his watch. Three more minutes.

"I want you to believe for your miracle. You can be healed tonight because God wants it."

Another mistake to add to the list. The music crescendoed as Edgar scribbled on his paper. When he finished jotting down his final comment he saw something move out of the corner of his right eye. At first he thought the women beside him was stretching. He turned his eyes without turning his head and what he saw convinced him he was dreaming.

The woman's eyes opened in amazement. She was scarcely able to breathe as she looked at her hands. She stretched them out effortlessly. No more bend to them, no more awkward twist. They were completely normal. She looked down at her legs that had somehow regained movement.

Edgar turned his head. He stared at the woman. His mouth dropped open. The music seemed distant. It was as though there was no one else in the arena except him and the woman. He looked at her face. It was difficult to tell if it was the same person as before. Her cheeks were not sunken in as they previously were. Now, they were full of color. She gingerly got out of her wheelchair and stood feebly on her feet. She put one foot ahead of the other and began to walk to the front. An usher came up to help her but she gently pushed his arms away.

"I'm walking," she said with whispered amazement and then spoke with more conviction. "I'm walking!"

Corvey stopped when he heard her and ordered the ushers to make room for her. A smile came over his face as he saw her approaching the platform.

Edgar stood up and watched in disbelief. He turned around trying to find the woman who was sitting beside him before. Impossible. Absolutely impossible.

The woman got on stage and gave an account in front of the capacity crowd as to how she had been miraculously healed from multiple sclerosis. She had never spoken in public before, yet she felt calm, as though she was talking to an audience of one. When she was finished speaking more than thirty people came on stage to give account of their healings, though none was as dramatic as the woman in the wheelchair.

Corvey concluded the evening with prayers of thanksgiving and was escorted off stage by his security personnel. Edgar sat down, his mouth open, and wondered what had just happened. He pretended to look at his notes on the chair beside him as his students walked by, and explained he was just "finishing up." The students left without him. Even after the arena had emptied Edgar would not leave. He could not leave. Not until he had it figured out. Not until he had an explanation. Edgar searched through his mind to find some way to understand what had happened. But he came up with nothing.

He looked to his left and saw the notes he had written on the theological mistakes made by Corvey. Then he turned to his right and saw the empty wheelchair.

The owner would not be needing it any time soon.

9

At first dawn, Lucas pulled out the scrap of paper. He held it up to the light and read it as many times as he could before the guards came by. It wasn't so much that he necessarily liked it—he wasn't sure if he did or not. It was that it was English. It gave him a mental break from the alienating feeling of the foreign language around him. Anything to provide comfort from his surroundings.

He stood up and found he was able to walk without assistance. His body was badly discolored from the beatings, but he took it as an indication that he was beginning to heal. To keep his mind from concentrating on the pain, Lucas read and re-read the piece of paper. After forty readings, he had the page memorized.

A guard (not the tall one) walked down the hallway to his cell. Lucas stuffed the paper into his uniform and pretended to lie down asleep. The guard banged on the door. Lucas got up. The guard shouted and another guard who had been speaking with one of the other prisoners came to the cell.

They led him outside to the work area. Lucas surveyed the depressing picture of a group of four hundred plus men who had given up on life. No parole board hearings. No media to plead their case. No chance for an appeal. They were like zombies, walking around and obeying every word the guards commanded them.

Part of Lucas hoped he would be assigned to weed-pulling duty where he could meet people and possibly eat the weeds so he wouldn't have to eat as much of the slop. Instead, the guard took him to the latrines.

He didn't argue this time. His shoulder was in no shape for a confrontation. He got down on his knees and scrubbed the floor. Back and forth. Back and forth. He glanced over his shoulder and saw that the guard was not paying attention to him. Lucas looked at the refuse box and wondered what might be waiting for him. He edged closer to it and searched through the stinking, soiled paper for anything that might resemble literature. His fingers touched a thicker piece of paper. He raised his hands to bring the paper into the shaft of light that was let in through the small window. Sure enough, it was English. It looked similar to the last page he found. He cleaned off the excrement as best he could. He read the first few lines. It was part of the second chapter.

Lucas returned to his cell and as soon as the guards had left he read the two pages that now comprised his entire library at Xaing Xaing. Years ago, the guards forbade prisoners from reading anything except the writings of Mao Tse-tung, the former Chairman of China. Even though China had since passed through their cultural revolution, a very small, stubborn group of guards in China, especially the tall guard, still clung to Mao's teachings. The rest of China had moved forward. They, however, had not. Massive reforms had spread throughout China. They had reached Xaing Xaing, but they failed to convince the tall guard and some of the others to abandon their disastrous ways. In the tall guard's mind English literature, especially a Bible, would not be tolerated.

To escape his boredom Lucas memorized the second page. It kept the hope of a world outside of Xaing Xaing alive. He refused to let his mind drift off into imagining the possibility of a rescue or a pardoning. It wasn't because he didn't believe it could happen—he did—it was because his new goal was to survive prison, not to cling to dreams.

The second chapter talked about people speaking in foreign languages and the working of miracles. He glanced at the first page again but could not make out the title of the book. Lucas memorized the passages until it was too dark to see. He hid the pages in a crack in the cobblestone and lay down on his back. How much longer would he be there? When would the door open so that he could go back? He recited the verses as best as he could remember them. They were a fence for him. Something to separate him from the world he now lived in.

The need for his two companions on his dresser at home came back to him. There in his cold cell he wished he could guzzle down a bottle of whiskey or brandy—anything other than the dreadful slop that would be arriving for breakfast the next morning.

Caesar tried everything he could to get Lucas out of China. A press conference had drawn some attention but not enough to encourage the Chinese government to release him. Caesar thought of Lucas. *How is he doing? How is he holding up under the pressure?* He felt responsible for Lucas' situation. He was the one who had told Lucas to go to China. No, he didn't know at the time of the decision how things were going to turn out. But he was the one who had given the final okay. Caesar lived under the guilt that people live under when they know their actions unwittingly played a role in some else's misfortune.

In his private study, with the lights turned down, he scribbled ideas on a scrap of paper. He had a company to run and Lucas was absorbing much of his energy. He had to get him back or recognize that after trying every conceivable angle without success, Lucas would never return to the Council. He finished his idea and called in his secretary. After the media, the government, the pleas, there was still an alternative.

It was one in which he hoped the Chinese would finally show some interest.

Tabitha came to work the morning after the crusade and poured herself a glass of distilled water from the water cooler. A real breakfast was too much work in the morning.

She sat down at her cubicle and got ready to prepare a follow-up article of the people who claimed to be healed at the Corvey Crusade. She wanted to discuss how the people who had experienced miracles, or alleged miracles, were now getting along. She turned on her computer, logged in and saw a message from Fat Chester. She was to see him in his office. Right away.

That was never a good sign.

She knocked on Chester's door and heard a faint "come in." She entered and saw him poke his head out from behind his computer. At first he was just curious who was there, but when he saw it was Tabitha he put on a frown that quickly turned to a look of disappointment. Tabitha froze in the doorway and wasn't sure if she should stand or sit down. Chester reached for his copy of today's *Observer* and threw it on the chair across from him

"Did you even go to the crusade last night?"

"I was there," she said, already feeling herself becoming defensive.

"You're sure?"

"Pretty sure, Chester." She wanted to say *Fat Chester* but she held her composure.

"Really? Because only a deaf and blind person could have written the article you wrote. Anybody with working eyes or ears would have written about what really happened!"

Tabitha didn't look at her story on the front page. She wrote it. She knew what was there. Chester calmed down a little and put a copy of the *Sun Times* in front of her. He was angry, and he realized he was angry, so he tried not to do any unnecessary damage.

Just take the blame and get out of his office, Tabitha thought, as she felt the aggravation that sometimes comes with having a boss of the opposite gender.

"Well?" he said.

"Well, what?"

"Tabitha, your article is a joke. It made us look bad. All of us. There was a woman with multiple sclerosis who came to the crusade in a wheelchair and then walked out with nothing. How's that for a story?"

Tabitha looked through the article in the competing paper. There, with a smile on her face, was a picture of the woman who had sat beside Edgar. Only this time she wasn't sitting. She was standing and looked as healthy as any of the other people in the picture. It bothered Tabitha. She wanted to say it was a fake, a forgery of sorts. But she knew she had been scooped. Seeing the woman who had been healed standing beside Corvey, Tabitha had nothing to say in reply.

"Well?" Chester asked.

"You can't believe an evangelist, Chester. You know that."

"Maybe not. But I can believe a medical report."

Sure enough. Halfway down the article a medical doctor confirmed the woman's instantaneous healing. Tabitha studied the paper only to avoid eye contact with Chester. She felt like a mouse that was about to be chased again by an angry cat.

"I'm sorry," she said. "You're right."

"Tabitha, the next time you go to an event, do us all a favor and stay to the end." Tabitha looked up from the paper and met his eyes. She felt three feet tall. She nodded and turned to leave but Chester stopped her. She sighed quietly to herself and wished for a chance to leave his presence. "I want you to continue following the Lucas Stephens story. A Chicagoan is imprisoned in China. He might be innocent and that makes big news."

Tabitha grinned and tried to give the impression that everything was going just the way she planned. "You got it."

The morning couldn't have gotten off to a worse start.

10

Pouring rain besieged the Notre Dame campus. It was the kind of rain people enjoy when they are indoors with friends, maybe at a cabin playing a game or watching a good movie. But Edgar was outside, sitting on a bench, partially protected by a tree. He had studied theology for five years at Notre Dame; some of that time was spent right on this bench with colleagues, engaging each other in what they learned. They had lively discussions while checking out the beautiful women, especially the rich ones, and he had enjoyed the companionship of people who held similar values. But today he was alone, with only the rain and a brown envelope in his hand to keep him company.

To his far right was the football stadium where he watched every Fighting Irish game. He loved the screaming crowds and the hot sun. Usually the Irish played a good game, too. He and his buddies always went for hot dogs at half time. They got the long ones with enough onions to chase those rich, beautiful girls away. They often left the stadium with hoarse throats from cheering for the players and yelling at the referees. They sat in the cheap seats but that didn't stop them from screaming at the men in the striped shirts if, when, they made a bad call.

To his left he saw the mural on the library building wall of Jesus blessings his disciples. The mural faced the stadium end zone and because Jesus had his hands lifted high above his disciples, the way a referee lifts his hands to signal a player has crossed the goal line, the mural was nicknamed *Touchdown Jesus*. Edgar remembered looking at the mural when he left the football games. Sometimes the Irish won. Sometimes they lost. But for Edgar, *Touchdown Jesus* gave the games a feeling of continuity, as if to say: *Win or lose, I'm still here.*

Only Jesus didn't seem to be saying that today.

On game day, the campus was packed to capacity with Domer fans. Grads from all over came to unite in the spirit of Notre Dame. Before the kickoff, Edgar would sit at his favorite bench, this bench, and reminisce with grads or with students about life and just relax in the feeling that comes with being in a place you enjoy. Today, however, was different. There was no one else outside and there was nothing to enjoy.

Rain dripped off his hair onto his partially unzipped jacket. It had gotten into his clothes and started sticking to his skin. He rubbed his face, partially to clear the water and partially to make the world go away, if even for a moment.

His class had had a heated discussion about the Corvey crusade. They had argued about the miracles that Edgar tried, with much conviction, to get out of his mind. He couldn't explain them and what he was unable to explain he was unwilling to discuss.

Handle and Sheath were pleased with his evaluation of the crusade but were extremely displeased with the "Corveymania" that had swept the class and was now in danger of sweeping the hallowed campus of Mount Carmel. But Mount Carmel, thirty miles away from Notre Dame, was now the least of Edgar's concerns.

On the top left corner of the brown envelope were a logo and a return address. His name stood in bold capital letters in the middle. He had received it early in the afternoon and after reading the contents he had canceled his classes for the remainder of the day. Without any warning life was taking a turn. A turn for the worst.

He got up from his beloved bench and looked up at *Touchdown Jesus*. He seemed so distant now, so impersonal up on that mural. Edgar once thought of himself as one of Jesus' disciples. Now he couldn't have felt further away.

He thought about going down to the Grotto to pray, as he often did while he was a student. The carved-out portion of the rock with its burning candles often gave him the powerful feeling of being completely protected. But now, in the pouring rain, even the prospect of being at the Grotto gave him little comfort.

Edgar's life had been all laid out. He had had plans to buy a sailboat and sail around Lake Michigan. Maybe he'd even have gone down to Florida and sailed in the Keys. His home was paid for and he had entertained thoughts of buying a small cottage. He had hoped to teach Monday to Thursday and then take off for a weekend of sailing. He'd have written books on Friday, theology books, and learned to fish and relax. The future had been all set for Edgar. But then he got his envelope.

That stupid brown envelope.

11

On his third day of cleaning the latrines Lucas retrieved the next page of the book. It wasn't stained as badly, which made it easier to read, both from a visual and smell point of view. Ironically, the bathroom became a welcome source of reading material. It was English. It was entertaining. It was his escape.

The third page had a story of a man being healed. He was a cripple since birth, poor and made to beg alms. Two people came to him and within moments he was completely healed. It was as though he was never sick. What interested Lucas was not just that the man was made healthy but that he was made healthy without prescription drugs.

Lucas memorized most of the third page that evening. By tomorrow he would have it all committed to memory and would destroy the pages to avoid the evidence. He would have the words stored in his mind, a safe place where the guards had no access.

That evening, in the latrine, the tall guard finished his evening ritual and instead of reaching for toilet paper he pulled out a small English Bible and tore out the next page. He had confiscated it from a prisoner who recently died at Xaing Xaing. The contraband was smuggled in, maybe through a sympathetic guard, but now the tall guard had it and he knew how to put the book to good use. One by one, page after page, latrine visit after latrine visit, he used the book the only way he saw fit.

That way he was assured no one else could be tempted by its poison.

Lucas awoke at the sound of boots hitting the cobblestone. He squinted his eyes through the darkness but couldn't make out any figures. The guards came to the cell and, to their surprise, they saw Lucas waiting for them. It was cause for the guards to be concerned. Often, they would shout at Lucas, open the door, kick him and drag him out. But this morning was different. Lucas stood at attention as if to inquire why the guards had taken so long to get him.

The tall guard took a step back and waited for some kind of attack. Another guard cautiously opened the door while staring Lucas directly in the eye. He'd make a good negotiator, Lucas thought. Lucas stepped out, walked past the guards and led the way to the latrines.

When they arrived the tall guard shouted at Lucas just to make it clear that he was still in charge. Lucas nodded, almost smiled, got down on his hands and knees and began scrubbing the floor. The tall guard told his subordinate to be careful. A change in behavior in a prisoner was a bad sign—perhaps it was an indication of an uprising or that a suicide might be attempted.

Lucas waited for the guards to move out of sight. The refuse box was in the corner. Just a few more minutes and he would have his treasure of the day.

By the end of the third week Lucas had managed to retrieve the entire book. Twenty-eight chapters in all. He memorized the first twenty-five chapters and regularly dumped them out with the waste from the latrines. Only the last three chapters remained in his cell and tomorrow they would be committed to memory and the pages would be discarded. He spent every waking minute of his day reciting the words in his mind and sometimes quietly to himself. He could be seen doing his work and mumbling under his breath.

The guards noticed Lucas talking to himself and wondered if he was becoming like the insane man in the cell across from him. On occasion, Lucas watched him. The guards left the man alone. Prisoners who were that far gone never posed a threat. The insane man did his work, if it could really be called work, and talked to the trees, the birds, the dirt, himself. The insane man was already dead; he just didn't know it yet.

With his body healed from pain (the scars, however, would probably never heal) Lucas spent the night on his back looking through his small window up at the evening sky. He recited his passages with a partial view of the moon and thought about life back in the Western world. He was once fascinated by stock charts and sales figures. But that world had since become so distant in so short a time. Now, a story of ordinary people with extraordinary abilities, especially that of healing the sick, had overtaken his interest.

The story he was memorizing had begun to consume him.

Lucas kept the last few pages rolled up, hidden in one of the cobblestone blocks. They were safe there, pretty safe, and it was better they stayed there than on his body. Strip searches at Xaing Xaing rarely revealed anything except emaciated bodies, but still, they were more common than cell searches.

On his twenty-eighth day in prison, Lucas followed the guards to the latrines. With his one month anniversary approaching, Lucas decided to keep track of time. When he had first arrived there had been no point because he knew he would be released soon. But the hours had dragged into a day. The days became a week. Now the weeks turned into a month. Would the months drag into a year? Two years? Forever? He thought of Mike's comment that a prisoner could remain in a labor camp indefinitely without a trial, a sentence, or without ever being officially charged.

The tall guard pushed him into the latrine and Lucas began scrubbing. When the guards left, Lucas moved to the waste box to search for his gold. He searched through the container but did not find any pages. This time all he found were soiled papers. Nothing else. Whatever trail he was following had ended.

He reached into his uniform for the remaining pages in order to throw them away with the waste. His body shot out a rush of adrenaline the way a body does when a sudden loud noise is heard or when a student sees they have just failed a course. Lucas couldn't believe it.

The pages were missing.

His heart pounded like a base drum at a rock concert. He checked the latrine floor for any indication that the pages were still with him. Nothing. His mind raced through the possibilities. If they had fallen out on the way to the latrine they would be on common paths where anyone could pick them up. But the excrement stains would give them away as having come from the refuse box and if a guard picked them up he was done for. If another prisoner discovered them that prisoner would undoubtedly bury them in the ground for fear of having a guard assume they were his. The only other alternative was that the pages were still hidden in the crack in the cobblestone floor at his cell. Every day was similar to the one before and, as much as he tried to replay the events of that morning, he couldn't remember if he had taken them out or not.

He finished his latrine duties and nearly broke into a light jog on the way back to his cell. He looked nervously at the guards for any hint of trouble. Nothing seemed different. The tall guard was as expressionless as always. If he had found something, Lucas would have been beaten unconscious by now.

He got back to his cell and waited the anxious moments until the guards were out of ear shot. Lucas immediately moved to the corner where the pages were buried. He dug his fingers between the stone and the dirt and made contact with paper. Lucas took in a deep breath. He wouldn't wait to throw them out tomorrow. He would review the last pages and eat them. They were a liability, now, more than ever.

He pulled out the paper and felt something different. They were smoother than he remembered. And the weight was all wrong. The rain must have gotten to them. But there were only two pages. This was not good. The first one had no writing on it. The second one had a picture on it. He held it up to the light. It was a scull and cross bones.

The sound of footsteps behind him caused Lucas to cram the pages back into the hole. He whirled around. The tall guard, with his dark, hollow eyes, looked straight through Lucas. There was a sinister presence in those eyes. It was the presence of evil, the presence of something void of any human concern. Behind him stood four other guards. Each of them carried a baton.

The tall guard held the pages Lucas had been memorizing in his hand. He pulled out a ring of keys and slotted one into the keyhole. Lucas pushed himself to the back of the cell like a wounded puppy. The tall guard turned the key and opened the door. Fear gripped Lucas. He began to recite his verses but it didn't take the feeling away. The tall guard pulled out a pack of matches and crouched down. His huge legs looked like trees on either side of his head. He lit a match and held it to the pages.

As they began to burn he whispered to Lucas. Who could tell what he was saying? Who could tell what was going on behind his expressionless face? Lucas didn't understand the words but he understood the message. It was a message deeper than hatred. To hate someone is to feel something for them; but there is an evil far beyond hatred and the tall guard was already there. He attached no value to Lucas. For him, Lucas was no longer a human being. He was nothing.

The pages caught fire. The tall guard looked at Lucas through the burning flame. Their eyes connected. He dropped the pages on the ground and turned to speak to the others. Lucas instinctively reached out to grab them. He didn't need the pages, he had them memorized and was going to throw them out anyway, but seeing them burning there on the ground just felt wrong to him.

As if on cue, the tall guard spun around, raised his boot and with incredible force smashed his heel down on Lucas' wrist. There was a tremendous cracking sound like the sound a branch makes when it breaks off a tree. A flood of heat and pain pounded in Lucas' body. He screamed and dragged his hand into his chest to cover it with his other hand. He hoped this would be the end of it.

But he was wrong.

The tall guard grabbed Lucas' sore hand and dragged him out of his cell. The fragile tendons and bones in his wrist hung feebly together making Lucas feel like his hand was going to separate from his arm. The tall guard stopped in the middle of the hallway and left Lucas with his outstretched arm for the nearby prisoners to see. Once again, he lifted his huge leg and came crashing down with his heel on Lucas' elbow. He missed somewhat and crushed the radius, one of the two bones connecting the wrist with the elbow. Lucas screamed again and tried desperately to pull his hand back but his arm would not respond. The shouting echoed throughout the cell block. The other prisoners turned away. They'd seen this before.

Lucas tried to get up but the tall guard grabbed him by the hair and smashed his head against the ground. A thumbnail wide gash split open above his ear. Blood trickled out and he felt light-headed the way people do when they've been in a car accident.

The tall guard yelled an instruction and immediately two guards grabbed hold of Lucas, one by his hair the other by his arm, and dragged him down the hallway. The tall guard yelled at the other prisoners that the punishment was for being in the possession of contraband.

They brought him to a cold, clammy room. A dim bulb hung down and put out only as much light as a few candles. A steel joist ran along the center of the ceiling. There were blood stains on the ground.

The tall guard fastened a handcuff to Lucas' right hand. One of the guards forced him to his feet. They swung the cuff around the joist and clasped it to Lucas' left hand. He stood on his toes, much like the way a ballerina does, to avoid the pain of his crushed wrist.

Lucas saw the tall guard in front of him. He held an object in his left hand. Part of Lucas didn't want to know what it was, the other part needed to know in order to brace himself for what was coming. It had a steel handle with pieces of leather strips hanging down from it. Lucas tried to reposition his wrists in the cuffs so that the steel would not cut into them. He felt blood trickle down his arm.

He looked past his arm and saw one of the other guards. This one had a baton in his hand, maybe made of rubber, maybe steel. He looked to his other side and saw another guard with a wooden stick with red stains all over it.

It hit Lucas that this was probably his death sentence. No firing squad, no gallows, just three guards—guards who didn't know his name and who didn't care who he was. It seemed so stupid to Lucas—to die at the hands of these people. And for what? A wrongful narcotics conviction that resulted in an unjustified prison sentence with no chance for an appeal.

Lucas looked at the tall guard. Instead of seeing a ruthless, amoral dictator, Lucas saw a man without hope, without compassion, without life. A man for whom all human decency had long since deteriorated. How does someone get to such a rotten state?

The tall guard tore the top off of Lucas' uniform to reveal his thinning body. He was once athletic and muscular. Now he was reduced to skin, bones and whatever courage he had left. The tall guard ripped off Lucas' pants too, leaving him naked in front of his assailants. One of the other guards made a joke and flung his cigarette at Lucas. The two guards laughed, but not the tall guard. His fun was just beginning.

The tall guard took the first swing at Lucas. The leather straps cut against Lucas' chest, leaving thick red stripes. Lucas clenched his jaw. It felt as though someone was slicing him open with a hot knife. The other guards whapped their sticks against Lucas, striking him in the face, the groin and on his back. The batons smashing against his body sounded like boards being hit together. Lucas tried as hard as he could to stay on his toes. If his legs gave way it would surely put too much stress on his damaged wrist and possibly his arm would tear off at the hand. He stayed as strong as he could, helpless against the blows of the guards.

The guards struck Lucas again and again. The tall guard shouted at him, taunted him and made fun of him. Lucas shifted his weight from one leg to the other but it didn't make standing there any easier. Blood shot out from his body with every hit, some of it hitting the small bulb above him making the room even darker, some of it landing on the guards. The smack of the whip against his back echoed in the small room.

The tall guard threw his whip away and stepped up to Lucas whose eyes were blurred from the beatings. Unconsciousness would be a welcome relief, but it would invariably place incredible strain on his wrist. If he blacked out now it might be the last time he would see his hand attached to his body. The tall guard formed his hand into a fist and struck Lucas in the face, catching him under the eye. Lucas' head snapped back. The end was fast approaching. The ability to reason had long since left him. Clear thinking was gone. Exhaustion had set in the way it does for amateurs finishing their first marathon. The second blow caught him square on the nose. A pop was heard and his eyes welled up with tears.

The tall guard lifted the burned pages to Lucas' bloodied face. His calves cramped as he struggled to maintain balance. With every breath, blood came out of his nose and his mouth. The tall guard dropped the pages into the blood beneath Lucas and slowly shook his finger at him. He pressed his face against Lucas' and looked him eyeball to eyeball. "No," he whispered.

Lucas had one final conscious thought. *Here comes the end.*

The tall guard stepped back and smashed his face directly between Lucas' eyes. Lucas blanked out immediately. The guards waited a moment and tried to catch their breath from the ordeal. Urine ran down Lucas' leg. He hung there like an animal in a slaughtering plant. Blood and sweat dripped from his body forming a puddle beneath him.

The tall guard whipped Lucas one last time. But there was no response. He released the handcuffs and Lucas' body slumped to the ground. The tall guard shouted at the other guards but neither reacted—it was as if the horror of what they had done was only now becoming clear in their minds. He shouted again and they reluctantly grabbed Lucas by the shoulders and dragged him out of the room.

The Cage, as it was called by the inmates, was a small concrete hole in the floor with a steel lid that acted as a door. It was the size of a cardboard box one might expect to be used as a transport casing for a new TV. It was too small for someone to stand up and too small to lie down. The only light came from a hole in the steel lid. It was Lucas' brand new home.

They dropped his body in, locked the lid and went to wipe the blood off their uniforms. Afterwards, the tall guard sat down at his desk, pulled out a book and began to read.

Lucas awoke a day later and quickly wished he hadn't. After his first beating at Xaing Xaing, Lucas felt his entire body with the exception of his fingers and toes. This time, however, everything hurt. Every breath, every blink, every heartbeat moved something in his body that caused him pain.

His head throbbed with so much force that it sounded as if a thousand mosquitoes were humming in his ears. His face was caked with dried blood. His head rested against the cold concrete wall but it hurt too much to move. He began to cry. The tears stung his eyes but he didn't have the strength in his arms to wipe them away. He told himself not to cry but soon realized it was involuntary, as if something deep inside him, much deeper than the wounds of his body, was desperately seeking to be healed.

He sat in the Cage with his knees tucked awkwardly under his chin and wondered if it was wrong to pray for death. He shivered and his teeth chattered uncontrollably. How good a swig, a whole bottle, of his brandy or whiskey would go down right now. He recalled the words from the pages he had memorized and recited them, in his mind, from beginning to end, over and over again.

It was the only thing he could do to keep his mind off the pain.

12

In the dark, cold Cage, Lucas sensed the horror that comes with being assigned an eternal sentence in isolation. For some people, time appears to be linear, giving them the feeling that the past is truly gone. For others, like Lucas, it's more circular—as though nothing can prevent them from reliving what has already happened. He felt like a kid on a merry-go-round whose every spin is exactly the same as the one before. At a park, the circular life can be the greatest reward. But in a seclusion cell at Xiang Xaing, it's the greatest punishment.

When the guards came to give him his daily bowl of slop, Lucas found himself unable to receive it from them. It took all his energy to simply look at them, leaving nothing to raise his fingers and accept the pathetic offering from their detestable hands. They mistook it for an act of defiance and swore at him as they slammed the lid shut. It was the only contact Lucas still had with the outside world.

The verses, the pain, the guards bringing him food. That's all Lucas had left.

But the pattern finally broke when something out of the ordinary happened. It occurred as he quoted some of his memorized pages. By the fiftieth time of reciting his passages (or maybe it was the seventieth or the thirtieth, he had lost the ability to keep track of time) Lucas felt an occasional jolt of electricity run through his body. It wasn't a huge surge, but the shock was distinct enough for him to know he wasn't imagining it. At first he thought it was the muscles in his body reattaching. But each time he quoted the passages his fingers felt the sensation. It was like the feeling a person gets when they've accidentally stuck the end of a screwdriver into an electrical socket. It troubled Lucas, not because he thought he was losing his mind, but because he couldn't tell if it was hurting him or healing him.

As he mumbled the verses through his swollen jaw his hands became warm. Speaking the verses was like turning the dial on a heater to make the room hotter. When the guards periodically opened the lid and the light shone in, Lucas looked at his fingers. Except for the swelling and bruising there was nothing unusual about their appearance. Everything looked normal. It was just that they *felt* so strange. He was able to move his wrist, at least slightly and he wondered how it was that just three short days ago it was completely useless to him.

That evening, much of his pain had subsided the way pain does after the body switches from defending itself to recovering. His beard had grown in and his once shaved head now showed the stubble growth of a brush cut. Reciting the verses helped Lucas keep his sanity, but it was coupled with a problem. His hands had now become uncomfortably hot.

He stopped saying the verses to let his hands cool down. But the moment he started again they heated up. It got to the point where his hands felt like they were on fire. He closed his lips and tried not to think of what was happening. But it was no use. His mind stayed focused on what he had memorized. His hands grew hotter. They took on a reddish color and almost glowed in the dark Cage. Lucas tried to blow cold air on them but nothing he tried could cool them down.

The heat moved up his hands as far as his wrist. His fingers got so hot he was sure they would explode out like bullets from a gun. In desperation he screamed and slammed his hands against the cobblestone wall. They sunk into the stone and then cooled down immediately. Steam rose up. He stopped panting and pulled his hands back across his chest.

There beside him in the wall were two indented handprints.

The Cage door opened and a guard looked inside. It surprised him to see Lucas squinting up at him. The Cage had not seen many survivors.

Two guards pulled him out. His head still hurt (he wondered if it always would) and he found it difficult to stand up straight.

They brought him down a hallway to the tall guard's office. One of the guards knocked on the door. A single syllable answer came from inside. They opened the door. They saw the tall guard.

He looked up from the book he was reading (Chairman Mao's book). When he saw Lucas he jerked his head back. He furrowed his brow then stood up from his desk. He waited there a moment as if he wasn't sure what was going on. He walked over to Lucas. Each step he took made him look bigger.

The tall guard looked at the guards, then at Lucas, then back at the guards as if he was trying to convince himself that Lucas was really there. His mouth dropped open. He said nothing. Didn't even look Lucas in the eye. For the first time, Lucas thought he could sense fear in the tall guard.

The tall guard turned around to hide the shock in his eyes. He mumbled to the guards in a barely audible voice that Lucas was to be assigned to weed pulling and garbage cleaning duty. It would be a welcome change for Lucas because he would get the opportunity to be with other prisoners, other people. Time would tell if that was a good thing or not.

He worked in the garden with a wooden hoe (metal was not allowed) and scraped at weeds. Afterwards, he picked up garbage around the prison. It was monotonous but at least it didn't stink like the latrines.

The rain drizzled down on him as he hacked into the tough soil. The water felt good on his body. He opened his mouth and stretched out his tongue to catch a clean drink. He closed his eyes and remembered the times when he would come home exhausted from a business trip and relax in the shower.

When he opened his eyes he noticed another prisoner working nearby. At first it meant nothing to Lucas but then it seemed that the man was making his way closer and closer to him. It was the insane man, the one from the cell across from him. Lucas turned his body in such a way so that he could work and maintain eye contact with the insane man. It was, after all, prison and he had never been in open population before. Not at Xaing Xaing.

The insane man shook his head with involuntary movements but did his work nonetheless. Lucas worked at clearing the weeds but the approaching man made it impossible for him to concentrate. He gripped his hoe and prepared to strike at the insane man in case he tried something. Occasionally, other prisoners looked in their direction as if they were waiting for something to happen. The guards were none the wiser. Just another day at Xaing Xaing.

Lucas deliberately moved away from the approaching enemy and glanced over his shoulder, hoping he would not follow. But he did follow, and right behind Lucas, until he stood a little more than a swing away. Again, Lucas walked away and again the insane man followed. He was pretending to dig in the weeds but he missed more than he pulled up.

Lucas turned around and looked him the eye. He braced himself in case of an attack. There would be no reasoning with him and no way of telling if he was going to attempt something. Their eyes locked and what Lucas saw concerned him. The insane man was looking right at him. Not around him, or through him, the way people do when they've lost their senses, but right into his pupils—it was if he was studying Lucas.

"You speak English?" asked the insane man.

Lucas turned around to check if someone was sneaking up on him. There wasn't. "Yes, I do."

"Keep working. Keep your head down."

Lucas did as he was told. Without realizing he turned his back on the insane man and half expected him to smash his hoe down on him.

The insane man spoke to Lucas without looking at him. "How many tons?"

Lucas assumed the insane man's English was so poor, or so outdated, that his translation skills were now inadequate. Lucas shrugged his shoulders to indicate he didn't know what the insane man wanted.

The insane man asked again. "How many tons?"

"I don't know what that means."

"How many tons of steamed corn?"

"I'm telling you, I don't know what you are talking about."

The insane man, who evidently wasn't so insane, explained in his broken English that prisoners used to receive approximately one pound of steamed corn for rations each day. In roughly five years, a prisoner would consume a ton of steamed corn. Prisoners at Xaing Xaing referred to the length of their sentences in terms of the tons of food they would consume during their imprisonment. A prisoner with a fifteen-year sentence, for example, would respond by saying he would eat three tons.

"I don't know what my sentence is. I haven't had a hearing yet."

"That concerns me."

"Why?"

"Were you in another cell before you came to the one across from mine?"

"No."

"That concerns me even more."

The insane man introduced himself as Sidong and explained that he had learned his English from a missionary. Now, as a prisoner, Sidong pretended to be insane in order to receive better treatment from the guards. They went easier on people, prisoners, who were mentally ill.

"What do you want from me?"

"We are planning an escape. In two days," Sidong said.

Lucas wondered if it was a trap. Maybe a guard paid Sidong off to keep an eye on him. Maybe Sidong was an informer. Maybe this was nothing but a set up.

"I don't think that would be such a good idea," Lucas said hoping Sidong would tell him otherwise.

"Forty of us. It's all planned. If you want in just say so."

"But if I wait for my hearing I might be out in a week."

"I'm sorry you believe that," Sidong said reaching down to pick up a weed that his hoe could not accomplish. "Have you ever noticed that you are not in a cell with others; that you're not with ten people, a toilet pail and a wash bucket all crowded into one tiny cell?"

"Yes, I've noticed."

"Do you know why?"

"No."

"Because you are scheduled to be executed."

Lucas stopped working. He felt sick in his stomach again. It was as though he was going to vomit his lungs out right there in the garden.

"You are strong?" Sidong asked.

"Strong enough."

"Are you with us?"

Lucas tried to control his breathing. That word continued to ring in his mind. *Executed. Executed. Executed.*

"Yes, or no?" Sidong said.

"Yeah, I want out."

"We have connections inside and outside. The day after tomorrow we make a break for it."

The following day, Lucas received instructions on how the jailbreak would take place. The advance warning gave Lucas time to rehearse his part. Familiarity would breed success. So they all hoped. And the next evening the adventure began.

At eight o'clock, a person wearing a guard's uniform entered the barracks. He carried a large bag and hurried to the end of the block to Sidong's cell. The guard produced a set of keys and unlocked Sidong's door. He opened the bag and gave Sidong one of the contents inside. A shotgun.

Within seconds he opened all of the cells and the prisoners got out. Every second prisoner received a shotgun, not Lucas, and they lined up to get ready for action. Lucas waited at the back of the line. His heart pounded like everyone else's. Freedom or death was just minutes away.

The make-believe guard left the barracks quietly and disappeared out of sight. He was on his way down the road to a delivery truck that would take the prisoners to safety. Lucas held his breath. Everything went quiet. His pulse throbbed so loud in his ears that it sounded like footsteps creeping up behind him.

Lucas looked at the shotguns. When he first came to Xaing Xaing he would have welcomed the opportunity to shoot every guard. But now he questioned those same feelings. Something felt very wrong, or different. He questioned himself if he would have the guts to actually take a guard's life. *Of course I can. Of course I can.*

To calm his nerves he began reciting the verses. His hands became warmer. Sidong nudged him; he turned around and received the last shotgun. As soon as Lucas grabbed it, his hands went as cold as the steel itself. He looked at the other prisoners who clutched their weapons like drowning swimmers clinging to life preservers.

The plan was simple. Sidong would wander aimlessly out to the courtyard pretending to speak with his imaginary friend. The guards would discover him and assume one of them had forgotten to lock his cell. When they would approach him to bring him back, Sidong would fake a temper tantrum as though he and his imaginary friend were having an argument. When the guards would get within firing range he would pull out his shotgun and blast the three or four guards nearest him into the next life. Then the rest of his block of armed prisoners would fire their way out of the prison gate, past the towers and race down the road to the delivery van. Conceptually, it was straight forward.

But it did not work out that way.

Sidong made it out to the courtyard undetected and, as was expected, one of the searchlights caught him. Two guards shouted at him as they approached. The other insurrectionists waited in the shadows for their opportunity. When the guards saw who it was they lowered their rifles. Sidong ranted and raved as loud as he could. Meanwhile, he reached into his uniform. When the guards were close enough, Sidong grabbed his shotgun. And that's when everything went wrong.

He had made the mistake of loading a shell into the chamber before hiding the gun in his uniform. He had figured it would save him a few precious seconds before getting the first round off and hoped it would provide him with a guaranteed advantage when he aimed it at the guards. But when he pulled it out the trigger caught on a button. The shotgun gave off an incredible bang and blew his head clear off his shoulders.

The guards immediately raised their rifles. The general alarm sounded. On the block, the prisoners panicked and raced down the hallway through the penitentiary. They made it as far as the courtyard entrance. When they opened the door they were greeted by five guards with shotguns who opened fire on them. The prisoners did not have time to react. Two prisoners were filled with bullets and flew back against the others, thereby protecting them from the second round of gunfire from the guards. The prisoners ran away in complete confusion. Pandemonium broke loose.

The next mistake came when the prisoners ran off in different directions. The plan had been botched and an alternate route had not been thought through. In the confusion, Lucas dropped his shotgun. He tried to go back for it but the onslaught of horrified prisoners made it impossible to retrieve. He ran off with another prisoner who was still armed. Lucas briefly considered returning to his cell, but after what happened when the tall guard discovered the English literature Lucas knew what would be waiting for him if he was caught after an attempted jailbreak.

Gun fire was heard throughout the penitentiary. Screams of people being shot echoed throughout the brick walls.

Lucas and the other prisoner ran down a stairwell. The commotion got further and further away from them. They came to a door and looked through the window. There in the distance was freedom—through the door, across the back yard of the prison and down the slope to the delivery van.

Lucas heard footsteps behind them. This time it wasn't his pulse. They were real boots on real concrete. Lucas and the prisoner pushed their backs up against the wall and tried to hide in the stairwell. The prisoner checked to make sure his gun was ready to fire. The steps grew closer. There was only one set of feet. Beads of sweat formed on their faces. Out of fear, Lucas began to quote verses in his mind. His lips moved as he said them.

The steps came closer and closer. Slower and slower. The prisoner clutched his shotgun. Inches away. Just inches away. Then, he appeared. It was the tall guard. He didn't notice them, not at first. Their presence took him completely by surprise. When he did see them (he probably *felt* their presence first) his eyes grew wide open. He sucked in air. He tried to aim his rifle at them but he was too late. The prisoner fired at the tall guard. There was a tremendous bang. Pellets raced out of the barrel. The force knocked the tall guard off his feet and blew him back against the wall. He stayed there for a moment with a look of horror and shock on his face. He stared at them with eyes that almost looked human, as if his mortality was only now being made known to him. He searched for his shotgun and saw that it was out of reach. He slid down the wall and fell with his back to the ground.

Without any hesitation the prisoner opened the door and ran to safety.

But Lucas froze.

The prisoner made it halfway through the courtyard and looked back in bewilderment at Lucas. He motioned for Lucas to join him. There were no guards to stop them. Lucas looked at the tall guard. He wasn't dead, though he was certainly on his way. The tall guard tried to move, but his body would not respond. He breathed in short small bursts, struggling to clear his throat to get what little air he could into his lungs.

Lucas looked back at the prisoner, then down the hallway. No one was coming. He glanced at the tall guard. He looked so strange and out of place lying there all by himself. This towering giant reduced to nothing more than a dying soul. Lucas left the door and walked to the tall guard. He checked over his shoulder and saw the prisoner vanish into the bush. Within minutes he would reach the delivery truck.

Lucas crouched down. He heard the tall guard wheeze as though he was overcome with a horrible case of asthma. It sounded like he was going to cut out all together any moment.

The gunfire upstairs had ceased. A hush had fallen on Xaing Xaing.

The tall guard focused on Lucas. His breathing slowed down. Some blood had soaked down his side, through his uniform and now spilled on to the floor. Lucas bent down and quietly recited his verses. He didn't have the courage to look the tall guard in the eye. He half expected him to pull out his whip and start beating him again. Although that would be impossible now given the circumstances, Lucas still felt scared in his presence.

He rested his hands on the tall guard's chest. He felt the blood and smelled the tall guard's piercing odor. Lucas prayed and quoted some of his verses. His hands became warm. His fingers began to tremble.

The fear left the tall guard's eyes. The atmosphere grew warmer. He looked at Lucas in amazement and wondered what he was doing. *Why wasn't he leaving? Why didn't he just go with the other prisoner? What was he still doing here?*

Whatever chance Lucas had at freedom was certainly gone now. The truck would have left. Suddenly, Lucas felt the tall guard's chest rise. Both of them were stunned.

The tall guard sputtered for air and then breathed in short pants. He took in a deeper breath and couldn't decide if he was already dead or simply experiencing a dream. A tear came down the tall guard's cheek. It dripped off his face and landed in the pool of blood beside him. Lucas removed his hand and looked at the chest. There was no wound whatsoever.

Lucas looked at his hands—his plain, unassuming hands, and then back at the chest. The tall guard swallowed. He breathed in, held it a moment and then let it out. The tall guard made eye contact with Lucas. What he saw shocked him. Instead of a prisoner he saw a person. Instead of uniform he saw a champion. He was then overcome with an unbearable sense of guilt and was about to feel remorse for all of his actions, but his attention was diverted to another guard who appeared from behind the doorway. The other guard saw Lucas touching the tall guard and raised the butt of his rifle. The tall guard tried to shout for him to stop. But the guard smashed his rifle onto the back of Lucas' head. He hit the ground and his face landed in the tall guard's pool of blood. The tall guard rolled over and tried to help his fallen comrade. As Lucas drifted off into unconsciousness he saw that the tall guard's chest was perfectly healed.

Lucas had seen his very first miracle.

13

Lucas was jolted awake by a bumpy ride in an armored vehicle. He felt the weight of an ice pack on his head where the guard hit him. His eyes readjusted and he moved his hands. There were no handcuffs.

Across from him sat a doctor with wire-rimmed glasses, slicked black hair and a concerned expression on his face. He came to Lucas' side and checked his head.

"Where am I going?"

"No English," said the doctor with a sheepish smile. He looked at Lucas' head and seemed to be content with the progress his wound was making. Lucas turned and noticed there was only one guard in the vehicle. As he sat up a rush of pain swelled in his head. The doctor repositioned the ice pack and grimaced as though he could feel the pain himself.

The absence of chains and the presence of a doctor gave Lucas the assurance he needed that he was not on the way to his execution. He laid his head back down and slept the rest of the ride.

The vehicle came to a stop. A knock at the door. The guard opened it and stepped out. A burst of sunlight filled the compartment. It was noisy outside, sounded like city traffic. The doctor helped Lucas to his feet the way a grandson helps his elderly grandmother and ushered him out of the vehicle.

Lucas was greeted by a team of soldiers. They weren't rough looking like the guards at Xaing Xaing. These were more dignified, almost noble looking. At the end of the row of soldiers came an attractive Chinese woman with long, straight black hair. She wore a knee-length gray skirt, a white blouse and a matching jacket. She shook Lucas' hand and smiled, revealing her perfect teeth.

"Welcome to the minister's office, Mr. Stephens." Lucas detected an accent. British, most likely. She was probably educated in England for a foreign relations position. She spoke to him in a diplomatic tone but when she saw the marks on his face her expression became concerned. She almost looked embarrassed, as if a deep, dark secret had just been revealed to her.

"Thank you," Lucas said. His eyes stayed focused on her. She had fair skin, a thin body—definitely an athlete. She gave off a faint trace of perfume that almost hypnotized him. It made him feel as though he could let down the walls of protection he had built in prison and collapse into her arms. Lucas desperately wanted her to hold him. He wanted her to take him away to someplace safe. She was the first female he had seen in such a long while.

There was something comforting about being in the presence of a woman.

"My name is Pan Chong. Won't you come in?"

He didn't know which minister he would be visiting or what Pan's function was in the office, but she could have asked him to follow her anywhere and he would have done it. He managed a smile and felt completely helpless. "Yes, I will."

They walked together into the large office building. Expensive cars dropped people off. Fancy suits and sharply dressed women cluttered the elaborate lobby. Lucas vaguely recalled a life like this.

Lucas and Pan arrived on the twenty-eighth floor. She led him down a hallway to a private room where new clothes had been laid out for him on the dresser. "How is your head, Mr. Stephens?"

"My head his fine," he lied, "and call me Lucas."

"As you wish, Lucas." The longer he looked at her the younger her appearance became. Late twenties, maybe thirty at the most. And she was intelligent, too. It wasn't so much what she said but, rather, the way in which she said it that attracted Lucas to her. She struck him as being compassionate, caring and yet unmistakably confident. He watched her, almost to the point of making her feel uncomfortable. He was captivated by her.

Prison does strange things to a man's emotions.

"Is there anything else I can get for you, Lucas?"

Yes, just stay here. I want to sit down here with you and get to know you. Tell me how you're doing. Smile, if you want to. Let me in on what makes you tick. What are you interested in? What are your goals? Your dreams? If you could succeed at anything in life what would it be? What's your favorite food? What do you sound like when you laugh, I mean, really laugh? Forget the minister. Let's go for coffee. Heck, forget the whole world. We'll get in one of those little taxis and you can show me around Beijing. You can get one of those cool, white umbrellas and we could spend the evening walking someplace safe. We could, I could, feel what's it's like to have companionship again.

"Nothing, I'm fine. Thank you." She was about to leave when Lucas stopped her. "Why am I here?"

"The details you get later." Pan smiled in a way that reached right inside of Lucas. She left the room and closed the door behind her.

That sinking feeling of being in a room, alone, returned.

Off to the left was a shower with all sorts of toiletries. In front of him, about a short football throw away, was a large bed with a huge dragon painting on top of it. He considered how awful he must smell. The things you get used to in prison. He walked past a mirror and proceeded to take off his shirt. He stopped and glanced at his face. His dark hair looked stringy and ragged. There was a scar above his left eye, swelling on the cheekbone below it. He wondered what his body might look like after the beatings. He closed his eyes and took off his shirt and pants. Some things are better left until later.

He turned on the shower and the warm water ran over his head. He kept his eyes shut the entire time but as he washed his torso with a bar of soap, he could feel them—the jagged marks where the whips and sticks had left their signature. The tears were no match for the pounding, refreshing water.

After his shower he changed into a dark blue Chinese suit. He looked good in the Mandarin style jacket that did not have any kind of a folded down collar the way Western suits do. Underneath he wore a crisp white shirt.

Lucas stepped out of the room and looked for Pan. She walked up to him and gave him a smile of approval. "You see. You look Chinese already." She motioned with her hand and the two of them walked down the hallway to a room where two guards stood at attention. Lucas could not look them in the eye. The guards nodded, opened the door and allowed Lucas in. He turned to Pan.

"You're not coming in?"

She shook her head to one side. "The minister will be with you shortly." She gave a short bow, so slight that it was hardly noticeable, turned and walked briskly down the hallway.

At the far end of the room Minister Chong sat at a table with a guard on either side of him. Another woman, in her forties and not as attractive as Pan, approached Lucas and ushered him to a seat across from the minister. Lucas noticed the table where Minister Chong sat was elevated. Lucas felt hopelessly small in front of him. He was surrounded by a sea of deep red carpet. Dragons decorated the walls.

"Please bow to Minister Chong and then sit down." Lucas did. "May I offer you some tea?"

"Thank you."

Minister Chong looked at Lucas through his glasses and gave no indication as to whether the meeting was for a good reason or a bad one. He stared at Lucas for longer than what would be considered polite, then took a drink of water and gave a frown.

"You are being released from prison." The words came to Lucas like cold water on a hot day. "We are dismissing your case and are sending you back to America." Lucas didn't know what to say. What was there to say?

Minister Chong looked at Lucas, at the marks on his face. He became quiet, almost unsure of what to say next. "We are still undergoing reform in China—and in our prisons."

"Not at Xaing Xaing, you're not."

Minister Chong pressed his lips together, as though fighting to refrain himself from saying something he would later regret. "Reform takes time. We still have some old thinking, even in our younger people."

Lucas studied Minister Chong's face and saw a resemblance between him and the tall guard. The sunken eyes gave it away.

Lucas thought back to the healing incident at Xaing Xaing and wondered what the tall guard thought of it. The tea arrived. "How is he?"

"He is not your concern. He is my concern."

"You know him?"

"I do."

"The guard is your son?"

Minister Chong nodded in a way that made him appear embarrassed.

At first it seemed clear to Lucas. The tall guard got miraculously healed and called in a favor from his father to get Lucas out.

But the logic didn't make sense to Lucas. Why would the tall guard, after being healed, want to get rid of Lucas? Maybe he was scared. Maybe he felt guilty over the way he treated Lucas. Possibly he did it out of honor, or respect—qualities the Chinese maintained even through their brutal revolution.

"We have made preparations for you to leave China," Minister Chong said.

"Have you spoken with your son?"

"Do not ask me about him again."

Lucas nodded his head but it didn't stop him from wanting to know about the tall guard, about what he thought of what had happened.

"He has taken a leave of absence," the minister said.

Lucas stood up, bowed and left the room.

The plane taxied down the runway. Lucas sat in first class, surrounded again by the Chinese language. The pain in his head subsided. He took some water and a painkiller to help it along. The roar of the engines comforted him. He glanced out of the window and saw the runway racing past him. The plane took off and the crowded city beneath him grew smaller and smaller.

Lucas was going home.

14

Lucas landed at O'Hare in the drizzling rain. He looked out from his window seat through the reduced visibility and recalled the last time he arrived in Chicago. It had been raining much harder that day. He had arrived on an Empirico jet just in time for the Council meeting where it was decided that he would go to China. This time, as Lucas filed out of the plane, he wasn't going to be giving instructions to company personnel. He wouldn't be hurrying off to a Council meeting. And there wouldn't be a driver waiting for him. Now, with the crowd of passengers pushing past him, he was on his own—but at least he was on his own at home.

He walked out of the terminal and something caught his attention. He thought just for a moment that he wasn't really in Chicago—that maybe his mind had played some cruel trick on him the way it does during a nightmare. What he saw surprised him, even concerned him. It was Caesar. His puffy eyes and thinning gray hair were unmistakable. Beside him stood one of the Empirico drivers. Lucas recognized him as Jonathan, father of two, basketball fan, grew up in Des Moines....

Caesar had a rare look of compassion in his eyes. It was the look a mother gets when she sees her child after he has successfully gone through surgery. He grinned, as much as men like Caesar do, and nodded his approval. His boy was home.

As touching, or as shocking, as it was to have Caesar there, it concerned Lucas. Caesar wouldn't have come to the airport even if had been for his own son, if he had one, and maybe not even under those circumstances. Caesar didn't come to meet people at airports. Ever.

"Caesar." It was all Lucas could say. One could guess Lucas should have had some idea about who would be at the airport, but then again, why should anyone have shown up at all? He left China without anyone knowing he was leaving, all except the tall guard and Minister Chong's office, and now he had shown up in the Windy City. But Caesar knew he'd be here. Somehow Caesar was always a step ahead of him.

And that would prove to be a major obstacle for Lucas.

"Welcome back from China," Caesar said.

"Thank you." Lucas turned to the driver. "Hello, Jonathan." Jonathan nodded.

"You must be tired," Caesar said. "I'm glad you're home."

"How did you know I'd be here?"

Caesar paused. He looked at Lucas and gave an even-toned answer that seemed rehearsed. "The airline told me. Be glad the media don't know yet."

They got into the limousine and Lucas felt the relaxation that comes from being with someone who knows all about you and yet still wants to be around you. On the way to Lucas' home they talked—really talked. They spoke about things that matter to people, not the endless drivel that most conversations are wasted on.

"What about Mike?" Lucas asked.

"He's out of town."

"Doing well?"

"Me or him?"

"Both of you."

"I'm relieved to see you alive. So I'm doing well, or at least I'm doing well now."

"And Mike?"

"Haven't talked to him the last three days. He left town on business."

They were quiet for a moment. Caesar was playing the line between employer and friend. It's a line that's not easily drawn and is even tougher to walk. "That must have been unspeakable. Being in that Chinese prison." Lucas tried to find a response but couldn't. "I know you don't want to talk about it. Believe me. I know." Caesar said that with such conviction, such understanding, it was as if he'd had been with Lucas in his cell and somehow knew exactly what he had been through. "What human beings can do to each other... it's as if some people can completely lose their humanity." Caesar looked like he was in a trance, like he was giving a confession to the police after a long, exhausting interrogation. "People. They turn into animals. Give them a little power, a little autonomy and what do they turn into? Savages. Rotten, filthy, cruel." His voice turned to anger and for the first time Lucas didn't feel just intimidated by Caesar, he felt downright scared. "But you're back now," Caesar said, hoping to change the subject. "You're back and that's what counts." He gave Lucas a playful slap on the knee. And for a moment Lucas felt what it might be like to have a relationship, any decent relationship, with a father.

A flight attendant noticed Lucas' name on the registry and, recalling the name from the newspaper stories, placed a call to the *Observer*. Tabitha, who was working late, answered her phone and received the news. An innocent man returning from a jail sentence would normally be a cause for celebration. But Tabitha was far from celebrating. She didn't want Lucas to return from that prison, maybe not ever. Having him in China was the easiest way to cover the story. Now that he was back in town she would have to schedule a face-to-face meeting with him. She dreaded the thought.

The limousine stopped outside a medical clinic and Caesar explained to Lucas that he wanted to make sure he was all right. Four doctors (one a psychiatrist) and a nurse spent an hour examining Lucas. They took X-rays of much of his body as well as blood and urine samples and gave him a complete physical. Plastic surgery might be needed to fix up some of the scars. Lucas answered a number of questions, the psychiatrist found nothing wrong with him and they released him.

The limo drove through the huge gates at Lucas' home and up the driveway. Caesar asked him, "Are you going to be all right tonight?"

"I think so," Lucas said, wondering if the memory of being in prison would keep him awake.

Lucas got out and thanked Caesar. It wasn't just a simple thank you, like the kind someone gives the pick-up window attendant at a fast food joint, but a real heartfelt thank you. He needed Caesar, he needed someone to connect with, to bring him back to Chicago and settle him down.

Lucas watched as the limo drove down the driveway, through the gates and out of sight. He opened the side door—there were no shadows moving inside this time, no surprise party either—and entered his home.

On his kitchen table, stacks of letters and junk mail were laid out perfectly by the house-cleaning crew. His fridge had been restocked and cleaned. He looked through the mail and found personal letters and lots of thinking-of-you cards. It was nice to know people hadn't given up hope.

He walked through his home and looked into each room, as if doing so could emotionally reattach him to his life there. It seemed so surreal, so distant that he had spent time rotting away in a Chinese prison. And yet, within a twenty-four hour period he was sitting in the lap of luxury.

Again.

He changed out of his Chinese suit and into a pair of jeans and a blue silk shirt. He checked his voice-mail and listened to a stream of messages. By the time he reached the last one he expected another hope-you're-home-soon from a friend, maybe even a call from one of those hot girls who had played basketball in his pool at his last party. But instead he heard something else. The voice was familiar. His mind searched through his memory to identify the owner but his heart found the answer first. His body pumped out a rush of adrenaline. It scared him. The past was barging into his life like a police raid. He hadn't heard the voice in years but he knew it well; there was no mistaking it. His mind finally caught up. And it then hit him. Of course. It was Tabitha Samos.

"Hello, Lucas. I heard you were back in town. It's Tabitha Samos calling, by the way. I've been assigned to your story. I hope you're doing well… I'd like to meet with you. Tomorrow. 7:00 at Navy Pier? If you can't make it please call. Otherwise I'll see you then… Bye."

He hadn't spoken with her in three years and that had suited them both just fine. There were probably ten reporters at the *Observer* who could have covered this story, maybe more; what were the odds that she would get the assignment?

When the initial shock passed he replayed the message and wondered what she looked like now. Still beautiful, he assumed, probably married. Attractive, smart women tended not to stay single as long in Chicago as they did in other cities like LA. The part about "I'd like to meet with you," was a truism. It was more like she *had* to meet with him. And now he, of course, *had* to meet with her.

Lucas pulled out a ginger ale from the fridge (there was no beer), sat down on his leather couch and recalled the time he met Tabitha while studying at Harvard Medical School. She had wanted to go to Notre Dame but because they didn't have a medical program she had tried her luck and succeeded at getting accepted at Harvard. A jolt of nervousness shot through him when he remembered the first time he saw her. There was something between them right from the start. He felt helpless then, the way a man does when he's in the presence of a woman he needs.

They connected in a way that only soulmates can. The two of them joined the same study team and usually found themselves in the top five percent of the class. They each had a bright future. Maybe even together. But that all came to a crashing halt. It was an event with results Lucas hoped could dissolve with time. Time, however, doesn't heal old wounds; it just tricks the mind into not remembering them. Lucas wanted to believe they were gone and forgotten, even though deep, down inside he knew those wounds were patiently waiting to be re-discovered.

He changed into his pajamas and sat down on the edge of his bed. He looked at the pictures of his sponsor children from around the world, then at the bottles of whiskey and brandy. He didn't need them, or so he tried to tell himself. He got under the covers, rolled over on his side and forced himself not to drink. *I don't need them.* But his throat told him otherwise. He felt like Pavlov's dog.

It seemed that by going to sleep in his own bed there was a conditioned response that left him with a craving for alcohol. He tried to relax and concentrated on how good if felt not to be on cobblestone, not to be worried about approaching footsteps, not be at Xaing Xaing.

15

When Lucas woke up at 5:00 a.m. the fear of being back in Xaing Xaing gripped him. It was as though cords had been wrapped around his chest to prevent him from breathing. But as his eyes adjusted he saw something other than bars and he smelled something other than sweat and vomit. He wasn't in prison. He was in his bedroom. Away from all of that. He had the same feeling of relief students get when they wake up to discover the horrendous exam period really is over. He stayed in bed another fifteen minutes, worried that if he should get out, his feet would touch cobblestone and life as number 430 would return.

No guards. No pain. If there was a heaven, this is probably what it was like. Lucas pulled back the covers and put his feet on the ground. No cobblestone either. Smooth, hardwood floor instead. He stood up and convinced himself he was at home. He could walk around as freely as he wanted to. Do what he wanted to do without fear of being beaten.

He walked to the door and was about to touch the handle when he stopped. A strange feeling of dread came over him. He told himself he was in no danger of the tall guard coming to attack him and that there was nothing to fear. But try as he could, he was unable to shake the sensation that something was drawing him to stay in the room. It was as though a magnet was pulling at him.

But the pull was not strong enough to force Lucas back. It was more like a beckoning. *What is this?* Still groggy, he turned back from the door and came to the bed. He felt exhausted and got down on his knees, much the way he did when he was cleaning the latrines. He wondered what was happening. It was eerie—unlike anything he had ever felt before.

Something was in the room with him.

He quoted some of his verses to calm himself down. He glanced around hoping to catch something out of the ordinary. The room seemed bigger. Although everything was perfectly quiet, it *felt* loud to Lucas—the way a person feels when they stand behind a waterfall. Everything looked the same. But there was something there, he was sure of it. Somehow it was more real to him than the floor he was kneeling on. He waited there a moment, trying to decide if the presence was evil or good. Powerful and gentle, horrifying and relaxing all at the same time. It scared Lucas, almost as much as the tall guard. Something *was* watching him, moving around him, right beside his ear and all around the room.

Are you God?

There was no response.

Lucas got behind the wheel of his Mercedes and headed down the driveway. The sunlight glittered through the trees beside him. The leather seats against his back and Harry Connick Jr. singing over his sound system helped him believe life as an Empirico executive had returned. He cruised off to work under a beautiful sky and wondered what his first day back at work would be like. And his encounter later in the day with Tabitha Samos.

He parked in his assigned stall and was about to walk into the building when a security guard stopped him. Lucas felt awkward. Embarrassed. Almost ashamed. Even though this was Empirico he could not bring himself to look the guard in the eye.

The guard told him the doors weren't working and that he would have to go around to the other side. Lucas nodded and walked out. When he got to the front of the building his heart skipped a beat. For a moment he had trouble believing that what he was seeing was really happening, like yesterday when he had seen Caesar at the airport.

All of the employees from Empirico's Chicago facility clapped and cheered for him. Above them hung a huge banner that read: WELCOME BACK HOME LUCAS. A huge burst of red, white and blue balloons took off into the air. Lucas calculated in his mind. Eight hundred employees at an average of $40 an hour for about fifteen minutes; this little welcome cost Caesar about $8,000. He shook hands with some of the Council, their coldness as noticeable as always, and greeted Caesar before talking with some of the employees.

Anne, the Danish bombshell, gave him a hug to welcome him back. He smelled the relaxing fragrance of her perfume and hung onto her probably longer than he should have. He didn't want to let go of her. The way she held him reassured him he was safe. There was something about being touched by a human who wasn't going to whip or beat him that made him feel good; it felt right. She escorted Lucas to the Council chambers and filled him in briefly on what had happened since he was gone.

Lucas entered and saw that most of the Council members were present. He shook hands with more of them and had no trouble deciding that they really didn't want him back. Claire shook his hand, wanting instead to wrap her arms around him. "I'm glad you're back, Lucas," she said in her French accent. He believed her.

Mike, who had just arrived back from his trip, pushed through the crowd to Lucas. He looked relieved to see him. "I can't believe it." He shook Lucas' hand and patted him on the shoulder. "How are you doing?"

"I'm alive, Mike"

Although they both laughed, Mike looked uneasy. Maybe he wasn't feeling well. The jet lag was probably catching up with him, too. "It makes me sick just thinking you were in that prison."

The mood got serious. Lucas recalled his beatings. He tried to force the memories away. "Me too."

Caesar came to the lectern and called everyone to attention.

"We are here to celebrate the return of our unjustly accused friend." He turned to Lucas with a wry grin, "or was it justly accused?" The Council laughed. "We are proud to have him back with us and we're glad he's in one piece." The room became quiet. "Here, at Empirico, we're a team. And the team sticks together. We're the best. And because we're the best there is nothing we can't do. We rely on each other and that's why we're glad you're home. Welcome back, Lucas."

They raised their glasses of orange juice or coffee (it being a little early for real drinks) and gave a cheer. Waiters emerged from the back pushing trays of breakfast food containing scrambled eggs, sausages, toast, fresh fruit, juices, cereals and more coffee.

After the meeting it was back to the reality of what they were all hired to do. Back to forcing pharmaceuticals down people's throats. Back to selling overpriced items to underpaid people. Back to doing what Empirico did best.

Lucas walked past his office to Mike's. He knocked on his door, let himself in and saw that Mike was on the phone.

Normally, Mike would acknowledge Lucas' presence and point to a seat opposite him. But this time he didn't do that, didn't even look up. Maybe he hadn't heard Lucas come in. Mike stayed glued to the phone for another few minutes.

When he finally hung up he let out a sigh. "That's it for me, Lucas. I'm off to Honduras."

"No plans for China?"

Mike shook his head and looked out the window. "I can't believe you had to go through that."

"Felt like an ongoing nightmare. Like the kind you know you're having but you can't wake yourself up from."

"I wouldn't know."

"Are you all right, Mike?"

Mike was about to answer with a *Sure, I'm fine, why? Do I look bad?* when Lucas continued. "You seem on edge, worried."

Mike froze a moment, as if someone had hit the pause button, then he came back to life. "I'm sorry, Lucas. I'm stressed." Mike eyed the door to make sure no one was listening. "It's getting to me a bit. All the deals, the pressure. Everyone here going for your job, my job. I mean, we're supposed to be a team, right? But we're not. We're after each other as much as we are after the competition."

"I know."

Mike looked at the door again as if he was a secret agent afraid the information he was giving would fall into enemy hands. "I can't lose my job."

"You're not going to lose your job." Lucas read the expression on Mike's face. "You're doing well, aren't you?"

Mike relaxed a bit, but not enough to convince Lucas that things were all right, or that they would become that way any time soon. "Yeah, good enough, I guess."

"Mike?"

Mike walked to the door and closed it. He didn't need to, really. There was no one within hearing distance.

"I'm behind in my sales. That's all." He drank from his coffee cup. "It'll turn up."

"You need a break," Lucas said.

"I don't need a break."

"Yeah, you do. Let's catch a Cubs game."

"Can't. Honduras, remember?"

Lucas wanted to believe that everything was going to be okay with Mike, but the way he talked and the way he looked didn't give Lucas any confidence. His friend seemed strangely distant. It wasn't just the stress; it was more than that. Maybe Mike was on some medication for his anxiety. Maybe the Empirico culture was bearing down on him more than it usually did.

One thing was for certain. One of them had changed.

Lucas sat down at his desk. He glanced out his window that looked over Empirico's private park. Even though he'd been with Empirico for two years he had never taken the time to see what was outside his office. Sure, he'd looked out the window from time to time to take a mental break, but not to concentrate on what was there. This time, however, he really looked. There were a few picnic tables and a beach volleyball court. A walkway path snaked its way through trees. Probably a great place to go jogging. The sun was perfect and there wasn't even so much as a gust of wind.

He turned on his new laptop (a new one was issued every six months by Empirico) and cycled through his client list. Normally he got such a rush out of planning his sales pitches and trips but this time felt different for him. He readjusted himself on his chair and tried to get back into gear. *It's just that I've been away for so long. I've never been out of the loop for more than a week. It'll click again.*

But it didn't click. Not the entire morning. They say once you learn to do something you never forget—like riding a bike, playing the piano, or working for a multinational pharmaceutical company. But as much as he worked that morning Lucas couldn't get his mind back into his routine. His office had once been a second, or first, home for him. Now it was like a graveyard.

It felt as though he was sitting in someone else's chair.

Lucas forced himself to carry on by organizing sales presentations to prospective clients. He skipped over the leads for China—he wouldn't be touching those for a while—and researched ideas for new markets.

He thought back to the Council meeting where the suggestion of selling to Africa was made. He reconsidered going there a moment and then turned it down again. There was a need for pharmaceuticals there, absolutely, but there was no chance of making any money. He recalled an article about a pharmaceutical philanthropic program that was started to protect the 3.5 million children who die each year from diarrheal diseases. He rubbed his hands over his face and thought about a report he had read on all the people in Zambia who were dying. He thought about how drastically different his life was from those destitute people and how they had done nothing to deserve that kind of life.

Anna came to the door bringing with her a smile and cup of coffee. The sun reflected off her straight blond hair making it look almost white. She made the room come alive the way some women can just by simply being there. She placed the cup of Irish cream on his desk and raised her eyebrows at him. "I'm only pouring this for you today to welcome you back, so don't get into thinking that this is new trend."

"Anna, I'm touched."

"You'll be happy to know that your efforts with Dr. Graves paid off. He signed on with us, again."

Anna smiled and left. The news of a successful sale did not make him as excited as it used to.

By 6:00 p.m. Lucas managed to accomplish what would normally have taken him thirty minutes. He wanted to attribute it to jet lag, first day back or that his body was recovering. But he couldn't shake the feeling that there was more to it than that. He left the office early (6:00 was considered *very* early by Council standards) and got into his beloved Mercedes. He checked his watch and drove out of the parking garage. He had a 7:00 appointment at Navy Pier that he hoped would have been canceled by now.

16

Lucas drove down Lake Shore Drive to Navy Pier. On his left was Lake Michigan. It was a calm evening. There were a few boats out. Joggers were scattered along the pathway.

He got a craving for a hot dog and realized he hadn't had one since before Xaing Xaing. Up ahead, on the right, he saw a vendor and pulled over. Nothing like a little taste of home. It wouldn't be a Cubs hot dog—nothing came close to a hot dog at The Friendly Confines—but it would, at the very least, be a Chicago hot dog.

He parked his car. As he approached the vendor he saw a boy, about twelve years old, sitting next to the hot dog cart in a wheelchair. He had short black hair and wore a bright red Manchester United soccer jersey. His legs hung down, motionless.

Lucas got in line and watched the boy give out change while his father filled orders. Some of the customers tried to make conversation with the boy, but he avoided eye contact with them as if doing so would prevent them from discovering his disability.

The boy looked through the lineup of customers, five deep now, to the soccer field across the street. There was a game going on and the players were roughly his age.

"What can I get for you?" the boy said without looking at Lucas.

Lucas reached in his wallet and pulled out a twenty. "A hot dog and a bottled water."

"You can get a smokey for only a dollar more."

Lucas admired the boy. A salesman in his own right. Who could refuse? "You got it."

"Four dollars."

Lucas gave the bill to the boy who fumbled in his money belt for change while concentrating on the soccer game. The shouts and cheers of the parents could be heard over the traffic. Lucas reached out his hand and received his change. As he did so he inadvertently touched the boy's hand. A jolt of electricity, like what he felt at Xaing Xaing, ran through his body. It scared Lucas at first because the feeling brought back memories of his prison cell, the Cage and the guards with evil looks in their eyes.

"What's your name?" Lucas said.

"David. What's yours?" The boy still didn't make eye contact. The game was more interesting. Besides, in a few minutes this customer would be gone and David would probably never remember him.

Probably.

"I'm Lucas. What happened to your legs?"

It was like the wind left the sail of David's ship—as though somehow David had managed to block his condition out of his mind only to have this customer drag him back to reality. He let out a breath and looked at Lucas. "A drunk driver. Paralyzed my legs."

"I'm sorry to hear that." Lucas searched for words and wondered if striking up a conversation with this boy was the best use of his time. He was on his way to Navy Pier and as much as he didn't want to meet with Tabitha he couldn't be late. Talking with David the paralytic was not going to get him there any faster. Part of him wanted to race back into his Mercedes. *Forget the hot dog and just get out of here!* The other part wanted to stay and talk with the boy.

"I'm never going to walk again," David said.

"Who told you that?"

David raised his brow the way kids do when adults ask them stupid questions. "The doctors did."

Lucas was about to respond, but the warming sensation in his hands startled him. He glanced down and wondered if he was inadvertently touching an element. He clenched his hands into a fist to let off some of the heat.

"They did?" Lucas said.

David looked up at him. "You don't believe doctors?"

"I believe doctors. Very much so. But maybe there's still a chance."

"What's that supposed to mean?"

Lucas crouched down and looked into David's curious eyes. "What if I told you that you could walk again?"

David pulled his head back. *Walk again?* He studied Lucas' face. There was a cut or a scar above his left eye and swelling below it. Nothing extremely noticeable, but it was obvious enough, the way personal defects are once you know where to look for them. It was, however, the eyes themselves and not the marks around them that stood out for David. They were so full of conviction, so full of compassion.

"If I could walk again, I'd run out there and start playing soccer."

Lucas shot his eyes to the left and to the right to see if anyone was looking their way. "Can I pray for you?"

David crossed his eyebrows again. His reaction said no, but the longer he looked at Lucas' eyes the more convinced he became.

"Pray?"

Lucas nodded.

"For me?"

Another nod.

"Why?"

"Because I think you can walk again," Lucas whispered.

"Me?"

"You."

"You think I'm gonna walk again?"

"Maybe."

"And that's gonna happen when you pray for me?"

Lucas swallowed. "I think there's a chance," he said as quietly as he could.

David shrugged his shoulders slightly, then nodded. "Okay."

Lucas placed his hands on David's legs. He prayed. Heat transmitted through his hands onto David's limbs. The street went quiet. It seemed as though the traffic had disappeared. David didn't dare close his eyes, not while he was holding the hot dog money. He could feel the warmth as well, like when his father put a heating blanket on him when he got sick. Lucas took his hands away and everything turned back the way it was. They heard the traffic. The sounds of Chicago. It seemed so weird to David. A customer prayed for him. Who ever heard of that? The father served his customers unaware of what was happening. But he *would* become aware. And very soon.

"If you want to play soccer again, stand up and do it."

David waited a moment. Then he edged his body forwards. He gave Lucas a skeptical look and decided to chance it. His feet touched the ground. David took in a deep breath and with his arms he pushed his body forward. His eyes were filled with curiosity and hope—the way a person's eyes get when they hear the lottery numbers being called out and the first few match their ticket. He transferred his weight to his feet. He stood up out of his wheelchair.

And then he crumpled to the ground, just as a paralytic would.

His father saw him lying there and quickly came to his aid. "Davey, are you all right?" Lucas and the father helped David get back into his wheelchair. "Davey?"

"I'm fine. I... I just slipped out that's all."

"You're sure you're okay? 'Cause you can tell me in front of all these people if you're hurt, right?"

"Dad, I'm okay." But he wasn't okay. Not on the outside and, now, not on the inside either. He hated himself for being such a sucker—for being a believer. He was embarrassed and felt like a fool in front of all the people. David didn't know for sure what was supposed to happen. But he did know one thing. The man in front of him, the one with the scar above his left eye, was a liar, a showman and a customer he hoped would never come back. He turned away from Lucas and looked at the soccer game.

Lucas' hot dog would be ready any moment. *Just take your hot dog this time and get out of here!* Lucas thought. But still he wouldn't leave.

Lucas crouched down again. "I don't know what to say."

"Don't say anything. Get your hot dog and your water and get out of here."

"Can I pray for you again?"

"You call that prayer?"

"I think so."

"I don't."

"I'm sorry. I really am." Lucas saw the hurt in David's eyes. He got angry with himself. He had wanted to make a bad situation good again, but all he had accomplished was to make it worse.

Lucas left the boy and got his hot dog. He poured on the mayonnaise and relish and decided against the onions. He loved them, but Tabitha, however, would not. He thanked the vendor and walked past David.

"Who were you praying to?" David asked, not taking his eyes off the game.

"What?" Lucas said as he got down on one knee beside David.

"Who were you praying to?"

"To God."

"God in Heaven?"

"You know another one?"

David shrugged his shoulders. "God in Heaven. That's what my coach used to say when I screwed up on the field."

Lucas felt awkward beside David, especially after what had happened. But like a man who doesn't learn his lesson, who is compelled to repeat his mistakes, Lucas wanted to give it another shot. "If you want me to pray again I will."

David looked at Lucas. Those eyes, there was something in Lucas' eyes that made David want to try again. He clutched onto his money belt even tighter. Maybe Lucas would try and steal it, maybe that's all this was about. Yet down inside, in that part that tells you it's okay to trust someone, David decided to give Lucas one last chance. "I don't want to fall down again."

"I don't want you to fall down, either," Lucas said.

"I don't really know the God you're praying to."

Lucas was about respond but then realized he didn't know much about the God he was praying to, either.

David continued. "The only God I know is the one who gets shouted at during soccer games."

"You mentioned."

David looked at the lineup of customers. "If you're going to do it, then do it quick."

Lucas rested his hands on David's legs and prayed the fastest prayer he'd ever prayed. Again, a short warmth shot through his body into David's legs. Lucas relaxed. Maybe the kid would walk, maybe he'd fall. Either way Lucas could head off to Navy Pier knowing he tried. In a way, it released him.

He thought about the possibility that the healing of the tall guard at the prison was an anomaly—that it was a random supernatural occurrence over which he had had no control. Maybe, in retrospect, the whole thing had just been an illusion. A man being healed of a gun shot at close range? That's craziness. Things like that don't happen. It made Lucas think that maybe they hadn't been real bullets. Maybe the guns the prisoners had were filled with rubber bullets. That would account for the blood on the tall guard's chest and would also explain why he didn't die. That whole thing with the tall guard probably never was a miracle.

Or maybe the tall guard did get shot with real bullets and really did recover miraculously. And maybe Lucas' encounter with healing was strictly a one-time thing that couldn't be repeated, least of all not with a paralytic boy sitting next to a hot dog vendor.

David pushed himself to the edge of the wheelchair. His feet touched the ground. He had made it as far as he did the last time.

The surrounding world left them. It was as if Lucas and David were the only two people on Lake Shore, maybe in all of Chicago.

David looked past Lucas at the soccer field in the distance. He released his hold of the wheelchair and transferred all of his weight to his legs. He wobbled for a moment, the way an infant does when taking its first step, then he regained his balance. Suddenly, there he was. David was standing.

"God in Heaven," David whispered to himself. He raised his right foot and shuffled it in front of him. He stretched out his hand for balance and then took his second step. He smiled, just for a moment and recalled what it was like to walk. He took his third step and never gave the wheelchair another thought. "Dad! Dad!"

The father didn't follow the sound of the voice. He knew it was his son calling out to him and so he instinctively looked at the wheelchair. But he found no one there. Fear hit him, the way fear hits a parent when their child is not where they think he should be. "Dad!" This time he did follow the voice. He looked down the sidewalk and saw his son walking away from him. At first the dad was relieved, but then he became confused.

"David?" The father left the hot dogs cooking on the barbecue and went after his son. "David?"

By now David was walking perfectly. It was as though he'd never been in that accident. His father caught up with him. His eyes grew wide. "What happened, son?"

"God in Heaven."

"David, what's going on?"

"Gonna go play a little soccer, Dad. That okay?" David broke into a light jog. His father followed after him, forgetting all about the hot dogs and the anxious customers. David ran as fast as he could. His father struggled to keep up. "You're running, Davey! You're running!" His father wasn't in the best shape and his son quickly ran ahead of him. But the dad never gave up. He followed behind his boy as best he could. *God in Heaven*, he thought, *my boy's running*.

Lucas looked down at his hands and instead of feeling peace he felt a sudden panic. He saw the father-son duo shouting at the top of their lungs on their way to the soccer field. He saw the bewildered customers standing in line for their hot dogs. Lucas turned and walked down the sidewalk to his car.

What's happening to me?

He got into his Mercedes and closed the door. The silence was a welcome relief from the commotion outside. He gripped the steering wheel as if hanging on to something tangible could assure his mind of the world he still lived in. *What was that? Did that kid really walk out the wheelchair? What is going on!?*

He thought back to the tall guard lying in a pool of blood on that cold floor. Something strange had happened there as well. It could have been dismissed as an out-of-the-blue occurrence. Couldn't it? But now, he had just seen a paralytic walk. What were the odds of something like this happening twice?

Lucas wanted to leave. He *had* to leave. He had to get out of this place. He put the car in drive and headed down Lake Shore. It was 6:45. He'd make it just in time. He turned up Harry Connick Jr.'s "Moment's Notice" hoping to switch his mind from the paralytic, now a healthy soccer player, to Tabitha. The entire way to Navy Pier he battled the feeling that comes with trying to understand something that can't be fully understood. He was in the realm of the miraculous—that's what he finally assumed it was—and felt completely inadequate to deal with it.

To make things more complicated, he was about to have an encounter with a reporter who had more in common with him than just the story of his time in prison.

17

Lucas made it to Navy Pier just before 7:00 and decided to calm his nerves with one his favorite drinks. He found the lemonade stand on the south side of Navy Pier. It was an addiction, one he had no trouble confessing. Four heaping scoops of sugar, freshly squeezed lemons and ice. He sucked back on the straw and felt the cool jolt against his throat. Five dollars never tasted so good.

He passed the tour boats to his right and the Shakespeare Theater to his left on his way to the point. He had come here often, sometimes with her; still, the excitement and relaxation he normally felt at Navy Pier were replaced with anxiety, even a touch of fear.

He glanced at the outdoor restaurants and looked for her among the groups of people gathered under umbrellas. Maybe she had put on weight. If she had gained fifty pounds he might not recognize her anymore. What if her complexion, her appearance, her good looks, what if all that had changed? He could be here for hours trying to find her.

By the time Lucas reached the end of the pier he had half-finished his lemonade. What a sugar rush. He wanted a second one, maybe even a third. He looked out ahead of him and that's when he saw her. Tabitha. She hadn't gained those extra pounds. Her face was turned slightly to the right as she watched the yachts and sailboats out on Lake Michigan. Her complexion hadn't changed, either. She had not gotten uglier. She'd gotten better, if that were even possible. She held a drink in her hand, lemonade too. Her shoulder-length, straight black hair blew gently in the Chicago wind. She wore a pair of white jeans that fit perfectly on her irresistible frame and a black sweater that hung comfortably around her. Her skin was darker than he remembered; maybe she'd been tanning. She wore glasses, though she didn't really need them. She looked better than ever.

In that split second he wished the past had never happened. He wished for a time machine, to go back and undo what was done and start all over. Even though she hadn't spoken a word yet, hadn't even noticed him, she still had this power over him. It was the kind of power a woman has over a man when he really wants to be with her, when deep down inside he wants her more than anyone else.

He swallowed, realizing that his feelings were foolishness.

She heard the footsteps behind her stop. It was 7:00. It had to be him. No matter how many times she rehearsed this moment in her mind it didn't make facing him any easier.

They both waited. Neither of them was prepared for the visit. Neither of them wanted it.

"Hello, Tabitha."

His voice was unmistakable. Even with the children playing and the babies crying around her she knew it was him. Should she smile or be straight-faced? Happy or serious? Business or pleasure? She didn't know how to respond to him, just that she *had* to say something. She turned around.

They made eye contact.

Just before she responded a sudden nervousness came over them. For years they had wondered if and when, this day would come. And now here it was. And for all their worrying, it wasn't what they had assumed it would be. He was just him and she was just her.

"Lucas," she said in as even a tone as she could manage. There were two of her at that moment. One that wanted to wrap her arms around Lucas, release him (and her) from the past and live as if it had never happened. The other one wanted to finish this interview and leave him, once and for all, both physically and emotionally.

There was an awkward silence between them. Sometimes those periods of silence go over well, as when lovers are staring into each other's eyes—words don't matter much then and they usually fall way short of expressing what's going on, anyway. But here, under the clouding Chicago sky, the silence was debilitating. Lucas searched his mind for the conversation tactics he had used when business deals got tense.

"Thanks for choosing Navy Pier."

Tabitha didn't answer right away. The part of her that wanted him out of her life was winning over the part that wanted to start over again. The struggle was like that of a boxer who was now easily in charge of what was once a close fight. The painful memory of what happened between them shot through her as though it was reoccurring right in front of them. In spite of the separate lives each of them had gone on to live, the hurt was just as fresh as it was when they last saw each other. Three years had past, but the wounds were still there. They were deeper and more painful now; time has a habit of doing that to things that don't get cleared up.

"Thanks for coming," Tabitha said.

He nodded and maintained eye contact. He wanted her to smile, if even just for a split second, to remind him that things had been good between them at some point.

She, however, was already feeling the weight of her mistake in meeting with him. She got a feeling that told her the meeting was not going to be what she wanted. She needed the facts to come out about his time at Xaing Xaing as fast as possible and then she'd be off. But no interview goes exactly the way it's planned, especially not between people who have more at stake than just a news story.

"You look good," Lucas said and then quickly realized it was a mistake. It was the truth. But it was flattery and that always made her feel embarrassed. She was beautiful, absolutely no mistake about that, but she was beautiful in a gentle sort of way. She didn't have an in-your-face model kind of look. Just, well, beautiful.

She put down her lemonade on a nearby bench and realized how cold her hand had gotten by holding it. She picked out her notepad and pen from her purse and without looking at him she fired off her first question. "Were you treated fairly in prison?"

"I guess that depends on what you mean by fair."

"Fair in your opinion?"

"Who gets treated fairly in prison?" It wasn't meant to come across as sarcastic but it did.

Tabitha looked away for a moment. *What am I doing here?* She pressed her lips together. Lucas was about to continue with his answer when Tabitha whirled her arm out and slapped Lucas in the face. Some slaps you can sense coming, like after you say something you really, really shouldn't have. But this one was not expected. Lucas was caught totally off guard. She had got her back into it and hit him well. Not as well as a Chinese prison guard but still hard enough to make it hurt.

It made her feel better, if only for a moment. Like a hole in the roof during a rain storm, the feelings of anger poured into her and she felt the same way she had before she hit him.

She repeated her first question. "Were you treated fairly in prison?"

"Tabitha, I think we need to sit down."

"Why did the Chinese government let you go?"

"Why did you ask me to come here?"

"Do you think the American government did all that it could to help you?"

Lucas looked out to the lake and then back at Tabitha. She was angry and hurt. A deadly combination. He wanted to reach out and hold her hand but he knew that would not be possible. At least not right now. He was about to answer when she interrupted him.

"And last, do you have any plans to attack Chinese judicial policy on foreigners?"

Her eyes looked directly into his. For an instant they passed the limiting shackles of language and connected with each other. It was like the way the picture on a TV suddenly goes clear for a moment after someone fiddles with the connection. He wasn't just looking at her. He was looking into her. He saw the woman he once loved. Maybe he still did.

"Thank you for your time," she said.

Tabitha put her paper and pen in her purse, picked up her lemonade and disappeared into the crowd of people who were enjoying the evening.

She walked as fast as she could, as though the speed with which she was walking would help her leave the memory of the meeting behind her. She regretted what had happened. She didn't know how it was supposed to turn out, just that it wasn't supposed turn out that way. But she assured herself that it was over. She had gotten her interview. The story was done. Lucas was back. And now he was gone, forever.

As she got to her yellow convertible her pager beeped. She unclipped it from her belt and read the message. There was a breaking story at a soccer field not too far away.

Something about a boy being miraculously healed.

18

Lucas finished his lemonade at Navy Pier and paid another five bucks for a second one. The girl behind the counter cut up the lemons in front of him, scooped in the sugar, mixed it together with the ice and handed it over. He took a long drink from it, thinking that maybe it would help him get over the encounter he'd just endured with Tabitha.

He got into his Mercedes and wished he could start the meeting over again, the way the losing team might want to re-start a championship game. He pushed the button to retract the sunroof and drove out of the parking lot not sure of where he was going. Maybe he'd drive through downtown. Maybe he'd enjoy the night life along North Michigan Avenue's Magnificent Mile. There was something refreshing about being behind the wheel of his car. Traffic would be normal by now (as normal as it gets in Chicago) and he would be able to clear his mind while looking at the city's incredible architecture. The sun had set and many of the buildings, especially the John Hancock, looked even better at night.

The image of Tabitha walking away from him stayed in his mind. He was concerned about her. When he heard her on his voice-mail it opened a jar that was better left untouched. The meeting had put them both in an awkward position. She was angry with him, that much was obvious. She hadn't forgotten their past (who could?) and now he wondered if they would ever return to their separate paths again.

He was reaching down to turn on the Cubs game—they were playing against the Diamondbacks in Phoenix—when his attention was suddenly diverted back to the road. A shadowy figure lay sprawled out in front of him. The body was about a stopping distance or so away, plus or minus. Lucas pounded on the brakes. His powerful Mercedes came to a shaking stop. Lucas heard the thumping in his chest. He opened his door and stepped out. The figure lay just in front of his tires.

He was fairly certain he hadn't hit the body. As he walked closer to look at it Lucas started breathing again. He wiped the sweat from his forehead, relieved that he hadn't run it over. He thought the horrendous sound of tires screeching against pavement would have jolted the body awake. But the body hadn't moved.

There wasn't much traffic, not on his side, as he looked around for witnesses. No one. He turned on his hazard lights and then came back to the body.

It was a man. White. He had long straggly hair. He wore a pair of old blue jeans, the kind that get worn for every occasion. He was lying face down, maybe passed out. Maybe dead.

"Hey. Hey, are you all right?"

Just then a car drove by. The driver glanced at the lifeless figure and quickly turned away the way people do when they don't want to get involved in something that may cost them time or effort. Lucas crouched down. He got a waft from the body—a brutal combination of booze, cigarettes and body odor.

"Hello? Are you okay?"

Another car drove by and looked at the scene but carried on. Lucas touched the body. He wondered if it might suddenly come to life, jump up and attack him. It was a man in his mid-fifties, strong build. Carried a pot belly.

Lucas tugged at the body's shoulder and, as if on cue, the man turned over, seemingly on his own. Lucas leaned closer and touched the man's neck. He felt a pulse. He shook the man who grunted in response. The man wore a ripped Hell's Angels shirt and pair of cowboy boots. In his right hand was a brown paper bag with a bottle inside.

Lucas shook the man again. He coughed and sputtered as if being woken from a dream. "What? What?" He opened his eyes. They were bloodshot and puffy. He rubbed them and let out a breath that could have killed a bed of flowers. He looked around in bewilderment, then stared up at Lucas. "What do you want?"

Lucas was not about to begin a conversation with a drunk. He looked down the road and tried to think of a solution. How was he going to get rid of this guy? A short distance away, within shouting range, he saw a soup kitchen. A faint neon cross above the door fizzled in and out like a creepy motel sign that can't decide if it has a vacancy or not. *Perfect.* Lucas breathed a sigh of relief. *I'll dump him off there.*

Lucas helped the drunk to his feet then hit the automatic lock on his key chain.

"I ain't your gonna help me," the drunk slurred.

"You're lying in the middle of the road."

"What's wrong with that?"

Lucas felt that the drunk was stronger than him. If he turned violent Lucas would stand no chance. "Because you can't lie in the road." Lucas spoke louder as if he were shouting to an old man who was hard of hearing. The frustration of what could have happened worked its way out. "I could have killed you!"

The drunk turned his head to Lucas. He was suddenly aware of what was going on. He looked at Lucas with empty eyes. What he said next froze Lucas' spine. "That was the whole point, you idiot."

The drunk looked back at the Mercedes and lowered his shoulders as if he had just found out he had failed at some crucial mission. He brought the bottle to his lips, finished the contents, then threw it away in disgust. With a swiping motion he hit Lucas. "I'm fine. I don't need you." The drunk took two steps and fell over.

Lucas picked him up again and half dragged, half carried the man to the Center City Mission. He knocked on the door but there was no response. He saw a note inside the window that said: AFTER HOURS PLEASE RING DOORBELL. Lucas pushed it. He noticed a few empty hairspray bottles and a mouthwash container on the sidewalk.

A medium-build, Native man came to the side window. He had a brush cut. He opened the door wide enough to see Lucas but not the drunk.

"We're closed."

Lucas put his foot in the door to prevent it from shutting. *Oh, gee, you're closed? That's just my luck. I wanted to come in and have a wonderful bowl of soup. Perhaps you didn't notice my $150 silk shirt, or maybe you missed my Mercedes in the background with the hazards blinking?* "I'm not here for me." Lucas pulled the drunk into view. "I found this guy on the street, passed out. I have to bring him in."

What he meant to say was that he wanted to drop him off and make a run for it. The Native man thought a moment and nodded. "Okay." The door opened wider and Lucas dragged him in. "Just bring him into the kitchen," the man said. "Check in the back for one of the volunteers. They can help you."

"I'm not here to go to the back. I'm here to drop him off."

"I'm on the phone talking with a lady who's got a gun to her head." The Native man said that with such force, like a drill sergeant commanding a cadet, that Lucas didn't argue. He grabbed the drunk around the shoulders and brought him down the hallway to the eating area at the back.

The Center City Mission referred to the eating area as the dining room, but that name gives the impression there are waiters, dishes and fancy tables for guests who pay for their meals. This wasn't a dining room. Not the way most people understand it. It had fifteen round tables with no linens. Each table had plastic forks and spoons, styrofoam cups and wooden chairs. It was a subsistence room, really; not that the food was bad; it wasn't. It was that this room was a lot more than just a place to get food. It was the last line of defense between people eating and people starving. If the least, the last and the lost of Chicago didn't get fed here or at some other inner city rescue, they'd resort to other things to fill the void. They'd walk the streets on empty stomachs, alone. And when they got really hungry the memories would come back (but only the bad memories, funny how that works) and they'd turn to alcohol, like the drunk did, or to getting high off hairspray and mouthwash.

The floors had been recently cleaned. Only one light was left on, just above the door. Lucas sat the drunk down and leaned him against the table. He walked through the dining room to the kitchen at the back and looked for any sign of help.

"Hello?"

Nobody answered. Lucas searched through the dark kitchen. He knew he wasn't likely to find anyone, but he wanted to keep what little hope he had alive of having someone take the drunk off his hands. He came back and sat down.

The drunk moaned as though he was trying to start talking. Lucas bent his head down to listen to him. The drunk opened his eyes and took in a deep breath. Without any warning, his cheeks filled up. Lucas tried to get out of the way but he was too late.

The chunks flew out the drunk's mouth. The spray splashed against Lucas' shirt and spread up his chin. Lucas jumped up in disgust. He swore. The drunk put his head back down on the table, exhausted from the ordeal.

Lucas left the dining room and found a bathroom. The stench of the drunk's vomit filled Lucas' nose. He turned the sink on full blast and washed the pieces off his face. He took off his shirt and ran the affected parts under the tap. It wasn't much use. The shirt was ruined. He put it back on and returned from the bathroom, determined to say goodbye to the drunk.

The Native man came back after finishing his phone call. "I see you've met Jake Rubenstein."

"Sort of."

The man proceeded to tell Lucas about his new drunk friend. Jake was a regular at the Mission. He had six children from three wives. One wife had died, the other two and all the kids had broken off contact with him. The last he heard they had gotten as far away from him as they could. He once owned a housing construction company and had as many as forty people working for him before it collapsed. He then went into the trucking business and when that ended he soon found himself living on government assistance. He spent what little he had on booze and ate all of his meals at the Mission. He occasionally ran drugs when money was short. He had two parents who wanted nothing to do with him.

Jake used to ride with the Hell's Angels in Los Angeles and moved to Chicago when his second wife died. He had been arrested on fifteen counts of aggravated assault, four counts of burglary, had served a twelve year sentence in prison for murdering a police officer during a botched drug trade and served another prison sentence of one year for killing two people. Since his release from jail he spent his life high on drugs and alcohol. He hung out at the Mission, at his apartment or, as was the case tonight, in the middle of the street.

Jake was a nobody.

Lucas shouted at him. “No more barfing!” Jake made no response.

“Well, I guess you can take it from here?” Lucas said to the Native man as more of a statement of fact than a question.

“No, actually, I don’t have any room for him. I’m not allowed to, but I could leave him with some blankets in the chapel. Thing is, he only lives a short car ride away. Maybe five minutes,” turning to Jake, “right Jake?”

Jake sat up in his chair and looked at the vomit stains on Lucas’ shirt. “What happened to you?”

The volunteer patted Lucas on the shoulder. “Jake can show you where he lives. You don’t mind taking him to his home, do you?”

Lucas avoided eye contact. *Yes, I do. I don’t want some stinking, putrid, disgusting…* Lucas stopped his thoughts. The smell of Jake was familiar now. None of the five senses triggers the memory as strongly as the sense of smell. Lucas could tell you why. The stench was unmistakable. It reminded him of Xaing Xaing. It reminded him of the rotting prisoners on the execution block.

“Of course not,” Lucas replied, wishing he wasn’t in this situation.

He took Jake out of the Mission, brought the car around and struggled to get him into the front seat. He leaned Jake’s head in the direction of the rolled down window.

“If you’re going to barf then barf out the window. Now where do you live?”

Jake said nothing. In his upper pocket was a bulge. Lucas opened up his jacket and found a mickey of Vodka. *What an idiot,* Lucas thought. Jake leaned his head against the headrest. Lucas moved it back to the open window.

“Where do you live?”

Jake stared out the window. He raised his finger and pointed south. Lucas turned his hazard lights off and chauffeured the drunk to his home, hoping Jake wouldn’t stink up his car too badly before he was gone. Lucas got on Dr. Martin Luther King Jr. Dr. and headed south. They drove a few minutes before Lucas asked, "Well, where is it?"

Jake looked around. He was lost, but as is the custom for some men he wasn't ready to admit it. Lucas was tired. His clothes stuck to him and between him and Jake they had managed to stink up a perfectly good Mercedes.

"Where is your home?"

Jake eyes searched the surroundings. Not finding anything familiar he turned to Lucas. "Where's your home?"

"Do you know where you live, or not?"

"Yes..."

"Where?"

"I just don't know right now."

"What's your address?"

"Not sure."

Jake closed his eyes and slumped back into the seat. Lucas slammed on the brakes. Neither he nor Jake had any idea where his home was, if it even existed. Lucas turned the car around and headed back to the place with the fizzling sign. "I'm not putting up with this."

At 9:00 Lucas stopped outside the Mission and knocked on the door. No response. Forgetting the lesson he recently learned, Lucas saw the note again and rang the bell. Still, there was no response. He banged on the door. It wasn't as loud as the bell but it helped him release some of the aggravation. "Open up!" No one came to the door. Not the Native man, not any of the residents.

Lucas got back into his car and slammed the door shut. He looked at Jake, who was sleeping against the door, then he looked at the door handle. All he would have to do is pull back on it, shove Jake out, drive off and he would be rid of him. He *wanted* to be rid of him. He could leave him there on the cold pavement, by himself, without anything to eat, without anyone to care for him or even know he was there.

Lucas closed his eyes. He rubbed his hands over his face and shook his head. *One night. I can put him up for one night.*

He put the car in drive, turned on the song "This time the dream's on me" and drove off to his home in Evanston. He would let the drunk spend the night. Heaven knew he had enough room for him. He let lots of his friends sleep over at his house, especially the ones who, like Jake, were too drunk to remember their name. But he'd never had a street person in his home before. And he hoped it would never happen again.

As he listened to the music he thought about his day thus far. A boy had been miraculously healed, he'd had an encounter with Tabitha and now he was taking a drunk home with him.

Deep down inside he wondered where all of this was leading him.

19

Tabitha got to the soccer field just as the players were leaving. A cool wind had picked up and it convinced her to wear her black leather jacket. She grabbed her camera and closed the top on her yellow convertible.

"Have any of you seen David?" The players turned and pointed to a kid on the field as though they had been asked that same question a hundred times. She looked out and saw a boy playing with a middle-aged, overweight man. *This is a hoax. There's no way that kid couldn't walk.*

"David?"

The boy stopped playing and looked at her. He smiled when he saw the camera. "Hey! A reporter!"

He ran up to her and got excited the way kids do when they think they'll get their picture in the paper.

"Are you David?"

David nodded.

"I'm Tabitha, Tabitha Samos. I'm with the *Observer*." His father came up, having overheard her introduction. "I've been hearing some strange things, David. Has anything out of the ordinary happened to you recently?"

"I'm walking."

That wasn't out of the ordinary. Not for most people.

"You couldn't before?"

David pointed in the distance to a wheelchair next to a closed hot dog vendor stand. "That used to be mine."

"Used to?" Tabitha said with enough expression to imply that she didn't believe him.

"That's right," the father said.

David told her that he had been paralyzed. A stranger visited him and after he prayed for him his legs just got stronger.

"What was his name?"

"I never asked him."

"What did he look like?"

David gave a vague description, the only detail being that the man had a scar over his left eye.

"You got up and started walking?"

"Yup."

"Just like that?"

"Just like that."

Tabitha bent down to look at David's legs, hoping they might reveal a clue as to what happened. But they said nothing to her.

Tabitha looked at the father. "Could I contact your doctor, to ask him a few questions?"

"You mean to find out if we're lying?"

"Yes." She realized her answer had not been very polite, but she was here to find concrete evidence and if that meant calling a disillusioned kid a liar then so be it.

The father reached inside his wallet and gave Tabitha the doctor's business card.

"Could I call him right now?"

The father nodded and Tabitha dialed on her cell phone. When the doctor answered she introduced herself and asked him if he recalled David. He did. She explained what had apparently happened and before she could ask to have David examined the doctor told her, practically commanded her, to bring him to his clinic at once.

Lucas brought Jake into his house and sat him down on a chair near the entrance. Jake seemed to be getting heavier and Lucas' body ached from holding him up. He took in a few breaths to supply more oxygen to his muscles. He told Jake to stand up, which he did, and Lucas took him upstairs in search of a room.

They pushed themselves down the hall like wounded soldiers walking waist deep in a swamp. He dropped Jake down on a bed in a spare room and got him a towel and some toiletries. Lucas would have offered him clothes but he had nothing that would fit. When he came back to Jake's room he saw him sound asleep. He looked dead, as though someone had shot him and dumped him down on the bed.

Lucas went to his room and locked the door. He took a hot shower and felt the relief that comes with being clean again. He thought about work. Tomorrow would be another day at Empirico. And for the first time since being hired on, Lucas regretted having to go there. It was strange. This was Empirico. He had a dream job. Great pay. The feelings, however, persisted. He shook his head as if doing so would clear the thoughts from his mind. But it didn't help. The thoughts of wondering why he was at Empirico and whether he should leave stayed with him. *Where else would I go? What else would I do?*

He dismissed this line of thinking on the grounds that it was completely irrational.

Lucas threw his shirt and pants in the garbage, he had plenty more of them, and collapsed into bed. He was drained, physically and emotionally.

He tried as best he could not to pay any attention to the two bottles on his dresser. He didn't need them anymore. He was past all that. He quoted some of his verses but his attention returned to whiskey and brandy. They always gave him such a refreshing kick. That wonderful shot of booze hitting the back of his throat as it warmed him on the way down felt fantastic. But he knew he could do without them. Tomorrow, he'd throw those bottles out.

He tore off the covers and grabbed the brandy bottle. In one hand he spun off the cap and poured himself a drink, more than a shot's worth, and downed it in one glorious gulp. He reached for the whiskey and did the same. The liquor ran down his throat into his stomach. It warmed him up and made him feel light-headed for a moment. He breathed out slowly. The waft of alcohol filled his nostrils. He got back into bed and pulled the covers over him as if to hide from what he had just done. He tried to convince himself that it wasn't a problem, that it was just a little habit that could easily be kicked. But inside him, the part of him he couldn't lie to no matter how hard he tried, he knew he had trouble refusing the bottles. They were like new people invited over for a house party, who turn out to become obnoxious and, even though the owner of the house wants them to leave, he can't force them out no matter what he does. Lucas had gotten to the point where people get when they have problems that are too big to handle, but he continued to tell himself that this would be the last time—that he could get over it with some more will power.

Before Lucas went to sleep he looked at the door to confirm that it was locked. It didn't really matter though. A guy with Jake's build could bust it down with one hard push if he wanted to.

Tabitha, David and his father drove up to the clinic under the dark sky. Dr. Feinberg waited at the entrance wearing his glasses to make sure his eyes wouldn't deceive him. David stepped out of the car and walked towards the clinic. Dr. Feinberg said nothing. He just watched, with his mouth slightly open, in a state of wonder at what was happening. He got down on his knees and touched David's spine. "Does it hurt?" David shook his head. "Can you bend down, touch your toes?" He did. "Can you come in for an X-ray?"

Dr. Feinberg took X-rays of David's back and then went to get the old X-rays from the file. When he returned he held them both together for them all to observe.

They compared the two X-rays. Dr. Feinberg wondered if the X-ray he had just taken would suddenly change appearance and materialize into the old one showing that David really was paralyzed. He expected David to fall down as though this was all some elaborate joke that was being played. But after reviewing the X-ray again he shook his head slightly. He was in complete awe of the discovery. Tabitha followed him until they were out of earshot of David and his father.

"Dr. Feinberg, isn't it possible that this could have happened on its own? That his body could have healed itself?"

"Possible?" Dr. Feinberg replied. "Anything's possible. I think what you mean is, how likely was this to happen?"

"And? How likely is this?"

"Between zero and none." He shot a quick glance at her. "Don't print that comment in your paper."

"But isn't there some way to explain this?"

Dr. Feinberg put the files away and thought so long about his answer that Tabitha wondered if he heard the question.

"In my profession I am supposed to provide some kind of an explanation for every case, every person, who walks through those doors. The three words that I hate to hear, and I mean hate, are 'I don't know.'"

"I don't know," replied Tabitha as though it were a secret code.

"Yes, I don't know. I wish I had an answer for you." He closed the filing cabinet and looked straight into her eyes. "But this is beyond me."

Back at the *Observer*, Tabitha finished her story on Lucas by making up answers to the questions she had asked him at Navy Pier. She felt uneasy about lying, but the only alternative was to schedule another visit with Lucas, and that wasn't going to happen.

She then got started on the story that really interested her—the story of David. She wrote about the mysterious man, the healed legs and quoted the doctor. *I don't know, I don't know, I don't know.* Those words repeated in her head like a three-year-old asking for a cookie over and over again. There was something very unsettling about what he said—that he didn't know.

But someone knew. Someone out there had done something to heal David. She desperately wanted to meet the stranger. Somehow, some way, she would find that person. No matter who it was.

Lucas woke up at 2:00 as though someone had shouted directly into his ears. He experienced that familiar dream again—the one where he stood in the middle of the desert. The sun scorched down on him. No water in sight. There was nothing around him except for sand. Everywhere he looked there was a sea of dull yellow sand. And for no apparent reason he began to feel anxious, worried; it was the kind of feeling a university student gets when he hasn't finished the exam and the clock is winding down.

He checked in on Jake, who was still asleep, and then walked downstairs. He put a pot of hot water on the stove and looked up at the full moon. It was so bright. It almost looked fake, as though someone had put special bulbs in it to make it glow like that. He thought about the space voyages and was amazed that people had really been there, that they had actually set foot on it. He made himself a cup of lemon herbal tea and added some honey before sitting down on his black leather sofa.

He thought about the tall guard at Xaing Xaing and the boy, David, who was running for the first time since his accident. The healing of the tall guard could have been considered a fluke. Things that happen out of the ordinary, such as a man being healed from a blast at close range for example, may happen on one occasion. But David was the second case that was out of the ordinary. People who are paralyzed don't get out of wheelchairs.

They just don't.

But the boy *had* walked out of the wheelchair and the tall guard *did* survive the gunshot. Something inside Lucas, or elsewhere, wanted that guard and the boy healed. But the thought that got Lucas out of bed that evening, the thought that kept him up for the rest of the night, was that maybe there were others who would be healed as well.

20

Edgar paced around his kitchen trying to make himself tired. He had used sleeping pills each of the previous five nights and their effect was now weakening. Reading used to help his sleeplessness but that remedy had since expired. Normally, he slept seven hours a night. Now, he was lucky if he got four.

He passed by the microwave and saw the digits shining 3:00. He looked outside at the full moon, so bright and beautiful against the night sky, and wondered how people ever got the courage to build a rocket and fly out there.

On his kitchen table was the brown envelope, the one he had held in his hand at Notre Dame when the rain poured down on him. Beside it was his Bible, the same Bible he brought to the Corvey Crusade. He hadn't opened it since he got the brown envelope. It just lay there, like some relic waiting to be discovered.

He tried to pray but the words didn't show up. He was like a man about to give a speech who had lost his notes. He sat down in his chair with the moonlight shining on him as if to keep him company. The only thought on his mind for the rest of the night was how he was going to make it through another day without any sleep.

Lucas finished his herbal tea and returned to his room around 5:00 a.m. When he closed the door behind him he immediately felt something strange—as though he had entered a different world. It was as if there was someone else in the room with him.

He breathed in slower than he normally would have and looked around the room. He saw nothing out of the ordinary. He opened his walk-in closet much the way parents do for kids when they're scared of the dark to prove there isn't anything to be afraid of. The closet was empty. Except, of course, for his massive wardrobe.

He pushed open the door to the adjoining bathroom half expecting something to jump out at him, the green monster from the hospital, perhaps. But there was nothing. His breathing got heavier. The feeling of someone sneaking up behind him grew stronger. Instead of turning around, Lucas hurried into the bathroom and closed the door behind him, hoping to escape it. It scared him in a way that made him wonder if he was losing his mind.

But whatever was in the bedroom had somehow made its way through the closed door and into the bathroom.

"What do you want?" Lucas said, sounding more afraid than he wanted to. It was all around him, filling the bathroom the way poison fills a gas chamber before an execution.

His hands felt numb. His blood ran slower. He closed his eyes and said his verses. The presence grew stronger and more powerful. And after a few moments, Lucas, still not daring to open his eyes, realized that as terrifying as the presence was, it wasn't there to hurt him.

Are you God?

The presence was all around him. It almost felt inside him. He felt like he could command an entire city to pick up and move into another state; and yet at the same time Lucas felt he was going to be vaporized like some piece of newspaper that gets thrown into a fireplace.

Who are you? What do you want? Why are you doing this to me?

Lucas waited but got no response.

You are God. Aren't you?

He stayed there for an entire hour, sitting on the ground with his back to the door. Unsure of what was going on.

He checked in on Jake and saw that the man hadn't moved. It was doubtful that Jake would remember Lucas or anything from the previous night. Lucas wrote a note that went something like this: *You are in my home in Evanston because I found you drunk on the road. I couldn't leave you there, or at the Mission, so here you are. There's food in the fridge. I'll check on you later.*

Jake would see the note taped up on the door and Lucas wondered how safe it was to have this drunk in his house.

Lucas changed into a dark blue blazer and selected his favorite of fourteen blue shirts. He left his house and decided to drive his BMW instead of his Mercedes to work.

He arrived at Empirico at 6:30. He walked down the hallway to his office and stopped outside the door. This had once been his battle ground. Now he could hardly identify with the war.

He forced himself through the doorway feeling like a robber breaking into someone's home. He sat down at his computer. *Get out. Get out, right now.* It sounded as if someone was really talking to him. It was as if Anna's voice was reaching him through the speakerphone.

But the phone didn't ring that morning and no one came by to see him. Lucas sat in his office staring sometimes at his computer and sometimes out the window. It was as though David's paralysis had worked its way into Lucas' arms, leaving him unable to type at his laptop or to pick up the phone and call a client.

Maybe there are others who need healing.

Lucas stood up. His office felt so foreign to him. He was like a kid who runs away from his mom in a mall only to find himself completely lost with nothing around looking remotely familiar. Lucas shook his head. And right there in the office he made up his mind.

He was going to quit Empirico.

Lucas knocked on Caesar's door.

"Come in, Lucas," Caesar said. He had watched him come down the hallway on the security cameras. Lucas entered. Caesar motioned to the seat in front of him. "What's on your mind, Lucas?"

Lucas sat down in the chair. He normally had the ability to come straight out with things. But this seemed different. This *was* different.

"Caesar, I just can't get my head back into things. I sit at my desk and I can't concentrate..."

"I understand."

"You do?"

"Of course."

"How?" Lucas wondered.

"How? How doesn't matter. Prison does strange things to a man." Caesar's voice grew stronger and quieter. "When a man is confronted by evil, by someone who wants to take away from him what is rightfully his, take away his freedom, for example, he is forced to become a different person, a survivor."

"A survivor?"

"In China you experienced what all of us know but deep down we don't want to admit. The human race is basically evil and thrown in here or there are some good people."

"I think there are many more good people than bad."

"That's because you're young. People are the way they are because their lifestyles are good. Put them in a starving country, put them in a sinking ship with not enough lifeboats, put them in charge of prisoners at a jail with no one to report to and what do they become?" Caesar looked at Lucas with his eyebrows lifted as if to say the answer was self-evident.

"I have to leave, Caesar."

And that's when the grenade exploded. If anyone turned from friend to foe in an instant it was Caesar Alexander. His jaw clenched together. He glared at Lucas, staring straight into him without blinking. It was as though some evil creature was going to jump out of Caesar's skin and tackle Lucas to the ground.

"You're not going anywhere." The comment froze Lucas in his chair. It was as though he was being hypnotized by some incredible force. He breathed as best he could but it felt like a wire rope was tying him back to the chair making it impossible to take in oxygen. Caesar's eyes burned at him; if they were guns Lucas would have been dead by now. "No, you're going to take some time off. But you're not leaving."

Lucas wanted to run. *Just get up out of the seat and race down the hallway.* But he felt strangely compelled to stay.

"You can take a leave of absence." It was supposed to sound compassionate but it came out sounding more like a stay of execution.

Lucas didn't want a leave of absence. He had made up his mind. He wanted out. Sometimes a man knows he's in the wrong place at the wrong time. And for Lucas the place was Empirico and the time was now.

He felt helpless, trapped in that chair. All he could get himself to say was a slight *okay.* The wire ropes around his chest loosened and Lucas stood up. Caesar's eyes followed him like a powerful lion stalking its prey. Lucas nodded, hoping the meeting was over. It was.

Caesar made no motion. Not a nod, not a gesture. He just sat with a mean look on his face. When Lucas thought about it later he recalled seeing that look before. That look of superiority, hatred, anger. Downright evil. It reminded him of the tall guard at Xaing Xaing. Lucas couldn't look Caesar in the eye on his way out.

Lucas left the office feeling as though he had held his breath the entire time. He walked down the hallway convinced the bridge behind him was burning.

It's just a phase, Caesar thought. *He's going through a phase. He'll be back soon.*

He'll be back.

Caesar announced to the Council that Lucas would be taking a leave of absence. The first thought that went through their minds was: *How long will he be gone?* For the time being, Caesar assigned Lucas' responsibilities to various members of the Council with the greatest share given to Mike, as was the case when Lucas was in prison. The increase in Mike's responsibilities would be rewarded with an increase in pay.

"We will be scheduling a press conference with Dr. Graves to announce our new leukemia product," Caesar said, standing in front of his soldiers. "This is a big one for Empirico. Lots of press will be there."

Caesar was to give a speech in the leukemia ward with the media recording his every word. Beside him, the leukemia-stricken children with their bald heads would be interviewed to say how grateful they were for Caesar and Empirico. Empirico (specifically Caesar) would look like the savior of these children. And for an added bonus the Council members would be present to answer any questions, especially questions pertaining to the personal satisfaction they were getting out of contributing to society in this manner.

The meeting ended but the Council didn't disperse as they usually did. They hung around talking with each other about what life without Lucas would be like. It was as though they were celebrating the death of someone they were glad to have gotten rid of.

In his office, Caesar finished a cup of Irish cream coffee with a teaspoon of cinnamon and a shot of Kahlúa to give it some kick. He glanced at the *Observer* next to him. The story Tabitha had written about David the soccer player caught his attention. He picked it up and skimmed over the article then put it down. He felt embarrassed for people who would be interested in a fluke healing. Pharmaceuticals were the real thing. People could depend on them.

Miracles were for the weak.

Edgar came in from his morning walk a little more tired than usual. He made himself a cup of instant coffee and sat down at his oak table. He spread butter and honey on his bread and popped a multivitamin into his mouth. It was a new habit he was getting himself into.

He folded his hands to pray but still nothing came out (or *in* for that matter). Normally prayer came easily to him. And why shouldn't it? He was a theologian. He knew all about prayer. And yet nothing came to his mind. No words. No thoughts. Nothing. He looked around his house and recalled the hilarious times he enjoyed with his colleagues playing Trivial Pursuit and other mentally stimulating games. He quickly mumbled something about being thankful for food and began to eat.

He put the *Observer* on the table and stirred milk into his coffee. The *Observer* was a new thing for him. He never bought it. But on his walk that morning he passed by a familiar corner store and for no apparent reason he picked up a copy. As he walked out of the store he second-guessed his purchase the way a person might regret buying something they didn't really need in the first place. But something made him buy. An impulse, maybe.

He brought the coffee to his lips, it wasn't too hot, and drank a mouthful. He was about to take a bite of his toast when he saw the story of the miracle soccer boy. He read the article over twice, especially the part about the mysterious miracle healer and the doctor not knowing how to explain the boy's recovery. *I don't know*, the doctor was quoted. And for Edgar, that line stood out of the article like a flower in the middle of a desert.

21

Lucas returned to his mansion thinking about what life without Empirico might be like. He forgot that Jake had spent the night at his place, but when he went upstairs he caught a whiff of a horrible stench and the events of the previous evening came back to him. Lucas opened the door to Jake's room. The air smelled so badly it was as if someone had dumped a pile of used baby diapers on the ground. The bed was empty. The towel was on the chair, unused, and the toiletries had not been touched.

For a moment Lucas thought Jake was gone. But sounds of splashing outside told him he was still around. Unfortunately. Lucas went downstairs and opened the glass door that led to the backyard. There was Jake, jumping around in the pool like a little kid.

"This is a great pool! I've never been in one so big before. Get your bathing suit on and come in!"

"No thanks," Lucas replied and made a mental note to shock the pool once Jake was gone.

Jake turned over on his back and laughed like a child who has just been tickled by its parents. His fat gut hung out like a big bowl of jelly as he pushed through the water. He pulled himself up on the side of the pool revealing two tattoos on his right arm—one was a sword and the second was a heart with a name in it that Lucas could not make out. Jake had a large scar on his chest, probably from a knife fight. Jake got out of the pool and Lucas was relieved to see he was at least wearing a pair of jeans.

"Say, what's your name?" Jake asked, sticking out his hand.

"Lucas Stephens."

"I'm Jake." Jake shook Lucas' hand so hard that it hurt him.

"You got a last name?"

"Doesn't everyone?"

Jake gave Lucas a playful punch in the arm that was forceful enough to convince Lucas it would leave a mark. But Lucas knew better. Any time someone refused to give him simple information it meant one thing: Jake had something to hide.

"Did you have a good sleep, Jake?"

"You know. When I woke up I thought for sure I was in Heaven. This place is amazing! Did you know you have two big screen TVs here?"

"Actually, there are three," Lucas replied.

"Your parents must be rich."

"I live here by myself."

"Then your parents must be proud of you."

Now it was Lucas' turn to avoid the question. "I have a good job." What Lucas should have said was that he *used to have* a good job, but it hadn't sunk in yet.

Jake picked up his shirt from the table where he had been tanning while reading the *Observer*. He shook his hair, the way a dog does, and put his stained shirt on. He smiled and chuckled to himself as he squinted in the light. He was poor and dirty, anyone could see that, but he had a confidence about him that told Lucas he hadn't always been on the bottom. Some people are born, raised and killed on the streets. It's as though they never had a chance—they lived in a part of the culture that was totally isolated from any escape routes. Jake wasn't what Lucas had expected from someone lying drunk in the middle of road.

"So, what are we doing today?" Jake asked like a neighborhood boy knocking on his friend's door on a Saturday morning. Lucas said nothing. He didn't know how to answer. The delay in response spoke volumes to Jake. His optimistic smile lost its momentum. He grinned politely and died a quiet death. No one else in society wanted him. Why should this multi-millionaire be any different?

"Well, that's okay," Jake lied. "I have things to do today, too," he lied again.

Lucas searched for words to say but his communication skills couldn't fill the void.

"I understand," Jake continued. "You don't have to explain."

"I'm sorry if I misled you." Lucas didn't regret taking Jake off the street, but he did regret taking him to his house. He had no idea who this man was or who he was connected to. What if someone was after him? What if they followed him here? What if Jake was a criminal? What if? What if? What if?

"You didn't mislead me. I mean, you went the second mile for me."

"Maybe."

"No, you did. When was the last time someone picked me off the street? When was the last time I got to drive in a Mercedes or swim in a pool? When was the last time I slept in a bed?"

A bed? Lucas nearly choked. *Is that what he said? A bed? What does he sleep on?* Lucas recalled that it wasn't too long ago that he, too, had slept without a bed.

"I can give you a ride to wherever you're going."

"Can you give me a ride home?"

Lucas nodded, then wondered if such a place existed for Jake. As they walked to the house, the *Observer* caught Lucas' attention. There, on the cover, was the picture of David the soccer player. Lucas quickly glanced through the article, the way a high school student cramming for an exam would, and read the part about the mysterious miracle man who was nowhere to be found.

Lucas figured the chlorine from the pool probably helped to disinfect Jake, but they got into the Mercedes all the same because there was no reason to stink up two perfectly good vehicles. They drove past the Mission to the South Side. On the right they saw an old man who was shriveled up as though he had just come out of a washing machine. He pushed a shopping cart filled with bags and aluminum eavestrough extensions. Garbage lay on the street, on the sidewalks. But it wasn't so much the garbage and uncleanliness that bothered Lucas. It wasn't even the gray color of everything. It was that there were so few people out. As though everybody was hiding. No kids playing, no pedestrians. It looked so empty.

"Up there, just ahead."

Lucas saw the house and wondered how Jake made it to the Mission, especially on those cold Chicago nights when the wind hits you in the face like a baseball you didn't see coming. And what about the danger? Jake was white. The neighborhood was black, well, mostly black. Some Hispanics and and a few whites. But each group had their neighborhood. Just like other big cities. It was as if some teacher had shouted at them as children in a classroom: *All the Hispanics over to that side, blacks over there and the whites over there. And don't any of you go to the parts where you don't belong.*

But Jake had. He was a white man in a black neighborhood. Never once, not one time since he lived there, did anyone ever hurt him. Sure, the occasional racial slur would come his way telling him to get his white behind out of the neighborhood but nothing really dangerous.

He lived in a blue house, or at least it used to be blue. The weather had beaten it up and turned it that unmistakable shade of gray that everything in the neighborhood seemed to turn to. He occupied an apartment on the main floor of a property that had been converted into a four-unit rental complex. The shingles were falling off and the paint had been peeling for years. The grass was grown over and the porch had a few steps missing. Jake took the steps two at a time to avoid the missing treads and cautioned Lucas to stay close to him. The other residents, he warned, were not as friendly as he was.

From the second floor window, a prostitute who was recovering from a beating the night before saw the two come in. *Drugs*, she thought. *Nobody in a Mercedes shows up without selling something, or someone.* She stared long and hard at Lucas. He looked good to her and she hoped his eyes would wander up to meet hers. Maybe she could reel him in. If she had been more presentable she would have introduced herself. But the bruises on her face lowered her street value. If Lucas turned out to be a rough one she might not survive it. She turned away from the window, put the ice packs back on her face and erased any thoughts of getting some work with a guy like Lucas. Rich boys were out of her league.

Jake opened the front door and had trouble closing it properly behind them. Ahead of them was a hardwood floor with some rotten boards. The radiator halfway down the hallway had been urinated on again the night before and it smelled bad enough to make someone throw up. To the left was a locked door that led upstairs to two units. At the back was a screen door that led outside where three youths were drinking beer and smoking marijuana. They were laughing hysterically. None of them had any shoes on and none of their parents knew where they were. On the right were two rooms. From the room farther down the hall came the sound of rock music and a monotone, bass voice. It was recorded music, but for Lucas it sounded more like some drunk was singing into a microphone. *At some point this building was brand new*, Lucas thought. It was hard for him to imagine what it would have looked like back then or who would have lived in it.

When Jake opened the door to his room Lucas immediately understood why Jake stank so ferociously. Lucas couldn't decide if it smelled worse in the hallway or in Jake's place. The stench forced Lucas to breath through his mouth. But Jake didn't flinch. He'd gotten used to the smell years ago.

"Here we are. Home sweet home."

It was a small unit and Lucas wondered why there was so little furniture. The room was practically empty. A rusted, old stove with only one working element stood in a corner. The hardwood floor was chewed up the way a floor gets when it doesn't get looked after. Large chunks of plaster had fallen off the light yellow walls. The only window in the place had been smashed and was poorly covered up with the cardboard from a cereal box. A pale green toilet and basin stood in another corner. The door to the bathroom had been broken in a fight. The shower never worked. There was one incandescent bulb screwed into the ceiling and it gave off enough energy to light up the room. Lucas figured the less light the better. It would prevent him from seeing other details. A T-shirt was rolled up against the wall and doubled as a pillow. A shower curtain covered with mold served as a blanket. The floor served as a bed.

It was Xaing Xaing all over again, except, of course, for the guards.

Jake pulled a stool out for himself and gave a wobbly metal chair to his honored guest. On the ground near Jake was a pitcher of water with a shot glass and a beer stein next to it.

"Can I offer you a drink?" Lucas shook his head as politely as he could. He was sure if he touched the water he would drop down dead. Jake continued. "It's a nice quiet neighborhood. The people are okay. I try to help out. Fix the place up when the landlord gives me some money."

The smell was really getting to Lucas. The sight of cockroaches in the corner made him wonder if it was acceptable to jump out of his chair and stomp on them. The music from next door pounded through the wall. It was probably some teenager blasting his music, oblivious to the fact that there might be other people around who didn't like it.

Jake lived in a hovel. But his deplorable living conditions weren't what bothered Lucas. What got to Lucas was that Jake seemed to be all right with it.

"You can't live here," Lucas said.

"Sure I can. My rent gets paid on time every month."

"I mean you can't exist here. I wouldn't let a dog live in here."

"Why not? I would love a dog."

Lucas had to get out. Like a person suffering from claustrophobia, Lucas felt as though the walls were closing in on him. It felt as if concrete was being poured around the window and door to seal them in. *This place should be bulldozed down and burned to the ground.*

"You can't stay here." Lucas stood up and walked to the door.

"You don't like my place?"

"Your place sucks, Jake."

Jake looked away from Lucas in humiliation. It was as though a school principal had just told him he was going to be held back a year. There in front of him was a man. Not even a man, a boy, practically. He was what? In his twenties? And he was a hundred, a thousand times better off. And here Jake was in his home, his garbage dump with a roof. Something inside him believed that he deserved better. Not necessarily a mansion like Lucas, but some place where there was hot water. Some place where the radiator didn't stink like an unflushed toilet. Some place where the neighbors talked to you and not just when they were drunk. Jake looked up at Lucas. His smile disappeared and his face blended in with the deplorable surroundings. "What are you suggesting?"

Lucas didn't want Jake to stay with him. He just didn't. But how could he turn his back on him? How could he pretend he was doing the best thing for Jake by leaving him here? Having Jake stay here would be as bad as taping a dog's mouth around the exhaust of a car.

Maybe worse.

What am I supposed to do? Go to everybody who lives in a dump and invite them over? What am I thinking with this guy? Leave him here, his mind told him. *Leave him here and forget about him. What is going on with you that you would even think about something like this? Are you stupid? Are you truly insane?*

"I don't know what I'm suggesting but you're not staying here. What's your rental agreement?"

"Month to month."

"What's your walk-out clause?"

"Anytime."

"That time is now."

Jake got off his stool and reached over to the floor to pick up a stack of clothes. There were two T-shirts with holes in them and a pair of jeans.

"Leave them there. You don't need them."

Jake dropped the clothes. He had no other possessions.

Lucas walked out of the room and left the house being careful not to fall through the missing steps. Jake wrote a note on the back of a soup can label informing his landlord of his decision. He took one last look at his place then stuck the note in the door as he closed it. He locked the door and was about to stuff the key under the door when he stopped to think about what he was doing. No, his home was not something to be proud of. But it was a home, his home. And if Mercedes Man over there on the street was lying to him then he stood to lose what pathetic accommodations he had.

Jake decided to risk it. The only reason Jake believed Lucas was that Lucas had stopped for him. It was enough to convince Jake to go with him. Lucas had stopped on the road to pick him up and, willingly or unwillingly, chose to take him to his home. Jake figured there was something trustworthy about a man who does things like that. Regardless of what car he drove, what his job was, or where he lived, a person who offered to take in a drunk was above most people. Jake pushed his key under the door out of reach and walked out of what he once called his home.

He jumped off the porch and left his rat hole for the Mercedes waiting for him on the street. He sat down next to Lucas. His smile returned. “So where to?”

Lucas switched the car in drive and couldn’t get away fast enough. “I have a promise to keep.”

22

When Lucas and Jake arrived at the hospital they noticed a group of parents preparing a colorful party in the front yard. A huge hand-painted banner hung between two poles that read: SURPRISE. The parents tucked bright red napkins underneath blue plates. Some of the mothers poured drinks into white cups and put them on top of the plates to keep them from flying away. The pizza would be arriving soon.

The party was being put on by family and friends of the leukemia patients. More than sixty people had come to show their love for the children who were on the slow boat to death. The parents talked with each other and compared how their children were doing. One of them checked his watch to make sure everything would be ready in time for when the children would come down. Two mothers cried as they set a table. The doctor had prepared them that their daughters would probably be next.

Lucas and Jake walked through the party to the front door. They signed in at the security desk and took the elevator to the children's cancer ward. Lucas searched his mind for the name of the girl he had promised to visit. Even though he could recall her face he couldn't draw out her name. Was it Amy? Andrea? Alana? He remembered that she had bright blue eyes and a lisp. She was the one with all the questions. The one who was dying.

They stopped outside the same room where Lucas had been the

day he met with Dr. Graves. Lucas looked inside and saw her resting in her bed. She was underweight the last time he was here, but now she looked even worse—like a balloon that was slowing losing air. Her eyes were open but she wasn't looking at anything.

A nurse stopped behind them. "Can I help you?"

"I'm here to see a patient." It bothered Lucas that he could not remember the girl's name.

"Which one?"

Lucas pointed to her.

"Angelina?"

"Yes."

"Are you a relative?"

"No. A friend. She asked me to come back to see her."

The nurse studied Lucas' eyes as if she were trying to tell the true nature of his intention. "All right. Ten minutes. But keep quiet, some of them are sleeping."

Lucas led the way to the room and stood at the end of her bed. She saw him out of the corner of her eye but didn't think it was a visitor for her. Her mom had come to see her with one of the other moms a few minutes ago. They had both left crying.

Lucas came to her bedside and knelt down to be at her level. He smiled when he saw her big blue eyes. He tried not to notice her bald head or the dark bags under her eyes.

"Angelina?"

She looked at his face, at each part individually to see if something would trigger her memory. She saw a scar above his left eye. Then she saw his eyes. They looked different, like a lighthouse that now had a brighter light burning inside. "I remember you now. You're the man who had to leave in such a hurry."

Angelina looked over at Jake. She wasn't too sure what to make of him. She hadn't seen him before either and he certainly, definitely, was not a doctor.

"I'm Jake."

"Hello."

"Are you warm enough? Do you need another blanket?" Jake asked.

Angelina sniffled the way kids do when they feel a cold coming on. She shook her head slightly. Jake would gladly have given her a blanket. He recently gave the woman in the apartment upstairs from him a blanket and found himself a used shower curtain in the garbage dump to use as a substitute.

"How are you feeling?" Lucas asked.

"Not so good. I'm always tired." She looked so helpless, so worn out, trapped there in her bed. A child her age should be running around, telling jokes, spilling Coke on herself at a fast food joint, not lying in a cancer ward. She had reached the point that sick people get to when they know, and people around them know, that everything's been tried. What should have worked, hadn't worked. Her parents and the medical staff continued to encourage her but she knew what was going on in their minds. The race was ending.

Lucas wished that speaking with her could somehow get the cancer to leave her body. He opened his mouth but the words were out of reach, like a bus pulling away from a passenger. He quietly began to quote the verses. Angelina heard him but didn't understand what he was doing. It didn't make him, or her, feel any different. Not right away.

"We had strawberry ice cream yesterday."

"You did? How did it taste?"

"Very, very cold."

Lucas smiled. She smiled too, but it faded quickly, as though the realization of some bad news was preventing her from laughing.

"Angelina, do you remember when we talked last time?" She nodded without breaking eye contact with Lucas. "I told you that our company could solve anything we put our minds to."

"I know."

"I told you that there was nothing we couldn't do. That we could find a cure to make you better. We could find a cure to make everybody better no matter what they had."

"I remember."

"Angelina, I was wrong."

"I know."

"You know?"

"I knew you thought you could do it. But I knew that you couldn't. I could see it in your eyes. You had the same look the doctors get when things are going bad and they don't want you to know it. You hoped that you could. But you couldn't." She looked through Lucas' eyes to investigate what was happening behind them. "But you have something different now."

"How do you know?"

"I can see it."

"You can see it?"

"Yes," Angelina said. "In your eyes. There's something there that was missing the last time you were here. What is it?"

"I don't know."

"You don't?"

"No. But I think I know that you can get better."

She tilted her head slightly. "How?"

It should have been easy enough for Lucas to explain. *I pray and it seems people get healed.* But it was too simple an explanation to possibly be right. He didn't understand how it worked. Maybe he never would.

"I think I have something that can make you healthy."

"Is it him?" Angelina said pointing to Jake.

Jake smiled and laughed with his smoker's cough laugh. "It's not me." He then became quiet, equally interested in what Lucas was getting at.

She looked around and saw nothing out of the ordinary. "Is it here?" she asked.

"Maybe."

"Maybe?"

Lucas glanced behind him as if doing so would give him the confidence that someone was going to materialize and heal this girl. "I think so."

"You think so? If you're not sure, then how am I going to get better?"

The nurse passed by the room and glanced in. He'd been there about five minutes. Another five and he would be asked to leave.

"I want to pray for you, Angelina. To get better. Not just for you to sleep better, but that you'd walk out of here and never have to come back."

Leave the hospital? Angelina thought. *The only kids who ever leave this ward are the ones you never hear from again.* She used to pretend in her mind about leaving the hospital, going with her mom for some strawberry ice cream, playing with the kids in the neighborhood. But circumstances had a way of eroding that world of make-believe.

"Where will I go?"

"To live with your parents, your brothers, sisters."

She vaguely recalled having a life outside of the hospital. She had a bedroom to herself. There was a dog in the backyard that barked whenever she had to take a nap. The neighborhood kids would come over for homemade popsicles, the kind you make when you put juice into ice trays and freeze them. There was a world out there with laughter, friends and playing outside. A world without pain.

"Could I chase the dog around the house again?"

"Only if your mom lets you."

Some of the other children had woken up and were listening in on the conversation. Whenever someone came to visit anyone in the room they came to visit everyone.

"What about popsicles?"

"What about them?"

"Do I get to have a strawberry one? On the porch?"

"I think your mom would do that for you."

"Could I have two?"

"I betcha if you asked, she'd give you as many as you wanted."

Angelina smiled in a way that looked painful. There was this life inside her, something separate from the decaying shell she was in, that wanted to get out and run around.

"Can you pray for me now?"

Angelina closed her eyes. Lucas put his hands on her head. Some of the children sat up in their beds and gave it their full attention the way they did when entertainers came to the ward.

Lucas recited portions of the pages he'd memorized at Xaing Xaing. His hands grew warmer. When he thought about how to make them even warmer they grew colder. But as he forgot about the sensation of heat and focused on the stories his hands became hot.

Lucas repeated some of the accounts of people getting healed. The more he spoke, the hotter his hands got. He could hear Angelina's breathing becoming deeper. His hands trembled from the heat. The room seemed strangely crowded, as though a thousand people had suddenly crammed in.

Lucas felt a poking sensation in the palms of his hands coming from Angelina's head. It was the kind of feeling a man gets when he rubs his face before shaving. Angelina sat up in her bed. She blinked like she had just woken up from a nap. She touched her head. Lucas removed his hands. Jake's mouth dropped open.

Patches of hair had grown on her head.

"I have hair," Angelina whispered.

Lucas touched her head and gently moved it over her scalp to feel the hair. He leaned closer for a better look. *She was bald before. She was. I saw it. There wasn't any hair before.* But now there was, not much of it, but it was there. There was something that scared Lucas about seeing an event that shouldn't be happening. It was the same feeling he got with the tall guard and the soccer player. There was something bigger, much bigger, at work here. He felt insignificant, the way the worst team in the league feels when they have to play the champions. It was like meeting an alien. At first it's interesting in a scary sort of way, but then you realize you are hopelessly ill prepared to be in its presence.

She rubbed her head from the back to the front. "But it's so short. I'm going to look like a boy."

Lucas focused on the hair. It seemed like it was growing right before his eyes. He shook his head in amazement, the way a scientist would whose experiment has just proven some incredible idea.

"I think you might be getting more hair."

Jake touched the top of her head. He looked into her eyes. There was more color in her face, more energy.

"It's time for you to get out of your bed, Angelina," Lucas said.

"I can't get out of bed. I have to stay here. I'm sick."

"I don't think so."

"This is my bed. These are my friends. This is my home. I can't leave. Not without them."

"Maybe we could go and help them together?"

The other children were on the edge of their beds. Angelina looked at them, then at Lucas. "I don't know if I can leave here."

"If you want to get better, take my hand and get out of the bed."

He offered her his hand. She took it and slid down onto the floor. She looked at the mirror behind her and ran her hand through her hair. It was long enough now that her fingers got lost in it. She stepped closer and admired herself. A smile came to her face and with a bolt of energy she turned to Lucas. "Let's go help my friends!"

She ran to her friend in the bed next to her. He was waiting at the edge with his hands stretched out. "Can I leave, too?" Lucas knelt down beside him and laid his hands on the boy's bald head. In a moment, it too showed growth.

The other children got out of their beds and gathered around Lucas. One by one he prayed over them. He placed his hands on their heads and saw them get healed.

The children began to cheer and shout. They ran to the mirrors and played with each others hair. Angelina's was now down to her shoulders, it didn't look like boys' hair anymore. They jumped up and down and hugged each other. One of the kids started shouting and that got the rest of them going. They ran to the door screaming for joy, pulling Lucas and Jake with them.

The nurse heard the commotion and came to the room. The children smashed through the door and knocked the woman off balance. "What in the world?" She saw the children in the hospital gowns run past her, yelling like kids do when they're having fun. But these weren't the sick kids, couldn't have been. These ones were running, laughing.

These ones had hair.

The children ran down the stairs shouting as loud as they could. Their little feet hurried down as fast as gravity could pull them. They reached the main floor and raced for the front door, running past all the curious onlookers.

Outside at the surprise party the parents heard the commotion. They stopped what they were doing and listened. It grew louder and louder and louder. Suddenly the doors burst open. They saw the children explode out of the hospital, like kids on the last day of school, and run down the steps towards them.

One by one the children found their parents. They jumped up to get a hug. The parents saw the hair and wondered what had happened. When they looked into their eyes they confirmed that these children were their own. Their babies. The ones they gave birth to—some of them right at this very hospital.

Angelina had not continued with the rest of her group. She stopped halfway down the stairs and ran back to see Lucas and Jake who were making their way down.

"Wait!" she called out to them. "Wait!" She stopped in front of them out of breath. "You'll have to forgive me. It's not every day I get to leave the hospital. My mom always said to say thanks and so here I am. Thanks."

The nurse opened the door to the stairs and looked down. She wanted to say something but couldn't find the words. She couldn't believe it. Maybe part of her didn't want to. The hair on the children's heads was so far out of the nurse's world, so far from her normal experience. It was as if someone had told her that her world was a pretend world and that there was something out there, something better and much, much more powerful.

Lucas bent down and touched Angelina's hair. He could have stayed there for hours being amazed at the miracle. It felt like silk in his hands. Unable to figure out how this had happened he touched her face and said, "I'm not sure I'm the one you should be thanking."

"Did that thing that shines in your eyes do this?"

"I think so."

"I think so, too."

She turned and quickly went down the stairs. Her blond hair bounced off her back as she negotiated the steps. The nurse ran back to tell a doctor that either the kids were healed or that she herself had gone crazy. Angelina stopped for the last time and called up to him. "You never told me your name."

"Lucas."

She smiled. "I like that name." And with that she ran out to reintroduce herself to her mother.

Angelina's mother searched through the crowd of kids looking for her daughter. "Mom!" She turned and saw Angelina running from the hospital. Her hair flew behind her like Batman's cape. She jumped into her mom's arms and hung on for dear life. Then Angelina's face became serious as she looked her mom square in the eye. "Strawberry, mom."

"Strawberry?"

"Yeah. And lots of it. We can sit out on the porch. You and me. The whole day."

"Okay," her mother said. There was more than just her daughter in her arms. What it was, she didn't know. But it was bigger than Angelina, bigger than a healing.

The pizza arrived on time and the surprise party could begin.

23

Tabitha pulled into a handicap parking spot. She grabbed her leather bag and tape recorder and hurried through the parking lot wondering about what she would see. When she first saw the message on her pager she thought it was a typo—that maybe someone in the office was in a hurry and didn't get the message right. Only the thought of David playing soccer again and the interview with the doctor afterward made the message more believable: LEUKEMIA WARD EMPTY.

The party was in full force. Kids playing. Parents laughing. Pizza boxes scattered over the ground. Tabitha noticed that some of the doctors were examining the children. It seemed strange to her that they would be doing this outside, especially since the kids looked perfectly healthy.

There were no other reporters at the scene, not yet. She walked through the party into the hospital and spoke with the receptionist who sat protected behind security glass.

"I'm looking for the leukemia patients."

"Outside," she replied, too busy to look at her.

"Where outside?"

The receptionist pointed back to the door. "The party?"

Tabitha didn't understand. She walked back outside. There were no sick children there. Maybe it was around the corner, a second party going on, perhaps. She walked through the pizza parade and Angelina's mother stopped her.

"Are you a reporter?"

Tabitha turned around and made eye contact with the woman who was speaking with her. "I'm trying to follow a children's leukemia story."

"Incredible, isn't it?" Angelina's mother said.

"Isn't what incredible?"

"The children."

Tabitha looked around unsure of what the woman was trying to say. "What about them?"

"They're all healed. The entire leukemia ward."

Tabitha suddenly sensed that same feeling she got when she used to read Nancy Drew books or watch *Charlie's Angels.* It was that feeling of being a super-sleuth trying to solve a mystery. Only this was real. And it was bigger than a mystery. The words of the doctor came back to her. *I don't know. I don't know.* She told herself that she was just a reporter, that her job was to report what was happening, not to explain it. But it was tough not to want things explained that were so completely out of normal experience.

"They're all healed?"

The mother nodded.

"These children are the leukemia patients?"

"They *were* the leukemia patients.

Tabitha looked around again. *There's no way these kids were sick.* "Can you tell me what happened?"

She called out to her daughter. "Angelina? Come here, sweetheart." Angelina came to her mom and sat on her lap. "Sweetheart, this is a reporter. She wants to know what happened."

Tabitha looked at Angelina's beautiful hair flowing around her. Her big blue eyes squinted in the sunlight.

"Well, I'll tell you," Angelina began. "First, I was sleeping. Well, I was supposed to be sleeping. But I couldn't. And then we got better."

It was so simple. No complicated X-rays to review. No doctor's tests. Just a testimony of a young child. The miracle was easy for Angelina to believe, impossible for Tabitha.

"How did you get better?"

"Someone came to visit us."

"Who?"

"This man."

"Did he give you his name?"

Angelina knew she asked him his name. She thought about the sound of his voice, that convincing look in his eyes, the warmth of his hands, but she couldn't recall his name. "I can't remember."

"What did he look like?"

"He was nice. Really nice. He had dark hair."

Great, Tabitha thought. *She's just finished describing ten million people.*

"And he had this sore spot right here," Angelina said pointing above her left eye.

"What kind of sore?"

"Like a cut."

Tabitha pulled out her notebook. Two separate healings, David and now the leukemia ward, done by a man with dark hair and scar over his left eye. It had to be the same person.

"Had you ever seen him before?"

"It was a while ago."

"A few years?"

"Maybe. Well, maybe less than that." She turned to her mother. "How long ago did Mickey die?"

"About six weeks, sweetheart."

Angelina looked at Tabitha. "Six weeks."

Usually Tabitha's notebook was just a polite way of showing she was interested in an otherwise boring conversation, but this time it was genuinely investigative. There was a man with healing power somewhere in Chicago. Everyone on earth would be running to him.

"Did he tell you where he was going?"

"No, they just left right after everyone was better."

"Who's they?"

"There was this really nice but really big man. He smelled a lot. I didn't say anything because I didn't want to hurt his feelings, but boy, did he stink."

Other reporters hurried to the scene. Soon, there were eight crews in total. The party's warmth and miraculous atmosphere was stifled by the onslaught of media.

Tabitha took a picture of the mother and daughter. She scribbled the title of her article into her notepad. MYSTERY HEALER STEERS CHILDREN CLEAR OF DEATH.

Two Empirico limousines pulled up. Security personnel stepped out and methodically glanced at the nearby crowd. They wore dark sunglasses, dark suits and somber faces. Various Empirico Council members emerged as well.

Thatcher and Ridley stood shoulder to shoulder with Caesar who was the last person to step out. He saw the party at the far side of the hospital grounds and smiled. *What a great day to deliver the news of a new leukemia medicine.*

When Caesar entered the hospital's main entrance he found it strange that the usual crowd of media weren't there to greet him. He was sure Empirico had sent out notices to all the major papers and TV stations. The Empirico team, ten in all, took the elevators to the leukemia ward. On the way up Caesar reviewed his speech, especially the part about what pride he felt over the new product.

The elevator opened and what Caesar saw forced him to double check that this was the right floor. Was this some sort of joke? Caesar stepped out and looked around. The floor was empty.

A few moments later a crowd of reporters, including Tabitha, came out of the stairwell and rushed up to Caesar. *Now this is more like it*, he thought. *But where are Dr. Graves and all the medical personnel? They should be groveling at my feet thanking me for developing such a drug.*

"Mr. Alexander! Mr. Alexander!" the reporters shouted.

Caesar took in a deep breath through his nose and got ready to deliver his prepared speech. Thatcher and Ridley were really unnecessary but they provided for a healthy company image. They kept the media back as best they could.

The reporters shoved their microphones into Caesar's face. Caesar cleared his throat, paused for effect, then spoke in as clear a voice as he could manage.

"It's a pleasure to be able to announce on behalf of the dedicated workers at Empirico—"

"What do you think about the miracles?" Tabitha interrupted.

"Does this affect your plans for the new drugs you're developing?" asked another reporter.

Caesar was caught off guard. What were they talking about? More people came up the stairs. Some of the children who were previously sick came in and showed their moms where the miracles took place. The doctor's came in as well, still shocked and amazed at what had happened.

"As I was mentioning," continued Caesar, "we are proud—"

"But what about the miracles? This has to be big news for a pharmaceutical company," said a reporter.

Caesar glanced to his assistant for help but all he got was a blank look.

"Does it bother you that the children were healed without medication?" Tabitha asked.

Caesar gave the predetermined nod to Thatcher which meant: *Get me out of here at all cost!* Thatcher ushered Caesar away from the reporters who tried in vain to get more information. Caesar's face grew red as a result of the combination of embarrassment and anger he felt. He had planned things out so that situations like this would be avoided.

Dr. Graves pushed his way through the crowd. "Caesar, welcome."

Dr. Graves extended his hand to Caesar. Normally, Caesar would shake hands and add a pleasant grin, but this time he just stopped and glared at Dr. Graves. He spoke to him in a harsh, quiet voice. "What kind of stunt are you pulling?"

"What?"

"You made me look like an idiot! How dare you?"

"Caesar, I can't explain it. They're healed."

"With whose medication?"

"I can only tell you what I know."

"Whose medication?"

Dr. Graves waited a moment. He looked liked a farmer trying to convince the police that a flying saucer really had landed on his property. "No one's."

Caesar knew he heard wrong. He shook his head at Dr. Graves and asked him to repeat himself.

"There was no medication, Caesar. This morning they were sick. Now, all our tests show them to be perfectly healthy. I can't say it more directly than that."

The doctor's lost it, thought Caesar. *A man younger than me losing his mind. No medication. What dream world is this idiot living in?*

Caesar pushed past Dr. Graves and looked into the leukemia ward. The bed covers were half off. A water cup had spilled on the floor. But what bothered Caesar was not the mess—it was that the room was empty.

The reporters left Caesar on the leukemia floor. They followed the healed children around as though they were football players who had just won the Superbowl. Today, the children were the center of attention and Caesar was not. This was supposed to be his day of recognition. His day of media coverage. His day of fame and glory. Sure, he'd had plenty of them before. But this was his show. The media were supposed to be there for him. The children had stolen his thunder.

And it drove Caesar to unbelievable jealousy.

24

Lucas and Jake left the hospital before the media showed up. Lucas wanted to avoid the attention until he had this healing phenomenon sorted out in his mind. Unlike his former boss, Lucas didn't like the media.

They arrived at the mansion still trying to understand how the children had been healed. They sat down in Lucas' living room and for the longest time they said nothing. It was as though they were in a state of shock, or they had just robbed a bank and were wondering if the cops were going to show up.

Lucas closed his eyes and tried to make sense of what he was experiencing. He thought about the incident with the tall guard. It must have been luck. It couldn't have been as miraculous as he originally thought. Maybe it was just a product of his mind. And the soccer player? Kids do recover from illnesses, even serious ones. And did those kids really have leukemia? It didn't make sense. None of it. It seemed so easy. It seemed like an illusion. He trusted his memory of the healings to be accurate, but, in the end, memory is not a record of what happened. It's just an imprint of an interpretation of what happened. It's a personal version of the events, only it keeps on changing the further away a person gets from it. And that's what was getting to Lucas. He was wondering if the events really had happened just as he remembered them.

"So you were in a prison?" Jake interrupted.

"Right."

"And you read pages that were used as toilet paper and now people are getting healed?"

"Something like that."

"That's not normal."

"That's what bothers me."

"I mean, that's really not normal."

"I know. It makes me wonder if something is wrong with me."

"Wrong with you?" Jake stood up. "A ward full of leukemia patients gets healed and you think there's something wrong with you?"

Lucas lifted his hands and held his palms in front of his face to study them. They looked like normal hands. Nothing special. But there *was* something inside them. Something warm and powerful. And when it came into contact with sick people it made them better.

"There's nothing wrong with you, Lucas."

"Do you understand how this healing is happening?"

"No," Jake said.

"Then how do you know nothing's wrong?"

"How could kids being healed be wrong?"

"What if there's a side effect? Or maybe this healing has a shelf life of, say, twenty people. Once the twentieth person gets healed, boom, I'm dead."

"I doubt it."

"Or worse, maybe it reverses itself. I have the touch now, but what if it changes? Makes people sick? Kills them?"

"You're asking the wrong guy."

Lucas rubbed his hands through his hair. He spoke to himself but it was loud enough to reach Jake. "Where do I go from here?"

That evening, they sat outside near the pool listening to the radio and eating barbecued hamburgers. Lucas finished two but Jake was still going strong after four. The radio had a news story about the healings that morning. The reporter talked about the healed children, the relieved parents and the doctors who were both thrilled and baffled over what had occurred. He finished his story by saying that no one had any idea of who was behind the healing miracles.

"I have a plan about what we should do next," Lucas said.

"Good. 'Cause I don't."

"Meet me in the living room. Tomorrow. 5:00."

"A.m. or p.m.?"

"Morning."

"What are we going to do?"

"Just be there."

"I'll be there." Jake took another bite of his hamburger; most of it fell onto his plate. "Just to be clear, I can stay here tonight?"

"Stay here as long as you want."

Jake had never heard those words before.

Lucas knelt at his bed. He prayed and recited his verses. The moon brought the only light into his room, not that he needed it. But it served as a time marker to tell him it was late which is why the knock at the downstairs door surprised him.

He passed the living room on his way to the front door and saw Jake engrossed in a book. Lucas felt bad for being surprised that Jake could read.

He opened the door without looking through the window first. When he saw who it was a rush of blood pounded through his veins. There stood Tabitha Samos. She had her beautiful black hair tied behind her. She wore a T-shirt, blue jeans and a pair of nervous eyes.

Part of Lucas hoped they would never meet again. But the other part, the part that was more convincing, knew that once their paths crossed they would stay crossed until their relationship was resolved, one way or the other.

"Tabitha."

She smiled. "I wondered if you were going to open the door."

Lucas figured Tabitha was here for one of two reasons, maybe both. Either she was here to discuss the falling out at Navy Pier or she was on to him about the leukemia ward. He thought of Jake. If Tabitha was looking for the two people who were involved in the healing at the hospital then Jake would be a giveaway.

"Care for a walk around the place?"

"You don't want to invite me inside?" Tabitha suddenly blushed. She opened her mouth slightly as if to suck back the words she had just said. She didn't mean it the way it came out. She smiled, feeling awkward. "A walk outside is fine."

They walked around to the backyard. Lucas tried to avoid eye contact as they walked past the tennis court. The lights from the house reflected off the pool and onto the small bridge that crossed over a creek. They made small talk the way people do when they are trying to avoid the real issue that's bothering them.

"I'm sorry, Lucas."

"Sorry?"

"Yes."

"About?"

"I shouldn't have hit you."

Lucas nodded and tilted his head slightly to indicate to her he was willing to put the incident behind them.

There was a silence between them. Neither of them knew how to continue so Lucas took a chance.

"Been fly-fishing much?"

She paused a moment and recalled the times she went with her father to their favorite river to go fly-fishing. Even though her dad was a politician he wasn't much of a talker, at least not with the family. Still, when Tabitha cast into the river with her father she felt close to him. The cold water rushing past them, the fresh air, the warm sun on their faces; it made fly-fishing with her dad a memorable experience. It reassured her of his interest in her life. Although her father was only a twelve-hour drive away, Tabitha had not seen him in more than two years. She missed fly-fishing. She missed her father.

"Not for a while," she said.

"How's your work at the *Observer*?"

"We had the story of our lives today. A leukemia ward was cleaned out."

"I saw it on the news."

"What's even more amazing is that none of us know who healed them."

"Apparently it was miraculous."

Tabitha leaned on the railing and took in the night air. The sound of water beneath them reminded her of fly-fishing. She pretended to make eye contact with Lucas but really she was looking for the scar above his left eye. Sure enough. It was there. She had checked the security sign-in sheet where she barely made out his scribbled name and that of a Jake Rubenstein. She figured Jake was inside, which would explain why Lucas didn't want her there. Angelina said the man who prayed for her had first come to see her about six weeks ago. Tabitha thought back to when Fat Chester assigned her the story. It was about six weeks as well. She couldn't believe her luck. Or was it misfortune? Black hair, male, scar above his left eye, the time factor. She was nearly certain.

"What would you do if you were the one who healed those kids?" she asked.

"I don't know. What would you do?"

"I'd do it again."

"When? On lunch breaks?"

"If I had that kind of power I'd quit everything and do it full time. Wouldn't you?"

"I wonder."

"How's your work?"

"It's good."

"Really?"

"Really."

"I phoned Empirico. They said you've taken a leave of absence."

Lucas felt unsure of himself. His disassociation with Empirico had not yet sunk in. "That's right," he said. "I've take a leave of absence."

"To do what?"

Lucas wished she would just stop with the questions. What business was it of hers anyway? Nosy reporter.

"You know. Everybody needs a break from time to time."

"But a leave of absence?"

"Yes. A leave of absence." He was becoming angry now and wanted her out of his backyard.

Tabitha nodded and observed the scar as discreetly as possible. "I wonder where a person like that gets their healing power."

"Could be a lot of places."

"I did a story on a boy named David who got out of a wheelchair yesterday."

"Lucky kid."

"Soccer player. Happened on Lake Shore. Not far from Navy Pier. Just before we met."

She's putting it together. But she doesn't know for certain. All she has is ideas, a few leads. Some coincidences. Nothing concrete. That's when he remembered the sign-in sheet at the hospital. He looked away from her, as though doing so could hide the truth being told in his eyes.

She glanced at the scar one more time. "I just came by to try and... well... you know, whatever."

"I'm glad you did.

"I need to go."

She got to her yellow convertible and backed out of the driveway. She dialed on her cell phone and got the printing room. "Stop the press," she said.

The voice at the other end laughed. Was this some sort of joke?

"I know the identity of the healer."

25

The sound of Jake coming down the stairs was unmistakable. He didn't walk down them the way most people do. He pounded down them, as though he was checking to see if he could smash through each step. He came into the living room at 5:00, just as they had agreed, and saw Lucas kneeling on the floor at the couch with his hands folded. Even with all the noise Jake made on the stairs Lucas did not hear him.

"What are you doing?" Jake asked.

Lucas looked up from his prayers. "I'm praying."

"That's not praying. Down on the ground there with your face buried in your hands? What, are you crying?"

"No."

"You're praying? Really?"

"Yes."

"Like that?"

"Do you know a better way?"

Jake laughed and revealed his dentures. "For starters, you stand and lift your hands, palms up as high as you can, like someone is going to pick you up."

"You do that?"

"No," Jake confessed. "It's just what this preacher I know at the Mission does when he prays."

"At the Mission?"

"You'd be surprised. You get some pretty good preachers there."

"And this preacher raises his hands?"

"All the time."

"That's not for me."

Jake shrugged his shoulders as if to say *suit yourself* and proceeded to lift up his hands. "So we's praying to God, right?"

"That's the plan."

"The Almighty?"

"To God in Heaven."

"God in Heaven it is."

It had been a long while since Jake prayed last. So long that he couldn't remember what he prayed about the last time he did. Might have been when he was running from the cops, or maybe when he was so stoned he thought he was going to die. No, not then. He remembered now. The last time he prayed. It was at the accident. The accident. The accident.

"So do we pray out loud or just quiet to ourselves?" Jake asked.

"I usually just pray quietly to myself. 'Course, I've never prayed with someone else before."

"Out loud then?"

"Out loud it is."

Jake rested his head back on his shoulders as if he were tanning. Somewhere, out there, at a place even spacecraft can't reach, was God. Sitting on his throne, maybe. Walking around, somehow able to hear and concentrate on the prayers of millions of people. And that's when Jake froze. *Yeah, right. God in Heaven. The Almighty. He's up there just waiting for me to pray. Probably got all the angels around, maybe even Jesus and Moses and the rest of them. All gathered around to hear me... I don't think so.*

"You first," Jake said lowering his hands and his arms.

"Okay. I'll go first." Lucas cleared his throat. "We're praying to you, God, this morning because we've seen some people get healed and we're thinking...well, I don't know what we're thinking. I've been reading your book and found out that you healed people back then. It seems like you're doing it today, too. I guess we're trying to see if we're supposed to be doing some more of this or if we just go back to what we were doing before."

There was a pause. Jake waited, wondering if Lucas was going to continue. "You finished?"

"Finished."

"That's it?"

"I haven't got anything else to say."

Jake looked up at the ceiling again, thinking that somewhere through it was God, up in the sky some place. He lowered his head. "God in Heaven… I'm calling you that 'cause that's what the preacher at the Mission always calls you. It's been a while since I've talked with you. I'll make this quick. I met this here guy Lucas on the street outside the Mission. He took me into his big house and here we are praying to you. I'm not sure what I'm asking for or if you're even listening. But if you are, if you really can hear me, then I'm just hoping that more of those sick people don't have to stay sick. That's about it. God. Amen."

They both opened their eyes. Jake looked at Lucas as if to say *what happens next?*

"I recite my verses."

"Your verses. The ones from prison?"

"Right."

"Okay. You go ahead. I'll just listen."

Jake listened as Lucas recited the entire passage. It took an hour and a half. Jake imagined the stories as Lucas told them and pretended to be the characters—the ones who got healed and the ones who touched them.

When Lucas was finished they became quiet. A hush fell over them.

"I had this dream last night," Jake said.

"Dream?"

"Yeah." Jake was visibly shaken, as though he had just walked away from what should have been a fatal car crash. "There was you and me and this third guy."

"A third one?"

"And he asked all kinds of questions. Always curious, trying to find stuff out."

"Sounds good."

"Didn't end that way."

"What happened?"

"We were screaming. Well, not screaming exactly. No. No, it was screaming, like pandemonium had broken loose. We were scared."

"The three of us?"

"More than that. The three of us were there, but there were others, too. I just remember how scared I was and that bothered me."

"Why?"

Jake looked up from the ground. Something was wrong. He turned to Lucas. "Because I don't get scared, Lucas."

There was a knock at the front door. It seemed louder than it was because of how quiet they were talking with each other.

"Hang on."

"Forget the door," Jake said.

"I have to see who's there."

Lucas walked to the front. When he was out of earshot Jake spoke again, more to himself than to Lucas. "You don't need what's at the door."

Lucas opened the door and saw a swarm of reporters with microphones and TV cameras.

"Where do your powers come from?" a reporter asked.

"Are you expecting to get paid, Mr. Stephens?" asked another.

"How does Empirico feel about your efforts?" asked another.

There were at least twenty of them. They shouted at him as if he was God, able to hear each person individually. One of them thrust the *Observer* into his face. The front page had a security camera picture from the hospital of Lucas and Jake. The headline read: LUCAS STEPHENS, THE HEALER.

Lucas looked for the name of the writer of the article. It wasn't to find out who had written it, it was to confirm his suspicion that it was a former friend of his. And it was. Tabitha Samos.

He closed the door on the bloodhounds and leaned up against it. Two things bothered him about the article. First, he hated the media attention. Second, Tabitha had lied to him. She had come over not to patch up their relationship, but to verify some facts of the story.

Jake heard the commotion and came over to see what was happening.

"You're famous?"

"We made the front page."

"Me too?"

"You too."

Lucas handed him the paper. Jake was amazed that he had gotten into the papers for something other than crime.

"It's time to decide what to do," Lucas said.

"Meaning?"

"Meaning you either quit this thing now or go forward with me."

"You've already decided?"

"I have to try."

"You're going out there?"

"Not out the front. But I am going out there. I'm gonna see what these hands are really all about. But you have to decide for yourself."

"I'm with you."

"Jake, I have no idea where this is going to lead us."

"That's okay. Do you have a plan?"

"I'm going to use this power to help as many people as I can. And I'm not letting anyone stand in my way."

"I like your attitude."

"Jake, I don't know what I'm pulling you into."

Jake smiled. "It's better than where I've been."

"All right, then."

Lucas changed into blue jeans and T-shirt. They both wore plain, unmarked caps and snuck out the verandah while the media continued to bang on the front door.

"So, where to?" Jake asked.

"I don't know. I'm making this up as I go."

"What about Wrigley Field?"

"Why there?"

"A huge crusade. Like Corvey. Thousands of people."

"What? Just walk in there and say we're having a healing crusade?"

"Sure."

"What if the Cubs are playing?"

"Then we'll watch the game first, Lucas."

"Wrigley Field?"

"Why not?"

Lucas stopped at the back gate of his property. He could hear the faint sound of the reporters still banging the door for his attention.

"Jake, if we go through this gate everything changes for us."

"You're wrong about that, Lucas."

"Why?"

"Because everything has already changed."

26

They didn't make it to Wrigley Field. Their feet wouldn't allow it. They walked as far as Lincoln Park before Jake nearly collapsed.

"We're almost there," Lucas said.

"I'm almost dead," Jake replied. He wanted Wrigley Field. Actually, he wanted to sit down at a restaurant right across from Cubs Park and taste the homemade hamburgers and the ice cold beer. But that would have to wait.

They sat down at a bench in Lincoln Park and observed the flower garden filled with a variety of colors. The grass was freshly cut. Jake took his shoes off and kept his eyes on two women in their early twenties as they jogged past him.

Nearby was a middle-aged man standing on the sidewalk. Dark skin. Thick sunglasses. A cane nearby. He had a perfect view of the park.

Except for the fact that he was blind.

"So who do we look for?" Jake asked as he rubbed his stinking feet. Lucas looked around, trying to find a sick person. "You're just going to walk up to someone and heal them?" Jake asked.

"It's as good a plan as any other."

"Who first?"

Lucas shrugged his shoulders. "I guess we just find someone."

"You found me, didn't you?" the blind man said. He felt his watch and chuckled. "You two are right on time."

Lucas turned to see the man. "What do you mean? Right on time?"

"I knew you two were going to show up."

"Show up?"

"Yes."

"Here? Right at this time?

"That's right."

"And how did you know that?"

"Because I was told so."

"By whom?"

"By a man in my dream. Said you two would be here."

"A man in your dream said that?"

"That's right."

"And what would happen when we got here?" Lucas asked.

"Didn't say exactly. Said you'd help me. Said one of you was really rich. I guess that means you're going to give me the money I need to get a safer place to live. Right?"

Lucas shook his head then realized that wasn't communicating anything to the blind man.

"I don't think I'm here to give you money."

"Yes, you are." The blind man laughed as though he'd heard a good story. "I thought it was foolishness when I woke up. Two guys showing up right at this time. But I came and here you are. And one of you is rich, right?"

"I'm well off," Lucas lied.

"Well, then give me your money."

Lucas looked over at Jake to see what he thought. Jake shrugged his shoulder as if to say: *You're the one with the magic touch.*

"I'm not here to give you money," Lucas said. "I'm here to give you what I got."

"And that is?"

Lucas got up and walked over to the man. "For you to see again."

The blind man became silent, as though he had just been told his wife was dead. He shook his head. "It was so real," he said under his breath as though he was trying to say it in his mind only it ended up getting spoken out loud instead. He picked up his cane and walked away. "I mean it was so real."

"Sir?" Lucas walked after him. "Sir, why are you leaving?"

"You fellows have a nice day." He said that in such an angry tone.

"Sir?"

The blind man turned around. "You fellows go back about your business and don't be talking to me no more."

"What was so real?"

The blind man stopped. He turned his head and for a moment Lucas thought he was actually looking at him. "Don't waste my time. And don't make me feel like an idiot! Someday when you have a health issue and when the money gets tight, maybe you'll realize how desperate you can get."

"I've heard," Lucas said.

"No, you haven't heard anything. When I mean desperate, I mean your mind. It begins to play tricks on you."

"Tricks?"

"Yeah. Weird things. Like guys showing up in your dreams, telling you your problems are gonna get better."

"You don't believe it?"

"I believe it as much as I believe blind people can receive their sight back."

The blind man walked farther away. Lucas called out to him. "Did he get the time right?"

The blind stopped. He dropped his shoulders like he was being given a heavy backpack to carry. "Get what time right?"

"The man in the dream. He told you we'd be here at a certain time. Only we couldn't have known anything about it. Was the time he gave you accurate?"

The blind man nodded to Lucas. "It was right."

"Exactly right?"

"Yes, exactly."

"You say money would make your money problems go away."

"Go figure."

"If you received your sight, couldn't you get a better job and earn the extra money you need?"

"I told you. I don't believe in blind people receiving their sight."

"Then maybe you have more problems than just money."

Jake walked over to Lucas and stood beside him. The blind man walked back to them at a quick pace, as if he was going to whack Lucas with his cane. Instead, he tapped Lucas on the shin and he stopped. "I'm not going to tell you that I don't believe in miracles because I actually do believe in them—that they really can happen. But a man in my position can't go believing things just 'cause people tell them. You do that with everything you hear and you end up in a world of hurt."

"I can only give you what I have," Lucas said.

"And what is that, young man?"

"Well, you see, that's where I have a difficult time explaining it."

"You have five seconds to explain it and if I don't like it, I turn around."

"That's not much time."

"I'm counting," the blind man said.

"I think God heals people through me."

"God?"

"God."

The blind man thought a moment. "You think it was God who talked to me last night in the dream?"

"It wasn't the one from hell, that I'm fairly certain of."

"This is where you start yapping about faith and believing and trusting and stuff."

"I'm not a preacher."

"Neither am I. But that's what you're going to start talking about right?"

"I don't know what those things are."

"Good. Cause I know exactly what they are. I also know I don't have a single one of them. And that, the preachers tell me, means I ain't never getting healed." He began smelling something. "And what is that stink?"

"Those are my feet," Jake said.

"Well, put your shoes back on! There are some nice-smelling flowers around here that are going to die if you don't!" Jake bent down and put his shoes on.

"Well?" the blind man said.

"Well, what?" Jake said.

"What are you doing here?"

"I walked here from Evanston on the way to Wrigley Field," Jake said. "I came here because we're looking for sick people. I'm not asking you to explain faith, forgiveness or whatever else it was you were saying. I just want to know if you want us, well, not me, my buddy here, to pray for you. We can't make you any promises, but we have to know one way or the other. Yes or no. Decide right now. 'Cause if it's no, we're moving on. So, what'll it be?"

Lucas turned his head slightly to see Jake. There was a fire in his eyes and in his voice, too. He had a conviction, a real belief in what he was saying. Lucas was impressed, as impressed as a man gets when he sees someone wearing a smelly pair of shoes and wearing a shirt covered in stains.

The blind man became serious. What were the odds? The man in his dream told him they'd be here and they were there. "I'm taking whatever you got."

Lucas whispered into the blind man's ear and placed his hand on his bare eyes. Lucas quoted some of the verses and prayed to God in Heaven, God Almighty.

"Oh my," the blind man said.

Lucas kept his hands on the blind man's eyes and continued speaking his verses. Jake watched Lucas' lips and studied the expression on the blind man's face. The blind man took in a deep breath and slowly opened his eyes.

"I can't see anything."

"That's because I haven't taken my hands away yet," Lucas replied.

Lucas pulled down his hands and the blind man's eyes grew wide. He began to laugh with excitement. He saw green carpet on the ground, huge brown pillars with green pages on them, small people, big people, fat people, thin people, different colors on people's skins, all walking around talking to each other. There was a flash of colors nearby. All mixed in together. Behind him cars zoomed by.

"Gentle Jesus, meek and mild," gasped the blind man. "That's a car?"

Jake patted the man on the back. "That's a car."

He looked over at the flash of colors. "That's a garden?"

"A flower garden," Lucas replied.

He looked at everything. He was amazed, like a two-year-old on his first trip to the zoo. He looked at a tall oak tree in the park.

"What's that?"

"A tree."

"They get that big?"

He walked to the pathway and shook people's hands at random introducing himself as the man who had just been healed. Then he ran and jumped and shouted as loud as he could. "I'm seeing! I'm looking at things and I'm seeing!"

He left his cane lying on the ground at Jake's feet.

"Now, can we go to Wrigley Field?" Jake asked.

They crossed over from Lincoln Park to Addison, the street that runs by Wrigley Field. The moment Lucas stepped on the street he felt a sudden chill, like a cold draft on a November evening.

"Something wrong?"

Lucas said nothing. He just stood there. There was something strange about Addison.

"Lucas? Is something wrong?"

"Yeah. Something's wrong." Lucas didn't know what it was. Nothing looked wrong, nothing sounded wrong either, but still, it felt wrong. He felt as if he was being led into a trap of sorts.

"It's just jitters."

"You're probably right."

But it wasn't jitters. It was more than that. It was a feeling he couldn't shake.

The blind man had gone to his favorite coffee shop where he normally ordered a café grande with some cinnamon. But this time he had a message for the people inside. At first the customers thought he was a tripped-out lunatic, but then many of them began to recognize him as being the blind man who used to stand at the outskirts of the park. It didn't take long before a call was placed into the *Observer*. Tabitha received a message through her pager. The healer was on the loose.

Again.

A woman in the coffee shop heard the news and ran out to find them. She carried with her a screaming child. She saw two men that matched the description the blind man gave and hurried up to them. "Are you that guy? The one with the healing power?" She had a youthful look about her, probably could have passed for an eighteen-year-old even though she was twenty-five. Lucas could barely hear her above the baby's screams. Practically deafening. A man ran from the direction of the coffee shop to see Lucas and Jake. Within seconds people crowded around Lucas, pushing and shoving to get closer as though he was giving away money. They asked questions like: *Are you the one? How do you do that? Can you heal me?*

The woman with the baby fought to stay in front of Lucas. She looked at him with her tired, bloodshot eyes and gave him her child.

"Can you help me?"

"What's the problem?"

"She screams."

"That's normal for a baby, ma'am."

"She screams every waking minute of the day. She has since she was born."

"You've taken her to the doctor?"

"Three of them. They don't know what's wrong."

"What kind of tests did they run?"

"Whatever the insurance companies allowed."

The woman had needle marks on her arm, no ring on her finger and bags under her eyes. She looked the way people do when they haven't slept properly in a long while. Her head was tilted to the side, as though too heavy to lift up straight.

"What's her name?"

"Damaris. After her mother."

"It's nice to meet you, Damaris."

"I'm not the mother. Damaris was murdered by her husband three weeks ago just before he killed himself."

Lucas felt her pain. "And you're looking after her?"

"Of course. But I sleep exactly three hours a night. I give her to my mom for seven hours a day so I can get to my job. The screaming bothers the whole apartment and the caretaker is threatening to take action if it doesn't stop. Can you help?"

"I know someone who might make a difference."

Great, thought the women. *Another referral to another doctor.*

"I can't explain why, or even how...."

"But?"

Lucas looked at the woman and wondered if she would think he was crazy for the answer he was about to give. "I think God heals people."

"God," said the woman, as though she hadn't heard the name in a long time.

"God."

"Well, whatever. I don't care how you do it, just make her better. Whether it's God or something else makes no difference to me."

Lucas switched the baby to his left arm to give his right ear a break from the screaming. "You have heard about God, haven't you?"

"Oh, yes. When I was twelve years old my momma took me to a church to hear all about God. One day the pastor and my momma went on a date. I never saw them again. Last I heard they were living together in Florida. My dad went to look for her and he never came back either. Yeah. I heard all about God."

"I haven't met that God," Lucas replied.

"That's the only God I know. Now are you going to help me or not?"

Lucas laid his hands on the child. He closed his eyes and began to recite his verses. The screaming changed to a loud cry. The loud cry turned into off and on bursts. And then it was quiet, or as quiet as it gets on Addison in the late afternoon. The mother heard birds singing for the first time in three weeks.

"How did you do that?"

Lucas didn't hear her. The crowd swelled around him like fans on a football field after their team wins the game. They pushed him and grabbed at him shouting for his attention. *I have an aunt who's sick! I have a bad back! My mom's dying!*

"One at a time!" Lucas shouted. Jake pushed out his arms to form a shield around Lucas and held the people back as best he could. Tabitha pulled up in her yellow convertible. She grabbed her camera and hurried out to the crowd.

By then the radio stations had announced that Lucas Stephens was at the corner of Addison and Pine Grove. A marketing executive overheard the radio announcement as she passed by the receptionist's desk. She told the receptionist she suddenly remembered she had a meeting and left the office. She got into her Lexus and drove off to meet the famed miracle worker. Maybe he could help her with her chronic migraines.

A factory worker heard the news, as well. He told his lead hand

and supervisor that he needed some time off work and quickly got into his car. With any luck his son would be home from school and he could take his diabetic boy to see the man from the newspaper.

All over Chicago people found (or invented) excuses to leave work. They hurried down to find the miracle man. They'd heard about him on the news, read about him in the papers. But the sick didn't want third party information. They wanted to see him in person.

They wanted to be well.

Vehicles parked up and down the neighboring streets. A line-up of cars stretched down Addison.

Tabitha came up beside Lucas. He pretended she was not there. He hoped, only for the next few minutes, that she would leave. He didn't want her around. But he would be needing her. Sooner than he thought.

He laid his hands on one person at a time. Each of them came to him with a variety of problems. One with a back problem, one with allergies (the kind that make your eyes water and your nose stuffy), one with arthritis in the left hand and a man in his sixties with hearing trouble. They were all healed. But just when things started to go well, a man with a skin disorder fought his way to Lucas. He was the twentieth person of the day. And he would be the last.

The skin on his face and arms was inflamed to such a degree that it was likely his whole body was covered with the disorder.

When people saw the man they pulled away in horror and hoped it wasn't contagious. The man really was ugly, like he had just walked off the set of a horror movie.

"You're the miracle man?"

Lucas didn't dare move. He was frightened. It looked like the man was dying right in front of him. "I think so."

"You were there when those kids got healed at the hospital, right?"

"I was there."

The man smiled as best he could. His dried face cracked around his mouth as he did so. He nodded, relieved; he had finally found what he was looking for. He lowered his head as though he was embarrassed to look up. "If you're able to do anything for me… I'd do anything in return."

Lucas laid his hands on the man. The warmth traveled through his finger tips into the man's arms. Suddenly, the man's skin began to grow together. The cracks dried up. The roughness left. It was as though a magic cloth had wiped away the sickness to reveal perfectly healthy skin. His skin stopped itching.

After taking his hands off the man's arms Lucas felt exhaustion come over him. Practically debilitating. There's a good kind of tired, like when you finish exercising. But there's a bad kind, too, like when you're struggling at work after getting only two hours of sleep during each of the previous two nights. This was the bad kind. The kind where you feel like you're not even really awake, like you're in a dream and yet you're still supposed to function.

Lucas swayed once to the left. Jake caught him. "You all right, chief?"

He turned his head to Tabitha who had been taking pictures and writing notes. "Get me out of here."

Tabitha didn't hear him. But when she saw the expression on his face she reached out to touch him. "Lucas? Lucas?" But he was already gone. Jake's powerful arms pulled him into Tabitha's car. The crowd pressed on after them. Their arms reached into the car trying to touch Lucas. Tabitha gunned the accelerator and drove off. Jake patted Lucas on the face the way a trainer pats a boxer when he's been knocked out. "Lucas? Lucas, wake up."

But Lucas didn't wake. He lay there, as though in a deep, deep sleep.

27

The TV at the Mount Carmel teacher's lounge carried the 6:00 news. Edgar and a few other professors had gotten together for a cup of coffee to unwind, but Edgar wasn't interested in conversation. He was only interested in the story of the miracle worker in Chicago. The professors tried to involve Edgar in their discussion but his one-word answers told them he had other things on his mind.

When the story ended he walked out of the room without saying goodbye to anyone. He got in to his car and drove off. Although Sheath and Handle, the brass from Mount Carmel, were in the building he left a voice-mail for them telling them he was taking a leave of absence for a few days.

Sheath and Handle normally expected a sit-down meeting before they allowed any kind of absence. But this was no time to play by the rules. This was a different matter entirely.

Edgar did not have time to deal with school policy.

Caesar sat down on a bench at the Empirico property overlooking a pond. The warm, humid air helped him breathe, unlike the cold Chicago winters. He often came to the pond to think through solutions to difficult problems. Being close to nature gave him a clean, refreshing environment to help him evaluate a particular situation. Normally, the pond was his place of peace. But he was not at peace tonight. He had Lucas to worry about.

He saw the news reports about the miracles. There weren't many healings, maybe forty or so in total including the children with cancer. There wasn't anything to be worried about. Still, something was eating away at Caesar. And the longer he sat there the worse it got.

His tired, puffy eyes looked out at the ducks gathered on the shore. He thought it strange that in all his struggles to become rich and have a place to live these ducks, which never worked a tenth of what he did, had food to eat and a place to live. The beautiful trees and flowers did nothing but stand there and yet they were more beautiful than all of his thousand-dollar suits. Above all, they did not have to understand what ulterior motive was driving Lucas Stephens.

Caesar's years of experience had taught him much about business. He gained knowledge of running his company that is only achieved through the struggles and successes of being in charge. But Lucas did not fit any problem he had previously encountered. He was determined to understand Lucas' behavior.

Mike watched Caesar from his office window at the pond. Seeing Caesar there concerned him. The length of time Caesar was spending there concerned him even more.

He joined his boss on the bench. He looked up and saw the stars were out. It was as if someone was poking a hole through the night sky to let the light in from a world outside. Mike didn't look for any ducks around him. He didn't care to. The environment was a waste of time for him. He didn't support the abuse of the world but he was sick of unemployed, left-wing tree huggers lying down in the middle of roads preventing people from getting to work and feeding their families.

"Been out here a long time."

Caesar responded with a slight nod. He was trying to understand if Lucas was a business problem, a personal problem, or both. Maybe he was just overreacting. Maybe Lucas was nothing to be concerned about.

"You saw the news?" Mike asked.

"Yes, I did."

"He's getting a lot of attention."

"Yes, he is."

Mike spotted a mother duck waddling to the water with her

faithful envoy of ducklings behind her. "Dr. Graves postponed his agreement for the leukemia medication."

"There will be other leukemia patients."

"That's what Dr. Graves said. And there are hospitals all over the country that want our product. It's really nothing."

"What's nothing?" Caesar said with such hostility that it made Mike uneasy.

"The healings. They're nothing. It's nothing to worry about." Mike laughed to lighten the mood but it didn't help.

"It's only nothing if he stops healing people."

"What more can he do? Even if he cleans out one ward a day he'll never amount to anything significant."

"You don't think he's anything to be concerned about?"

Mike swallowed. "It would be better if he wasn't around at all. But so what? In spite of what's happened or what could happen, he's no threat. He's no threat." Mike repeated the last line to assure himself that Lucas was not a problem.

It was peanuts. The sales they lost because of Lucas' activities at the leukemia ward amounted to a grain of sand on Empirico's financial beach. And the people healed on Chicago's streets earlier today were nothing. Twenty people today, was that it? And how many of those would need pharmaceuticals? How many of those would need pharmaceuticals from Empirico? There was no financial loss from the street healings. But Caesar wouldn't let it go.

"I think we should keep an eye on Mr. Stephens," Caesar said in a tone more commanding than usual.

"Consider it done."

Mike walked away with an eerie feeling. It was the first time Caesar had not used Lucas' first name.

Lucas stood in the middle of the desert. The hot, blistering sun baked down from above and the equally uncomfortable sand burned beneath him. The dry air burned the inside of his lungs. There wasn't a cloud in the sky. He looked ahead to the point where the land and the sky become the same thing and saw nothing but endless gray. Then he heard it. Behind him. A rumbling, like the sound a train makes when it's off in the distance. The rumbling grew louder. It wasn't sneaking up. It was roaring up to him. Faster and faster. Louder and louder. Like a huge wave that's about to crash down on children playing on the beach. Lucas turned his head to see what was coming.

He awoke and looked into Tabitha's eyes. Her black hair fell down around her soft face. She had a cool cloth in her right hand which she dabbed onto his forehead the way a mother would her sick child. A sudden nervousness came over her.

"Lucas."

"What happened?"

"You blacked out."

Lucas thought about getting up but changed his mind. It felt good to have her with him. There was a beauty about her and not just in her appearance. Any man who saw her could appreciate the way she looked. This was different. There was a warmth in her, a gentle, yet strong compassion that was coming from inside her like a light giving off heat. A compassion that only the people who knew her could appreciate.

"I'm at home?"

She nodded as though they didn't have to say anything in order to communicate. It was as if for a moment the past had been erased, as though they were back in medical school with a clean slate.

Lucas took in a breath and blinked his eyes. The exhaustion that he felt in the healing line had lifted. It was like waking from a Sunday afternoon nap. He sat up next to her and felt the armor falling off his body. He didn't need defenses any more. So he thought. It was like old times. Just the two of them. He reached over and touched her shoulder. "Thank you."

Tabitha stood up. There was an invisible barrier between them and Lucas had crossed it without her being ready. "I have to go."

"Tabitha, you don't have to leave."

"No, I think it's best."

Lucas saw Jake outside at the pool barbecuing hamburgers. Tabitha got to the front door. Lucas called out to her. "Why did you help me?"

She shook her head the way a woman does when she is both angry and in love at the same time. "Why wouldn't I help you?" There was an awkward silence, then she opened the door and walked out without another word. Lucas watched as she got into her yellow Mustang and drove off.

"She likes you!" yelled Jake from behind the smoke of his barbecue.

"I don't think so."

Jake brought in the hamburgers. The smell of garlic and onion filled the room. Lucas realized how hungry he was. Jake had everything ready. The condiments were out. Cold beer. A bag of chips. Plates, too.

"She does, man. Any woman who sits at a man's side taking care of him, that's love."

"How long was I out for?"

"An hour."

"I can't believe that happened."

"You got tired."

"This was more than tired."

Lucas was about to take a bite of his hamburger when Jake stopped him. "You're not going to pray?"

"Are we supposed to?"

Jake shrugged his shoulders. Lucas mumbled something and starting eating.

"It was strange. Blacking out like that with all those people there."

"Strange as in bad?" Jake asked.

"Strange as in it felt like the power left me."

28

Lucas and Jake didn't say much. They munched away on their hamburgers and chips and felt the relaxation that comes with having a full stomach. Jake ate five hamburgers, Lucas three. The cold beer calmed their nerves, maybe too much so, because both of them barely heard the knock at the door. Lucas turned down the volume of the TV.

"Did you hear that?"

"No."

The Cubs game ended. Chicago won. Another knock at the door.

"Go away!" Jake shouted.

Lucas went to open the door. He hoped it would be Tabitha, but when he opened the door no one was there.

"You probably scared off whoever it was," Lucas said.

"You probably took too long in getting there."

Lucas came back to the living room and saw Jake peering through the windows as though looking for an intruder.

"What?"

Jake held up a finger to his mouth for Lucas to be quiet. Lucas approached.

"What?" Lucas whispered.

"There's someone out there," Jake said.

"How do you know?"

"I just know."

They opened the door to the pool area and heard nothing.

"You're sure you saw someone?"

Jake didn't answer. His face was stern. Mean. Like he was going to beat somebody up.

"Whoever you are, you better come out!" Jake was looking for a fight. His fists were clenched.

"Take it easy, Jake. We don't know who this is." But Jake didn't care. He hurried outside to the front of the house without finding anybody. "There's nobody out here," Lucas said.

"Then who knocked at the door?"

"Take it as proof that if anybody's here they mean us no harm."

Jake thrust a finger at Lucas. "Just because they knock, doesn't mean they're nice."

Lucas realized Jake was right. They walked back to the pool and then stopped. There was a rustling in the bush. "Get out of there!" Jake shouted louder than he needed to. They waited a moment without any response. Jake ran up to the bush. "I said get out of there!"

"Jake, wait."

But he didn't. He reached behind the bush, grabbed onto a collar and dragged something out. It was a man. Probably mid- to late thirties, but it was hard to tell under the night sky. The man tripped and fell to the ground. Jake jumped on top of the man like a wrestler, pinning the assailant's face down on the ground and bending his arm behind his back.

"Who are you?" Lucas demanded.

"Get off of me!"

"Who are you?"

Jake lifted the man's head. His glasses were pushed off his face but not broken. Jake was ready to hit him. Lucas stepped closer and bent down.

"You have three seconds to give me your name."

Lucas saw the man was no danger. Dress pants, dress shirt and a sweater hardly matched the attire of a robber. The man tried to catch his breath. Lucas tapped Jake on the shoulder to get him to release the man. Jake waited a moment, wondering if the man would turn on him, then decided to let go.

The man rolled over and sat on the ground. He rotated his shoulder hoping he wasn't hurt. He adjusted his glasses and looked up at Lucas. Jake recognized the man but couldn't remember where he had seen him last. The Mission, maybe?

"My name is Edgar Sardisan."

"A reporter."

"No. I'm not a reporter. I'm a theologian."

"What are you doing here?"

"I heard about you in the news. I wanted to investigate you."

"A reporter."

"No. I tried your front door. There was no answer. I came around to the back. I heard shouting and got scared. I thought about cutting a hole in your roof and getting in that way."

"A hole in my roof?"

"I'm sorry. That was a joke. I'm a teacher at Mount Carmel, not far from Notre Dame."

"A Fighting Irish fan?" Jake asked.

Edgar rotated his shoulder a few more times and thanked God it was not out of place. "Yes. You too?" Jake nodded. Edgar recalled Jake as well, only Edgar's memory was better than Jake's. "The Sheridan Corvey Crusade, right?"

"That's right. You looked familiar."

"You know each other?" Lucas asked.

"We met. Well, briefly," Edgar said.

They introduced each other and shook hands. Odd, Lucas thought, that two men who met at a healing crusade were on his property. "You want to come in?" Lucas offered.

They sat down in the living room. The smell of hamburgers still lingered in the air. Edgar accepted a cup of decaffeinated coffee because he wanted to keep what little hope he had of sleeping alive. He talked about the Sheridan Corvey Crusade, how he had previously been convinced that miracle working was a sham but that now he could see there was something more to it.

"So the professor is here to learn from us?" Jake said with a laugh.

"Something like that."

"We don't have anything to teach," Lucas said.

"Nothing to teach? A boy who was previously unable to walk is now playing on a soccer team. Children in a leukemia ward walk away in perfect health. A crowd of people near Lincoln Park are healed from all sorts of things and you say you have nothing to teach?"

"Exactly."

"How can you say that?"

"Because I don't understand it myself."

"How can you not understand what you're doing?"

Jake grabbed two beers out of the fridge and rejoined them in the living room. Lucas held out his hand expecting to get one from Jake. "These were both for me," Jake said. But Lucas didn't laugh; he just held his hand out and Jake gave him his second bottle.

"So you walk around, lay your hands on people and things just happen?"

"I told you, I don't know."

"Have you always had this power?"

"No."

"When did it start?"

"When I was in prison."

"In China."

"Right."

"And since then, you've had it? The power to heal."

It's been said that more than ninety percent of communication is non-verbal. Lucas had a tough time believing Edgar's reason for visiting him. What Edgar was saying seemed honest enough. He looked like a theologian and he probably *was* interested in healing. But the vibe Lucas was getting didn't match. Something wasn't quite right.

"How did you find me?" Lucas asked.

"You're all over the news. I read Tabitha's article. Nice girl."

"You know Tabitha?" Lucas asked.

"A little. You?"

"We've met."

Jake finished his bottle, his fourth of the night. He tried to resist the urge to get another one but he felt so alone, so insecure without a beer in his hand. He got up to get one more soldier.

"I find it suspicious that a theologian from Notre Dame—"

"I'm not from Notre Dame," Edgar interrupted. It came out more like *if only I could be so lucky to teach at Notre Dame.* His eyes lowered, as if embarrassed about what he would say next. "I teach at Mount Carmel."

"Fine. Mount Carmel. But you're a theologian nonetheless and you come to my house late at night hiding in the bushes."

"I was scared." Edgar felt like the uninvited guest that he was. He put his coffee down and paused a moment. "If you want me to go, I'll go."

"I didn't ask you to come and I'm not asking to leave. I just want to know. Why are you here?"

Edgar took off his glasses. He was used to speaking with people who were pursuing degrees in theology, not with high powered executives and people like Jake.

"I want to join."

Lucas jolted his head back. "Join what?"

"Your team. I want to know how the two of you do what you do."

"It's what he does," Jake said pointing to Lucas. "I'm just the hired help."

Lucas wasn't buying Edgar. His reason for being here was rational but not believable. "We have no plan. No direction. I don't even know Jake's last name."

"Rubenstein."

"I now know his last name. But we really don't know what's going to happen. If anything."

That was fine with Edgar. He didn't need a plan. He just needed to be with them.

"So, I'm in?"

Lucas looked to Jake for his opinion. Jake shrugged his shoulders. He was fine either way.

"You're in."

"Thank you."

And it was that simple. There they were. Just the three of them. Sitting in the living room. Together for the first time.

"Now, back to your time in prison," Edgar said.

"Why do you want to know all this?" Lucas asked.

"Don't you want to understand this power? I mean, the ability to heal... it's been all but extinct."

"You're the theologian. You tell me."

Edgar cleared his throat trying to buy time for an answer. He had studied the Bible since he was able to read. He had received his doctorate at twenty-eight and knew many of the big guns in the theology community. But he did not have an answer as to how the people were being healed.

"Healing isn't very big in the theology community."

"Why not?" Jake asked.

"It's out of the norm."

"What's the norm?" Jake asked. Lucas didn't know either.

"Forget I mentioned it. Healing is seen as a cop-out. As trying to make life easy."

"Healing is a bad thing?" Lucas asked.

"No, not bad. Bad is not the right word. But it's certainly not God's will to heal. At least not that often."

"How do you know that?" Lucas asked.

"You can't possibly believe that God wants to heal everyone."

"I don't know. Doesn't He?"

"This is the problem. You are confusing a theology of God's sovereignty with a theology of his specific will for each person. You are classifying what God did for one person as being normative for everyone."

Lucas looked at Jake. Jake was lost a long time ago.

"I think we should set a ground rule right from the beginning," Lucas said. "What's the last grade you finished, Jake?"

"Ten. Well, nine. I dropped out in grade ten."

"The rule is that you only use words that Jake, and I, can understand."

Edgar felt embarrassed. He didn't mean to exclude Jake from the conversation.

"Of course. I'm sorry. What I'm saying is that God might want to speak to people through their sickness."

"You think that's possible?"

"C. S. Lewis once said that 'God whispers to us in our pleasures, speaks in our conscience, but shouts in our pain: it is His megaphone to rouse a deaf world.'"

"What then? Do I just leave kids sick in a leukemia ward because God wants to talk to them?" Lucas asked.

"That's what I'm here to find out."

Lucas looked at the clock. 1:30.

"All I know is that I memorized these pages from the Bible and this power came. I think those two events are connected. But I don't know for certain."

"Pages from the Bible?" Edgar said sitting up in his chair.

"I think so."

"Which book?"

"I don't know."

"How does it go?" Edgar asked the questions as though inquiring the route to a secret treasure.

"'The first account I composed Theophilus—'"

"Acts," Edgar stood up from his chair as if he had just heard the most important news of his life. "The book of Acts," he said, barely loud enough for the others to hear. "You memorized this book?"

Lucas nodded. "I quoted it as often as I could in prison. Still do."

"And this is what does it?" A confused expression crossed Edgar's face. It almost looked like he was in pain. "This is what gives you the power?"

"I'm telling you for the last time. I don't know."

"You have no degree in theology?"

"No."

"You pray and read the Bible? That's it?"

Jake finished his fifth beer and cut in. "No, we also get out there and do whatever we can."

"But your basis is reading and praying?"

"Is something wrong with that?"

Edgar searched his mind for an answer. "No, I guess not."

"Well, I think there are a ward of kids who used to have leukemia who think it works just fine."

"Evidently," Edgar replied. He felt in a different world. He was in awe, not of Lucas and Jake, but of what he was discovering. "You believe in God?"

"I do," Lucas said.

"And you believe that God has the ability to heal people?"

"Yes, I do." Lucas stood up and wished them both a good evening. "You're welcome to hang out with us. If you can figure out what's going on here I'd be happy to listen."

"Thank you. Can I spend the night?"

"No. You stay outside. In the bushes."

Jake laughed. But Edgar didn't get it. He nodded his head wondering how cold it would get. Lucas shook his head and smiled at Jake before looking at Edgar. "That's a joke."

"Right."

"Down the hall. There are three bedrooms. Pick the one you want."

They went to their respective rooms and tried to salvage what they could from an already short evening. Edgar lay down on his bed and thought about what he was doing. He thought about Sheath and Handle back at Mount Carmel who would no doubt be wondering what had happened to him. He thought about the woman who had been healed at the Corvey Crusade, the one who had left her wheelchair beside him. He thought about the book of Acts, which he had taught for years.

He turned on his night light, pulled out his pocket Bible and turned to chapter one.

29

Lucas, Jake and Edgar met for prayers at 6:00. It was supposed to be 5:00, should have been 5:00, but they were exhausted, especially Lucas who was worried about what happened to him the day before. One moment he was fine, people were being healed and the next moment he was losing energy. It was as if his batteries had been drained right before his eyes.

Jake and Lucas prayed first using short, to-the-point petitions. Nothing complicated. Edgar prayed the longest. On and on and on he went, using words neither Lucas or Jake had ever heard. The two of them exchanged glances of boredom. Long prayers might be effective but they were tough to listen to.

"Wrigley Field?" Jake asked, already tasting the hamburgers at the ball park.

"Why are you so intent on Wrigley Field?" Lucas asked.

"Exposure. If you have people getting healed out there it will be the biggest thing."

"I don't know if that's what we want."

They put on their caps and dressed in jeans—except, of course, for Edgar who couldn't possibly wear anything but his dress pants, dress shirt and sweater. He was like one of those dolls in a store that only comes with one set of clothing.

"What is it that you *do* want, Lucas?" Edgar asked.

Lucas shrugged his shoulders. Being without a plan was a new approach to life for him. And it suited him just fine. Since being released from jail three years before (that was the first time he went to jail, Xaing Xaing was the second time) his life was on a preset course. But Xaing Xaing had changed that, freed him up, and life was becoming more adventurous because of it.

Jake was the first to get to the front door. He glanced out the window. "They're here." *Who's here?* the other two thought. "I've never seen so many at one time." And then they realized what he was talking about.

Lucas looked as well. The entire driveway, more than that—most of the front yard, was filled with reporters.

"We're never getting out of here," Edgar said.

"That's the spirit, Edgar. Stay positive," Jake said, sounding more angry than sarcastic. "We'll take the back door." Jake went to the door leading to the pool area and opened the shades. It was bright outside, no clouds. Reporters were there as well. "They're everywhere."

"Can we take a car?" Edgar asked.

"We'd be followed the whole day," Lucas said.

"You're going to attract a crowd no matter where you go." Edgar sounded less worried about the reporters and more concerned about his friend's safety. "You have to get used to that."

Lucas put his hand on the door handle and prepared himself for the onslaught of questions. He didn't want the spotlight, didn't need it. But it was out there. waiting for him. And it would only get more intense. Anonymity was a thing of the past.

"Are we ready?" Lucas asked. The other two nodded.

Lucas opened the door. The reporters, more than fifty of them, conversed with one another the way reporters do before press conferences. The three stepped out of the house and walked down the stairs. The reporters were so busy talking they didn't even notice them coming. Any second now. One of the reporters would see them and make a mad dash.

They walked past the first few reporters and Lucas saw that it was more than the Chicago media who were present. The national media were present as was the BBC and others from around Europe. The reporters talked with each other and speculated about how a young, multi-millionaire pharmaceutical salesman got the ability to heal.

One thought it was a secret drug. Another thought it was a hypnotic tool to trick people into thinking they were healed and that the symptoms would return as soon as the power wore off.

The three walked past the next cluster of reporters who didn't notice them either. One reporter spoke into his cell phone as Lucas passed by and said the trio had yet to emerge from the house. People looked right at them, but it seemed to Lucas that they were actually looking through them.

Jake leaned over to Lucas to whisper in his ear. "Do you know what's happening?"

"I don't have a clue."

"Do you think we're dead?"

"I guess we'll find out."

They walked to the end of the driveway. It was as if they were in a shopping center and all the reporters were mannequins. Jake and Edgar stopped to look directly at a tall brunette. "Hello?" they both said to her. She made no response. Jake smiled at her. "If you're free later, maybe we can get together?" Jake loved it. Talking to beautiful women without them walking away was fantastic. But Edgar had a different take on the situation. He thought he was in the twilight zone.

"This is freaking me out!" he said, breathing faster. "What's wrong with us? What's happening?"

"Just keep walking," Lucas said as he went to the end of the driveway.

But Edgar stopped. His hands began to tremble. Jake went back to help him.

Lucas reached the end of the driveway. Either there was a strong gust of wind or the gates opened by themselves. Lucas walked through them and saw Tabitha pull up in her yellow convertible. She turned off the engine and checked inside her leather bag to make sure everything she needed was there.

"Tabitha?"

She didn't hear him. Didn't see him either for that matter.

She moved her head and threw her black hair over to the other side. She didn't wear a lot of makeup, didn't have to. White T-shirt and blue jeans. Simple and cool. That's what attracted Lucas to her in the first place. He stepped up to her car and crouched down so that their faces were at the same level.

"I hope we'll get a chance to talk sometime. I mean really talk. No cameras. No people. Not your job, not my job. Just you and me. Maybe like it used to be."

Lucas got out of the way as she opened the door. She had a confidence about her. Not arrogance, that's different. She was sure of herself. Did her job well, handled herself well with people. Lucas needed that. He didn't want to admit it. But he needed her.

"I miss you, Tabitha." She walked away from her car to meet him at the front door when he came out. "I miss you."

She turned into the gates and out of sight. Jake and Edgar came to join him.

"Well, Edgar?" Lucas said.

"Well, what?" Edgar looked like a child who had just come out of their first horror film. "What was that?"

"You tell me," Lucas said.

"I have no idea what that was."

"You see, Edgar? You're going to fit in just fine."

The three got onto a bus headed to Wrigley Field, Edgar still convinced he was having an out of body experience. He didn't say much. He was afraid. He sat in his seat wondering about what he had gotten himself into.

As they traveled down Clark, Jake got up and headed to the door for the next stop. He couldn't wait. It was as if those hamburgers were pulling him in like a fish at the end of a line. He'd have three of them. Beer, too. Lots of it. They'd eat, do interviews for the media. Then they'd go out to center field, no, not center field, they were the big time now! They would go to the pitcher's mound and have huge lineups and cameras.

But Lucas didn't get up. He stayed in his seat. He looked out the window and saw Wrigley Field approaching. *This is it. Get up and get out. They'll come running to you. Everybody. This is it!*

But it wasn't it. Not today, anyway. All he had to do was stand up and walk out there. It was his for the taking.

And yet, there was a hush inside him that made him turn down Wrigley Field. It seemed so stupid. Here was Cubs Park, waiting for them to take over like a house that is about to occupied by new owners.

"Sit down, Jake," Lucas said.

"Believe me. I know when the Wrigley Field stop is."

"Jake. Sit down."

Jake pushed his hands out, palms up, like a magician about to do a magic trick. "This is Wrigley Field, Lucas."

"Jake."

Jake's face became angry. He didn't like being told what to do, especially not by someone half his age. He turned back from the door and sat down across from Lucas. The bus stopped near Wrigley Field, let out some passengers and then continued on.

"Well, there it goes," Jake said. "Wrigley Field. Everybody wave goodbye now."

Jake let out a sigh of frustration. He glanced up at Lucas for an explanation.

"We're not going to Wrigley Field," he said.

Edgar turned his head to Lucas. "So where, then?"

30

They transferred buses and as they continued south of downtown Chicago, Edgar became increasingly nervous. It wasn't the length of the ride that was making him feel uneasy, it was the deteriorating condition of the neighborhood. The streets were getting dirtier. The houses grayer. The people darker. The poverty surrounded him like a pack of wolves ready to attack. For Edgar it was claustrophobia.

For everyone else it was the South Side.

The bus came to a stop. Lucas and Jake got off first. Edgar looked out through a window and nearly choked. "Here?"

The warm air filled Lucas' lungs. Although he was unsure about being in an unknown area he knew this was the place to be. Sometimes a man knows he's in the right spot at the right time. "Here."

It was Edgar's first trip to a black neighborhood and already he hoped it would be his last. He was scared the way people are when they're around things unfamiliar to them. "It's nothing to worry about, Edgar," Jake said.

Edgar stepped off the bus. "Then why is that guy staring at us?" Edgar pointed to a man looking at them from his backyard.

"He won't bite you," Lucas said.

They walked down the sidewalk and Edgar couldn't help but think that he would feel happier driving the area in a car with bulletproof glass. In the distance, down an adjacent street, a baseball game was being played. Little League, no doubt. Chicago had plenty of volunteers from the surrounding neighborhoods and all over Chicago that gave of their time to coach teams.

"Where to, Captain?" Jake said.

Lucas pointed ahead. "The white house."

"The white one it is," Jake replied.

Edgar reached out his hand and grabbed Lucas by the shoulder. "Now, explain that to me. Why are you choosing the white house?"

"I don't have a reason," Lucas said continuing. "It's a hunch."

"You're guessing, then."

Lucas stopped. "It's not arbitrary if that's what you mean."

"Then how do you know you're right?"

"About the white house?"

"Yes."

"I don't."

"Then going there could be a mistake. We could just as easily pick any other house."

"We could. But my conscience tells me to go to the white one."

"Your conscience? That's what you are basing this decision on?"

Lucas scratched his head. "Edgar, I can't prove to you this is the right solution. I could be completely wrong about this."

Edgar evaluated Lucas' answer. "Fair enough. Off to the white house."

Actually, the house was *mostly* white. Some of the paint was peeling, especially around the windows. The grass was overgrown, what little there was, and the chain-linked fence sagged outward, as though kids had been sitting on it. There was a pathway through the grass to the front door on sidewalk pads that were uneven. The three walked up to the door, their shadows stretching out in front of them as if to test the waters to see if everything was safe.

"Okay, Edgar. Knock on the door," Lucas said.

"I'm not knocking on that door."

Lucas frowned at him and knocked. There was no response. Lucas elbowed Edgar in the arm. "You wanted to know what's it's like," Lucas knocked again, "so you're going to find out."

From the back of the house came a low, mean voice, as though someone had already seen them but didn't want to talk to them. "I don't want to buy nothing."

"We're not here to sell anything."

"Then leave." There was a muffled conversation inside the house, then a pause. "Come around to the back," the voice said. But it didn't sound very inviting.

The three walked through the grass, stepping on animal droppings on the way to the back. There was a shed, about the size of a small bedroom and a doghouse. No grass. Lots of flies.

Lucas knocked on the back door. "We're at the back." There was no response. "Hello, we're at the back."

"And don't not one of you put your hands in your pockets or I'll send you where you're going," said the same voice, only this time it was behind them and holding a gun.

The three turned around. Edgar nearly died. He'd never seen a gun in someone's hand before. Hunting rifles, yes. Handguns, no. Of course he'd seen handguns under the counter at stores, but somehow that's not the same as when you're on someone else's property and it's being pointed at your heart.

"We're here to help," Jake said as cool as if the man didn't have a gun.

"Help?" the man said. He was in his late fifties. Taller than average but not that tall that he would stand out much. He wore an undershirt and a pair of black pants. His head was bald and sweaty. He seemed more scared of the gun than they were. "I don't want your help."

From upstairs through the only open window that faced the back came a quiet female voice. "Daddy?"

"Baby, you just go back to sleep. Ain't nobody here."

"Who are you talking to?" The voice sounded as if every word took a great deal of effort to come out of her mouth, much less down to within hearing distance in the backyard.

"Baby, I'll be up in a minute." The man's face appeared meaner when he turned back to the three. He looked desperate. "Now, I ain't asking you. I'm telling you. Get out."

"We're not dealers," Jake said as if he had a direct connection to the man's brain.

"I don't care," the man said.

"My friend is right. We're here to help," Lucas said, hoping the man would put the gun down. Edgar shook so bad, like a brutal case of Parkinson's, that Lucas wondered if he would die of fright.

"What's wrong with the woman upstairs?" Edgar asked and then wished he hadn't said anything.

The man pointed the gun at Edgar. "It don't matter to you."

One pull of the trigger, even if he didn't mean to, and the man could have Edgar dead. He swore at Edgar, telling him he was the man with the gun and they were going to get off his property. Jake saw that the man's hand, the one with the gun, was lowering. "Your gun's slipping. You gotta keep it pointed up." The man looked at Jake. "Actually, keep it pointed on me, these guys ain't so used to it."

"Daddy." The voice sounded so faint now, as if all the energy was spent on her last words. "You leave those men alone. And you let them come up here." It wasn't a request. It was a command.

"Baby, you go back to bed now."

"It's them, Daddy."

The man looked up at the window. Lucas looked, too, but there was no one there.

"It's not. Baby, I told you. That guy lives in a mansion in Evanston. Ain't nobody coming from Evanston to see us." But the more the man looked at Lucas the more he wondered if this was *the* Lucas from TV. Something triggered in his mind. He became frightened. He felt as though his gun were nothing more than a piece of wood in his hand, as though the three standing there had the power to do whatever they wanted and he could do nothing about it.

"I've got six bullets in this gun, that's more than what I need to kill the three of you."

"I'm Lucas Stephens."

The man took a step back. His mouth dropped open and he lowered his gun. "You can't be. It don't work that way. It just don't work that way."

"Your daughter wants us to go see her?" Lucas asked.

"That's right," the man said. He felt as though the President or a famous sports icon had just come to his house.

"I think she would want you to put the gun away, too," Edgar added.

The man hesitated and tried to assure himself that none of them would pull out a piece. He lowered his gun. "Step away from the door."

They moved to the side and the man led the way into his house. They introduced themselves—the man's name was Arthur—and the three declined anything to drink.

To the right was a kitchen with dishes piled up looking like they were about to fall. To the left was a TV and dining room. A table had a half-finished puzzle on it. Down the hall was the front door and the staircase leading upstairs.

"Daddy? Are they coming?"

"Yes, baby." Arthur whispered to the three. "She's not herself anymore. In the middle of the night she sometimes calls out for Jerome."

"Jerome?" Lucas asked.

"Her husband. Or he was supposed to be."

"He took off?"

"When he heard the news that she contracted this virus and that she might never recover he suddenly found someone new." The man pressed his lips together. He tried to calm himself down. "That was twelve days before the wedding." He shook his head. "Now she just lies there like a little baby, hardly able to move. Exhausted all the time."

"Daddy?" The voice was so weak, as though every syllable took all her strength to get out. "It's them, right? The ones from TV?"

"Baby, we'll be right up."

Arthur opened the door to her room. A frail woman lay on the bed next to a window facing the backyard. Early twenties perhaps, but it's always hard to tell when they've lost so much weight. The table next to her had pictures of school children. Get-better-soon-Ms. Parker cards and hand-drawn posters decorated her walls. A bed pan lay beside her, empty. She tilted her head to see them. She closed her eyes and a smile came to her face. She opened her eyes again. "Hello."

"Baby, these are the ones from TV."

"I know, Daddy."

"They gonna talk with you a while, okay?" She nodded and looked like she was going to fall asleep. "You need anything?"

She started to shake her head but then a slight smile came to her face. "I'm still waiting for my strawberry ice cream."

Arthur let out a sigh like a student who walks into a classroom only to be reminded that there is a test that day. "I'm going, baby. This time I ain't forgetting." To the three: "You boys want some'in?"

They didn't and the man went downstairs.

"I'm Lucas."

She smiled. "I know that." Looking to Jake, " I know you, too." When she looked at Edgar she raised one side of her mouth. "But you, I don't."

"I'm Edgar."

"Are you a healer?"

"No. No, I'm... I'm the student here."

"Well, me too, I guess." She adjusted herself on her bed as though something underneath was bothering her. She introduced herself as Dorothy. "So, y'all here to make me better?" Her voice was nothing more than a faint whisper now, as though it was about to cut out all together. Lucas gave no answer. He didn't need to. She saw it in his eyes. She said, "This is the first time I'm talking to a man who's not my dad or my doctor since..." Her voice trailed off as if she was headed somewhere she didn't want to go. "Well, you know how it is. Boys don't want sick girls, I guess."

Downstairs, the man scooped out strawberry ice cream from the plastic container into glass bowl. Beside him, one of the stacked dishes began to slide. He reached over to grab it. As soon as he did that, one of the other dishes fell in the opposite direction. His other hand held the ice cream and he couldn't grab the falling dish in time. A plate slipped off the stack and fell to the floor. He stuck out his foot to cushion the fall and prevented it from breaking. Just when he thought things were under control three bowls slipped off the side and crashed on the yellow tile floor. He cursed at himself for not cleaning the dishes earlier and pushed them over as best he could to prevent more from falling. He scooped more strawberry ice cream into the bowl and passed by the front door on the way to the stairs. A voice from the street called out to him.

"Well, let's go!"

Arthur looked outside. A group of fifteen or so people had gathered at his fence. He opened the door. "What do you people want?"

A fat old man took a cigar out of his mouth. "We hear you got the healer people in there. Bring 'em out."

"I ain't got nothing, you fat pig, now get lost."

"You ain't got nothing?"

"That's right."

"You ain't got nothing in your head, Arthur!" They all laughed.

"You get lost or I'll use you for a bowlin' ball and roll you into next week."

The group laughed again. The fat old man got more serious; he wasn't joking anymore. "You're lying to me, Arthur. I don't like you lying."

"I ain't lying. Now get away from me."

"You know how I know you're lying, Arthur?"

"I don't know and I don't care."

"I know you're lying because your daughter is standing right behind you."

"You're a stupid, fat old man, you know that? My baby's not well." Arthur's voice turned from angry to hurt, as though a gush of pain was released by telling people how badly off his daughter was. "And that's how I know that there ain't nobody behind me!"

Arthur turned around to prove to the fat old man that he was right. But he wasn't right. It was the fat man who was right. And it was Arthur who was wrong.

Dorothy was standing. Nobody was helping her. Arthur looked behind her to see who was holding her up.

"Baby? Baby, are you standing?"

"I'm standing, Daddy. I'm standing."

"You feeling okay?"

"I'm feeling better."

"You see, you dumb old coot," shouted the fat man. "You got them healers in there. Now let 'em out! You ain't the only one with sick people."

Tears came to Arthur's eyes as he touched his daughter's back and arms. It was so out of the ordinary. So unusual. So foreign to everything he had ever experienced before.

"How'd you do that?" Arthur asked. Deep down, though, he knew. He knew that somehow his daughter's prayers had helped. He'd prayed with her as well. But it was one thing for Arthur to ask for a miracle, a different thing entirely to accept it when it was standing in front of him.

Lucas, Jake and Edgar left the house and walked to the people gathered on the street. The number of those gathered was bigger than it had been a few minutes ago; there were about thirty people now. As Lucas began to converse with them, Edgar turned around and went back to the house. Arthur and Dorothy hugged each other.

"How did you know we would be here?" Edgar asked.

Dorothy turned away from her father for a moment. "I'm sorry, Edgar. What did you say?"

"How did you know we would be here?"

Dorothy had a radiance about her. It was as if she was shining. "You're a praying man?"

"Most of the time."

Dorothy smiled and looked at him with the sun reflecting off her face. "Then why don't you understand that I knew you would be here?"

Edgar nodded. "I'm sorry, Dorothy. I'm a little new at this."

The three spent the rest of the day in front of the house. When more healings started it didn't take long for others to hear about it. Crowds of people from the South Side and all over Chicago came to them. Tabitha and other reporters got the news while waiting at Lucas' mansion. Confused, they hurried into their cars and off to Lucas' location and wondered how he got out of the house without any of them seeing him. Within minutes, TV stations were interrupting regularly scheduled programs to bring their viewers live coverage of the healings.

Caesar sucked back on his cigar at his Empirico office. He leaned back in his leather chair with a scowl on his face as he watched his boy, his property, on TV healing people. He let out a puff of smoke and shook his head. The healing of David, the soccer player, was nothing more than amusing. The leukemia healings, however, had embarrassed him. The miracles at Addison and Pine Grove had given him cause to be concerned. Now, the South Side healings were making him angry. *They're poor people,* he tried to convince himself. *They don't have decent insurance and they don't have money for real pharmaceuticals. They don't count.* He tried to convince himself that sick or healthy, the people who got healed didn't affect his financial figures. How could a measly few hundred people matter to his big company?

But then Caesar heard the news report that people from the Loop and all over Chicago were coming to see Lucas. People with the ability to pay for pharmaceuticals were getting a free ride from Lucas. *They should be getting their healing from me.*

A hundred? Five hundred? Caesar convinced himself that even if a thousand got healed it wouldn't hurt Empirico any. With Empirico's market share it would take a lot more to affect their financial strength. Still, the healings bothered Caesar. One of his own was ripping him off. Stealing from under his nose. *How dare Lucas do that. How dare he.*

All across Chicago, people raced out of work, got into their cars and hurried to the South Side. Doctors, engineers, teachers, dental assistants, laborers. They came from all over just to get a chance to be touched by him. The streets became jam-packed. Cars could not travel within a five-block radius of Lucas. People parked as far as ten blocks away just for chance to see him. Thirty police officers tried desperately to keep control of the situation.

Great crowds came to Lucas bringing those afflicted with cancer, AIDS, diabetes, arthritis, those who were blind, deaf, mute and many others and they were all healed.

Edgar and Jake allowed one person through at a time. Lucas touched them, prayed and saw them get well. His mind and his eyes fought with each other to confirm that time and time again a miracle was being performed. He was confused and excited, happy and terrified, all at the same time. He wished moments like this could last a lifetime.

Shouts of joy erupted in the South Side. The rich had come, the poor had come. The old had come, the young had come. But most importantly, the sick had come. They came in sick and walked away healthy.

When evening had come more than fifteen hundred people had been healed from every kind of illness and every kind of disease. Thousands more, however, were still waiting.

As Lucas laid his hands on a small child the crowd suddenly grew strangely quiet. It was as though they weren't there anymore. Jake looked over at Lucas. "You all right, big guy?" But he didn't need an answer. Lucas wasn't all right. He was tired, exhausted. A light-headed feeling had come over him.

"I'm getting that tired feeling again."

"You sure?"

"I have to go," Lucas whispered. "I can't be here any longer."

Jake grabbed Lucas under the arms, trying to be as nonchalant about it as possible. Policemen directed the three to one of their cruisers. Tabitha tried to get to him but her shouts were no match for the sick who desperately wanted to touch him. "Lucas! Lucas" she screamed. But it did no good. Lucas got into the cruiser without hearing her.

The cruiser left the South Side and headed for Evanston.

When the crowds finished celebrating and the reporters had left, the city clean-up crew got to work. The area was littered with papers, drink bottles, wrappers, crutches, bandages and wheelchairs. It took a crew of ten until the next morning to clean it all up. They loaded the wheelchairs onto trucks and wondered if the owners would ever be calling for them.

The three arrived at Lucas' mansion. The police had set up a barricade to prevent reporters and sick people from getting in. After an exhausting day they were home. Away from the crowds. Away from the reporters. Away from the spotlight.

Lucas had regained some of his strength and was looking forward to a hot shower and a pillow. They entered the house and Jake made the comment that he was going to barbecue them a huge hamburger before bed. Edgar was about to say that he wasn't hungry when Lucas stopped mid-stride. A shadow moved behind a wall. They all saw it.

"It's just a surprise party," Lucas said, hoping that's what it was.

He called out to whoever was behind the wall. "Nice try, guys. I'm not fooled this time." His voice cracked a couple of times as he said that. He was hardly convincing.

"When's your birthday?" Jake asked.

Lucas' heart sank. His birthday was months ago.

He turned on the lights. Five strong-looking men wearing balaclavas bolted towards them. Jake hit one of them in the face sending the assailant backwards. Edgar, however, never stood a chance. He was elbowed in the chest with such force that his head snapped back and crashed against the door. He fell to the ground in a daze.

Lucas grabbed one of them by the neck and punched him in the throat. Another masked man over-powered him and drove his head into the banister. He was punched twice in the face, fell to the ground and was kicked in the side. He tried to protect himself but it was to no avail.

Jake got a kick in his big stomach. It knocked the wind clear out of him. He fell to the ground gasping for breath. A heavy punch to the side of his head sent him to the ground unconscious.

The attackers left. The three lay motionless on the ground. The police outside stood their guard, hearing nothing.

31

Lucas was the first to sit up. He rotated his head and felt a throbbing pain in his cheekbone. "You alive, Jake?" No response. "Jake?"

"Yeah, I'm here. What's left of me."

"Edgar? Edgar?"

Jake reached over to Edgar's neck for a pulse and found one. He shook Edgar and woke him up. "Feels like a hangover, doesn't it, Eddie?"

Edgar held his hand to the back of his head. "I wouldn't know. And my name's Edgar."

Jake laughed, then winced in pain. He leaned his head back down and felt the relaxation that comes after a fight is finished. The three of them lay there a few minutes comparing stories of other times when they'd been beaten up. Jake went first, listing off a series of brutal beatings involving chains, knives and guns. He'd been shot twice.

"I was elbowed once," Edgar said. "In the nose. During a basketball game."

"Well, you've gotten the worst of it now, haven't you?" Jake said.

They stood up. Edgar protested that his basketball injury *was* serious, it even needed ice. They entered the kitchen to clean themselves up. Lucas touched his hand to the sore spot on his face and said his verses. But the pain wouldn't go away.

"Are you healing yourself?" Edgar asked.

"Trying to."

"Is it working?"

"Doesn't seem to be."

"Why not?"

"Maybe it's only meant for serious stuff. Cancer, AIDS."

"You're not worried?"

"About?"

"That you've lost it."

"The power to heal?"

"Have you?"

"I'll find out tomorrow, won't I? It's just bruising, Edgar. And we have lots of ice." Lucas threw him a gel pack, but Edgar did not seem relieved.

He closed the freezer door and that's when they all saw it. In bold, red letters, spray-painted across the cabinets was written: STOP IT.

"It's just a threat," Jake said, hoping to lighten the mood. "If they wanted us dead they would have killed us."

It was logical and it comforted Lucas. Somewhat.

Still, he couldn't shake the feeling that he was no longer safe in his own home.

Lucas sat down on his bed and looked at the pictures of his sponsor kids. If it wasn't for their identification listed below he wouldn't have known their names. He tried to memorize them once but the names of those kids from foreign countries were too long to remember. He picked up one of the cards. A boy, maybe ten—yes, ten, he looked at the birthdate—smiled for the camera. He wore a black suit jacket, T-shirt, shorts, but no shoes. The suit jacket was dusty and dated, obviously too big for him. His mother probably made him wear it to make him look as sharp as possible. Having a kid wear a suit jacket without any shoes on his feet didn't make any sense to Lucas. The boy was from Kenya. His name was Mumina. Lucas said a prayer for him. Nothing very long, just for him to get some shoes.

It seemed so dumb, a kid without shoes.

He passed by the bottles of liquor and was determined not to touch them. His caller ID showed that a hundred and forty people had called. He made a mental note to cancel his number, but he would not get around to doing it any time soon. He repeatedly hit the delete button to rid himself of the unwanted messages. When he got to the end he saw two from Tabitha. He pressed the dial button and lifted the receiver. It rang twice.

"Hello?" a soft voice answered.

"Tabitha?"

There was a pause. It was the kind of pause you get on the phone when you're wondering if someone is glad to hear from you or if they're wishing you hadn't called.

"Lucas? Is that you?"

"It's me."

"Thanks for calling back."

She *did* want to talk to him. He could feel it in her voice. He repositioned himself on the bed and looked at the faces of the children ahead of him, Mumina in particular. "What's on your mind?" he said.

"It's not about the paper, Lucas. Don't worry." They both let out a brief laugh before Tabitha continued. "I... I just wanted to call. I didn't have a reason." Tabitha closed her laptop at her wood table in the kitchen of her spotless apartment. She'd finished her story for the day and nursed a cup of herbal tea to help her sleep.

"Sometimes that's the best reason for talking," Lucas said.

There was another pause. Not an awkward one. Sometimes people can wait a long time in a phone conversation without either person saying anything and it still works.

"Lucas? What's happened to you?"

I went to jail, discovered this healing power, quit my job and now walk around like an itinerant miracle worker. "I went to prison, Tab." The line went quiet. Tab. That's what he'd called her in medical school. She liked the name. Her dad called her Tabby. Her mom, Tabitha Jane. It was as if each special person in her life had a special name for her.

"That's where this all started?"

"It seems that way." Lucas took the ice pack off his face and wiggled his cheek muscles. Still sore.

"And now this power operates through you to heal people?"

"I think so. I'm still working on an explanation."

"It's strange."

"How do you mean?"

"It's supernatural. I mean, this is just weird."

"I know."

Tabitha took a sip of her tea. The warmth ran down her throat. It was as if the liquid knew how to reach each of her tense muscles and put them at ease. As she relaxed in her chair she remembered why she had called him in the first place. Yes, it was just to talk, but there was something else that had been bothering her ever since she saw him last. "So can you tell me how you made it out of your house without anyone of us finding out about it?"

"You ever seen the movie *Batman*?"

"Twice. Once with you."

"Right." He remembered now and felt embarrassed for asking her the question. "I have a secret cave where I can get away in my special car."

"Lucas."

"I even have a butler. He keeps the car in top condition."

"Lucas, how did you get out?" There was a tone of worry in her voice.

"I have an underground entrance so I can come and go like a ghost."

"Stop it."

The line went quiet. He didn't want to answer her question. His mind was already having enough trouble dealing with the healings. He didn't have the energy to investigate how he was able to walk past people without them seeing.

"I don't want to talk about it."

"How did you leave your house?"

"Tab."

"Lucas, please. I won't write anything about how you did it. You have my word. I just want to know. How is it possible to have someone leave a house that is surrounded by reporters and not have anyone see it?"

"'Possible?' I'm no longer certain of what that word is supposed to mean."

Tabitha took another sip of her tea. "You know, I had the strangest feeling this morning as I was getting out of my car—when I was parked in front of your house. It felt like you were there. It was almost as though you were talking to me. I know that sounds stupid. But it's how I felt."

"It's not stupid."

"When I got to your gate I looked back because I expected to see you."

"What did you see?"

"That's the strange part. My eyes saw nothing. But it was as though a part of my brain was registering that you really were there. That you were walking away, but still within shouting distance. I wanted to call out. Maybe I should have." She took another sip. She held the tea in her mouth, breathed in and swallowed it. "Forget I said anything. It doesn't make sense."

"You felt it?"

"No. I felt you."

"But you didn't see anything?"

"Nothing. Yet I knew you were there. Don't ask me how. I just did."

"If I could explain it I would tell you."

"I know." She finished her tea and poured herself another cup. "You had a busy day today."

"Had some company when I got back."

"That's good."

"Not these guys."

"No?"

"They wore balaclavas."

"Lucas!"

"They're gone now."

"Were you hurt?"

"I got a good one in the face, nothing serious."

He stretched his face muscles again. It wasn't as serious as he first thought.

"Using ice?"

"Fifteen on. Fifteen off."

"No, no, Lucas. Half hour on. Half hour off."

"It'll be fine."

"It's not going to be fine. Leave it on for half an hour."

"Tab."

"Do you have it on right now?"

"No."

"Lucas. You need it on for a half an hour."

Lucas put the ice pack back on his face. "It's on."

"Leave it there."

"I will."

"Half an hour."

"I will," he said.

"Lucas?"

"I promise."

"You don't know who they were?"

"I have my ideas."

Tabitha crossed her legs on her chair and breathed in the steam from her tea. She thought about the possible identity of the assailants who had attacked Lucas. She took a drink and thought carefully about her answer. Then she volunteered her idea of who was behind the attack. "Empirico?"

Lucas took the ice pack off. His skin was frozen. He checked his watch then put the pack back on again. It hadn't been a half a hour yet. "I'm wondering the same thing, myself."

32

The team met at 5:00 for prayers. Edgar prayed the longest, again, causing Jake to finally cut in. "Why do you pray so long?"

"I don't think God cares how long they are."

"Maybe He doesn't. But I do. Why don't you just get to the point?"

Edgar was tired, a little sore and ready to snap at Jake. He breathed in through his nose to help him calm down and then continued praying.

The three prayed for each other to stay open to where they would be directed that day and, of course, for the sick to be made well. Edgar was becoming more comfortable with the thought of miracles—not because he understood them, he didn't, but because he had seen them. There's a confidence that grows with familiarity. Still, Edgar wondered what Mount Carmel thought of his involvement with a miracle worker. He had been on the news and no doubt Sheath and Handle would be feeling the embarrassment and shame of having one of their professors tied in with a fanatic. He speculated about how long his position there would last.

When they finished praying Lucas glanced at the *Observer* headline: HEALERMANIA HITS SOUTH SIDE. He was about to pick it up when he heard something coming from outside. He listened. There was shouting going on.

Lucas went to the window and saw a mass of people gathered outside the gate of his home. The police were there holding them back. It brought Lucas comfort to know they weren't on his property. It was as though his front yard was a buffer zone giving him the security of knowing they couldn't charge after him. They yelled out from the street. *Lucas! Lucas!* The media were there. So was Tabitha. He knew he had to go out there and see the people. He was *expected* to be out there. More sick people, more healings, more of the same.

For Lucas, the thought of sick people getting healed was amazing and horrifying at the same time. It wasn't like seeing a cold go away. This was entirely different. Cancer, paralysis and all the other kinds of sicknesses that meant the average person was not in control anymore were being cured without a trace of ever having been present.

As he watched the crowd get bigger and as he heard them get louder he wondered how long his healing gift would last. What if it didn't work today? What if he was like a rookie sports figure who storms into the league only to fizzle out and never be heard from again? How long could he keep this up for? He felt as though he had stepped onto a treadmill without any chance of getting off. He'd gotten what could only be compared to a Midas Touch and now he was traveling a road that was leading to an unknown destination.

"You don't have to go out there if you don't want to, boss," Jake said as if he was reading Lucas' mind.

"Yeah, I do."

"Why?"

"You think I can have what I have and sit in front of the TV all day?"

"It's your call."

Lucas closed his eyes. "I know."

"Are you afraid of being attacked again?" Edgar asked.

"Yes."

"Do you know who is after you?"

"I think it may have been Empirico."

Edgar pulled a carton of orange juice out of the fridge and poured himself a glass. "Your company?"

"My former company." Lucas glanced at the crowd again. They

were even louder now. If it weren't for the police the crowd would be banging on the door, maybe smashing windows to get in. "I don't know for sure. It seems logical."

"You think it's because of the healings? In the South Side?" Jake asked.

"I think it's because of all the healings. The leukemia ward. The South Side. I mean, there have been more healed each time. There were hundreds healed yesterday. Now look at what we have today."

"Could be thousands of people out there."

"But that's my point. They're not people. Not to Empirico. They're a market. Like cattle to a rancher. It's money slipping through their fingers."

"It's money slipping through the fingers of all of the pharmaceutical companies."

Lucas swallowed. That feeling of fear was back. It was as though an evil draft of air had washed over them. "But the other companies don't have Caesar Alexander as their president."

He looked at Edgar and Jake. Although they were his teammates in this mission he knew Caesar wasn't after them. Caesar could not have cared less about Jake and Edgar. Lucas looked back at the crowd. *All I have to do is quit and go back to Caesar. Then everything returns to normal.* While working at Empirico Lucas was proud to have a powerful boss like Caesar. Now Lucas was feeling the anxiety of what it meant to go up against him. It was as if Lucas had become Caesar's enemy.

And vice versa, of course.

"You don't want to go out there, do you?" Edgar said.

"No, Edgar. I don't."

"Tired?"

"Yup."

"Scared?"

"Scared, too."

"All set, then?"

"Ready when you are."

They walked to the front door wondering what adventures the day had in store for them. Jake wore his ripped jeans and stained, white T-shirt. Edgar wore his dress pants, dress shirt and sweater.

Lucas wore jeans, black leather shoes and a button-down red shirt. They opened the door and walked down the driveway. No reporters, no people on the property. Thank goodness.

The people outside the gate saw them coming and started screaming. The three were like rock stars taking the stage at a concert. The news cameras caught them and TV programs were interrupted to bring live coverage.

Lucas opened the gate. The crowd went crazy. They filled the entire street as far as Lucas could see in either direction. They were holding signs, shouting, clapping, pushing their way closer to get to him. Thousands were there. Maybe as many as ten thousand had shown up. It felt like a sold-out Blackhawks playoff game to Lucas. Wheelchairs, cameras, people everywhere. Begging for a chance to be touched by him.

And the only thought running through Lucas' mind was that he didn't want to be here.

The crowd screamed so loud that even though Jake was right beside Lucas he had to shout at him to get his attention. "There's no way, Lucas. You won't be able to get to them all," Edgar said.

"Just stick close to me."

One of the people held a poster that read: HEALERMANIA. Lucas spoke with a police officer and explained that one person at a time should be let through. The officer nodded.

Lucas looked out on the crowd and felt compassion for them. There were so many sick people, so many in need of a miraculous touch. It weighed on him that he had no chance of reaching even half of them. Lucas and Edgar stood right beside him, as did five million TV viewers.

A man with a skin disorder came to Lucas. His face and hands were completely deformed. Jake and Edgar pulled back. The man stood before Lucas and fought to hold back tears. He was a disgusting mess. "I've been praying for years to be healed," he began.

"Not much has happened for you."

"No. I understand that God can do everything. And I know He has the ability to heal me." The crowd became restless and shouted at Lucas to hurry up with the man. "But," the man continued, "is He really willing to heal me?"

Lucas thought back to the beatings he got in prison. He recalled how the tall guard had nearly killed him as he hung hand-cuffed in that dimly-lit room. Had God been willing to help him then? If so, where had He been? Why hadn't He stopped the guards from beating him? He thought back to the incident with Tabitha in medical school. Where was God then? Now, here was a sick man wondering if God wanted him well.

Lucas placed his hands on the man's neck and felt his bubbling and scaling skin. He prayed and hoped there wouldn't be more people like him in the crowd. The skin around his neck felt softer. Lucas felt the bubbling disappearing underneath his hands. People around him gasped in amazement. The healing spread around the man's body turning the rest of his skin to normal.

The reporters hounded the healed man like he was a survivor of a plane crash. But the man didn't pay attention to them. He looked up at the sky as though he were trying to find someone. He stretched out his arms and closed his eyes. It felt so good, so unusual, to be without pain. He leaned his head back and felt relief as the sun shone down on him.

Next came a man in his mid-twenties. He had an eye illness that he had carried with him for six years. He picked up an infection during a stressful university exam period that left his nose chronically stuffed and his eyes a perpetual bloodshot red. He had seen seven doctors on fourteen occasions, had undergone surgery, spent a small fortune on medications, had attended more than fifty healing services and knew the miracle stories of the Bible better than Lucas. And he was still sick. He congratulated Lucas on an incredible ministry and related his story.

"You're very persistent," Lucas said.

"Sometimes you have to keep after the judge to get justice."

"But does the judge always give justice?" It wasn't rhetorical. Lucas really didn't know.

"I know he always wants to. Whether it always happens, I can't say."

"Me neither."

Lucas laid his hands on the man's eyes and felt a faint surge of electricity. When he took his hands away he noticed there had been no recovery.

The man blinked a few times. "It didn't work," he said.

The crowd grew fierce the way a packed stadium gets when their starting quarterback has a bad game.

"Go and show your doctor," Lucas said as though a voice inside him had prompted him to do so. The man turned away dejected and passed by the reporters. Once again his hopes of recovery were smashed. He got into his car and drove off to see his doctor. He tried not to lose hope, but still he felt the way people do when they've exhausted every possible option without getting any results. He was about to put on his sunglasses when he caught a glimpse of his face in the rear view mirror. He put his foot on the brake and looked simultaneously at the road and at his reflection. His car came to a stop. It didn't matter to him that he was in the middle lane of a three lane street. Didn't matter to him that traffic was backing up behind him. Didn't even matter when people started honking and shouting at him to get going. What mattered to him was that he could breathe perfectly through his nose and that his eyes were crystal clear. He stayed there, admiring himself in the mirror. Cars honked ferociously at him. He closed his eyes and then reopened them. He laughed. He looked away again to make sure it wasn't a fluke. He hit the retract button on his sunroof and looked at the mirror again. Side to side he moved his head and saw the perfect whites of his eyes. He smiled. Then he laughed again. He gave a shout through the sunroof. Finally. Finally, he had gotten his healing. He had been to the harbor on more than sixty-five occasions.

This time his ship had come in.

Jake cut in after another person got healed. He grabbed Lucas hard by the shoulder and turned him away from the camera. "Lucas, you have to speed it up."

"I can't."

"Well, you're going to have to try!" His face became red with anger.

"I am trying."

"Then try harder! Forget the twenty questions with everybody."

"I think it's important to listen to people. I don't want to treat them like a number. Like some file."

"No one is saying you have to. But why should a few hundred get to share their stories when thousands more are waiting?"

Now, more than ever, Lucas wanted out. How fair is it to have a gift that can't be accessed by everyone who needs it? He wanted to sit by the pool in his house. Have five, maybe ten people come by in an afternoon, see them get healed and go back to watching the Cubs games or working on his stock portfolio. So many people begging for his attention. And he wouldn't get them. Not all of them.

Not by a long shot.

The smoke from Caesar's cigar piled up in the ceiling. He was preparing a sales strategy and felt encouraged by the progress his company was making. But his good mood became sour when he turned on the news. There, again, was Lucas healing all kinds of people. He turned it off in disgust and looked at the *Chicago Observer* on his desk. Lucas was on the cover. Caesar skimmed the article and read about the people who had been healed so far. Day one—a boy, the son of a hot dog vendor, healed of paralysis. Day two—thirteen children in a leukemia ward. Day three—South Side Chicago, hundreds. And today, maybe thousands. The trend was growing. And as far as Caesar was concerned it was growing in the wrong direction. Caesar swore quietly under his breath. Caesar then cursed so loud that Anne could hear it at her reception desk. He threw the paper at the wall. Then he got up and clenched his jaw. He walked over to the paper and spit on Lucas' face.

Caesar called Mike into his office. Mike entered and nearly choked on the cloud of smoke.

"Things are not improving with Mr. Stephens," Caesar said. His face was red. His breathing grew louder.

"Should we meet with the Council?"

"No. Not yet. I have another idea. You're Lucas' friend?"

Mike nodded and wondered what he was getting himself into.

When evening came the crowd outside Lucas' home grew more and more impatient. It was as if the sinking sun was an indication of the chances they had of getting healed. The gathering was effective for the two thousand, eight hundred people who were fortunate enough to be prayed for by Lucas, but hopelessly impractical for the remaining thousands who had not and would not, get through.

The crowd pushed harder and harder against the wall of security bars. The police tried to hold the crowd back but pandemonium had broken loose. A section of the barricade collapsed and the people rushed through to be touched by Lucas. The crowd pressed against Lucas to such an extent that they almost crushed him.

Tabitha shouted at Lucas to get back onto the property. The two of them, plus Edgar, Jake and two officers, made it onto the driveway. Lucas closed the gate.

"They're going to come over the wall," one of the officers said.

And they did. Like spiders, people started climbing onto the iron fence, trying to jump over. "Let's move it!" the officer shouted. They ran down the driveway. Lucas glanced over his shoulders. It wasn't a group of people seeking healing who were after him. It was a mob.

The crowd shouted at him to get back and heal them. The officer barked an instruction into his radio. All Lucas could hear were screams. Edgar was more scared now than when Arthur from the South Side had pointed a gun at him. Lucas ran to the front door, but the officer told him not to go in. "They'll come through the windows," he said. And that's when they all felt as scared as Edgar.

They hurried to the back of the property and exited through a gate onto a pathway. Two police cruisers arrived for them. They were about to get in when Lucas saw a man running towards them from the opposite direction. He carried something in his arms. When he got closer Lucas saw that it was a teenage girl.

"Hang on," he said.

"I don't think that would be wise, Mr. Stephens," the officer said.

"Just wait."

Jake and Edgar got into the first cruiser. The screams were getting closer. It wouldn't take the crowd long to figure out where they had gone. Lucas was worried, wishing the man hadn't shown up.

The man ran up to the cruiser. He collapsed in front of it completely exhausted.

"Please. Help my daughter," he said.

He was a stockbroker and a successful one. He had more than a million dollars in the market before his daughter got sick. Since then he had spent everything he had to make her well. His last bit of money was used to buy plane tickets from Flagstaff to Chicago. This was his last chance.

The girl's curly brown hair hid the left side of her face. She was thin, almost as though she had a bad case of anorexia. Her joints were out of place. Her tongue hung partially out of her mouth.

"She has Huntington's disease. It's—"

"I know what it is," Lucas said.

The crowd grew closer.

Lucas bent down and kissed her on the cheek. Her skin felt cold and sweaty. He whispered "God loves you" in her ear and then placed his hands on the sides of her neck. He looked up and saw that the evening sky had turned out its first star. Part of him wanted to make a wish just then. A wish that this would be the last person he would have to heal. No more crowds. No more healings. But he didn't make that wish. Instead, he prayed. A jolt ran through his fingers and flowed into her body. The power went through him at the threshold between pain and pleasure. The girl opened her eyes. She retracted her tongue into her mouth. Although her body still looked malnourished her face was suddenly full of life. It was as though someone had turned a light on inside of her. She smiled slightly the way a child would when they are given a kiss good night.

The crowd grew closer.

"Thank you," the man said.

"I'm not the one you should be thanking."

The man reached inside his shirt and pulled out a gold medal. "I won this in the Olympics years ago."

"I can't. I have to go."

The man took it off and gave it to Lucas.

The screams were even louder now. The people were all over his property, like enemy soldiers searching out his hiding spot.

"My wife's family has a tradition that says you exchange gifts with someone when they have gone out of their way to help you. I want you to wear this. As a thank you."

Instead of arguing, Lucas took it and ran to the car. He remembered hearing the man say the word "exchange" so he took off his watch. It was expensive but Lucas didn't care. He had to get out of there. He threw it at the man. "Here."

"But you've already given me my gift," the man said.

Lucas had no time to respond. The crowd found the gate and ran after him. The first cruiser raced away. Lucas jumped into the second cruiser. It took off with the door still open. Some of the crowd managed to keep up for a moment and banged on the back of the car. He sat next to Tabitha, her heart pounding like everyone else's. In a moment the house was far behind them, though the screams continued in their ears.

The police cruiser took them to the Palmer House Hilton. Tabitha got out first and reserved three rooms. With the help of a hotel security officer they opened a side door and let the three in. They hurried up the stairs. Jake and Edgar collapsed in their rooms as Tabitha took Lucas to his. She opened the door. Her cell phone rang.

"Tabitha Samos... No, No I have no idea where they are... Bye." She entered the room.

"How long will it be before they find us?" Lucas asked.

"Nobody knows you're here."

"They'll find us." There was panic in his voice. Fear. Real fear. He breathed in and out trying to get his breath but it wasn't helping. Tabitha pulled the plastic liner from the garbage can and gave it to him.

"Breathe into this."

He shook his head because he was unable to say anything. His breathing was out of control. Faster and faster; it was as though he was running only he wasn't getting anywhere.

"Take it," she said sounding more commanding.

He took the bag and formed a seal around his mouth. He breathed in and out a few times and within seconds the carbon dioxide level in his blood increased to normal levels. He began to feel better. He took the bag off and slumped down in a chair the way sick people do when they've just finished vomiting. Tabitha sat on the bed next to him.

"What have you gotten yourself into, Lucas?"

He didn't answer. The screams of those people chasing after him kept ringing in his brain like the sound of a guilty verdict in the mind of the defendant.

"They climbed over walls," he finally said.

"You need some rest."

"Over the walls."

He leaned his head back. Tabitha brought him a glass of water. He looked at it but didn't take it. "Drink it," she demanded. Lucas shook his head. She reached for his jaw and poured the water into his mouth.

"You're exhausted and dehydrated. Now take it."

He did. Not because he wanted to, but because she told him to. That wooziness was back. The same kind he felt in the South Side. This time it was more debilitating, as though the strength was being completely sapped out of him. He finished his glass of water, got out of his chair and fell into bed.

Tabitha looked at him lying on the bed. He was already asleep. She wanted to build a wall around him to shield him from having anybody find him. He seemed so helpless. So in need of protection. She closed the door behind her wondering if she should have called a doctor.

Lucas felt himself drifting off into a deep slumber. Panic gripped his mind. *They'll get me. They'll track me down. They'll find me. And then they'll finish me off.*

He fell asleep wishing he had never found those pages in prison, never discovered the healing ability and never touched that guard whose chest had been full of holes. He wanted desperately to turn the clock back—to get out of his life. Like the time in the Cage, Lucas again wished for rescuing. But this time he had the feeling that it might not come.

33

Tabitha knocked on Lucas' door the next morning. He hadn't moved since the night before when he had fallen asleep in his clothes. She had the spare key and opened the door. "Lucas?"

He opened his eyes. She brought him some water.

"Don't argue this time," she said. And he didn't. He looked around as though he was trying to figure out where he was.

"The whole city is wondering where you are," she said. Lucas took a drink. "Your friend Mike called me. He wants to know where you are. I told him I didn't know."

"Mike?" Lucas said as he began to recall the near disaster at his home last night. He had slept for ten hours. Still, he didn't feel refreshed, more exhausted if anything.

"He wants to have the three of you over for dinner tonight."

"You should come too," Lucas said.

"I wasn't invited."

"I'm sure Mike wanted you there as well."

"I don't think so."

"But I want you there."

"Why are you even going?"

A knock at the door. Tabitha checked through the peephole and saw it was Edgar and Jake. She opened the door. They were shocked to see her.

"I just got here," she said. But neither of them knew what to believe.

Jake saw Lucas in bed. "How you doing, guy?"

Lucas looked up at them and finished his glass of water. "Should we have supper with people who hate us?"

Empirico offered to send a limo to pick them up but Lucas turned the notion down (though Jake liked the thought of it). It wasn't about the limousine anyway. If they arrived in an Empirico limousine it would show they were dependent on them. If they arrived themselves, even if they had to go by foot, it showed they didn't need Empirico's help. It was a game, really. And because Lucas wasn't sure why Caesar had called the meeting he decided to get there on his own. Tabitha called a limo company to arrange a pickup for 7:00.

Shortly before then she arrived back at the Palmer House Hilton with three tuxes and her new dress, all paid for by Lucas. Lucas put on his tux with a Mandarin collar. He glanced in the mirror and noticed how similar he looked to the time he wore the blue suit after being released from Xiang Xiang. Lucas waited in Jake's room until Tabitha was finished getting ready in his room. She phoned him to tell him she was all set to go and he came to see her.

She opened the door. When Lucas saw her he felt a rush of helplessness come over him. Although she didn't know it, she had that power over him. She wore an off-the-shoulder black dress that extended to mid-calf length. Her hair was tied behind her with a curl coming down in front of each ear. She wore flat black shoes and a faint trace of a perfume. She fit perfectly into that dress. But it wasn't her appearance that got to Lucas. It was the look in her eye, the sound of her voice, the smile that she gave him—all the things a woman can do regardless of her size. In an instant she had conveyed what every man wants in a woman—someone who likes being with him. Someone who admires him. Someone who feels comfortable and free to be themselves and not someone else.

"I'm too nervous to say anything," Lucas said.

"Quiet, you. Are the others ready?"

"Yeah." He was in a daze. "They're ready."

"Well?"

"You look great, Tabitha."

"I meant, how are you feeling?"

"Better."

Tabitha walked past him into the hallway. "I'll check to make sure it's safe downstairs." She went down the stairwell and Lucas knocked on Jake and Edgar's doors. They came out wearing their tuxes. Edgar looked good in it, as though he had a touch of chivalry behind that studious look. Jake, however, looked uncomfortable. His shirt barely closed around his barrel chest. His pants were oversized to accommodate for his huge stomach. "This is stupid," Jake said, messing with his jacket the way a kid does when he hates the dress clothes he's wearing.

"You don't have to wear it, Jake," Lucas said.

"I don't have a choice now. My jeans are drying out in the bathroom."

Tabitha opened the door from the stairwell. "Let's go."

The three followed her. Jake watched Tabitha hurry down the stairs and whispered to Lucas. "You got one like her for me, too?"

When they arrived at Empirico, Thatcher and Ridley met them at the front entrance. They patted them down as a security precaution, something Tabitha did not appreciate, and led the way through a security door down a hallway. They said nothing. Thatcher and Ridley were not gifted conversationalists. Their shoes echoed on the black marble floor until they reached another door. Thatcher opened it and the four walked through. "Up the stairs," Ridley said.

They walked up a spiraling glass staircase to a mezzanine floor overlooking the property. The secluded area was enclosed by one-way windows. There were skylights above them and a fireplace off to the left. To the right was a long black table with tall black chairs and white table cloths and napkins. The floor was a soft-colored, wide strip hardwood. The lights were turned down leaving it bright enough to let them see across to the other side. Jazz could be heard playing through speakers.

At the far corner of the room Caesar and Mike turned from their view of the park as though they hadn't been expecting them so soon.

Caesar wore a tuxedo—white jacket, black pants and a white bow tie. Mike wore a black tux with a Chinese Mandarin collar and a shirt without a tie. It scared Lucas how similar they looked.

"Welcome here," Caesar said, his voice was muffled by the cigars he had been smoking that day. He and Mike walked toward them. They all shook hands and introduced each other. Caesar's handshake felt different to Lucas, it was harder, firmer—it almost hurt him. Caesar looked briefly into Lucas' eyes and then looked away, the way friends avoid eye contact when there's been a problem.

"Please, sit down," Caesar said motioning to the table.

They seated themselves at the table, Caesar at one end, Lucas at the other. Tabitha and Mike sat together on one side (it felt pre-arranged to Lucas), Edgar and Jake on the other. Waiters in white jackets appeared offering white and red wine. They brought out appetizers—a combination plate of steamed salmon, carrot soup and lake trout.

Caesar, Mike and Tabitha starting eating as soon as the food arrived. Lucas, Jake and Edgar bowed their heads for a short prayer. Caesar noticed but didn't care.

"It's a pleasure to have such famous people with us," Caesar said, lifting his glass. The others did the same. "To health," he said and they took a drink. Jake finished his entire glass. As he put it down a waiter filled it immediately. Jake smiled. Heaven.

"It's good to see you again, Caesar. And it's nice to be invited to have dinner with you and Mike," Lucas said.

"Wait 'till you see what the chef has prepared. It sounds fantastic. Though I must confess I couldn't pronounce it." They all laughed. Normally, it would have put Lucas at ease but tonight he had deep reservations about Caesar. He was fairly certain that Caesar had sent the attackers to his home; maybe Thatcher and Ridley were part of it. And behind the good food and the expensive wine was a catch. He was, after all, with Caesar.

There was always a catch.

When the meal and the small talk were finished the dessert came out, along with a new sweet wine. There was an assortment of cakes and puddings to choose from. Jake chose three.

"So tell me. How does this healing ability work?" Caesar asked, as if it was something he might be interesting in bidding on if the price was right.

"That's a good question," Lucas began. He wasn't sure how to finish his thought.

"Did it start in prison?" Mike asked, not looking up from his double chocolate cake.

"Yes."

"And after prison you began healing people right here in Chicago," Caesar said. He had lost interest in his fried bananas and ice cream and focused his attention on Lucas. He folded his hands in the form of a steeple in front of him as though evaluating Lucas.

"First," Jake began in between bites of his desserts. He clutched his fork like a hammer in his left hand and shoveled food into his mouth. "He nearly ran me over."

Lucas laughed. No one else understood what was so funny. Caesar kept his focus on Lucas. It felt to Lucas as though Caesar was trying to read his mind. "And this power takes sickness away?"

Tabitha took a sip of her coffee. She looked at Caesar and wondered what was wrong with his tired, pink eyes. "Numerous medical doctors have documented the healings—paralysis, cancer, AIDS, diabetes... hundreds."

"Thousands, actually," Caesar said, as though he'd been waiting to get the number out. "Depending on the source, it's estimated that more than four thousand people have been healed. That's a lot."

Lucas wasn't sure if *a lot* was referring to the number of people healed or the number of pharmaceutical drugs that would no longer be needed. "It is," was all he could say in reply.

"And so how does this all happen?"

Edgar cleared his throat. "We get up in the morning. We pray—sometimes for two hours straight." Jake wanted to cut in and say that when Edgar prayed it felt more like ten hours but he continued working on his desserts, loosening his belt to make room for his expanding gut.

"Then we get out there and do what needs to get done," Lucas said.

"So you do whatever it takes to accomplish your goals?" Caesar said it innocently enough, but the meaning behind the words carried a lot of weight. Everyone stopped eating. No one knew how to respond. Lucas looked across the table at Caesar whose face was full of arrogance and determination. It was as if they were having a blinking contest. Caesar's eyes, partially hidden by the puffy pink around them, looked like they were going to burst out of his skull and attack Lucas.

"We don't really have goals, Caesar," Edgar said trying to calm the mood.

"No goals? A man without goals is a failure waiting to happen. You have to have goals."

Lucas glanced around the elegant room. For a split second he felt a tinge, a nudge that reminded him that his old life was just within arm's reach. The power, the women, the money. It was all here for him, waiting to be put on like a favorite jacket.

"When things settle down, if they settle down, maybe we'll get to goals. Until then we just keep going," Lucas said.

"It seems like more and more people are getting healed every day. There must be a limit?"

"If there is, I'm sure we'll find out."

"Well, it's exciting to say the least," lied Caesar, and everyone knew it.

The waiters cleared away the dessert, asked if anyone wanted something more to drink (Jake wanted another glass of red wine), then went back through a door to the kitchen. The four thanked the waiters. Caesar and Mike didn't acknowledge their servers the entire evening.

Caesar leaned forward, blinking his tired eyes. "There's something on my mind that I wanted to share."

Here it comes, they all thought. *We've been wondering when you were going to drop the bomb.*

And then it came. Right out of the air. Exploding right around them. Caesar looked each of them briefly in the eye and said, "I want the four of you to work for me at Empirico."

34

The group froze at Caesar's job offer. They were expecting something out of the ordinary but not this. Lucas immediately thought it was a trap. Tabitha thought about the huge increase in pay. Edgar wondered what possible services a theologian could offer a pharmaceutical company. Jake almost laughed. An ex-biker at Empirico. As what? Security?

"I wondered how that would go over," Caesar said. A waiter came to him with a small wooden box. He opened it, revealing an assortment of cigars. Caesar studied the selection and took one out. The waiter clipped the end. Caesar put the cigar in his mouth and the waiter lit it. He sucked back on it and let out a big puff of smoke. The waiter offered cigars to the others. Only Jake accepted.

"What exactly did you have in mind?" Lucas asked. He wasn't interested in the offer. At least not at first. He asked the question to feign interest. That way when he said no it would seem as if he had thought it over.

"Let me give it to you briefly here, then we can go for a walk and think it over. Take in the beautiful night air." He waved his cigar and managed a smile. "There's no point to Empirico being involved in countries that don't make economic sense. We do some humanitarian work in third world countries and we've thought about increasing our efforts. Take Zambia, for instance. The masses there can't afford medicine. With your healing powers, Lucas, you and your team could help them. With our financial powers you would have the security and the backing you need to get the job done without having people attack you. Tabitha could be able to cover the stories and give Empirico a better image."

He leaned his elbows on the table and pulled his cigar close to his mouth. The end turned fiery red when he inhaled. *It looks just like his eyes*, Lucas thought. Caesar exhaled across the table as though he was breathing out venom. Tabitha coughed. She hated smoke. "And I think when we combine our efforts we'll both be pleased with the results."

A number of stars shone down on the Empirico property and a soft breeze was barely noticeable. Caesar and Lucas walked along the pathway in the wooded area ahead of the group. Within a few minutes they had lost them completely. This was Caesar's intention and it made Lucas wonder about what Caesar would say.

"Lucas, I'm confused."

"What about?"

"A lot can be said about a man based on the company he keeps. When I look at your friends I am concerned for you. A drunken bum and a stuffy academic. They're not you, Lucas. Why are you with them, exactly?"

They walked slowly. It was all Caesar could manage.

"It's just the way that it's worked out. Life's taken me down a different path than the one I had prepared for myself."

"I can see that." Caesar took the cigar out of his mouth and let out a puff. The smoke didn't seem to fit with the night air. He turned and looked at Lucas. "But is it the right path?"

Lucas glanced at the stars as if the answer was somehow encoded in the firmament above. "How does anyone really know for sure that they are on the right path?"

As Tabitha and Mike walked along he offered her his jacket to protect her from the cool evening. She put it on and kept hoping she would hear Caesar and Lucas' voices ahead or Edgar and Jake's voices behind. But she heard nothing except the sound of their own feet on the pathway getting farther away from the complex.

"What's it like covering the healings?" Mike asked.

"It's different. You watch as the sick people, I mean really sick people, go up there for a healing and in your mind you think this can't possibly happen. But it does."

"That's incredible."

"If you go to cover a sports event it may or may not be interesting. If you attend a press conference that, too, might be a total waste of time. But every healing event is something different."

Mike nodded, waiting for her to finish her answer so he could rifle off his next question. "How do you enjoy your work at the *Observer*?"

"Covering this story is interesting. It's what we as reporters live for. How about your work?"

He moved closer to her as though he wanted to wrap his arm around her waist. Tabitha re-adjusted the jacket on her shoulders to ward him off. Where were the others?

"My work is good. Empirico is a good company, you know. You'd be paid well if you came on board."

"You think Empirico needs a reporter?"

"Not just *a* reporter. We need a *good* reporter. Someone with experience who cares about the job. Someone who can act as a spokesman, spokesperson, for the company on matters of supernatural healing. You'd look good in front of a camera."

Normally, flattery made Tabitha feel good in a shy kind of way. But under the stars, on a dark path, away from the others, coming from someone she hardly knew, it sounded like a decoy. It was as though he was using it for ulterior purposes.

And, of course, he was.

Edgar and Jake stood on a small bridge crossing a creek. They had lost the group a while ago and gave up trying to find them. Jake clutched a beer bottle in his hand, leaned on the railing and listened as the slow-moving water passed by them. *Money buys a lot of things,* Jake thought and wondered how much they would offer him.

"What do you figure?" Jake asked.

"You think the offer applies to us?"

"Of course it does."

"But only because we're part of the team. He doesn't want us. Doesn't even want Tabitha. He wants Lucas."

"Could you quit your job teaching?"

"At Mount Carmel?" Edgar shrugged his shoulders. Now that he was away from the campus for a while he didn't feel as attached to it. It was like having a friend move away and only then realizing they didn't mean as much as you thought. "I guess I could."

"But if you don't take Caesar's offer then you'd have to go back? I mean, you do teach there, don't you?"

"I do. I'll have to go back. Sometime soon."

Jake imagined what it might be like having money. He'd buy a house. A nice car, too. He shook his head, realizing it was probably just wishful thinking. "So. Are you learning?"

"Learning?"

"You said you wanted to join the team to learn about what Lucas did."

"I think I am. I'm not sure."

Jake finished his beer bottle and wished he had taken two along. "You really left your teaching position?"

"Yes."

"To hang with us?"

"Who wouldn't?"

"A teacher of theology wouldn't, that's who," Jake said this making eye contact with Edgar. They stared at each other. The only sound was the creek beneath them. The water seemed louder the way quiet things do when you spend enough time around them.

"I'm not sure what you're getting at."

"You left. Just like that? You upped and walked out of your teaching job to come join us. People get fired for stuff like that, you know?"

"I realize that."

"But you came anyway."

"Yes. I thought it would be good for the students to gain an insight into how, or if, the spiritual world and the physical world are connected in terms of healing."

"What?"

"Oscar Wilde said 'the separation of spirit from matter was a mystery and the union of spirit with matter was a mystery also.'"

"So you came here...?"

"To gain insight."

"I don't buy it," Jake said shaking his head.

"Pardon?"

"I don't believe you, Edgar."

"You don't believe me?"

"That's right, Edgar. I think you're standing on this bridge, looking me in the eye and lying to me."

"The path you're on right now, Lucas, is causing me a lot of concern." They stopped and sat down on a bench. Caesar didn't want any more of his cigar. He butted it out on the arm of the bench and dropped it in a garbage can. "You don't have a plan. You're with people you'd never have associated with before. And you're with that girl again? I mean she's good to look at, but so are a hundred other women. Why on earth are you with her? She was with you during a part of your life that you don't want to go back to."

"Caesar, it's just the way it worked out."

"No!" Caesar said that with such force that the bench shook. "Things never just work out, Lucas! They happen because *you* make them happen. Look around you." He pointed his hand in a sweeping motion at the grounds. The main Empirico building was ahead of them. It lit up beautifully in the night sky. "Do you think this just happened?" His voice became softer. He looked at Lucas. "This happened because I made it happen. No government hand-outs. No lucky breaks. No mentors helping me along. Skill. Hard work. The right people. And nerves of steel. That's what did it."

"Then how do you explain the people who get healed supernaturally?"

Caesar stood up and looked at his building. "Your powers are beyond my comprehension as I am sure they are for you." He paused a moment and turned back to Lucas. "But at least with my help you won't have to go through the near disastrous experiences you've had with crowds nearly crushing you to death."

"I've been led this far safely."

"Led? If you think it through, how all this healing happened for you, you'll see that *you* initiated it and that you are the driving force."

Lucas stood up beside Caesar. He was about to take a step away from Caesar to get some distance when Caesar stretched out his arm and grabbed onto Lucas' shoulder. His grip was tight, not angry, but tight enough to make Lucas realize this wasn't a joke.

"Would those people have gotten healed without you making the effort to help them?" Caesar said.

"No."

"Would that healing power have come unless you searched for it?"

"No."

"Would you have made it as far as you have without pursuing this power relentlessly?"

"No."

"Then, there you have it. It all comes down to you, Lucas. You are the driving force in your life. Just like I am in mine."

He smiled in a way that bothered Lucas and they started their journey back to Empirico.

"I'm feeling a little cold out here, Mike," Tabitha said. "Which way is back?"

Their eyes met and Tabitha felt ice water run through her veins. She had no reason to doubt Mike's integrity, but the feeling of uncertainty was unmistakable. He was a millionaire and a respected employee, she told herself, but it didn't make her feel any better. They were alone, in a place not familiar to her and he was only a few feet away. Where was Lucas? Mike moved closer. She tried not to flinch. If he took another step towards her she would kick him as hard as she could and leave.

"It's to the right." Then he laughed. "To your left, that is."

Tabitha laughed, too. It wasn't that the situation was funny. It was anything but that. It was that she wanted to break the mood. She wanted to get away from him. The evening had started off well but it was ending poorly—if, indeed, it was ending at all.

But Mike didn't move. He stayed there looking at her. Tabitha kept smiling as though it was the only thing that could prevent the ice water from coming back. "I think you should encourage Lucas to seriously consider coming back to work for Empirico." The words weren't what got to her. It was the way he said it. So direct, so pointed, so mean. It was as though he was commanding her.

"I thought I was offered a position, as well," she said.

His eyes stayed locked on her the way a dog's eyes stay locked on a person before it attacks. "All of you are welcome at Empirico. I think Caesar made that clear. But you, more than the other two, will have influence on Lucas. I think he trusts you. Maybe more than that."

A smirk came to his face. He tried to make it seem as if they were having a lighthearted chat under the stars, but it didn't work. "Think it through, carefully."

Dumb as he looked, those words etched a place in her mind. *Think it through, carefully.* She nodded slightly.

The ice water returned.

"I'm not lying to you."

"And I'm not going to argue with you, Edgar. I've been lied to enough times in my life to know when someone isn't on the level with me and you know what? I see the same look in your eyes."

"You can tell if I'm lying because of the look in my eyes?"

"That's right, Edgar. I can look into your eyes and see that there isn't a shred of truth to anything you've told me. You're standing there in your tux looking all prim and proper hoping to convince me of something that I don't believe is true."

"You're messed up, you know that?"

"Yeah, I know that. I've been messed up for years. But I'm not on drugs and I'm not drunk, not now, and I know what I'm saying."

"I'm here to learn. Can someone of your understanding comprehend that?" Edgar's face was red. He took in a breath and looked back over the creek.

"You're not fooling me, Edgar."

"Forget I said anything."

Jake touched the bottle to his lips and only then remembered it was empty. The seconds dragged on. "I'm not accusing you of anything, Edgar. I'm just saying if you want to talk we can talk. Okay?"

Edgar nodded and then shrugged his shoulders as though everything was cool.

But things weren't cool.

Things were far from being cool.

The ride back to the Palmer House Hilton was quiet. No one commented on the food or the job offer. Lucas, Jake and Edgar got out at the hotel and Tabitha continued on to her apartment. She wished she hadn't come. In the back of her mind, playing over and over again, were those words. *Think it through, carefully.*

The thought stayed with her the entire night.

35

The three met in Lucas' room. Jake took off his jacket and opened the fridge to look for a bottle of beer. Lucas walked to the window and looked down on Monroe.

Edgar sat in a chair and rubbed his face tiredly. "Can someone please tell me what just happened there?" he asked.

"We were offered a buy-out," Lucas said.

"You think he means what he said?" Jake asked.

"I don't think he's lying."

"You're not considering the offer, are you?" Edgar asked. He blinked his eyes and slumped back in the chair. He opened his mouth and let out a big yawn.

"If we take it we'll have their protection. But then we don't get to choose where we go anymore."

"Then pick up the phone and tell him your answer is no," Edgar said.

"I'm not doing that. Not yet, anyway."

"Then you're considering it."

"I'm not considering it. I just don't want to lose him."

"What do you think Caesar really wants from you?"

"I know where you're going with this."

"Then why don't you call it off?" Edgar asked.

"Because Caesar needs us."

Edgar rubbed his eyes again. This time it was more than just being tired. He looked exhausted, as though he had stayed up all night with an infant. "He doesn't need us, and you know what? We don't need him."

"Maybe we can turn him around," Lucas said, trying to urge his friends to see things his way.

"Lucas, figure it out," Jake said swallowing a gulp from his bottle. "He's buying you off and getting you out of the picture."

Lucas stood up and pointed a finger at Jake. "I know that! Why can't you people see the good in him? If we could convince him—"

"You're not going to convince him of anything," Jake interrupted. "Why don't you just drop him?"

Lucas lost the energy to argue and turned to the window. He looked down on the cars driving by and envied them. He wanted to get into one and leave, go wherever, just escape his problems. But that option was not open to him. Not anymore. Sometimes a person starts on a path and they can't turn back no matter how tough it gets. He wished right then that he didn't have the gift. He wished for nothing more than a small apartment, an unassuming job and no fame. He let out a sigh. "I'm afraid," he said.

"Of what he'll do if you say no?" Jake asked.

Lucas didn't say anything. Didn't have to. Jake leaned against the wall and finished his drink. Edgar leaned his head back in his chair looking as if he was going to fall asleep.

Jake put his bottle on the fridge, shook his head and said, "We're all going to die."

The room stayed quiet for quite a while. Lucas turned from the window. He saw Edgar exhausted in his chair. His face looked pale. Jake looked over at the fridge wondering if he should grab another bottle.

"We're not going to die," Lucas said. He didn't know for sure, of course. He just wanted something to break the silence. He ran his fingers through his hair and then loosened his bow tie. "We can get Caesar to see things our way. I know we can."

Edgar stood up and let out a sigh of frustration. "Don't be so stupid."

"We're going to explore the possibility. Is that all right with you, Edgar?"

"I'm not sure that we elected you to decide on a course of action for us," Edgar said.

"Maybe not. But I am sure that we never elected you."

"Would you guys shut up," Jake said. "You sound like five-year-olds."

"Thank you Jake, but I think Lucas and I can take care of this."

"Sit down, you two," Jake insisted. Neither moved. Jake stood between them. "Sit down and shut the—"

"He will pay you a lot of money, cloud your thinking and all the good you wanted to do will be lost. We're not going back to Caesar and that's final," Edgar said.

"If you want it to be final then it can be final for you," Lucas said.

The room went quiet again, as if someone pushed the mute button on the remote control.

"Are you saying you want me out?" Edgar asked.

"I'm saying that I'm not having you charge around here like some pompous bull telling me what I should or should not do."

"If the eccentric, self-indulgent millionaire would take one minute to listen to reason he would see that Caesar is laying a trap. And you're headed right in."

"I appreciate your concern. But I don't share it."

"Edgar's right," Jake said.

"I'm not backing down," Lucas said.

"You're not thinking this through."

"If we go against him, he'll come after us. If we go with him we still have a chance."

"You're backing down."

"I'm not backing down! I'm trying to look at this rationally."

"You're an idiot," Edgar said.

"Would the two of you please just shut up!"

"I'm not blindly going to follow along," continued Edgar.

"If you want out, you got out."

"Unbelievable," Edgar said. He shook his head the way a player does at a ref when a bad call has been made. "You want me out?"

"No one's forcing you to stay."

Edgar lifted up his hands. "If that's what you want."

Lucas rubbed his eyes already regretting the way the conversation had turned out. He let out a sigh and changed the tone in his voice. "Why are you really here, Edgar?"

"I told you. I'm an academic and I wanted an opportunity to get hands-on experience with something I'd otherwise never associate myself with."

"I still don't believe you," Jake said.

"I don't care what you believe. You people are impossible." Edgar walked to the door and then stopped. He had his hand on the door handle ready to leave, but then he took it off.

"Well," Lucas said. "Let's have it. Why are you here?"

Edgar turned his face from the other two. He was sure he felt his eyes getting moist. He took a few breaths to get himself under control. He thought back to the crowds of people that had been healed. He thought about his job at Mount Carmel. Then he remembered that day at Notre Dame when he sat under the tree on the park bench in the pouring rain. He thought about the brown envelope. That stupid brown envelope. The contents had shot through him like a bullet. He turned to Lucas and Jake. "I have cancer," he said. "I'm dying."

36

As shocking as the news was it didn't surprise either Lucas or Jake. A theologian who claimed to have left his teaching job so he could investigate healing was reasonable enough, but for Lucas and Jake it was never entirely believable. Knowing Edgar had cancer made everything clear again, as when a detective finally gets the missing piece of a murder mystery.

Revealing his circumstances brought relief to Edgar. He stayed at the door wondering how they were going to react. His cancer was out in the open now. No more secrets. No more internalizing the truth. It was as if saying those words brought him on the road to healing.

"I came here for two reasons. First, I really did want to know how all this healing worked. But the reason I wanted to know was because..." It was tougher for him the second time around. He felt as though he would collapse on the floor like a small child and cry for hours. Maybe he should have. Heaven knows he wanted to. "Because I have cancer."

Lucas and Jake wanted to say something, but nothing came to mind. Inside, Lucas didn't see the problem. Cancer is bad, really bad, but not if you have someone in front of you who can make you well in an instant. "Why didn't you just tell us you were sick when you showed up at my place the night Jake caught you sneaking around in the bushes?"

"I should have. I don't know why I didn't. Maybe I was in denial. Maybe I was afraid you wouldn't let me join you. Maybe I was afraid God would say no to healing me."

"But then since that time why haven't you asked me to pray for you?"

"Because I need to know if God really wants me healthy. Maybe He's angry with me for some evil I did. Maybe He's punishing me for something my parents or my grandparents did. Maybe God doesn't want me better. Maybe by getting healed I will be thwarting His plan. And besides, how does healing actually happen? I mean, how am I supposed to understand it?"

"Understand it?"

"I don't see what's wrong with trying to understand this."

"Edgar, you've been with us. You've seen the healings. You tell me how we're supposed to understand this."

Edgar sat down in his chair again. "I haven't come to any conclusions yet. Just that it doesn't make sense. You have this gift. But there's no real reason for you to have it."

"I agree, Edgar. So what does that tell us?"

Edgar raised his eyebrows. "It means we still have lots to learn. Maybe there are more effective ways of administering the healing. Maybe there is more we can discover from other passages about how to be healed."

"So you came here on a combined research project and healing request?"

Edgar nodded his head. He reached for a glass of water and took a drink. "I knew healing was a sham. I mean I *knew* it. Corvey and all the rest were money hungry, power maniacs. And while I still don't agree with the money they make I can see firsthand that healing is legit. It's just that I can't explain why."

"Should you be able to?" Jake asked.

"Yes. We have a long way to go, but we have a starting point. We know God works through you to heal people. But why? Why does He heal them? Why does He use you and not others?"

"Maybe God wants to use others. Maybe for some reason God can't. Or won't."

"They say you won't believe in miracles until life hangs in the balance. Well, my life is hanging in the balance and I want a miracle. I don't know if I believe in a world greater than my own, a world with miracles. I mean I know it exists. I know it's out there. It's just that I'm not sure I have access to it. C. S. Lewis asked the question, 'How could you ever have thought this was the ultimate reality?' And now I think I know what he meant."

"But still you feel a need to prove this," Jake said.

"My colleagues, I'm sure, think I'm nuts—that I've abandoned sound reason. But I believe there is sound reason in healing and I need to prove it."

"Why?" asked Lucas, searching for any way to show compassion.

"Because we all don't need to get up and shout 'Glory' a hundred times in church and go running after flamboyant preachers. Just because we don't do cartwheels in the aisles and we prefer to sing older hymns doesn't mean we're any less holy. If healing truly is for real, as I think it is, then it should stand up to logical, theological, reasoning. There should be a way, maybe not to explain healing completely, but to at least provide a framework."

"So what I'm doing is wrong?"

"It's not wrong, Lucas. I'm just not sure it's seeing the whole picture."

"And academics, with their noses stuck in books, carry on their theological debates while thousands and millions are sick—do they have the whole picture?"

"We don't have it either. Though many of us think we do," Edgar said, drinking his water. "And the more time I spend with you I realize we might not have it by a long shot. But I think you'd be wise to look at things critically to really determine what it is you are doing."

Lucas glanced out the window as if there was an answer waiting for him on the street below. He thought back to the verses he'd memorized at Xaing Xaing. Certainly Edgar had read the passages over more often than Lucas, so why didn't the sick get cured by Edgar's hands? Why did it fall to him in the first place, anyway? Lucas turned from the window. Edgar was across the room from Lucas but he felt miles away.

"So, as a theologian you admit you've neglected people's health. Fine. Now, let's move on," Lucas said.

"I may have neglected their health. But you've neglected their souls."

Lucas sat down trying to understand what Edgar meant. To avoid feeling awkward he fired off a question as fast as he could think of one. "What do you mean?"

"What do you do, Lucas?" Edgar asked.

Lucas swallowed and cleared his throat. "I lay hands on sick people."

"And what happens?"

"The sick get healed."

"And what happens then?"

"Then they go on living their lives."

"Then?"

"Then eventually they die."

The room went quiet as Lucas felt the weight of Edgar's next question. "And what happens to them then, Lucas?"

Lucas didn't know how to respond. He looked at Jake for his thoughts but Jake just shrugged his shoulders. "This isn't about what happens to people after they die."

"You're sure?"

"Ever since I walked out of Xaing Xaing I haven't been sure of anything except people being healed." He looked right at Edgar. "So, do you want me to pray for you or not?"

Tabitha finished her cup of herbal tea and proofread her article on the whereabouts of Lucas Stephens. She had previously wondered if Healermania would have died down by now, like a clothing fad gone out of style, but it had every indication of exactly the opposite. Pollsters released information indicating that the approval rating for Lucas by the people of Chicago was at ninety percent. Not even JFK had enjoyed stats like that.

Healermania was spreading and Tabitha didn't know what to make of it, or of Lucas, either. She went to bed wondering how he was doing. She wondered how much danger he was in. Wondered where all of this was leading him. Wondered if he still had any interest in her.

And whether she had any interest in him.

Edgar stood in front of Lucas with his eyes closed. He didn't have the courage to raise his hands. They stayed stuffed in his pockets. "Do I have to lift my hands?"

Lucas shook his head. "Only if you want to."

"Will it make any difference?"

"I don't think so. What kind of cancer is it?"

Edgar spoke quietly; it was almost as if he didn't want the others to hear. "Brain cancer."

Lucas laid his hands on Edgar's head. Edgar took in a breath and tried to relax. Lucas prayed and quoted some of his verses. He didn't feel his hands getting warm. Didn't have the same peace that he normally felt with the other healings. He waited a moment and then took his hands off.

"Is that it?" Edgar asked.

"I think so."

Edgar blinked his eyes and moved his fingers as if he was expecting a pulse of heat to have passed through him. He looked at Lucas and swallowed. "It didn't work."

"How can you say that?"

"Because the pounding in my head is still there." Edgar tried to keep himself from panicking. "Try it again."

Lucas closed his eyes and laid his hands on Edgar. He prayed, said a few verses and still nothing happened.

"This is supposed to work! Why isn't it happening? Come on, do something!"

"Okay. Take it easy, Edgar."

"I'm not taking it easy! Now try it again."

"Edgar."

"Just try it again? Would you?"

This time Edgar lifted his hands as though he was calling out to Heaven. He breathed in and tried to be patient, but it was hard to be patient when the clock was counting down and the results weren't coming. Lucas prayed a third time. But again nothing happened. It was like an evacuation bell had sounded and the healing power had left the building.

Edgar backed away from Lucas and sat down in his chair. He closed his eyes a moment to absorb the pain from his headache. "Maybe it's a gradual miracle," Edgar said trying to convince himself of something he hoped was happening. "A lot of miracles are gradual, aren't they?"

"Could be. But not the ones we've seen."

Edgar reached for more water. He drank a swig then rubbed his hands through his hair. "Why isn't it working?"

"Do you think you've lost the power, Lucas?" Jake asked.

"No," Lucas said, not knowing for sure.

"Well, this is fair."

"We'll figure it out."

"We better," Edgar said. There was a pause. Nobody knew how to react. Edgar breathed at a faster rate. His face told the story of a sick person losing hope. "You see?"

"See what?" Lucas asked.

"God doesn't want everybody healed."

"Edgar, you don't know that."

Edgar stood up fast. "Don't tell me what I know!" His voice was so loud it surely reached the other rooms. He tried to calm himself down. Anxiety shot through him like a tranquilizer, debilitating him, making him wonder if the end was now truly within sight. He sat down in his chair. There was chemo, he told himself. There was still a chance. How good the chance was he didn't know. Nobody knew. He took a drink of water, closed his eyes a moment, then looked at Lucas and Jake. "Dietrich Bonhoeffer said that 'danger and distress can only drive us closer to him.' Maybe this is God's way of bringing me closer to his purpose."

They spoke quietly.

"That would mean the same God who heals thousands is the same God who makes people sick? I have a problem with that, Edgar," Lucas said.

"So do I," Edgar replied. "Maybe He doesn't make them sick. Maybe He allows it, even though He doesn't truly want to. I don't know. I don't know. I'm getting tired of thinking."

"So, what happens now?" Jake asked.

"Now I try and figure out what this healing thing is really all about," Edgar said.

"How are you going to do that?" Lucas asked.

Edgar placed his hand on his forehead. "I'm going to think through the stories you memorized in Acts and I'm going to look at the stories in the other books."

"Why?"

Edgar took another drink of water. He held it in his mouth a moment to cool him down and then swallowed it. "Because I think each healing story might be different. Unique. It's as though together they form a treasure map for discovering the message of healing."

"The stories? They're different?"

Edgar nodded his head. "On one occasion a man asks Jesus if he is *willing* to heal him. On another he asks if He is *able* to heal him. Then one time Jesus asks a man if he really *wants* to get well."

"You don't think every person wants to get well?" Jake asked.

"What about the husband who stays at home not having to deal with the pressures of work because he's on sick leave? Or the elderly woman who loves the attention of everyone's sympathy toward her illness? And the young man who uses his sickness as an excuse for his failures in life? No, I'm sure not everyone really wants to get well."

"You could be right," Lucas said.

Edgar stood up and walked to the door. He looked visibly shaken. Lucas called out to him. "Edgar?" Edgar turned around and looked at Lucas. "I'm sorry, Edgar."

"It's not your fault," Edgar said.

"No, I mean I'm sorry about the way I spoke to you. I said some things tonight that I shouldn't have. You should know that I want you on this team. And I'm not just saying that. I mean it."

"I know." Edgar opened the door. "Now if you'll excuse me, I have a lot of thinking to do."

Jake followed Edgar out of Lucas' room and stopped him in the hallway. "I wish I could tell you something that would help."

"Tell me my cancer will go away."

"I'd like to." They stayed there a moment not saying anything. It occurred to them that another hotel guest might come out of their room and spot them but they were too tired to care.

"I've seen lots in my pathetic life, Edgar. I've seen girls who grew up in abusive homes become prostitutes and end up dying in some cheap motel. Seen businessmen who lose everything and then get hooked on drugs to cope with the pain. I seen people who hate God get healed and now I've seen people like you who serve Him everyday but stay sick—or at least they don't get healed right away."

"What are you trying to tell me, Jake?"

"I'm telling you that life is not a payback system for how you live. The good don't always get rewarded and the bad don't always get punished. I don't know why. It's just the way things are."

"Well, somehow it's harder to take when you get the short end of the stick."

Jake nodded his head. He understood Edgar perfectly. Maybe too perfectly. "I used to sit up at night after bad things happened to me. I'd wonder if maybe life had handed me loaded dice so that no matter what I did things would turn out wrong. I'd ask, 'Why, God? Why did this happen to me?' And you know what his response was? God said, 'Why not?'"

Edgar nodded his head. He had asked God the same question a number of times himself.

"Look," Jake continued. "I don't understand either you or Lucas. Lucas has this magic touch. You have the brains. I don't have either. I'm sure somewhere between you and Lucas there is an answer for all this. Maybe not a full answer. Maybe it's just a better understanding. But even if we don't get there, Edgar, I want you to know that I'm with you. I'll stand by you no matter what happens."

Jake stretched out his hand to Edgar. Edgar grasped it firmly. "Thank you, Jake."

"You're welcome."

"Good night."

"Good night, Edgar."

Edgar closed the door behind him but didn't make it to his bed. He collapsed on the floor and began to cry. All those alcoholics, prostitutes and drug addicts got healed. Business people, mothers, daughters, husbands, fathers—all healed. And there he was. A man of the cloth, so to speak. Followed God his whole life. His reward? Cancer.

Jake was right. Whatever else life was, it was not fair.

Edgar wiped the tears from his wet face. He folded his hands and tried to pray, but nothing came out. Finally, after an hour of saying nothing he quietly whispered to God above hoping he would be heard. "I believe Lord," he said. "But help my unbelief."

37

Handle joined Sheath in his office for an early morning meeting to discuss Edgar, their lost sheep. Edgar's name and his affiliation with Mount Carmel had appeared in many of the articles and news broadcasts concerning the healings. It infuriated Sheath. Their reputation and the reputation of Mount Carmel was on the line all because of a theology professor who had decided to take leave of his work (and his sense, too, they thought) to chase after some crazed miracle worker.

On Sheath's desk were two stacks of letters and e-mail printouts. They were from parents and, more importantly, financial contributors to the university. The first stack supported Edgar. The other expressed concern over how a teacher at Mount Carmel could be swept away into such fanaticism; it outweighed the support pile two to one.

"We're in trouble," Sheath said, slurping his second cup of coffee.

"It's not a problem. Not yet."

Sheath pointed to the stack on his desk, the negative stack, and looked at Handle with a frustrated expression. "Then what do you call all these?" Handle was about to respond but Sheath continued. "I have prospective students calling and asking how they can register for our 'healing program.' On the other hand I have parents saying they will take their kids out unless we get rid of Edgar."

"Then we need to decide what we're going to do about it."

"Either we keep him on and endorse him or we fire him."

Sheath's phone rang. Normally, he wouldn't have answered it during a meeting but his mind was stalling and he needed to shift focus. He picked up the phone. When he heard the voice at the other end his mouth dropped open. "I'm fine, how are you?" He shook his head in amazement at Handle. "Can I put you on speakerphone?" He put the call on hold.

"Who is it?"

"It's Edgar."

Handle closed his eyes a moment to absorb the shock.

Sheath hit the speakerphone button and took Edgar off hold. "Edgar, so good to hear your voice again. I'm here with Glenn." Sheath's voice was upbeat, friendly, he pretended nothing was wrong. They exchanged greetings.

Edgar stood in front of the mirror in his hotel room. He often felt intimidated speaking with the brass at Mount Carmel. But today was different. Today he felt confident, not arrogant, just content that he didn't have to suck up to them. He felt he could speak his mind without having to necessarily give the answers they wanted to hear.

"Edgar, we're concerned," Sheath said.

"What about?"

"We're not sure about your involvement with this healing phenomenon."

"It's a little out of the ordinary isn't it?" Edgar said.

"Yes, it is. How do you see your involvement in this... Healer-mania?"

Edgar sat down on his bed and took a drink of water. "I plan on staying on. I'm curious as to where all of this is leading."

Sheath dropped his head as though he had just lost a game. "You plan on staying on indefinitely?"

"Why don't the two of you come and join me? It might interest you."

Sheath stood up and banged his fist down on his desk hard enough to make the stack of papers rattle. He was about to yell at Edgar but he managed to get himself under control. Edgar was slipping away from him. "Our current situation does not allow us to take leave of our jobs to go running around with a… whatever you call him."

"So what do we do about it?" Edgar asked. He was content either way—or as content as a man can be about potentially losing his job.

Sheath put him on hold and turned to Handle desperately looking for an answer. "What do we do?"

Handle shrugged his shoulders as if to say, *I'm not going to be responsible for what happens.*

Sheath finished his coffee. "If we keep him on our staff it will look like we support what he is doing and we'll lose major financial contributions. If we axe him then the students, and prospective students, will be disappointed and might not come back."

"He's got us either way."

Sheath hit the speaker button. "Edgar, we… we like what's going on," he nearly choked saying it, "and we think for the time being you should continue."

"That's great," Edgar replied.

Sheath wanted to hang up. "Thanks for calling, Edgar." He didn't even wait for Edgar's response. He hit a button and the line went dead.

"I don't think this is as bad as you're making it out to be," Handle said.

"You're right," Sheath said sitting down in his chair. "It's worse."

The three met in Lucas' room for their morning prayers. Jake stood with his arms stretched out above him, Edgar sat in a chair with his hands folded and Lucas knelt at his bed with his head resting on the palms of his hands. They took turns praying for the sick, for each other and especially for Edgar.

Outside, the traffic got louder. Then it sounded as though there was some kind of trouble on the streets. There was shouting as though angry protesters had gathered. The three tried to continue with their prayers but the yelling only grew louder.

Suddenly, there came a frantic knock at the door. Lucas looked through the peephole and saw a young man in a suit wearing a hotel badge that said MANAGER. Lucas opened the door. The young man's eyebrows raised in amazement.

"It *is* you," he said. Immediately, Lucas knew this was their last night at the Palmer House Hilton. "They said you were here, but I didn't believe them."

Maybe the limousine driver had spilled their location. Or maybe someone at the desk had figured out that three guests staying at the hotel under Tabitha's name might have something to do with the disappearance of Chicago's most famous trio.

"What do you want?" Lucas asked, wondering where they would go next.

"They're all waiting for you."

"Who is?"

"Everybody. Looks like all of Chicago is out there."

"Out where?" Lucas didn't wait for an answer. He went to the window, opened the curtains and looked down on Monroe. People filled the entire street. They packed together as though they were on a massive dance floor.

"The Mayor's here as well. He wants to see you as soon as you can make it," the manager said. Lucas looked at Jake who shrugged his shoulders in a way that said he was impressed. The Mayor was trying to schedule an appointment with *him?*

Jake and Edgar came to the window. Jake leaned against it to see how far the crowd extended. "It's at least three blocks."

"Five," the manager said. "West to LaSalle. East to North Michigan. But that was ten minutes ago. It's more by now. For sure."

"We'll be down in a minute," Lucas said, trying to comprehend the mass of people. The manager closed the door and ran down the hallway.

"You all right, boss?" Jake asked.

Lucas nodded. "I hope so."

"You hope so?"

"There's so many. I could spend a week down there and not get to them all."

Edgar turned his head slightly to look at Lucas. He mulled a thought over in his mind trying to find a solution. "Does it spread?"

"Spread?" Lucas asked.

"Yeah. Spread."

"Does what spread?"

"The healing power you have. Can anybody get it?" Edgar asked.

"Anybody meaning you?"

"Anybody meaning anybody. Look outside. There are more people out there than there are fans at a Fighting Irish home opener. You're not going to get them alone. So does it spread?"

"We can find out," Lucas said.

"How?"

Lucas felt like a student who opens his exam and doesn't recognize any of the questions. He didn't know what to do. Below, the crowds grew louder and bigger.

"We have to get out there," Jake said.

"I know. I know. Just let me think."

Lucas searched his mind but came up with nothing. He shook his head. "I'm drawing a blank." He shrugged his shoulders. "I can take you all back to Xaing Xaing and show you how I got it."

"That won't be happening," Jake said.

"Lucas, do you think God will give it to more than one person?" Edgar asked.

"You tell me."

"It's possible. I mean, he gave it to you, right?"

"Right."

"You think it could come to us?"

"We're not together by accident."

They looked at each other and wondered what might happen.

"Well," Lucas said. "Let's give it a shot."

They put their arms on each other's shoulders like football players in a huddle.

"On Blue 42?" Jake said, imitating a quarterback. Lucas laughed.

"Yeah," said Edgar. "And the play's to me. Fifty yard streak down the sideline."

"Can you even run fifty yards?" Jake asked. They all laughed. Really laughed, especially Jake whose big gut rumbled.

"Depends on who's chasing me," Edgar replied.

Lucas took in a deep breath, closed his eyes and got real quiet. "Well, God," he started. "It's us. We're here at the Palmer House Hilton in Chicago. Got a lot of people waiting outside. The manager figures it's at least all the way from North Michigan to LaSalle. A lot of these people are sick and so far it's only been me laying hands on them." Lucas felt himself beginning to cry. He hated it. He felt embarrassed. *Get yourself under control.* But he couldn't. Three grown men in a room. One of them crying. It felt worse than women watching a sappy movie. He fought back the tears and continued. "There's so many of them, God. If you can move this healing power around to Edgar and to Jake, I think a lot of people down there would appreciate it."

Lucas broke off suddenly, and walked to the door. "You guys coming?"

They walked down the stairs to the lobby. The press saw them and started shouting for their attention. Tabitha said nothing. She would get her interview later. A slight smile crossed her face when Lucas saw her. "Good luck," she mouthed.

When the crowd heard that Lucas was in the lobby some of them started screaming. The crowd had arrived without any concrete confirmation of his location. But when they saw him it brought relief. It assured them they hadn't skipped work and school for nothing.

Mayor Gibbs hurried up to Lucas. Beside him were two of his assistants. He looked flushed, worried, not the sort of composure Chicagoans had come to expect from him. He nodded briefly to Lucas. "I need to talk with you."

"Sure."

"In private."

They walked to the end of a hallway and the noise grew quieter.

"Lucas, I'm Bill Gibbs."

"I know who you are."

Mayor Gibbs let out a sigh as if a long manhunt had finally ended. "I don't know how to start." He began pacing and rubbed his hand through his hair. He loosened his tie. He stopped moving and put his hands on his hips. "We have a serious problem."

"How so?"

"How so? How so?" Mayor Gibbs wondered if Lucas had any idea how much stress he was causing him. "Have you seen outside?"

"A lot of people there."

"Like sixty thousand worth, Lucas!" He was angry now. He turned his head to the ground. He closed his eyes and tried to get himself under control. He looked back at Lucas the way a man does when he's begging for a favor. "I'm the Mayor of Chicago. I like you. I think what you're doing is beyond comprehension. I think it's the wildest thing to happen to Chicago since Elliot Ness and his band of Untouchables."

Lucas could hear a 'but' coming.

"But," Mayor Gibbs continued, "you are a problem."

"A problem?"

"Lucas, Chicago can't function with you here. I've shut down Washington, Madison, Monroe, Adams, Jackson—some companies have closed for the day because their employees are all outside waiting for you."

The crowd was chanting something about healing. Lucas couldn't make it out. It was as if he and Gibbs were in a shelter, if only for a while, to protect them from the world they had to go out to.

"What do you want?" Lucas asked.

"You can't stay in Chicago. The crowds are too big."

"I can't leave Chicago."

"Yes, you will." Mayor Gibbs was stern now. His face was intense. This was not a bartering session. He was giving orders. "Here's what I'm prepared to do. You and your two friends will get your day at Wrigley Field."

"A final send-off?"

"Right. That way I keep you happy. That way I keep the employers happy. And that way I keep the voters happy. You see? Everybody stays happy when you leave Chicago."

"What about the sick?"

"The sick will travel to you wherever you go. You have today at the Palmer House Hilton. After that, Wrigley Field. And then, you're out."

Mayor Gibbs' assistants as well as Edgar and Jake stood guard at the hallway. The reporters were determined to speak with them and tried to figure out what they were talking about for so long.

"What's left to say?" Lucas was not happy about the solution. He knew Mayor Gibbs was right; the downtown streets were plugged up. How long could this go on? Today was a working day. If he stayed in Chicago, people would continue to show up. Day after day after day after….

Mayor Gibbs gave Lucas a pat on the shoulder and walked down the hallway. Lucas thought about the offer, the command. Then he thought of Jake. He'd get his day at Wrigley Field after all.

The shouting grew louder. A burst of nervous energy shot through Lucas.

The people were waiting.

38

Lucas came out of the hallway and saw Tabitha waiting for him. "A podium has been set up for you. A microphone, too. The sound system won't carry you to all the people so a couple of the radio stations are broadcasting you live—as are TV stations."

Lucas nodded in a way that made Tabitha wonder if he heard what she had said. The crowd saw him through the doors and shouted louder. "You okay?" she asked.

Lucas nodded again without looking at her. He wasn't fine. He was far from fine. His stomach felt like he was going to be sick. He breathed in longer stretches to help him cope with speaking to the public. But the feeling of uneasiness remained.

Instead of being confident and ready to tackle the world, Lucas sensed a problem. *It's just jitters. I'll get over it.* Something was not right. It was as though everyone was gathered there to set him up, a charade to get him out into the open where he would be attacked.

There was a heaviness in the air in spite of the people present. He stepped onto the podium. The crowd went crazy. They shouted and screamed the way fans do when their team takes the field. The bright sunlight made Lucas squint. He searched the tops of the buildings and then scanned the first few rows of the crowd.

He tried to speak but nothing came out. The crowd didn't notice. They were so excited to have him there that by just standing in front of them he was fulfilling a desire. He forced himself to get his first words out and wondered if they would be his last.

"Good morning."

More cheers. People waved banners. Those at the front were the happiest. Odds were that Lucas would get to them. But a block, two blocks, five blocks away people in wheelchairs, those with cancer and other illnesses had a heavy question on their minds: *will he get to me today?*

"I want to thank each of you for coming."

The crowd became quiet the way a raging sea does when it suddenly turns to glass. There wasn't so much as a whisper. The pushing and shoving stopped as Lucas spoke. The only other sound in that part of Chicago was the train as it passed by.

"I know that many of you have come here looking for a miracle."

News cameras captured his every word. Tabitha stood behind him, notepad in hand, writing down some of the catch phrases she would later use in her article. Something impressed her about Lucas. Seeing him up on that podium, addressing the people gathered, broadcasting to Chicago, the US and other parts of the world. He was not the man she once knew.

"Many of you have come long distances to be freed from the illnesses that are destroying you. Leukemia, chronic pain, arthritis, allergies, headaches, the list is endless. I want you to know that God is a healing God."

The crowd screamed with such fanaticism that it would have blown away any sports crowd. The echo bounced off the buildings and sounded like nothing Lucas had ever heard before. Edgar listened and noticed how similar the atmosphere was to when he was at the Corvey crusade.

"There's a story of two blind men who wanted to be healed. They stood at the side of the road waiting for their chance. When Jesus passed by they shouted out for him. But the crowd told them to shut up. The blind men didn't care. They kept after Him. The two men seemed like insignificant outcasts compared to the mass of the crowd. But there is something that really strikes me in what happened in that story. The story says that Jesus *stopped*. He refused to be pushed along by the crowd. He refused to ignore the cry of two people. He stopped for them. He healed them and the story says they followed Jesus."

Lucas paused a moment and wished he had prepared a speech. All those people standing there. All those watching TV and listening to the radio. He searched his mind for something else to say. "I can't explain why some people get healed and others don't. And I'm thankful and support every doctor and every member of the medical field who has done their best to help people get better. And even when modern medicine can't solve something there is still hope. There is a supernatural God who still heals today—through doctors, through healthy living and through miracles."

The crowd yelled with such passion that Lucas feared for his life. Police line or not, this crowd could break through the barrier and rush Lucas before he had time to react.

He stepped off the podium and turned to Jake and Edgar. "You guys ready?"

"What if it doesn't work?" Jake asked.

"With the exception of Edgar, it's always worked."

"Not for you. For me. What if the news cameras are on me and someone doesn't get healed?"

"Then pass whoever comes to you down to me."

"But what if it never works for me?"

"Well Jake, then it doesn't work."

"I'll look like a fool."

"You might."

Lucas nodded to one of the officers who proceeded to let the first person through. Jake stood still a moment, not being sure of what he should do. He turned to Edgar. "Well?"

Edgar felt the nervousness that comes with being forced to make a decision in a hurry. This was it. The time to experience the difference between being on the bench and being in the game came down to his choice. He looked at Jake. "Well, we're not going to find out how it works by standing here wondering, are we?"

Jake looked over his shoulder. People shouted for attention. A grin came to his face. Courage rose in his veins. "Edgar. You're right."

"Of course I'm right."

They laughed in a nervous sort of way and went to the other

side. Their smiles faded quickly, though. The sight of thousands of sick people in desperate need of help can wipe the smile off anyone. *If only we could clone Lucas,* Jake thought.

Jake nodded to another officer who then let a biker through. He was about Jake's age. He wore a Hell's Angels jacket. Injection marks spotted his arms.

"You ride?" Jake asked.

"Used to. You?"

Jake nodded. He felt uncomfortable and wished the stupid cameras would stop trying to get a better angle on him. The man explained that he had picked up AIDS during a drug party a year ago. Jake had been at those parties, too. Loud, blaring music. Half dressed women. Dim lights. An endless stream of booze. A variety of drugs.

"I'm gonna pray for you, all right?" The man nodded. Jake and Edgar put their hands on the man. "God in Heaven, you see this man who's sick...." As they prayed, Jake could feel a perfect peace around them. The crowd suddenly seemed miles away as though they weren't even there.

"You feel any different?" Jake asked after they finished praying.

"No. Should I?"

"I'm new at this."

"Me too," the biker said.

Jake motioned for the biker to go to Lucas, to be sure the man left healthy.

Jake whispered to Edgar. "I feel like an idiot."

"Should we run inside? Hide?"

Jake wasn't sure if Edgar was joking. Edgar wasn't sure either.

Jake instructed the cameras to stand behind the barrier to give them some privacy. "We can't quit. We just can't," Edgar said. Jake nodded and the next person came through.

The three spent the entire day praying for people. To Edgar and Jake's knowledge not one person got healed as a result of their prayers. Lucas, who was on the other side of the barricade, was successful as usual. Every person he touched got healed. Fevers were gone in an instant. The deaf could hear. The crippled could walk. People with chronic headaches suddenly felt what it was like to live without pain. Jake never felt more useless in his entire life.

The sun had already set. Night was upon them. Lucas came over to see Jake and Edgar and they agreed to pray for one more each before calling it quits for the day. Lucas was exhausted. Edgar was frustrated. Jake was discouraged. "Good," he whispered. "The sooner I get out of here the better."

Jake nodded for the last time to a police officer who let in two Asian children. Jake didn't make eye contact with them. He couldn't. He wouldn't.

"Mister?" a small voice said.

Jake forced himself to look down. There stood an Asian boy, maybe eight years old, with his seven-year-old sister. Jake knelt down. One more failure he could handle. Then he'd be gone. He'd never lay hands on a sick person again. That he was sure of. He'd stick it out with Lucas. Be his bodyguard, confidant, friend. But the healing was not his thing. He felt stupid for thinking it might have been.

"Yes." Jake felt like Santa at the mall, promising kids gifts he knew he couldn't deliver.

"First, don't tell my parents I'm here," the boy said.

"You're on TV, kid. They're gonna know."

The boy realized he was caught. Didn't matter now. He may as well finish what he came here for. Jake laughed his smoker's-cough laugh. "What are you sick with?"

"It's not me. It's my sister. We're both supposed to be in school. But we didn't go today because we wanted to come here."

"Your parents are worried about you by now, you know that?"

"They probably won't be as mad if my sister gets better."

Lucas announced to the crowd that he was done for the evening. That wooziness had come over him again. He nodded to Jake and then went with Tabitha into the hotel.

"You're right," Jake said. "But next time, tell your folks."

"There won't be a next time. 'Cause my sister is walking away healed."

Jake closed his eyes and again wished that he wasn't there. He turned around but Lucas was gone. Poor kids.

"What do you have?" Jake asked the little girl.

The girl looked down at the ground, embarrassed.

"She doesn't talk," her brother said. "Not anymore."

"I… I can pray for her." *Why did I ever agree to this?* He put his hands on the girl's head and prayed so quietly that Edgar, who was crouching next to him, couldn't hear him. "God, I can't do this. I don't have what it takes. I should never have come here. All the same I'd like for you to help this girl."

Jake stood up, said goodbye without looking at the Asian kids and headed into the hotel. When the reporters saw Jake and Edgar they fired questions in their direction. But Jake was not interested.

"You all right?" Lucas asked.

"Can we get out of here?" Jake said.

"I have a car waiting for us," Tabitha said.

They got into a brand new sport utility vehicle and drove off leaving the dispersing crowd behind them. They passed people on the sidewalks. Some of them had been healed, but many others went away disappointed. Jake couldn't look.

"You all right?" Lucas asked again.

Jake tried to brush it off. "It didn't work, that's all."

"We've had a long day."

"It's got nothing to do with that… Forget it. It just didn't work. That's all."

Tabitha drove them out of the downtown area then turned to Lucas. "Any idea where we're going?"

Lucas shook his head. "Can't go to my place."

"You could try mine," she offered.

"They'll find us there, too."

"Schaumberg," Edgar said.

"Why there?"

"I have a cousin who runs a motel near there. He'll put us up."

"Can we trust him?" Lucas asked, knowing that if their location was discovered they would be harassed all night.

"I guess we'll find out."

The Asian boy took his little sister by the hand and led her through the maze of people walking down the sidewalk. They came to an ice cream store and he told her he would buy her whatever she wanted for being such a good sport and sticking it out the whole day in the heat. They waited in front of the ice cream containers and stared at the brilliant colors. Bright blue, chocolate, vanilla.

"What can I get you?" said the lady behind the counter.

"Could I please have a chocolate cone?"

"Sure. And for you?"

The girl looked at all the flavors until a reddish-pink one caught her attention. Her brother leaned over her not taking his eyes off the containers. "Just point to the one you want. I'll tell the lady." The girl thought about her choice. She considered the vanilla but then came back to the reddish-pink color.

"Strawberry," the girl said.

The boy looked up at the lady behind the counter to nod his approval. She grabbed two cones and began scooping out the ice cream. Suddenly, the boy felt colder than the ice cream he was about to eat. He looked at his sister. His mouth dropped open, his eyes grew wide. She looked back at him wondering what the problem was. She shrugged her shoulders. "I like strawberry."

Outside the ice cream shop the Asian boy found a pay phone and called home. A stressed woman answered the phone.

The boy swallowed. "Mom?"

The voice on the other end went hysterical. "Where are you? We've been worried sick about you! Why haven't you called? Are you all right? Has something happened?"

"Mom?" the boy continued. "Someone wants to talk to you."

39

Caesar watched the recap of the day's events in his office. He sat in his chair, shook his head at what he was seeing and debated if his lost sheep was ever going to come back. But inside he already knew the answer. Lucas was no longer part of his company, no longer a member of the Council. And in light of the miracles taking place, Caesar put him in another category.

Lucas was now a competitor.

All those people being healed. All those sales out the window. And the problem was only getting worse. Lucas, by himself, was healing thousands. Now it looked as though his sidekicks were getting in on the action. If Lucas continued his healings at his present pace, Empirico would encounter a significant, perhaps catastrophic, loss. And with the other two potentially being involved in the healings the problem could be three times as bad. If still others got involved they would have a disaster on their hands. And Caesar was not prepared to let that happen.

He called Mike into his office.

"I think he's a problem," Caesar said.

"He can't touch us. He's one man."

Caesar turned his chair, it squeaked as he did so, and shot a look at Mike that caused him to rethink what he said. "He's already embarrassed this company."

"He'll die out. It's just a fad."

"Oh? Does it look that way to you, Mike? Because I've seen today's news and it doesn't give any indication that he is fading away at all!" Caesar's voice was loud enough to be heard down the hall. He turned back to the TV and hit the remote to turn it off.

"You're concerned our market share will drop?" Mike asked.

"No. Our market share will remain the same. It's the market itself that will drop."

"Lucas can do that?"

"This is not only about what Lucas is doing right now; it's about what he and others like him could be doing in the near future. Even by himself he's inflicting damage; imagine what can happen down the road."

"Do you have figures?"

"Per capita drug spending in this country is about $416 per year. That's for the whole population, not just people who use prescription drugs. If we use that number and multiply it by the people who've been healed which is, I don't know, I'm guessing by now close to ten thousand, and multiply that by our four percent market share—that means we've lost more than a hundred and sixty thousand in one week. That doesn't sound like much, and it isn't, but at this rate, in a year he'll have cost this company well over eight million. And if others get involved then the rate of the healings increases through the roof. We could easily be talking hundreds of millions of dollars. This could get very ugly."

Mike sat back in his chair. "What are you suggesting?"

Caesar turned his head to Mike as if to say *Are you stupid?* Mike swallowed. Ice water ran through his spine. Caesar stared so long into Mike's eyes that it felt as though he was being hypnotized. "It's time that Mr. Stephens be encouraged with a little more force to reconsider his charade."

They arrived at the motel just outside Schaumberg, northwest of Chicago. The trip was successful; Tabitha brought them there without being followed. Edgar's cousin showed Edgar and Jake to their rooms. Lucas turned back to Tabitha who waited in the SUV.

"Thanks for helping us."

Tabitha put the vehicle in park and nodded her head. Lucas looked as if he had just worked three shifts in a row. "Get some rest," she said.

"I'll try."

She raised her index finger to Lucas as if to tell him she just remembered something. He came to the vehicle. Tabitha reached into her purse. She produced a new watch, still in its case.

"You gave your last one away. Thought you might want another one."

"Thanks. Again." He took it out of the box and noticed its heavy stainless steel backing. He buckled the black leather straps together and admired the silver and blue look.

"It suits you," she said.

Lucas turned around and was about to walk to his room when Tabitha called out to him. "Lucas?" He turned around. "Where is this all going?"

Lucas looked up for a moment. The night was dark, the stars were out. He looked into her eyes. "I guess I'll find out."

She said goodbye and drove off. The sound of her vehicle faded away.

Lucas was walking back to his room when Edgar opened his door.

"Everything all right?" Lucas asked.

"I think I'm okay."

"You have that look on your face, Edgar."

Edgar smiled. "What look?"

"The look that tells me you are about to ask me another question for which I don't have an answer."

Edgar let out a laugh. "You're right." Then the mood changed. Edgar's smile vanished. He looked at Lucas momentarily then stared up at the stars as if to rehearse what he was about to say. "You think it's because of my lack of faith?"

"Edgar."

"No, I need an answer. Tell me what you think. Straight up. I really need your opinion. Yes or no. Is it because I have a lack of faith?"

Lucas let out a breath and felt what it was like to have so many questions and so very few answers. "Define faith."

"A trust in God."

"Then my answer to you would be no. You being sick is not a result of a lack of faith."

"Then tell me. Why can all those people be healed but not me? What do they have that I don't? Am I being too rational? Am I looking for too much proof? Should I just forget all the thinking and—"

"No. Don't stop thinking. I wasn't sure we needed you on the night you came to my house. But I am now. This team needs brains. Your kind of brains."

Lucas' comment brought Edgar relief. "I'm not sure if I'm angry with God. I know there is at least part of me that is still objective. I'm curious. I know that's a strange thing to be when you're sick. But I'm curious as to why God would heal others and not me."

"Maybe it's timing."

"What if it isn't?"

"Then you keep trusting."

"But how do I do that? How do I keep from losing my faith?"

They heard a car drive by. They waited to make sure it didn't recognize them.

"Edgar, you know more about faith than I do."

"Lucas, I need more than what I have. I need what you have."

"Me?"

"Yes, you."

"Okay. Here's my reason for believing. Ready?" Edgar nodded. "I have none."

"What?"

"I have no reason. I rotted away in a Chinese prison and I somehow received the ability to heal."

"That's a reason to believe."

"Yes, if that happened to every prisoner then, yes, it would be a reason to believe. But it didn't happen to every prisoner. It happened to me. It worked out for me. There are lots of people who don't see the results. They don't get to see how the pieces fit together. Those are the people with real faith. Those are the ones who have no proof in their lives of God's involvement, at least not that they can see, and they keep on going. What I'm saying is that those kinds of people are way further ahead than people like me."

"So how do I make the cancer go away?"

"Edgar, it's not your job or my job to make sickness go away."

Edgar nodded his head a few times as if annoyed with how Lucas was avoiding the crux of the matter. "I understand that God does the healing, but how do I get Him to heal me?"

Lucas saw the vulnerability in Edgar's eyes. Edgar would have sold all his possessions and given all his money away if he thought it would bring him healing.

"Maybe it has to do with staying close to God, staying close to the stories and doing what's right. Then we've done what we can do and we leave the miracle part up to Him. I wish I knew what else to say, but I don't. I'm sorry. I am."

"It's okay," Edgar said, giving Lucas a pat on the shoulder.

"Somehow I know that I haven't given you the answer you need."

"Sometimes it's relief enough to know that I could at least ask the questions."

Lucas nodded.

"Good night, Lucas."

"You too."

Edgar closed the door. It hurt Lucas to know Edgar was in pain. He closed his eyes and thought about how the two of them could just as easily have had their positions reversed.

Lucas entered his room. He collapsed on his bed but strangely enough he didn't feel sleepy. He just lay there. His body was tired, but his mind still raced along.

He took a shower to calm himself down, said some of his verses and got into bed. But still he couldn't sleep.

He got dressed, put on a cap, turned up his collar and took a walk. He stopped at a nearby park and lay down on the bench. It was quiet. Cool, but quiet. There was something refreshing about not hearing a crowd—about not having to be around people begging for his attention.

Wrigley Field was next. He wondered how many people would get healed. He wondered what would happen afterwards.

He looked up at the sky again. Somewhere up there was God Almighty, looking down on him perhaps. "Where's this all going?" Lucas asked. Part of him figured he'd get an audible response. Maybe God in Heaven would call down to his man in the park to let him know what was going to happen. But there was no response. The only sound was the cars from the highway. No one else walking around. No people.

Anonymity was bliss.

Lucas got back to the motel at midnight. He was about to enter his room when he noticed that Jake's door was open just a crack. Lucas knocked. No response. He opened the door and spoke without looking in. "Jake?"

Still no response.

A little louder, "Jake?"

Nothing.

Lucas opened the door farther. There was no one on the bed. The bathroom light was off. "Jake?" The room was dark. The curtains were shut. There was no sign of a struggle. Maybe Jake had gone out for a walk to clear his mind.

Lucas' eyes adjusted. Against the far wall he saw a figure. It was slumped on the floor, back against the wall. Motionless.

"Jake?"

Lucas walked toward him. Why was he sitting on the floor? His foot struck an object. At first he thought it was the leg of the bed. But the object rolled and hit another part of the bed. Jake's eyes were open. In his right hand was a bottle. Vodka. Beside him, some rum.

It relieved Lucas to see the bottles. The shock of his friend on the floor brought other thoughts to Lucas' mind; perhaps Thatcher and Ridley had paid him a visit. But it had been booze and not fists that sent Jake to the ground.

Lucas closed the door. He sat down on the floor and leaned his back up against the bed. The stench of hard alcohol filled his nostrils. It reminded him of the stench in Jake's old place and the smell of his own whiskey and brandy bottles.

"Busy day today."

"Yeah," Jake said, as he let out a sigh. Lucas was sure he could get high off the fumes. Jake put his hand on his forehead. At first, Lucas thought it was because Jake was tired. But then Jake started to cry. Almost uncontrollably. It lasted only a few seconds but it was so deep, so desperate that it scared Lucas.

"Irish have a big game tomorrow," Lucas said.

"Think it'll be close?"

"No. Blowout."

"For or against?"

Lucas smiled. "For them. I'm predicting 67–13."

Jake put his bottle down and looked through the space between the curtains. He had a view of a single star shining through that small opening. Part of Lucas wanted to grab that rum bottle and join Jake. The hard bite of alcohol against the back of his throat would settle him down. *Just a drink,* he thought. *Just one drink before bed.*

Later, he told himself.

Jake's straggly hair flowed over his ears. Who knew how long he'd been at it. Probably got the bottles from the station across the road. Lucas figured that because of the cap and jacket on the bed. Jake must have disguised himself to buy it.

Jake never seemed to Lucas as one of those born and raised on the streets. He must have had a decent life at some point. He was smart, not educated, but sharp enough to make Lucas realize he was a guy who ended up at the bottom instead of one who started out there. Some of the ones that survive off soup kitchens and rescue missions seem predestined to be there. Bad parents, (or no parents present during upbringing), bad childhoods, bad breaks—it all contributed to a street person's demise. Lucas figured that Jake, though, was better off than many of those at or near the bottom. He used to have a place of his own. And he had optimism—the currency of the destitute.

The booze, the drugs, the women—it had all helped Jake deal with the pain. His addictions worked, or at least they seemed to work, short term. Trouble was, they made their way in, put down roots and no matter how hard he chopped at them afterwards, those trees stayed put. They were like guests who become rowdy and refuse to leave and a person regrets the minute they ever laid eyes on them.

Jake grabbed the neck of the bottle with his right hand and drank about two shots worth. "They better start using their passing game more. All this running. It won't work."

"I agree," Lucas said. "When teams know you can't throw then the safety starts cheating. Especially if they have good corners."

"That's right."

Jake put the bottle down and buried his face in his hands. He sobbed again, a little longer than before. He was like a kid crying at recess after no one picks him for their sports team. Jake only paused for a minute or so before talking again, but it felt like a lot more.

"It was a sunny day," Jake began. "Perfect sunny day. You know the kind?"

Lucas nodded. The room felt colder all of a sudden. As though someone had opened the door on a cold day.

"Not a cloud in the sky. That's rare, you know. There's usually some cloud somewhere on the horizon. But this day was perfect."

Jake's voice was solemn. He stared ahead as though he were in a trance. He guzzled some more of the bottle, trying to get the strength for what he had to say.

"The bride and groom left the church and got into their car. Black Buick. Four door. New. People threw that paper stuff at them..." he looked to Lucas for a response.

"Confetti."

Jake nodded. "They were going to spend the evening in town then catch a plane the next day for Disney World... or Disneyland, I can never remember which one it was."

Jake closed his eyes again. The tears were about to start again. But he held them back as best he could, the way a dam holds back a river. But Jake's dam wasn't so strong. And that river. That river pushing behind him was so powerful.

He gulped down a swig from his bottle. He held it in his mouth a moment then choked it down. "The family waved goodbye to them. The groomsmen. They hurried into their sports cars, determined to follow them. They zoomed down the street. Not speeding. Just cruising. You know? That feeling of having the windows down, driving down the road."

Lucas nodded. Jake got quieter. He spoke slower.

"The couple had been driving for about five minutes. That's when the groom spotted a truck out of the corner of his eye. He slammed on the brakes. The car screeched. But it was too late. And I think he knew it was too late. I think when he saw that truck, in that instant, he knew it was over. Maybe people get that feeling before it happens to them. It becomes suddenly clear to them and they realize: This is it. I'm finished."

Jake sucked back on his bottle. The last of the contents was too much to fit into his mouth. Some of it poured onto his shirt. He kept what was in his mouth for a while, it burned against his gums, and then he swallowed it. He would need it to get through the next part.

"The truck rammed the car so hard that it flipped it right over. The groom died on impact, that's what they said. The bride was smashed against the side of the car so hard that her head went through the window."

Jake's eyes scanned the floor for his second bottle. He found it near Lucas and ripped off the top. He sucked back on it the way a runner drinks water after coming in from a jog.

"The groomsmen ran out from their car. The best man got there first. The door was open. The bride was half in the car, half on the street. Her body was covered in blood. That white dress was coated in deep, deep red. She knew it was over. The best man knew it, too. It was down to the waiting part now. He looked into her eyes. She looked at him with that bewilderment and that hopelessness that comes when you know nothing can bring you back from the course you're now traveling. The life slowly faded out of her eyes, like a flashlight that loses power and finally goes out, until there was nothing left but a hollow shell."

He didn't take another drink. Didn't need to. The dam broke and that river came pounding through. Jake cried uncontrollably. It wasn't just sobbing. It was loud.

A while later he settled down and Lucas waited until he thought the moment was right. "You were the best man?"

Jake closed his eyes and shook his head. "I was the truck driver."

It was Jake who broke the long silence. It took so long for either of them to say something that Lucas assumed they would just sit there the whole night, staring at the walls, feeling the weight of pain that comes from living life here.

"I saw that biker in the healing line today and it reminded me of what I was. Maybe of what I still am. He didn't get healed. Not by me, anyway. None of them did. And by the end of the day it hit me that I don't deserve to be here, Lucas. I don't deserve to be part of this team. I'm not like you. My life is a mess. There's a thousand guys who would be better at this than me."

"Me too," Lucas said. He repositioned himself on the floor to prevent a cramp from setting in. Through the window he caught a view of part of the moon and remembered the light it gave to his cell while he was at Xaing Xaing.

"How do you know Tabitha?" Jake asked.

It was Lucas' turn to talk about his past, he knew that, but he didn't want to spill his guts. He sat there, hoping the question would go away. But it didn't.

"Lucas?"

Lucas stood up. "Maybe later." What he meant was that he hoped Jake, being drunk, would forget about wondering how he and Tabitha knew each other. But drunks, even when they're in the tank, have a strange ability to remember things.

"You all right?" Lucas asked.

Jake nodded that he was.

Lucas closed the door behind him and admitted to himself that he needed to tell Jake about what happened between him and Tabitha. Not that Jake could help. He couldn't. But sometimes there's a healing that happens when things are out in the open, when things get shared with someone who is trustworthy. Even if it's a drunk from a rescue mission.

He wanted Jake to know. Really, he did. But there wasn't enough alcohol in all of Illinois to help Lucas get through it.

Not tonight.

Jake took a shower and fell into bed. He turned on the TV for a preview of the upcoming Notre Dame game but what he found instead was a story of the Palmer House Hilton event. He saw two Asian kids and their mom being interviewed. It triggered something in his mind and he wondered if he knew them. But sometimes the longer a person looks at someone the more they seem like someone they've met before. He couldn't place them until he thought of the last people he saw in the healing line that day. He studied the TV. It looked like the girl who couldn't talk. Well, at least she couldn't talk then. Now, she was answering questions as any speaking person would. Was this really her?

He hoped it wasn't the booze.

40

"And why would I do that?" Senator Turtle said from his phone at his DC office.

Caesar stood up from his desk at Empirico. He had been talking on speakerphone but obviously he wasn't getting through to the senator. Caesar picked up the receiver. "So that people can see what's really going on!"

There was a pause on the other end of the line. It was as though Senator Turtle had lost interest in the conversation.

"What's really going on?" the senator asked.

"People are being deceived."

Another pause. "Caesar, you want me to hold a Senate hearing on the miracles Lucas Stephens is performing because the public is being deceived?"

"Call it whatever you want. Hearings are nothing more than publicity stunts anyway. The truth never comes out. Doesn't even factor into it!"

A longer pause this time. Senator Turtle was putting the pieces together. "You want Lucas to stop?"

"What difference does it make what my reasons are?"

"Why would you want him to stop?" And suddenly, the senator knew. "You're afraid? Of Lucas?"

"You've seen the numbers."

"So what?"

"So what?" Caesar said. "So what? If people stop needing the drugs what do you think will happen to employees at pharmaceutical companies?"

"But the public loves him. For me to do anything but praise him would be suicide for my career," Senator Turtle said.

"And if Lucas continues what happens to the hundreds, the thousands of people who earn their living in the medical field?"

Senator Turtle paused again. He wished this phone call had never come. "I think you're overreacting."

"Ten thousand healed in, what, a week? Seven measly days and he's already cured that many? Who's drugs are they going to buy if they aren't sick? Which doctors will get paid to help them recover when they're already healed?"

"I see your point."

"No, you don't! You haven't even begun to see my point! If you did, you'd be as concerned as I am. We're not only talking about people getting healed. We're talking about people losing their jobs. Lucas is bad enough. And if he can transfer his power to others to help him cure people then there's no end to this. Over nine million people are employed in healthcare. If one percent become redundant because of the decrease in patients as a result of Lucas' healings then ninety thousand people are out of work. What do you think that means to the economy?"

Senator Turtle closed his eyes and rubbed the bridge of his nose with his thumb and index finger. It was a tough call either way. "Well, what then? Even if I do call a hearing, what am I trying to accomplish?"

"I have a plan."

Lucas forced himself out of bed at 5:00 a.m. to start on his prayers. His knees touched the ground. He rested his head sideways on the blankets. He tried to pray but he was too exhausted to get the words out of his mouth. Within a few minutes Lucas was drifting off to sleep again, enjoying that feeling of leaving consciousness into a world beyond. But the dream he was about to have made him wish later that he had forced himself to pray no matter how tired he was.

He found himself in the same desert as always. Hotter this time, if that was even possible. The blistering air filled his lungs and dried out his mouth immediately. He heard a rumbling sound behind him. He turned his head. There was a hill not too far away. Lucas lifted his legs and walked through the sand, feeling the soles of his bare feet sting with pain. There was no water around. No place to cool off.

He collapsed at the hill. Using his shoulders and his knees he dragged himself to the top. Each pull felt as though a heavy weight was attached to him. His heart pounded faster. He wanted to leave. To run away. But there was nothing but desert around him. He forced his head to peer over and see what was on the other side.

A knock at his motel room door. Lucas woke up. He was relieved. He didn't care who was there. He was just glad to be out of his dream. His nightmare. He looked at the clock. It was eight. His prayer time was lost.

He staggered to the door and without looking through the peephole he opened it.

"Short night?" Tabitha asked.

"You too, I guess."

"I have bad news."

Lucas was getting used to bad news. "What does Caesar want this time?"

"It's not Caesar. It's Senator Turtle."

The name 'Turtle' jumped out at Lucas. He thought of the child's tale of the tortoise and the hare. Sometimes a story comes to mind and no matter how hard you try the images don't leave. He remembered the scene of the hare waking up and realizing how far ahead the tortoise had gotten.

"I told Gibbs I wouldn't go back to Chicago," Lucas said.

"It's more serious than that."

Senator Turtle spent the evening before the Senate hearing staring out of his living room window at his backyard lawn. In his hand he held a glass of red wine. He rarely drank, even at social functions—didn't like what it did to some people. But tonight he was nervous and he hoped the drink would bring calmness to him. It was, however, his second drink and his mind showed no signs of slowing down.

Caesar weighed on him more than Lucas. He had contributed to his election campaign and Senator Turtle felt obligated to help him out. But he didn't like the idea of the hearing. What was he supposed to do with it, anyway? Lucas posed a problem—or maybe he was just a potential problem. Trouble was, the senator was caught either way. Lucas was in danger of costing people their jobs. But if Senator Turtle came down on Lucas, as Caesar wanted him to, then the public might turn on him and his chances of re-election would be as likely as winning a lottery. Maybe less.

He wondered about asking Lucas how he felt about the medical jobs that would be lost—doctors, nurses, therapists—all because of his healings. But those people, with some retraining if necessary, could find jobs elsewhere. Couldn't they? Just as during the industrial revolution when machines replaced workers; most of those workers found other jobs. Didn't they?

Senator Turtle didn't know whether Lucas was a threat or a help.

The red wine didn't taste so good. Maybe it was because he wasn't used to it. He finished his glass and decided to get another bottle. When he turned around he nearly screamed.

It was his wife. Just standing there. Arm's length away from him. Her white nightgown hung around her, almost giving her the appearance that she wasn't really visible. Her curly blond hair was darker than it usually looked. Maybe it was just the light. How she got there without him hearing he didn't know. His heartbeat pounded in his neck. He half expected her to have a knife in her hand. It was just so spooky.

"I had a dream," she said.

Senator Turtle wasn't sure if she was awake or not. She had that look in her eye people get when they're sleepwalking. "What about?" he asked.

"Don't do him any harm." He was going to ask to whom she was referring but he realized she could only have meant one person. "I saw him in my dream. In the desert. It was so hot that he couldn't move. Yet, he did. He started. Crawling. Even though it would have been easier to give up, he continued on."

She was scaring him now. That look in her eyes. It was as if she was gazing right through his body at someone behind him. It would have made him feel better if she was sleepwalking—that could have excused her behavior. But she was awake, or at least that's what it seemed like to him. Without saying anything more she walked away, as though in a trance, until she turned the corner out of sight. Strange, he thought, that he could hear her going up the stairs but had failed to recognize her coming down.

Don't do him any harm. He stayed at the window with those words playing over in his mind. He tried to think about something else but his thoughts kept coming back to Lucas and the words his wife had spoken. *Don't do him any harm.*

What little chance he had of getting any sleep was now lost.

41

The *Chicago Observer* sent Tabitha to cover the hearing. She flew in to Washington four hours before Lucas did and used that time to dig up information. She didn't get to interview Senator Turtle, no reporters did, not now, and the news she obtained from others involved was vague. It wasn't that they were trying to avoid her, it was that they didn't seem to know why the hearing was taking place.

It appeared as though Lucas was making the wrong people angry.

Lucas, Jake and Edgar worked on their opening statements on the plane. They thought about preparing answers to possible questions but decided against it. They were tired. Lucas used the time to pray. The longer they stayed in the air, the worse he felt.

The hearing room was not very big, and it seemed even smaller with all the reporters crammed into the back half of it. At the other end was a raised platform. Maybe a shoe-length or so off the ground, but high enough to give the impression that whoever was up there was important. On the platform stood fifteen black leather chairs arranged in a semi-circle behind a large curved table. One chair, for Senator Turtle, was dead center; the rest were spaced out evenly on either side of him. Behind the leather chairs stood thirty or so stacking chairs. The senators would occupy the leather chairs and their assistants would sit behind them.

Directly in front of where Senator Turtle would sit was a table with a white cloth on it. Three chairs were at the table, looking dwarfed by the huge black chairs in front of them. Lucas, Jake and Edgar were brought in and they sat down at the table. Lucas sat in the middle, Jake to his right, Edgar to his left.

"Any idea what happens?" Edgar asked.

"No."

"Can they send us to jail?"

"This is a hearing, not a trial, Edgar."

Jake was the most relaxed out of the three. Being in front of legal authorities was nothing new for him.

The senators took their places as did their aids behind them. Senator Turtle read off his introductory comments hoping he was winning points with the viewers watching across the nation. In the back, Caesar waited patiently for Lucas to be made a fool of.

Lucas checked behind him and saw Tabitha in the first row. Her hair was tied behind her. She wore a white shirt under a blue blazer. She smiled slightly, hoping things would go well for him and recalled that three years earlier they had sat together on the defense side in their court case.

"The three of you recognize that you are not being charged with anything, this is strictly a hearing," Senator Turtle said.

Jake leaned forward to his microphone. "Pardon?"

"This is a hearing."

Jake rubbed his ear as though they were clogged with wax. "A what?"

"A hearing."

The crowd laughed. Senator Turtle cracked a smile.

"For the record, could each of you please state your name."

"My name is Jake Rubenstein."

"Lucas Stephens."

"Edgar Sardisan."

"Would the three of you please state your occupations, as well?"

Lucas reached for the water jug in front of him. He hadn't said much yet but his throat was dry, like it was closing around him, choking him off. He drank a bit, feeling the way he did in the desert during his dream. "I used to work at Empirico in a marketing capacity."

"I'm a professor of theology at Mount Carmel University."

Back at the professor's lounge, Handle and Sheath had hoped Edgar would have left out the Mount Carmel part. They could already hear the voices of major contributors on the phone canceling their future donations. They blamed themselves. They felt responsible for creating such a misguided soul.

Jake pulled the microphone closer to him. "I don't do anything."

The media laughed.

Senator Turtle looked down at his sheet and skipped over some of the questions he had prepared in order to get right to the point.

"The three of you are involved in a... I don't even know what to call it... a crusade of sorts. It's really got Chicago turned upside down. There have been numerous allegations—that's not the right word—ideas as to what you people are up to. I know the people of Chicago, including people from other parts of our nation and around the world, hold you in high respect. Our goal here is simply to ascertain the motivation behind what you are doing."

Caesar smiled. He loved it.

Lucas took another drink. The water was losing the cold bite it once had. It seemed no matter how much he drank he couldn't relieve the dryness in his throat.

"This is a power we haven't seen before," Senator Turtle said.

"That's unfortunate," Lucas said. Senator Turtle heard it, he just didn't know how to respond so he kept on going.

"What exactly happens when you put your hands on a person?"

"Power flows through me and burns away the sickness."

"Where does this power come from?"

Another glass of water. It was starting to look strange to people. Jake glanced at him as if to ask him if he was all right. Lucas nodded and answered the question. "It comes from God."

"God?" Senator Turtle said, already knowing what the answer was going to be. "And you have no control over it?"

"I do. We do. Our role is to transmit."

"Transmit?"

"Right. The power it... burns through us."

Senator Turtle's mind found a familiar record and began to play *Don't do him any harm* over and over again. "What we've seen so far is that this power of yours produces healing miracles. But like all power this could have a negative use. How do we know you can't make everyone sick?"

Lucas felt the way little kids do when they've walked away from their family at the park only to realize later that they're lost. Edgar pulled the microphone closer to let Lucas know he was stepping in. "This power comes from God. And we believe that God is a good God. If evil is the disintegration of good and if God cannot change, then there can be no sinister outworking of this power."

Senator Turtle continued. "When Pharaoh refused to let the Israelites go, God himself sent ten plagues on Egypt—one of which was the death of the first born of all children."

The room went quiet. The people who watched TV sensed it was taking a long time to answer. Senator Turtle was angry with himself for asking the question. He didn't want to ask it, not in retrospect. It was just that the question was on the sheet. Now he sat there, hoping Lucas would answer quickly.

"That was done because Pharaoh rejected God."

Senator Turtle announced that he was done asking questions. *Don't do him any harm* beat like a drum in his mind. Next to him, Senator Darwin, the highest ranking member, started his questions.

"Does this mean that if some of the sick people who come to get healed don't believe in God they will get diseases instead of a cure?"

"We're not here to destroy anyone," Lucas replied.

"I'm not saying you are. But this power...."

"Comes from God."

"Yes, you claim it comes from God. But can you prove this?"

Lucas turned to Jake who gave him a look that said *don't ask me.* He turned to Edgar who raised his eyebrows to indicate he didn't know either. The pause created an embarrassing silence. Senator Darwin continued. "We're not suggesting that you're doing anything wrong. And I want to make it clear that I, for one, am thankful for the three of you." Senator Turtle wished he could have made it clear that he, too, was in favor of the team. "But lots of people credit and blame God for all kinds of things. How do we know that wherever this power comes from it will continue to heal people instead of make them worse?"

Lucas didn't bother to look at either Jake or Edgar this time. He cleared his throat and took yet another drink. "All we have is a track record of the people who've been healed. That's it."

Senator Aimes, to Turtle's left, continued. "One of the issues we are facing here is the pandemonium that has broken loose in Chicago. It is my understanding that you are having one final crusade in Chicago," he looked down at his notes to verify something, "at Wrigley Field and after that you are not being permitted to re-enter. How do you plan on continuing this work if you can't get into Chicago or other cities?"

"We'll set up shop outside the cities. The outskirts. Maybe in designated areas."

"The pharmaceutical industry may experience…changes…if that's the right word, because of your activities. The fear has been expressed that if the trend of healings continues then people in the medical field will lose their jobs because of a lack of need. How do you respond to those claims?"

Caesar edged himself forward. Lucas took a drink of water and answered.

"I used to work in the pharmaceutical industry. And I was once a medical student. I find it difficult to believe that should some professionals become redundant they couldn't be transferred to other areas. Research for example."

"Are your healing activities a substitute for medicine?"

"Absolutely not."

Senator Turtle looked at the clock and declared a thirty-minute recess. He wished right then that he had stood up to Caesar before this whole thing got started. Even though Lucas looked so small in that chair, Senator Turtle felt powerless against him.

Senator Turtle met with the other senators during the break to discuss the matter. None of them wanted to deal with Lucas. They didn't want to be associated with him. "The conclusion is this," Senator Turtle began, "if we come down on Lucas we'll look like idiots. The public loves him and they'll turn on us. If we let him run loose then there will be people in the medical and pharmaceutical industries who will lose jobs."

"They *might* lose their jobs," clarified Senator Aimes.

Senator Turtle nodded. "In the end it's better that they lose their jobs than it is that we lose ours. Besides, it's what the people want. Lucas stays. Any problems?"

Senator Aimes agreed. "There's no other solution. If this hearing goes to any kind of a trial, we're dead. Even if a governing body tells him to stop with his healings he won't do it. We all know that. Just let him be. Let the individual states and city governments handle him. I don't want any part of it."

Senator Turtle relaxed a bit. That warning from his wife just wouldn't leave him alone.

A few minutes later, as Senator Turtle sat behind his desk alone in his office, Caesar stormed in demanding an explanation. He was the last person Senator Turtle wanted to see.

"What's happening?" Caesar demanded.

"I'm holding a hearing."

"You call that a hearing? A man is practicing medicine without a license and you're not doing anything about it!"

"Caesar, sit down."

"I don't want to sit down."

"You're all worked up, now sit down."

"Don't tell me what to do!"

"Have a seat and we can discuss this."

"I'm not sitting down! Now get out there and get those guys!"

Senator Turtle stood up. He did not appreciate being bullied. "It is not my job to 'get' anyone. I'm here to search out the truth."

"The truth? The truth? This is a hearing! A publicity stunt! The truth has nothing to do with it!"

"What did you expect? That the public would be made aware that Lucas might be costing them jobs in the future and turn on him?"

"Exactly!"

"Well, they didn't bite. What were they supposed to conclude? That it's better for thousands to stay sick in order to preserve jobs in the medical and pharmaceutical fields?"

Caesar's face got red. His puffy eyes got even puffier. He was like a balloon that gets over-inflated and is in danger of bursting. He knew he'd been beaten. That made him mad. But what put him over the edge was all the money he had given to Senator Turtle's election campaign. Why on earth would anyone support someone without expecting something in return? *What kind of world are we living in when money can't buy us what we want?*

"This is what I get? This is the thanks I get?"

"Think of our current healthcare situation. Think of the seniors in this country. Baby Boomers are getting older. The Congressional Budget Office predicts that Medicare spending will more than double in the next decade. You think we have the money for that? Lucas is helping."

"Not me, he's not."

"Caesar, I did what I could."

"I don't think so."

"If Lucas really is such a threat, why haven't any of the other top ten pharmaceutical companies complained?" Senator Turtle did not wait for a reply. "Lucas is a strange phenomenon. But in the end he stays."

Caesar nodded his head. He wasn't agreeing, he was simply telling Senator Turtle that he had heard what was said. Caesar turned and walked out of the room.

Senator Turtle sat down at his desk feeling the fine line politicians walk between helping the people who voted them in and helping the financial backers that made it all possible. He knew that when Caesar walked out he was losing a major contributor. But there was more money to be had in Chicago than just Caesar's. Much more.

Caesar walked down the hall literally bumping into people, not caring who they were. He got into his limousine and drove off to the airport. *But in the end he stays.*

Caesar said nothing the whole way back.

Senator Turtle adjourned the hearing. There would be no further questions. No further inquiries, for now.

Tabitha walked with the three out of the building. Thousands had gathered outside. Reporters shouted at them as police escorted them to a cruiser. Sick people desperately stretched through the crowd just to get a touch of Lucas.

All these people, Lucas thought. In spite of all that had been accomplished, his group of three was still hopelessly inadequate to meet the need.

They needed more people to join their efforts.

On their way to the airport, Tabitha, Jake and Edgar discussed the hearing—what they thought of it, what it felt like and the media attention that had surrounded them. Lucas, however, said nothing. He looked out the window the entire way back, not concentrating on what he was seeing. *That* they were called to appear at a Senate hearing did not interest him as much as to *why* they were called in the first place. He knew Caesar was behind this, he just didn't know why. Why a hearing? Why now? But whatever Caesar had hoped to achieve with it, he had failed. For most people, that would be the end of things. But not for Caesar. Caesar was not a quitter.

And that's what was scaring Lucas.

42

Caesar stood at his lectern and addressed the Council. Empirico had dealt with opposition before, but this was something different. This time, it had not been an international merger that was threatening them. It had not even been a start-up company that was causing them undue stress.

It had been one of their own.

Caesar looked up with his puffy eyes and tired face. He wished he had a strong cigar or a stiff drink to rid himself of the tension he faced. "What started out as an anomaly, something that was just plain unique and out of the ordinary, has now become a problem. A serious problem."

He took a drink of water. He felt tired, more so than usual. He promised himself he would take a nap to try and take the edge off. But as long as the Lucas Stephens problem remained, relaxation was going to be difficult. "Any ideas?"

Claire was the only Council member who didn't agree with Caesar. For her, Lucas wasn't a problem. He was a solution. Why should they see him as a threat? "I don't think there's anything left for us to do," she said. She felt the tension from the other Council members, their anger burned towards her. It was as though she was suddenly unwelcome, as though the Council (Caesar especially) had turned on her. "Let's let him do what he does and let's stay focused on what we do."

There was a long silence. It was the kind of quiet people hear after a stupid suggestion has been made. Claire swallowed. The room felt colder. Smaller. As if someone had pushed the walls in.

"Perhaps you're right," Caesar said nodding his head. "Perhaps we should adjourn. We could use a break. Especially me."

They stood up and Claire was the first one out of the room. She opened the door, walked past Thatcher and Ridley, then hurried down the hallway. She almost broke into a jog as she went through the lobby. When she got outside she sucked in as much air as she could, feeling that the Council room had somehow stolen oxygen from her body. What she felt in there was worse than claustrophobia. Much worse. It was like a cloud had gathered over them.

It was evil.

Once Claire was gone Thatcher and Ridley closed the doors and the rest of the Council reconvened their meeting.

"Anyone else?" Caesar said.

No one moved. It was Mike's turn to swallow. Something inside told him that he would not like what was coming next.

They had tried to intimidate Lucas by roughing him up at his home. They had tried to lure him back with money and a position. Then they had tried to use the government to put pressure on his public image. But everything had failed.

Caesar stepped out from behind his lectern and stood in front of them. He looked out at his soldiers knowing they would respond to their call to duty.

The Council began to plot their last solution.

Lucas, Jake and Edgar originally planned to return to the motel run by Edgar's cousin in Schaumberg. Trouble was, word had somehow gotten out that they had been there and now more than a thousand people were crammed around the motel hoping the trio would arrive. One person even offered Edgar's cousin a thousand dollars to stay in the same room Lucas had.

Instead, the three decided on a Jesuit center not far from Lincoln Park. Edgar had a Jesuit friend from Notre Dame named Mick who had told him he was always welcome to stay there if he needed a place in Chicago. Tabitha drove them to her apartment and Mick picked the three up from there and took them to his little hideaway.

It was an unassuming building from the outside. The front door looked more like an entrance to a run-down building. But once inside, the place took on a different look. On the main floor was a huge kitchen and an incredible living room with leather couches, books, artwork and a hardwood floor. An elevator serviced the three-storey building. Each floor had about seven units—each with two to three beds in separate rooms. Mick showed them to their rooms on the third floor and told them dinner would be ready soon.

After getting settled in, Lucas, Jake and Edgar joined Mick in the dining room. He created a pasta dish for them with an incredible chicken/tomato sauce. They shared a bottle of red wine and laughed together over the stories Mick told them about some of his travels. He loved California. He'd been to LA, Palm Springs, Sacramento, San Francisco and San Diego. He'd also been to Vegas but not to gamble, he said, just to watch a live boxing match. His favorite road in all of the US was Highway One along the Pacific Ocean to LA. He talked about his teaching experiences in Peru, his missions work in Mexico and the time he got lost in a part of China where no one spoke any English or French or Spanish. He was really something to listen to. After a chocolate fondue dessert Mick entertained them with his rendition of Frank Sinatra's "Chicago."

At 8:00 Mick announced he had a meeting to attend. The three begged him for another song and after singing "New York, New York," Mick said goodbye. The three thanked their host and as soon as he left, the room felt strangely empty. They cleaned up the dishes and went to their adjoining rooms. For a few hours they had escaped.

The wood staircase on the outside of the back of the building doubled as a balcony. Lucas left his room and came outside. It was a quiet evening, which was strange considering how close they were to major streets. In a couple of hours the bars and cafés would be filled with people.

Lucas thought about the next day and their final Chicago event at Wrigley Field. All the major papers and news stations had hyped it up. They expected huge crowds. Maybe as many as a hundred thousand people would be lined up along Clark for their chance to get into the Friendly Confines. Lucas tried not to think past tomorrow.

He had no idea what he would be doing. *Just take it one day at a time*, he told himself.

And what a day that would end up being.

Edgar came to the balcony a few minutes later. He stood beside Lucas. Neither of them said anything for a while. It was nice to be under the Chicago sky, not having to answer questions, or run from a mob, or be in a crowd. Serenity. What a cherished commodity.

"I've decided to go back to Mount Carmel after Wrigley Field," Edgar said.

Lucas nodded. "I'm sorry you didn't get what you came for, Edgar."

"I don't know about that. I think I just may have gotten what I was looking for."

"How's that?"

"I didn't get rid of my cancer. That's the bad part. But I've had a chance to see things that I didn't think were possible. Just knowing that these things—these healings—really happen..." He got quiet and then continued. "They've done something for me."

"What's your plan?"

"I'll finish the semester. Then I'm going to get myself a sailboat."

"A sailboat?" Lucas said, a smile coming to his face.

"I'm going to sail around Lake Michigan. Bring my Bible with me. Visit as many churches as I can. See if I can't make some sense of all this healing business."

"Visit some of the beaches, Edgar. There are some incredible women in Illinois."

They both laughed. Edgar turned a little red, as though Lucas had read his mind. "You think so?"

"Oh, I know so. Smart, fun, outgoing women. It's one of the pluses of living here. You be sure to keep your eyes open."

Edgar laughed again and for a moment he forgot about his cancer. But the memory of his illness quickly came back to him the way it does for people who live in pain. His sickness was never more than a thought away.

"Thanks, Lucas."

"Thank you, Edgar."

They shook hands and Edgar noticed a touch of fear in Lucas' eyes.

"You all right?"

"I'm fine."

"No, you're not."

Lucas turned and looked out at the street. "I'm a little concerned."

"About tomorrow?"

"About everything. I'm concerned about where I'm going. About whether I'll be able to handle it."

"Tolkien said that 'deep roots are not reached by the frost.' You're going to do fine, Lucas." Edgar left and Lucas nodded, hoping Edgar was right.

Edgar retired to his room. Normally he stayed awake until 11:00 or so, reading or talking with friends. But it was only 8:30 and already he was in bed. It seemed as if there wasn't as much time in the days as there once was.

His first chemotherapy session was in four days.

A few minutes later, Jake came out to the balcony. "Tomorrow's the big day," he said like a kid who can't wait to get to the ball game.

"Yes, it is," Lucas said not taking his eye off the night sky.

Jake leaned against the railing. His heavy frame was almost in danger of pushing the whole thing over. He had come outside to ask Lucas about Tabitha but didn't know how to broach the subject. It wasn't that he wanted to pry into Lucas' private life. That wasn't it at all. But he could tell there was trouble between Lucas and Tabitha. The two of them were carrying on the way people do when there's something between them that they don't want to discuss—hoping that the situation will just take care of itself somehow.

Which, of course, it never does.

"What about you?" Lucas asked.

"What about me?"

"What's your plan after Wrigley Field?"

"I'm with you, Lucas. Wherever you go, I go."

Those words would not have been welcomed by Lucas had Jake told him that during their first meeting when Jake had vomited all over him at the rescue mission. Yet now, on the balcony at a Jesuit center, on the evening before his biggest healing event ever, it was comforting to know someone was with him. Lucas wasn't above friendship the way some men are. And right now, a dedicated friend who happened to be a recovering drunk and drug addict was just what Lucas needed.

"I don't know where I'm going, Jake."

"Great. Then I'll follow you to nowhere."

They laughed, their voices carried across the parking lot to the street.

"Tabitha called," Jake said. "Wanted to know if we got here okay."

The quiet night got even quieter, as if someone had turned the volume right down.

"Nice of her to call."

Jake realized the timing wasn't right. He gave Lucas a pat on his shoulder and left. Lucas looked at his watch, feeling the solid stainless steel backing against his wrist. It reminded him of the gold medal he had received from the man whose daughter was healed outside Lucas' home. Lucas wondered where that medal was now. Probably in with his things, he guessed.

The night was still young. He wanted to call Tabitha back, let her know they were okay. She probably already knew that, he told himself. But he had to talk to her. In all the excitement about the healings they never took the time to discuss each other, to discuss their situation. He felt a tug in his chest. Some things a person can avoid for only so long.

He went back inside then down the stairs to the main floor. It was dimly lit but he found his way to the kitchen. He poured himself a glass of distilled water. The cold water against the back of his throat felt good. He saw the phone. He put his hand on it. He knew her number. He waited a moment, hoping for a sudden rush of courage to show up. It never came. He picked up the receiver and was about to dial when he heard something in the living room.

He came in and found Jake sitting on the couch, reading. Lucas sat down across from him and Jake put his book down. They weren't in a confession booth. But they may as well have been.

"You were about to call her?"

Lucas nodded.

"You want a glass of wine?" Jake asked.

Yes, I do. Actually, I want the entire bottle. No, wait. I want the whole case. Bring everything you can find. I want to get all loaded up and spill my guts. It doesn't hurt as much when you're drunk. "No, thanks. Nothing for me."

They sat there for a long while not saying anything, occupying themselves with their own thoughts. Even though Lucas had resolved himself to sharing something personal it still took an incredible amount of courage to get those first words out.

"Well, it's your call," Jake said. "If you want to talk about something, I'm here. You don't have to. I'm cool either way."

Jake looked at Lucas. But Lucas couldn't look back. He closed his eyes for a moment as if to draw strength for what he was about to say.

"I left Vancouver to go to medical school. Harvard. I met Tabitha there. We were at the top of our class."

It felt surreal to Lucas, the way things feel when a person is revealing something dark from their past. He had tried to forget about the whole event. Tried to put it behind him. He had hoped that serving his time in prison would have cleared his conscience. But it hadn't. The law had said he had paid his debt to society. But inside, Lucas was still paying for his mistake. He wondered if he would ever pay enough.

"She even took me fly-fishing with her father. It was a father-daughter thing they had going. Every Saturday morning for years they would go to their favorite river. Her father still goes there. Far as I know."

Lucas took a drink of his water wishing instead it was whiskey or rum. Anything stronger than water. He wondered how much wine was left in that bottle they had for supper.

"Her father decided to run for office. While he maintained that women should have a legal right to choose, he made it clear to everyone that he thought abortion was wrong."

He took another drink of water. The tough part was coming.

"Tabitha got by okay being away from home. But her sister didn't. She was a year younger and studied at Harvard as well. She got pregnant. Never found out who the father was. It happened when she got drunk at an off-campus party. She kept it a secret for a while—even Tab and I didn't know. Then it got down to crunch time. Right during her father's campaign. If the truth came out her dad would be ruined. She couldn't go to a clinic or a hospital for her abortion. A reporter might have found out; they always seem to find things out during elections. We told her to keep her child but she was too humiliated to go through with it. Daddy's little girl screwed up. A future Harvard grad. Part of the famous Samos family. Soon to be a mother with no idea who the father was." Lucas bent his head down and covered his face with his hands. He ran his fingers through his hair and continued. "Against our advice, she decided to get rid of it. Didn't want to live with the embarrassment. Didn't want to tarnish her dad's chances. She asked Tabitha and I to abort the baby."

Lucas stopped. He brought the glass to his lips but the water was gone. He clutched it in his hands as though doing so would help him get through the next part.

"I miscalculated the medicine to give Tabitha's sister. We raced her to the hospital but there was nothing anyone could do. She died. So did the baby."

He said that last part so fast. It was as if every word was like a knife being drawn out from his stomach, through his throat and out his mouth.

"We were both kicked out of medical school. I was sent to jail. Served a year. Tabitha's dad lost. Far as I know, he and Tab haven't spoken a word ever since."

Jake had a rare wisdom that knew when words were unnecessary. He looked at Lucas and nodded, knowing all too well the power the past can have over a person. Lucas buried his face in his hands. Tears came from his eyes but he made no sound. The two of them stayed there, in the dimly-lit, quiet room. Neither of them moved.

Lucas dialed her number. It rang four times and when he heard a clicking sound, he was sure it was the voice-mail starting up. But it wasn't. It was Tabitha. She responded with a simple hello. It caught him off guard and in his panic he was about to hang up. But there was something reassuring in her voice. Something calming that kept him on the line.

"Tabitha?"

She told him she was glad they had made it there okay and asked if they were all set for tomorrow. Lucas said that they were ready. And then things went still like the way a lake gets before, or after, a storm.

"Tabitha? Can we talk?"

43

Lucas put on a red cap and caught a cab to Buckingham Fountain. He walked through the park until he came to the brownish gravel area and stopped by a tree. He looked around for Tabitha but didn't find her. He checked his watch. It was 9:00. In front of him he saw the streams of water shooting out from the largest fountain he had ever seen.

Off to the right, coming from Columbus Drive, Tabitha walked towards the fountain. She wore her black leather jacket, white jeans and a black shirt. Her hair hung down around her shoulders, her eyes scanned the area looking for him.

When he saw her, a pulse of nervous energy shot through him. She looked so content, so confident. And he hated having to delve into the past, which would undoubtedly alter her otherwise happy mood. Part of him wanted to forget what happened—to pretend that everything was already dealt with. That it was all in the past.

And it *was* in the past. It was just that the past had a strange habit of showing up in the present from time to time.

She nearly walked right by him and would have if he hadn't called out to her.

"Tabitha."

He startled her. She was expecting him to be up at the fountain instead. She turned, relieved. "It's not polite to scare people, you know."

She said that in such a suave, cool manner that it made it even tougher for Lucas to talk to her about what was on his mind. He wished she could have been angry or worried—anything but the way she was right now. She saw the look on his face and got serious quickly.

"You have time to talk?" was all he could manage.

She raised her eyebrows and gave a slight smile to tell him that was what she was there for.

The park wasn't very full but all the same they stayed away from the fountain to avoid being recognized. The huge water bursts shot out occasionally and sometimes quite high. The sound was refreshing. It gave them the feeling they weren't the only ones there. They stopped at a bench and sat down. Some things can't be said standing up.

Lucas' mind stalled. He sat, looking at her, wanting to say something but not knowing where to start. Before he had got there he'd thought about preparing something, then decided he would just wing it. Say whatever would come naturally. Now, being in front of her, he felt hopelessly inadequate to explain what was on his mind. It reminded him of their conversation at Navy Pier where he had drunk his freshly-squeezed lemonade. He hoped this encounter would go better.

He let out a nervous laugh and said, "I don't know how to begin."

Her fears about this meeting being about something more than the healings were confirmed. And that could only mean one thing. "Pretend you're in a beautiful park sitting in front of a woman who wants to know why she's here."

He looked at the fountain. The lights really made it look incredible. He thought it interesting how water could capture a person's attention.

"Tabitha, I didn't think I'd ever see you again."

She nodded as though she knew he was going to say that.

"At least not this soon." He paused before continuing. "I guess what I'm trying to say is that I don't know how to make things right between us."

"That's what you want?" Their eyes met. "To make things right?"

"If it's possible," he said.

The communication helped to calm them. There was something therapeutic about talking.

"I'm not sure where we start," she said. The memories of her sister and that fateful event were coming back now. Memories never really leave, anyway. They just get put in a closet someplace and you forget about them, until one day you see something or hear something and it triggers what happened years ago. She felt it all over again at that moment. Anger at him. Anger at herself. Even anger at her sister. She felt tremendous regret over their decision to attempt an abortion. She forced herself to admit that it was their decision and not just Lucas'. A flood of sadness gripped her and she felt the way people do when they beat themselves up at night knowing that one small change of events, one different decision, could have avoided a whole life of pain and misery.

"It was my fault," he said.

Tabitha immediately shook her head. "It wasn't." She ran her fingers over her forehead trying to figure out what to say next. Lucas was about to continue when she cut him off. "And this isn't about blame. I could have stopped her. You could have stopped her."

"We should have."

"And she shouldn't have gotten pregnant in the first place." She wished she hadn't said that, at least not in that way. It felt as though she had betrayed her sister's memory.

"Tabitha, I'm sorry for what I did."

There was a long silence.

She said, "We all agreed to it, Lucas. We could have made other choices. Things could have turned out differently. But they didn't." She closed her eyes, knowing that life only moves forward and that one of the few things that can travel back in time is our memory.

She looked out at the traffic on Lake Shore and it hit her how all those people driving by knew nothing of what she and Lucas were talking about. Even though they were sorting through a crucial point in each of their lives, it meant nothing to the hundreds passing by who had their own problems to deal with.

"And all I know is that after the newspaper articles and after the healings, you and I are still a mess," she said.

"We don't have to stay this way."

"Can we get out?"

"Do you want to?"

"I know that we can't go on like this," Tabitha said.

"Then it starts with your answer."

"Answer?"

"I said I was sorry."

"How can I forgive you when I am equally to blame?"

"We have to start somewhere."

She didn't know what to say. It didn't feel right. For either of them. Here they were on a park bench in Chicago discussing a horrible event, a tragedy, and somehow it was all going to be made better in one conversation? It didn't feel simple. It felt wrong.

"Then why don't we start with me?"

"Because I'm taking responsibility."

"That's not fair," she said. Their eyes locked. For the first time since meeting again they really saw each other. They didn't just look at each other. They looked into each other. And it frightened Lucas to notice how similar she was to him.

"Why not?" he said.

"Because I need from you the same thing you need from me."

The decision to kill Lucas came easily to the Council. In the end it was the only logical conclusion. Lucas on the loose spelled trouble for them and he had to be stopped. He could have taken the offer to join them. But he hadn't.

Really, it was his own fault.

The Council (except for Claire who had left for the day and was none the wiser) agreed that the identity of the killer and the method of murder would be kept a secret. They decided that one of them would be chosen by random selection to take Lucas' life. That way, all of them had conspired to kill Lucas but only one of them would actually do it. The reason for keeping things anonymous was to prevent a Council member from getting an attack of morality and spilling their guts. Secrecy prevented anything from being spilled.

Except blood, of course.

Caesar gave each of them a glass of red wine and an envelope.

"I want you all to take an oath with me," he said in a strangely calm voice. Mike was sure that conspiring to kill someone would cause them all to become tense and nervous. But Caesar stood there as though he was giving any other kind of address. It was business to Caesar. It was personal, too.

Caesar raised his glass. The Council members lifted theirs. Mike hated red wine. Everything felt so eerie to him. A toast, it seemed, to Lucas' death.

"When you take this wine you promise that you will neither eat or drink until Lucas is dead." He looked each one of them in the eye. Mike felt that the look alone could kill. "This is not to be taken lightly. If you cannot agree then leave now, quickly!"

Nobody moved. The time to bail out came and went.

"Then it is settled. Take and drink."

The Council drank their wine. Caesar finished his whole drink in one gulp. He didn't smile. No evil glare. No cackling laugh. No *heh-heh-heh I've got you now* look on his face. He just put down his glass and told them to be seated. It was all so matter of fact. Mike was the last to sit down. The whole thing should have spooked him. It should have caused him to get up and run out.

Scary thing was, after drinking that wine he felt completely at home.

"I have envelopes for each of you. And in each envelope is a card. Every card is blank except for one. One of the cards carries a black X. If you receive the card with the black X, this will tell you that fate has selected you to serve your Council in the matter of Mr. Stephens."

They had never sat so still in all their lives. It was as if they had become wax statues. Sure, they decided as a team that one of them would rub Lucas out, but now that it was crunch time things seemed a lot more complicated. It was the moment of reality, as when players look at the list on the coach's office to see if they made the team. There were forty of them in that room. Only one black X. Each person had a little more than a two percent chance of being chosen. And oh, how big that two percent suddenly felt when the weight of a human life was being thrown around.

Caesar distributed the white and gold envelopes to each of the Council members. They held them in their hands. The envelopes seemed heavier than they actually were.

"Each of you will leave without speaking a word. You will drive off the property to a quiet place and open your envelope. Whoever has the black X will return and meet with me in my office."

No one said anything.

"You are all bound by your oath. We are dismissed."

And that was it. They got up and walked out. Just like any other board meeting. Just like any other day.

They got into their cars—their Porsches, BMWs, Mercedes and

drove off. As Mike watched the vehicles leave it seemed odd to him that the burden of murder sat inside one of those machines.

Mike drove for a while and passed various suitable locations. He wasn't sure where to stop. Where exactly do you open an envelope like this? He traveled down Jackson and looked at the clock. It was 9:30. Surely by now the others had opened their envelopes.

He parked his car near Lake Shore, grabbed the envelope and got out. He walked towards the fountain, his footsteps sounding louder than they normally did. Then he stopped. It was time to find out. One way or the other.

He lifted up the envelope. He swallowed. Sweat formed on his head. He took in a breath. He felt nauseous.

In the distance something caught his eye. It looked like lovers on a park bench. Just sitting there. But they looked familiar to Mike. Certainly that was Tabitha. Her dark hair was unmistakable. But who was she with? A young man in a red cap.

His heart stopped.

The park went quiet.

It was Lucas.

Mike's knees felt weak, as though someone had just told him he was about to die. He lifted up the envelope in order to see both Lucas and the card at the same time. He broke the seal and pulled out the card.

He opened it up. His eyes froze.

The card was blank.

He felt like falling to the ground, or screaming, or running. He took in a few deep breaths, grateful that he was cleared from this horrible responsibility. He looked back at Lucas. One way or the other the man's minutes were counting down now.

Mike looked up at the sky then closed his eyes. He was relieved that the ordeal was over. He tried to convince himself that he was fine, or as fine as a man can be after nearly finding out he would become a murderer. He pulled the card back into view to double check the result. He opened it up. Again, no X. He stared at the blank card trying to prove to his mind that there really was nothing written on it and that there was no reason to feel anxious.

He looked back at Lucas. Then back at the card.

He turned it over and was about to put it into the envelope when he noticed there was something inscribed on the back. He took a closer look.

Fate can be a cruel enemy.

"What's wrong?" Tabitha asked.

Lucas felt strange, the way people feel when they think someone is watching them. He looked around, convinced someone was spying on him but saw no one. The only evidence he had was the feeling of dread that suddenly came over him.

"Lucas?" she asked again this time getting worried.

"I'm okay," he lied. "I... I..." He shook his head. "Forget it." He looked back at her. "Where were we?"

Mike entered Caesar's office hoping his breath didn't stink—not that his breath was his biggest problem. It wasn't. It was just that he had vomited three times on the way back to Empirico and he couldn't get the smell out of his nostrils. Caesar looked happy that it was Mike, as though he would have picked him if he had the choice. Mike dropped the card on Caesar's desk. The black X facing up.

"Welcome," Caesar said.

The lights were dim. It was tough to see Caesar's eyes. "Let's get this over with," Mike said.

Caesar pulled out a map. It was when Mike sat down that he nearly died of fright. His heart pounded with such a boom that he felt it was going to burst out of his chest and explode in the room. There, behind him to the right, he saw Thatcher and Ridley. No expressions. No greetings. No acknowledgments. They just stood there as quiet as if they were pieces of furniture.

The sweat on Mike's body began to cool. The whole room seemed chilly. That sick feeling came back to him again.

"The three of you will make up the team. Tomorrow."

It should have felt more intense to Mike, more cloak-and-daggerish. But it didn't. It was all so trivial. So common. As if they were about to talk about the Cubs game from the night before.

"Three shooters." Caesar pointed to the map. "Here, here and here." He indicated one would be behind the Cubs sign at Wrigley Field. One would be stationed in the new apartment building on Clark. The third, Mike, would be on a rooftop overlooking the Addison and Clark intersection. The exit routes were also marked.

"Won't the shooter behind the sign get noticed?"

Caesar shook his head. "Wrigley Field stays empty until Lucas arrives. He's the first one through."

"So we get him outside? At the corner of Addison and Clark?"

Caesar nodded. "You will each have ear pieces and you will wait for my signal. I will either say 'Abort' or 'Action.'"

One word from Caesar was all it would take. Either way. He looked up at them as if to tell whether they would have the guts to carry it out. Thatcher and Ridley had fired weapons at people (they referred to them as *targets*) many times before, but for Mike—this was a first.

"I don't think you have the guts to do it, Mike," Caesar said.

Mike was offended. The comment was out of place. He glared at Caesar as though he was somehow able to transmit poison with his eyes. "I can take care of myself. Just make sure your two thugs here don't jam out on me."

Caesar scowled at him. He clenched his jaw. But Mike didn't back down. Not a chance. Inside, Caesar was totally satisfied. He'd never been more proud of Mike.

They went over the plan. It was straightforward. Fire three shots. Drop the weapons. Leave via the escape routes. And after some more discussion the three left. They decided to drive to the site in order to make sure they understood exactly how the triangulation crossfire would work.

Caesar got up from his chair and buzzed the front to tell them he would be leaving soon. He picked up his jacket and pulled out a cigar for the trip home. He looked back at his desk and noticed a brown envelope.

It was addressed to him.

Lucas and Tabitha got up from the park bench, neither of them really sure about what they had accomplished. The fountain could still be heard behind them.

"That's it?" she asked.

"I guess."

"Feels so strange."

"It does."

It was hard for both of them to believe that in less than half an hour the past had been talked through. Not cleared up, though. That's different. And that wasn't the point of their conversation. Sometimes things just need to be expressed. Sometimes they don't need a solution. At least not right away.

"Need a lift back?" she asked.

He was staying not too far from where Tabitha lived, but he wasn't heading back to the Jesuit center. Not yet.

"I want to see Caesar."

"You think that's a good idea?" She said that with enough emphasis to let him know that she didn't like it.

"I'm about to find out."

45

Caesar arrived at his home and sat down at his dining room table. He stared at the brown envelope and debated about whether or not he should open it. It wasn't good news. That much he knew. The question he was mulling over in his mind was how bad it would really be. He picked it up and opened it with a knife. His doctor had left numerous messages requesting that the two of them meet. But Caesar didn't want to. He told the doctor to send any health issues to his office. If Caesar wanted a visit with the doctor, he'd let him know.

As he pulled out the letter he got the feeling that whatever the doctor had found it would be something manageable. High blood pressure. Cholesterol maybe. He promised himself he wouldn't eat any more of those homemade pastries, no matter how good they tasted.

When he read the letter he discovered it *was* bad news—and that it was worse than he thought. The good doctor had discovered cancer. Caesar had three months to live.

If he was lucky.

"Sir." It was his butler. "You have a visitor."

His first thought was that it was Mike. *He better not be having second thoughts about shooting Lucas.*

"Who?"

"Mr. Stephens, sir."

Caesar closed his eyes. He couldn't believe it. The next time Caesar wanted to see Lucas was in a casket—provided, of course, there was enough of Lucas left to put in a casket. "Show him into the study."

"Should I provide you with anything?"

Caesar didn't respond. He didn't have to. The butler would figure out that the answer was no.

Caesar's study was on the second floor; it overlooked his indoor pool. There were two original Picassos among other paintings on the walls and a large aquarium the size of a car at the far end. Caesar looked at his exotic tropical fish, their bright colors flickering against the back lighting. He used to know what they were called, but he had since lost interest. He heard Lucas at the door. The butler introduced him and left. Caesar turned around.

"You know," Caesar began. "When I heard you were at the door I thought to myself—maybe he's going to come back to work for me." He laughed, but neither of them thought it was funny.

"I can't do that."

"And why not?" Caesar sat down in one of the two maroon leather couches. "Why can't you come back to Empirico?"

"I just can't."

"That's not a very good answer."

Lucas sat down opposite Caesar. He looked at the aquarium and wondered why someone would need such a huge collection of exotic, dangerous fish. Lucas thought the glass might break any second and that the deadly creatures would jump out and attack him. "Sometimes a man has to do things he's called to do as opposed to the things he wants to do."

"And you do your healings because you're called to, even though you want to work for me?"

Lucas searched for the right words to say. "I know that I couldn't carry on with what I was doing knowing what I had to offer people."

Caesar nodded his head pretending to understand and poured himself a bourbon from the tray beside him. He offered one to his guest. Lucas refused, but inside he wanted the whole bottle. Caesar drank a sip and looked carefully at Lucas. The man in front of him was going to be dead in twenty-four hours. Caesar felt like a priest administering last rites. Like a warden talking with a death-row inmate.

"What did you come here for, Lucas?"

"I think you were behind the attack at my home. I think you offered me and the rest of the team positions at Empirico to get me off of the healings. And I think you pulled strings to have the Senate hearing."

Caesar gave no indication that he was guilty. He didn't care if Lucas knew or not. "Is that what you came here for?"

There was a pause. Lucas eyed the bourbon. There was more than just bourbon on that tray. Behind Caesar, in a glass case, were still more bottles. That thirst burned in Lucas. He closed his eyes a moment, as if doing so could shut away the temptation. "I came here to tell you that I'm not backing down from what I'm doing."

You stupid fool, thought Caesar. *You stupid, stupid fool!* "Why are you doing this, Lucas? You gave up a wealthy position. Arguably, it's the best position on planet earth for anyone your age. And to do what? Hand out free medical services?"

"To help people," Lucas said.

"They're not helped and you know it. You and I are *not* in the business of helping people."

"Of course we are."

"No, we're not. We are in the business of prolonging agony."

Lucas shook his head. "People who are healed are not in agony."

"Nobody gets healed, Lucas. We all die. You know that. And I know that. All I do is provide medications to people who want to pretend that being here longer will make some kind of a positive difference in this world."

Caesar got up from his chair. A rush of exhaustion suddenly came over him. Maybe it was the cancer beginning to take its toll on his body. He poured himself another drink and decided to entertain Lucas a short while longer before retiring for bed.

Tomorrow was going to be a busy day.

"We help people lead more fulfilling lives," Lucas said.

Caesar sat down in a chair that was closer to Lucas than the couch. He hoped it would help Lucas understand him better. "We sell illusions, Lucas. I do it by selling pharmaceuticals and you do it by giving out free miracles. People want to think that once they are healthy their lives will be good. And we help them believe it's possible."

"You don't think life gets better with health?"

"Absolutely not. Health is the biggest farce on earth. It's a big business because it plays on the basic human need to be free from the evil effects of this world."

"There's nothing wrong with that."

"Everything is wrong with assuming you can have something that will never happen."

"Never happen?"

"There is nothing you can do about evil in this world. You can't escape it no matter how hard you try. Sick people think that being healthy will make their world better. Victims think that justice will make their world better. Poor people think having money will make their world better. It's all illusions, Lucas. If you solve a person's health problem it only opens their eyes to the wider realities of life. We assume that all it takes is to get healed, to get justice, to get money, to get this, to get that. It's all vanity, Lucas."

"You're talking from personal experience."

"We always talk from personal experience," Caesar said.

"A boy gets healed of paralysis and plays soccer. That's not a good thing?"

"Of course it's a good thing. But what has it accomplished? Maybe that kid being in a wheelchair had a chance to learn things about life he will now never have a clue about because he is healthy."

"A father spends all his money to have his daughter healed of an unknown disease. Now she's better."

"You only think she's better. What has that healing really done for her? It's given her a free ticket out. It's told her that all she has to do is persistently run to you, a miracle man, or to me, a drug man, to make the world go away. The father and the daughter wanted the same thing—to live in a better illusion. To live in a better make-believe world."

Caesar was a full head shorter than Lucas, but he felt ten feet taller. He looked at Lucas with more certainty now, more purpose. "Now I want the truth out of you. Why are you here?"

Lucas readjusted himself on his chair. "I want you to join me at tomorrow's healing event."

"And I want you to quit your occult, witch doctor routine and get back to your job where you belong."

"I don't belong there, Caesar."

"You don't?"

"No."

"Did you belong when you came begging me for a job?"

Lucas said nothing.

"When no one else would take you in? When your life was reduced to that of released convict, imprisoned for murder, did you belong then?"

Still nothing.

"And what about in China? When I paid a boat load of money to get you out?" Lucas' eyes met Caesar's. "Oh, yes. You didn't know about that, did you? It was me who got you out of that prison. Not God. Not luck. Me. I was the one who forked over the money. When I got you out of that prison, did you belong to Empirico then?"

"I thought I did."

"You thought?"

"I was wrong, Caesar."

Caesar put down his bourbon, got up and walked to Lucas. It scared Lucas. Weak and feeble as Caesar was, he had this power over Lucas. Caesar stretched out his arms and put his hands on Lucas' shoulder. It relieved Lucas. At first, he thought Caesar was going to choke him.

"I'm willing to forget everything and give it all back to you. The money. The prestige. The women. The future. It's so bright you can't even imagine. Pharmaceuticals were only the beginning. I'm working on a hotel in Las Vegas. It's going to be called the Avalanche. And I'm starting a film production company in Hollywood. You are the man to take all this on. This is for you, Lucas. I know it's for you because I know you the best."

"You know me?"

"Yes. I saw potential in you when everyone else saw failure. I took a chance on you when no one else dared. And I wasn't wrong. You know why?"

"Because you know me?" Lucas said.

"That's right."

"I don't think so."

Caesar stepped back, offended. He froze there, staring at Lucas, almost seeming he was going to fall over. "Then there isn't much left to say? Is there?"

He said that with such a low tone that it worried Lucas.

Caesar opened the door to the hallway and expected Lucas to show himself out. They each went their separate directions. Lucas stopped near the stairs and caught Caesar before he walked out of sight.

"Why do you want to stop me?"

Caesar turned around. He looked at Lucas like a prodigal son who was insisting on staying away. "Because you're in the healing business, too, Lucas. And if you hadn't noticed, we're not on the same team."

Lucas walked down the stairs and headed down the long hallway for the door. Caesar entered his bedroom and shook his head in disgust over Lucas' mutiny. He ripped open the drawer of his night table and looked at his gun. He thought about using it, but then decided against killing Lucas here, in his mansion, tonight.

A dead body lying face down in the front hallway with a bullet in the back would be awfully difficult to explain to the police.

46

Jake stood alone on the balcony watching the night sky. It was quiet, finally. The traffic had died down. The once crowded sidewalks, bars and cafés were empty. Only a few cars now. He should have had a peaceful feeling as he looked out at the stars and sensed the gentle wind. But Jake was uneasy. He couldn't determine exactly what was wrong. Only that there was something out there.

Something evil.

In his right hand he held Lucas' belt. He had thought, at first, that it was his own and had taken it with him after his shower. When he got outside he realized his mistake. He was going to bring it back inside but something about the belt concerned him. It was as though it was trying to warn him about an upcoming event. Lucas and Edgar were sound asleep in their rooms. Jake wondered why they weren't as worried as he was.

He prayed the entire night. Right on the balcony. His wrists became sore from leaning on the railing. But the pain didn't bother him. What bothered him was the creepy feeling that someone was behind him.

On a number of occasions he turned around, being certain that someone, or something, was there. Although his eyes didn't see anything, he was still convinced he was being watched. He had the feeling people get when they see a scary movie in a house by themselves. The house hasn't changed, only their perception about what's going on inside it has. It prevented Jake from praying longer than five minutes at a time. The feeling was all around him. Laughing at him. Mocking him. Plotting against them all. Waiting for it's chance to do evil—which was coming sooner than Jake realized.

At 5:00, Lucas met Jake on the balcony. One look at him and Lucas knew where he had spent the evening. He was exhausted. His scraggly hair hung down to his shoulders. All was not well with Jake Rubenstein.

"Jake?"

Jake had fear in his eyes. He looked at Lucas trying to determine if he was really there. "Lucas?" he said, hoping it wasn't an apparition.

"Rough night?"

Jake didn't smile. Didn't even nod. He just swallowed and said, "You can't go out there today."

"I can't?"

"No. None of us can."

"Why not?"

"You can't go near that crowd today. You just can't."

Lucas was concerned now. Worried. "What do you know, Jake?"

Jake hated the question. He had no proof, only a gut reaction. An instinct. Hardly the kind of evidence that would convince Lucas. "I just know."

"It's jitters," Lucas said. But inside he knew it was more than that.

"It's not jitters!" Jake controlled himself before continuing. "Something is wrong."

Lucas saw his belt in Jake's hand. He chuckled and tried his luck with changing the mood. "You've got my belt, you know?"

The mood did change. It got more serious.

"You're not getting it, Lucas."

"What am I not getting?"

Jake wrapped the ends of Lucas' belt in his hands, as though he were getting ready to strangle him and held it out in front of him. "Whoever owns this belt is falling into a trap."

"Jake, you're worrying me." Their eyes stayed focused on each other. "Are you all right?" Lucas was afraid. Any second Jake would snap out with that belt, wrap it around Lucas' neck and choke him to death.

"I'm fine," Jake said, his eyelids pulled back to reveal the whites of his eyes. "It's you I'm worried about." Jake released his grip on the belt but didn't take his eyes off Lucas. He gave it back to him.

"I'm not backing down, Jake. I'm not afraid. Whatever it is."

"I don't know how it ends."

"I didn't come here to quit when it got rough."

"Well," Jake said. "It's rough."

Lucas leaned against the railing and shook his head trying to figure out what was wrong. "Where are you getting this from?"

"Maybe from the same place you get your healing."

They stood there a moment, looking out at the night sky. Lucas could sense it now as well. Something *was* wrong. Very wrong. Jake walked past him to the doorway then turned back. "It's time for prayers."

Mike, Ridley and Thatcher went over the plan one last time to be sure there would be no glitches. They reviewed the triangular crossfire and, almost more importantly, their escape routes. They got into a white van, Mike drove, headed to their appointment at Wrigley Field.

Tabitha interviewed some of the people gathered outside the ballpark. Many of them were sick, unable to be cured by any means known to doctors or herbalists. Others came out of interest—to catch a look at a real miracle. Police had shut down the Clark and Addison intersection and were beginning to close off intersections five blocks in every direction. Hundreds were arriving every minute. More than ten thousand had already gathered, waiting to get into Wrigley Field.

Tabitha crossed the Seminary and Waveland intersection and walked in the direction of Clark when a white van drove up. It stopped on Waveland, behind the outfield. A man got out. He had a strong, tall build. He walked away from Tabitha and disappeared into the crowd.

The white van drove past Tabitha then stopped again. Another man with a strong build got out. It was when she recognized the man as being Ridley that her mind replayed the scene of the white van driving by her. She knew the driver.

It was Mike.

The white van drove down Waveland to Clark and out of sight. Ridley walked down Clark and turned into a work zone sectioned off by an orange fence. An apartment complex was undergoing construction. Fifteen stories high. It had a perfect view of Wrigley Field.

Clark and Addison, too.

Police vehicles escorted Lucas, Jake and Edgar down Clark to Wrigley Field. At 11:30 it was reported that fifty thousand people had arrived with still more on the way. Lucas saw the people walking on the crowded sidewalks. Some of the sick had others to walk the journey with them to Wrigley Field. Others had to walk it themselves.

"We'll stop at Clark and Addison," Lucas said.

The police officer nodded his head. "That's a good idea. Clark is jammed all the way to Buckingham."

"We'll get out there and walk the rest of the way."

Again, the policeman nodded.

Lucas looked at Jake. "It's going to be all right." He said that hoping Jake had changed his mind.

But he hadn't.

Thatcher positioned himself on the sundeck of Wrigley Field behind the Cubs sign. His rifle was in a marked package on the ground beside him. He wore a jacket with a courier uniform underneath, which he'd use as part of his getaway. He looked out at the intersection. The shot would be so simple. The line on Lucas was perfect. Thatcher figured he didn't even need the other two shooters. One clear shot was all it would take.

He glanced at his watch. 11:46. In less than fifteen minutes Lucas would arrive. Thatcher's plan was to take out his rifle at the last possible moment, assemble it, get off his shots and hurry outside. It was just a matter of execution. And it would have worked out that way if it wasn't for the voice he heard behind him.

"What are you doing here?"

Thatcher looked like an idiot, crouched down on the ground, peering out from behind the Cubs sign. He turned around and saw a security guard, no gun, standing at the entrance to the sundeck. Thatcher took in a breath and felt his handgun at his chest. He was smart enough to have put a silencer on it but dumb enough to have come this early and have someone spot him.

"You're not allowed to be here," the guard continued.

Thatcher thought about his options. He could pull out his gun and put a bullet through the guard's head before he could even understand what had happened. And Thatcher was going to do exactly that when he heard more voices. A few seconds later he saw two women in their twenties come in and stand next to the guard. They were attendants who helped people find their seats.

"I just thought I'd get a better view," Thatcher said.

"You're not allowed to be up here."

"That's what you said. People are coming in sooner or later, right?" He smiled. None of the others noticed the package on the ground.

One of the women shrugged her shoulders. "Why not?"

The guard left but the two girls came onto the sundeck and stood next to Thatcher. They looked out at the Addison and Clark intersection and noticed how great the view was.

Thatcher saw the smiles on their faces, one of them wore a wedding ring. They laughed with each other as though they were about to see the President or one of their favorite singers pass by. *Why don't they just leave?* He felt his gun again. Could probably take them both out with the same bullet. The shot of Addison and Clark was perfect. He couldn't give it up. *Why are they ruining it?* It wasn't that he *wanted* them dead, it was that he *needed* them dead. They were in the way. He'd cap them off, find a way to barricade the doors shut, get his shot off on Lucas and make his escape.

"I'll see you later," he said taking his package with him. They nodded and smiled as they said goodbye. One of them frowned when she saw the package. Strange. She turned back to her view of the intersection and didn't give it another thought.

Thatcher hurried out of the Friendly Confines not making eye contact with any of the other people. How could he have been so unprepared? He cursed to himself when he got out of the ball park.

By now he figured Mike would be in position. He glanced at his watch. 11:50. He put on his ear piece. In ten minutes he'd get the command from Caesar.

Caesar watched the live coverage on his flat screen TV in his office. He had a map on his desk of where the shooters would be positioned. Ten minutes and counting. He turned on his communication system that connected with the shooters.

"Get ready," he said.

The final command was fast approaching. Action or abort. Strange how a life can come down to one word. Inside, Caesar hoped that Lucas would turn away—that he would forget all the miracle working and come back to Empirico. But either way, Lucas had to quit his healings. Caesar wanted Lucas dead or alive.

But preferably dead.

Ridley picked up the rifle that was stashed on top of a heating duct on the seventh floor of the apartment building. The building extended another three floors higher, but the seventh was the highest level with a floor already constructed. He checked through the scope and saw a perfect shot of Addison and Clark.

Four feet back from the window was a large opening through the floor that extended all the way down. He had nearly fallen into it when he'd entered the room for the first time yesterday on their scouting mission. He made a mental note not to hurry backwards after the shooting. It had all seemed so simple last night. They discussed the shooting angles like a director shooting a movie. But now even the simple parts—the shots, the hole behind him, the escape route—became increasingly complicated.

His watch read 11:53. Seven minutes. The waiting was the hardest thing.

Mike hurried to the roof of a building on Addison west of Clark. It took him longer than they had thought to get to the building. He was supposed to be there ten minutes to twelve. Now, it was already five minutes to noon. But that would still be enough time. He crouched down on the roof. The parapet was high enough to protect him from the view of the surrounding buildings. *Just get it over with,* he told himself. He would fire his three shots, drop the rifle and go to his escape route.

His rifle was still where they had left it the night before, tucked in behind a sign structure. It was when he picked it up that he began to have second thoughts. He tried to convince himself by saying *I'm really going to do it.* But it didn't work. His conscience got in the way. It wasn't as strong a voice as he thought he would have heard. It was quiet. Almost as if it wasn't there. It was like a little kid in a crib calling out to him softly to stop instead of some loud booming voice screaming at him to put down the rifle.

That voice got quieter the longer Mike ignored it.

The police cars stopped and the three got out. Lucas felt the sunshine on his face. What a perfect day for a healing event. The crowd screamed like fans cheering for their team. Cameras focused on him. The police held the masses back. People shouted at him to let them touch him.

Thatcher got into a building on Addison east of Clark. He found the staircase and got onto the roof. He could see Lucas—for that he was grateful—and looked at his watch. 11:56. The plan was to shoot at noon but Caesar could give the command any time now. That meant he'd have to spend as much as four minutes looking through a scope at a man he was about to kill. Thatcher looked at the street below. There were so many people around. Someone would see. Someone would hear. But he couldn't worry about that anymore. He had to focus on the job. He had to fire off the shots, get back into the building, pull off the jacket to reveal the uniform and call it a day.

Things at the apartment building weren't going so well. Ridley cursed to himself when a news truck pulled right into his line of fire. Five feet higher and he would be fine. But that truck. It was right in his way. He wanted to abort the whole thing. He looked around for a ladder and found nothing. He glanced at his watch. 11:57. He swore again. The other two were in such good positions that the operation didn't really need him. He thought about packing it in.

He thought about ditching his rifle, getting on a plane and leaving his life behind him. He had enough money. He could sit on beach for the rest of his life. He wouldn't be able to afford an expensive beach, but he could certainly land some place nice and out of the way. He didn't need this job anymore. Last one, he told himself, then he'd retire.

Tabitha entered the apartment building after losing sight of the white van. She was sure the other two men she saw were Thatcher and Ridley. She climbed over the orange fencing and fell to the ground. Her ankle hurt immediately, but she refused to give it any thought. She got inside the apartment building and hurried up the stairs.

Her eyes readjusted to the light. She looked around the main floor and saw the construction work that was taking place. To her right she saw a staircase and went up.

She was going to stop on the fifth floor to look for Ridley when she heard a scraping noise upstairs. It sounded as though something was being dragged. She went higher, to the seventh floor. The sound grew louder, sounding like fingernails on a chalk board. And then it stopped. It got quiet.

She edged her way along the hallway, keeping her back to the wall. *Just leave! Just get out of here!* But the curiosity kept her going. She got to the door and turned her face to catch a glimpse of the room. She saw a ladder. Aluminum. Maybe ten feet high. At the top of it, Ridley stood with a rifle clutched in his arm pointing down at the intersection below.

She knew she had to do something. But what? She stood there for only a few seconds, but it felt a lot longer. It was as though the world had stopped and only she had continued. She couldn't attack him. He'd shoot her before she'd get close to him. She could yell and then run away. But where would she go? The hallway was so long. He would certainly be able to kill her and then he'd return to the room where he would shoot down at the intersection. At the people below.

At Lucas.

She went back to the stairs and raced down them as fast as possible. When she got to the second floor her feet slipped out from under her. She tried to grab the handrail to steady herself but she didn't reach it in time. She got that sick feeling in her stomach that people get when they know they are about to get hurt. She wished in that moment for her parachute and a soft landing. The first thing to make contact with the steps was her right foot. Her ankle turned inward and she landed with all of her weight on the outside of her foot. There was a tremendous crack like a branch being broken. A flush of heat burned through her body. Her throat closed up as though she was going to vomit. She crashed down the stairs and landed at the bottom.

Thatcher, Ridley and Mike had Lucas lined up in their scopes. 11:58.

The shooters were ready.

47

A little boy broke through the crowd. A police officer was about to grab him when Lucas told the officer to let him through. The boy looked perfectly healthy.

"You here all by yourself?" Lucas asked.

The boy nodded. Lucas knelt down so the boy could look into his eyes at an even level.

The crosshairs of all the rifles were pointed directly at Lucas. Thatcher aimed for the heart. Ridley did as well. Mike moved all over Lucas, as though he wasn't sure where to shoot. His heart pounded so hard he could feel the pulse in his ears. *I'm really going to do it? I can't do this. What am I doing?*

Lucas looked into the boy's blue eyes. "Your parents didn't want to come?"

The boy shook his head. "I guess not."

"You don't know where they are, do you?"

"I don't know *who* they are."

Lucas touched the boy's hand and could feel him trembling. He grabbed hold of his other hand. The shaking slowed down and then stopped.

Tabitha pulled herself off the floor. She reached for her cell phone then realized it was gone. She dragged herself out of the apartment building to the street. Her eyes welled up with tears of pain. A few more steps and she'd be within shouting distance.

The boy continued. "The only thing I know about my mom was that she had AIDS."

"What do you want done for you today?"

The boy jerked his head back. "I want to be healed."

Lucas lifted his hands to touch the boy. As he did so he noticed his watch. 12:00. Exactly.

Tabitha got to the fence and screamed as loud as she could. "Gunman! Lucas! They're going to kill you!" The people around heard her and wondered if it was a joke. They looked around for shooters. They saw nothing. A policewoman ran towards her. Tabitha collapsed against the fence. She used all her strength for her last warning. "Lucas!"

Caesar lifted his radio to his mouth. The shooters steadied their positions. His face turned a fiery red. Lucas suddenly felt cold. A chill ran down his spine. He was sure he could hear Tabitha's voice in the distance. He looked up and saw a rifle pointed at him. Jake saw it as well. He started running towards Lucas wondering if he could beat the bullet. Lucas pushed the boy out of the way.

At that moment Mike knew he had been wrong. It was as though he awoke from hypnosis, wondering who that person was who had agreed to kill Lucas.

Caesar screamed into his radio as loud as he could. "ACTION!"

The first bullet raced out of Thatcher's rifle and struck Lucas square on the gold medal around his chest. The bullet lodged into it but no farther. The force was so powerful that it knocked Lucas back. The second bullet came from Ridley's rifle at the apartment building. It was slightly off target because of the blow from the first bullet. The bullet was directed at his head but Lucas' hand came up and it smashed into his stainless steel watch, redirected through the bones in his hand and deflected into a police cruiser.

Panic broke loose and suddenly the clear shot the shooters once had was now replaced by a frenzy of people running in every direction. Mike heard the command but could not bring himself to shoot. He wanted the shooting to stop. But it was like a train that was off it's railing. Whatever course it was on, it would continue until it lost momentum.

The third and fourth bullets missed completely, striking the concrete and bouncing off into the crowd. A woman pregnant with twins was struck in the belly killing her instantaneously.

Jake nearly reached Lucas before the next round of bullets. But he wouldn't make it in time. The fifth bullet struck Lucas in the shoulder.

The sixth bullet struck him in the forehead.

Ridley clutched the rifle for his last shot. As he repositioned himself he inadvertently moved the ladder back to the opening. The ladder gave way and Ridley's rifle slipped against the window opening. He accidentally fired his weapon. The bullet raced out of the rifle across the street and pierced through Thatcher's eye. His body dropped against the parapet, blood dripping down on the grass beneath.

Ridley fell off the ladder and crashed through the opening below. He tried to grab onto the floor as it passed by him but it was no use. His neck hit a steel beam on the way down and decapitated him. His lifeless body slammed into the floor. His head came down a moment later and smashed on the ground. The last sensation Ridley had was of his feet becoming extremely hot.

The police formed a barricade around Lucas. They pointed their guns up at the buildings but they found no targets. Edgar and Jake tried to help Lucas but police held them back to make room for the paramedics. "I can help him!" Jake screamed. He didn't know for sure if he could help. It just seemed right to him at the time. They looked at their friend who was lying lifeless in a pool of his own blood. The boy beside him sat on the ground in horror. Lucas' blood seeped into the boy's jeans. The boy would discover later that he was completely healed of AIDS.

They got Lucas into an ambulance and hurried off. Jake prayed over Lucas, but the beep on the heart monitor got weaker and weaker.

The paramedics worked as fast as they knew how. Jake and Edgar prayed as best they could. It was loud in that ambulance. People shouting and praying. But somehow, over all the noise, the steady hum of a flatline was heard by all.

48

The medical staff succeeded in bringing back Lucas' pulse. At this point they weren't optimistic that Lucas would ever gain consciousness again. They felt he was fortunate to have made it this far considering what he had been through. Worst case scenario, Lucas would die. Best case, he'd be a vegetable; if that could be considered a best case.

Reporters went crazy outside, speculating if the miracle worker who had been involved in thousands of healings could, in fact, heal himself.

Tabitha, Jake and Edgar sat in a cordoned off area in the waiting room. Tabitha was treated for a badly sprained ankle. She was surprised and thankful it wasn't more serious, but in light of what happened to Lucas it wouldn't have mattered to her even if it had been broken.

Twelve hours after the shooting a doctor came to them and told them they were finished operating. Tabitha thought that meant Lucas was dead. But the doctor assured them he wasn't. He said they operated as quickly and as carefully as they could to remove the bullet lodged inside his brain. But the way he said that made them all wonder if the doctor thought Lucas would ever recover.

"We've done what we can do," the doctor said, then he invited them to see Lucas.

They wore masks, gloves and gowns and stood around Lucas in the intensive care unit. He was once so powerful, so full of healing energy. Now, he was helpless. Like a baby, not able to care for itself. Jake touched him and prayed. Nothing happened, at least not anything noticeable.

They stood around him not being sure of what to do. It felt so awkward. Lucas was always the center of attention. He was the one with the most drive. Now he was nothing more than a corpse being kept alive by a machine.

The three drove back to the Jesuit center. Tabitha parked her car in the parking lot. But no one got out. No one wanted to. They sat there, in the quiet, wondering what was going to happen.

"What if he dies?" Edgar asked.

"He's not going to die," Jake said softly. But inside he wasn't so certain.

Things had been going so well, Tabitha thought. The healings were making a huge difference to the people of Chicago and to all the people who came in from other parts. She had finally been able to sit down with Lucas and start the process of working through their common past. But now that all had come to a crashing halt.

They stayed in the car for hours not saying a thing. Not having Lucas with them left a huge hole. There was a sense that if the three could stay together, maybe just for the evening, the pain wouldn't be as great. It was as though the four of them together made one complete person. Now, one of them was not there.

And it felt awful.

When Lucas awoke he didn't find himself in the Intensive Care Unit. He didn't find himself anywhere in the hospital.

He found himself in the desert.

The blistering sand burned under his feet. The sun beat mercilessly down on him. Behind him, in the distance, he heard a rumbling—like waves breaking far out in the ocean that can barely be heard on shore. He turned around and saw the sand rising in front of him. He walked in that direction. The heat made him feel like a snowman in spring that gets slowly transformed into an inevitable end.

When he got to the top of the ridge he looked down and saw a small building. He could make it there, he figured. Probably die when he reached it, but it was worth a try. In the distance he heard the rumbling, louder this time, but he still couldn't see what it was.

He forced his body through the sand. His eyes were too tired to move from their fixed position on the small building. The sand became heavier. The air, hotter. He felt as if his lungs were burning.

Paint peeled off the white building. It was one storey, about the size of a three-bedroom house. But when he got closer he realized it wasn't a home. It was a restaurant. There was nothing around for miles, maybe days. But there it was.

He reached the porch, went up the stairs and opened the door. It looked like a fifties diner. Bar stools, red booths, jukebox, long counter, black and white tile flooring.

But no people.

Lucas walked behind to the counter and struggled to keep from collapsing. He opened the fridge door and felt the blast of the cold air. He pulled out a bottle of water and sat down on the floor. With his last bit of strength he twisted off the cap. He brought the bottle to his lips and drank his first sip. It hurt. Not what he expected. His second and third gulps started to bring relief.

Just as he was getting his senses back the lights turned off. Outside, the sky turned a purple-black color the way a sky does when a storm is coming. The wind picked up. The floor trembled.

He felt something to his left. He looked and saw a door. But there was something, or someone, behind it. He could feel it. Lucas froze his attention on it. Any minute, something was coming.

He held his bottle in his hands but couldn't drink. Terror gripped him. It was as though he had become a statue. He watched the door and felt the presence of evil.

The door smashed open. Smoke erupted, making it impossible for Lucas to see who it was. A figure emerged, not standing, but running directly for him. In his right hand, the figure held a wooden club. Lucas recognized the man.

It was the tall guard.

Lucas was too exhausted to move out of the way or to defend himself. The tall guard raised his wooden club and screamed so loud it hurt Lucas to hear it. He came down on Lucas with all of his force. Just as the club was about to smash Lucas' head the tall guard exploded. Then there was no trace of him.

Lucas took in a deep breath. Sweat dripped from his forehead. He stood up. The restaurant was now packed to capacity. People laughing, eating, drinking. The rumbling in the distance got louder.

A small child came up to the counter. "Mister?" she said.

Lucas looked down. She was young. Dark hair. Dark eyes. Maybe the same age as Angelina. "Yes?"

"Could I have an ice cream?"

Lucas nodded. He glanced around the restaurant again. And that's when it caught his attention. Sometimes things feel out of the ordinary even when at first they look right. But Lucas knew what was wrong—or at least what was strange. In a restaurant crowded with forty people, all of them were eating ice cream. No hamburgers, no drinks, no fries. Ice cream.

He opened the glass door. The cool of the ice cream containers felt good. "Which kind?"

"Strawberry," she said.

Lucas looked at the containers. Of all the different flavors, the strawberry one was the only one that hadn't been touched.

He scooped out the strawberry and gave her the cone. She thanked him and Lucas walked with her outside.

"What's that noise?" she asked.

It was louder now. Much louder. That feeling of terror was back again. It was as though someone had reached into his heart and made it stop.

Then it came. It was huge. Moving fast. A massive tidal wave of fire. As far to the right or to the left as they could see. Coming at them. Getting louder and louder.

Lucas smashed open the door. He stared in awe at the wall of fire coming directly for them. He yelled at the people. "Fire!"

The people said nothing. It was as though they weren't really there. He looked at the fire. It was much closer now and it looked even bigger and more powerful than before. He screamed at the people again. "Fire!" Some of them looked in his direction but they made no response.

Lucas picked up the girl and ran in the opposite direction. His feet hurt against the blistering sand. *Where am I running to? I can't beat the fire!* The people came onto the porch. Lucas looked back. The fire was nearly at the restaurant. It's scorching flame leapt out in front of it, hitting the people. Their faces melted. The clothes and skin on their bodies were burned by the flames. Only their bones remained. Their skeletons stood there until the fire wave swept by and disintegrated them.

The fire raged behind Lucas. He fell to the sand. Lucas turned to see thc approaching fire. He protected the little girl with his arms and screamed because this was the end.

The wall of fire stopped in front of them. What surprised Lucas was the coolness he suddenly felt. The sand was comfortable. The wind refreshing. He didn't have that dry sensation in his mouth anymore.

They stood an arm's length from the blazing fire. It was an infinite wall that spread out all around them. Breathtaking in appearance. Lucas reached out and put his hand into the flame. He pulled it out again. His skin had not been touched.

The wall of fire burned in front of them as if it were an alien life form trying to understand them. Then it moved toward them, into them and past them. The cloud cover above turned into a thick, white foam to shield them from the sun. The fire passed out of sight.

The little girl held his hand, licking her ice cream cone.

49

This time when Lucas woke up he *was* in the hospital. Tabitha was resting her hand on his. She readjusted herself in her chair to confirm that his eyes were open. She leaned forward to make it easier for him to see.

"Lucas?"

He closed his eyes and reopened them. She came into focus. Her black hair fell down around her shoulders. Her eyes, genuine and concerned, were like windows allowing Lucas to see into her. He felt so light, a visitor inside his own body.

She went to get the doctor and after a series of tests and questions the doctor left. Jake and Edgar came to the room.

"You see?" Jake said. "Taking a bullet ain't so bad." He bent down and whispered to Lucas. "But you took one in the head. I've never had that before," glancing at the others. "You make me jealous, kid."

Lucas managed a smile. Edgar came to Lucas' side.

"Hard to believe you made it through this."

Lucas nodded. There were words he wanted to say but they were out of his reach.

They all talked for a while. Lucas just listened.

After a pause Edgar said, "I'm going back to Mount Carmel, Lucas." Lucas closed his eyes momentarily to indicate he understood. "I'm starting my treatment soon." It was suddenly quiet. Being together again gave the four of them a sense of belonging, a sense of peace, a belief that everything they had worked so hard for had not been lost.

"Thank you for everything, Lucas." Another close of the eyes. Edgar touched him on the shoulder and walked to the door. He put his hand on the door knob and was about to leave when he turned around. "Where does it go from here?" It wasn't a question as much as it was a statement about the way he felt. Nobody said anything. Nobody had an answer. He gave a slight nod and then, as though he was never there, he left the room.

Tabitha looked at Lucas and a smile came to her face. She wondered if she should kiss him or not. Just on the cheek. Do friends do that? If not, why did she feel the way she did? She stopped short of him and looked into his eyes. "I'll come by again tomorrow." Lucas lifted his fingers to touch her hand. She wished he wouldn't have done that. Leaving his side would have been easy. But not now. There was something about his touch that made it more personal than words—giving her the indication that she was not alone.

She turned and walked out of the room, leaving behind the relaxing smell of her perfume and the memory of a relationship that had been resurrected.

"Well, boss?"

Lucas wanted to laugh. Jake did. A huge laugh came out, the kind that made his fat stomach jiggle. Lucas began to feel as if he was in his body again.

Jake sat down. "So, what happens now?"

Tabitha and Edgar said goodbye in the parking lot. She got into her yellow Mustang and drove off. Edgar watched her longer than he normally would have.

Her black hair blew in the draft. She breathed in and out noticeably for the first time since hearing those shots ring out above her head. Somehow things had gotten back to the realm most people refer to as normal—if that's what surviving a triangular crossfire can be called.

In the back seat was her fly-fishing gear—waders, fly rod, vest, boots, jacket, hat and flies. They felt like old friends coming together for a reunion after a long separation. She'd make her favorite river by Saturday morning. Regardless of the weather she would be in that water. So would someone else she knew.

Tabitha swallowed and wondered if this was the right thing to do. She thought about calling him first. To let him know she was coming. To warn him in advance. But she decided against it. One way or the other she would find out. No more guessing. Maybe things would work out. Maybe they wouldn't. She'd meet him out there on the water. Maybe they wouldn't say anything. Maybe they wouldn't need to. She could stand there in the water for hours with him. Casting. Feeling the sun on her face, the water rushing by them.

Hoping for a miracle.

Edgar was about to open the door to his office at Mount Carmel when he found a note stuck on the window. It was a message from Sheath and Handle. Edgar was fired. Effective immediately. No meeting. No personal words of gratitude. No explanation. Just a dismissal.

It was evening. The campus was quiet. No students around. Probably a movie or a bowling night or something. He stepped outside and looked up at the night sky. The stars flooded the canopy. Although he had cancer, although he just lost his job, for the first time in his life Edgar felt free.

He left the Mount Carmel parking lot and drove off to Notre Dame. He walked through the beautiful campus and passed by the mural of Jesus on the library, *Touchdown Jesus.* He sat down momentarily on his favorite bench. His situation hadn't changed since the last time he had been here, he still had cancer, but somehow he felt a confidence that even though his circumstances had not improved he could still consider himself a disciple.

He walked down to the Grotto. The caved-out portion of the rock had a number of candles burning in it. He was the only one there. Edgar knelt down in the front, closed his eyes and prayed. He didn't say anything and he stayed in the quiet, feeling the joy he felt while attending here as a student.

In spite of everything that happened, in spite of everything on his mind, the only thought he could think of was of all the ducks that walked around on campus. He used to feed them, or tried to. It amazed him how all those little ducks followed their mother around, so confident that they were being led in the right direction.

He'd get that sailboat. He'd do his research on healing and learn about how the power came to Lucas and whether that power could come to others. The healings were legit. He knew that now. He just didn't know why.

But there at the Grotto his shoulders felt lighter. It wasn't that someone had taken the burden from him, but, rather, that there was a strength inside him carrying it for him—or through him. His circumstances were the worst they'd ever been. But there was peace. There was a comfort in knowing that he didn't need to have the answers. It was okay that he didn't know. It was okay to wonder.

It was okay to be without an explanation.

When Lucas arrived at the prison he felt a chill come over him. But Lucas pushed himself through. He was led to the visitor booths and a guard showed him to the last stall.

Mike sat on the other side only a few inches away wearing a prisoner uniform. Although they were separated by protective glass Mike was in another world. One that Lucas was all too familiar with.

They picked up their phones and talked a few minutes about the things people talk about when they're trying to get a conversation started. Lucas knew Mike hadn't shot at him. What bothered him was that at one point Mike had intended to.

There was a long silence. Long enough to make Lucas realize that Mike was trying to say something but was having a hard time getting it out. Mike forced himself to make eye contact with Lucas. He turned his eyes down again but the look was long enough for Lucas to see the guilt in them.

"You remember when we were in China?" Mike said.

"What about China?"

"You were imprisoned because of drugs."

Lucas nodded, not sure where this was going.

"You never found out how those drugs got there," Mike said.

Lucas shrugged his shoulders. Then he realized.

Mike shook his head, then rested it in his hands as though it was too heavy for him to keep up anymore. He wished he could make the clock turn back. If only there was a way to redo everything, but there wasn't. Time only goes forward. Like it or not.

Mike hung up the phone and turned around, unable to face Lucas.

Lucas wanted to say something, anything, but with Mike away from the phone there was no chance of him hearing. He didn't want to end things this way. It didn't seem right. Lucas watched Mike being taken away by guards.

He got up from his chair and felt relief with every step he took to the exit door. He got into his car and drove off from the prison. He watched it fade away in his rearview mirror and thought about how strange the origin of his adventure had been.

Sometimes bad things really do get turned into good things, he thought.

Sometimes.

Lucas and Jake stopped outside a security checkpoint at O'Hare. It had been ten days since Lucas had awakened. The doctors had done an incredible job in surgery. His recovery was faster than they had expected.

"You're sure about this, Jake?"

"Of course."

"It could be dangerous."

"It's always been dangerous," Jake said with a laugh.

Lucas nodded. "I'm going to miss you."

Jake pointed a finger at Lucas. "Don't you start crying on me."

"I'm not going to cry."

"Lucas?"

"I'm not going to cry."

"Good. I don't want you embarrassing me in front of all these people."

Lucas smiled and then a puzzled look came over him as though he was trying to remember something. "How did we meet, again?"

"The street."

Lucas nodded, amazed at how their friendship began. "Right."

"You're going to be late," Jake said.

"You're going to come later? You promise?"

"I'll come. I'll be there. I just need to take care of this one thing first."

"Good luck."

"You, too." Jake gave Lucas a playful punch in the shoulder. Lucas told himself that someday he would be strong enough to handle those blows. Jake turned and walked away. He blended in with the crowd of people and then disappeared all together.

Lucas reached the aircraft at the end of the tunnel. He handed the attendant his boarding pass. She smiled and was about to give it back to him when she suddenly stopped. Something looked awfully familiar about him.

"Don't I know you?"

Lucas lifted his shoulders indicating he had never met her before.

"Wait a minute." She studied his face a moment to confirm her suspicions. "Are you the healer?"

Lucas took his boarding pass, picked up his bag and gave a slight smile. "No, I'm not."

He walked to the very back of the plane and sat down beside parents with screaming children. Nothing quite like flying hospitality class.

As the plane taxied to the runway a flight attendant announced that lunch would be served in about forty minutes. *Perfect. Just enough time to think through the passages I memorized in prison.* He leaned back in his chair and wondered what it would be like when he got to his destination.

He'd never been to Zambia before.

Lucas thought through the events of the last few months, fresh as they were in his mind. He recalled the tall guard in China, with those hollow eyes—never being sure of what was going on behind them. He thought of Edgar, the faithful theologian who was still sick—even though hundreds, thousands were healed in front of his very eyes. He wondered how a man like that was able to hang onto his faith.

There was Jake—a criminal, an addict and a friend who gave up nothing to be part of something. And then there was, of course, Tabitha, the woman he thought he would never see again. He was, however, wrong about that, as he had been about a great many things.

But what ran through Lucas as the plane took off was not a thought. It was a feeling. A feeling of insecurity, almost terror. A man gets that way when he has enemies.

Lucas said his verses quietly to himself, but the fear kept pounding at his heart's door. It was more than the tall guard. More than Caesar and the Council. Much more.

There was something out there waiting for him.